Providence Road

Detective Billie McCoy, Volume 2

Carol Marvell

Published by Carol Marvell, 2024.

This is a work of fiction. Similarities to real people, places, or events are entirely coincidental.

PROVIDENCE ROAD

First edition. October 11, 2024.

Copyright © 2024 Carol Marvell.

ISBN: 979-8227810496

Written by Carol Marvell.

Also by Carol Marvell

Detective Billie McCoy
Providence Road
Cold Bars
The Black Mamba
Judas Kiss
Cross the Line
Unmasked

To Shannon

Chapter One

Detective Billie McCoy groaned. A vile aroma drifted into her numbed awareness, drawing her from the sanctuary of sleep. She rolled her head to escape it. Free of the stifling odour, she settled. Although her sluggish body wasn't ready to wake, her mind stirred with the unexpected stench. She was having trouble gathering her thoughts. Why was that? Despite the misty cloud smothering her senses, a vague recollection of the bush sat in her last memories.

As her awareness sharpened, the aches from hard boards beneath her grew. Was she lying on a table? Or maybe a floor?

The smell suddenly returned, intruding into her thoughts and drawing her out of her slumber. Billie jerked her head away. Her eyes shot open. For a minute, she stared blankly at the shape looming above her. Its poised hand held a small bottle; smelling salts. Her focus honed in on the face, and instantly her blood turned cold.

Bland.

A well-muscled woman in her forties, Bland's dark, oily, bob-styled hair clung to the rounded face; her neck hidden beneath a double chin. Tattoos of crouching tigers stained the tight biceps on each arm under the rolled-up sleeves of her blotted army shirt.

It took all Billie's willpower to control the shock gripping her, to hold back the fear and panic threatening to take over. The events and horrors of recent days flooded her mind. Billie had found herself caught up in a ring of human trafficking, organised by Bland's associate, Captain Joseph Bates, Chief of Missing Persons, a member of the very same police force Billie worked for in Sydney. Billie and six young women, all fresh out of prison and carrying a strong dislike for cops, had found themselves kidnapped and whisked away in the back of a truck, travelling north under the cruel reign of Bland. Having been sold to a sheik at the end of their journey, Billie had managed to escape. Freeing the three remaining prisoners, she and the girls had hijacked a vehicle and fled for their lives, until they'd been ambushed and fired upon with tranquiliser darts, which had led to their recapture. Billie suddenly recalled Bates and Bland making their appearance moments before she'd passed out. Damn it. Of course they'd been behind the trap. But how had they found them? How did they know they'd be on that road?

Her stomach tightened as she came to terms with this grim predicament.

"Hello, McCoy," Bland said in a quiet, controlled tone. "Thought you could outrun us, did you? Well, this is our country, and we have friends where you wouldn't believe. Breaking out was the biggest mistake of your life. And then to kill the sheik's best girl, well . . . that was probably your second biggest mistake. He is very, *very* upset with you."

The detective kept her facial expression blank, hiding her struggling emotions and willing herself to stay calm. Something wasn't right. She couldn't believe how composed this usually loud, intimidating, and oversized monster acted. Bland was *too* composed. Billie lay motionless and met the woman's unfriendly gaze with an impassive expression, offering no sign of weakness or distress that might feed Bland's ego.

Bland's dark eyes narrowed. Her voice hardened as she spat out her next words. "You made us out to look like fools, and for that, I'm going to make you wish you were dead."

Anger and loathing burst through Billie's initial shock. Sitting forward in a sudden lunge, she grabbed a fistful of Bland's shirt with all intentions of pushing her out of her face. Only then did she register her hands were cuffed. Before she could shove Bland back, a pistol appeared centimetres from her nose. Billie froze. Her focus jumped to the .38. The small, ominous hole of the barrel staring her in the face carried a powerful message. She looked back into

Bland's savage eyes, ignoring the twisted grimace fixed upon her ugly features.

"You think I'm that stupid?" Bland sneered. "You have a lot to answer for, and if you want to start now, go right ahead."

For a long moment, the two stared at each other. Slowly, Billie let go of the shirt and sank to the floor, resting her head on the hard boards.

"That was a dirty trick with the truck," Billie said with distaste. Set up to look like it had lost control, an old Bedford truck with a flat tyre had smashed into a tree and taken up the entire road, forcing them to stop and setting them up for the ambush.

"It worked though, didn't it. We got what we wanted." Bland's sneer softened to a smug smile. "When we heard about the brother and sister hiding you down in the caves, it was only a matter of time before you surfaced. Thanks to our good friend, Mr Smith – you met him at the truck with the boy." An evil grin lit up her face. "He explained there was only one road out of there that met the main highway, and as he knew the area so well, he was very keen to assist us. Yes, it was worth the wait for a few days in the bush. We couldn't let our biggest trade simply drive off into the sunset."

Billie didn't answer. The last thing she wanted was to fuel Bland's sick, twisted mind with any added conquest.

Bland rested the gun under the cop's chin and went on in a quiet voice, each word enunciated to emphasise them. "Seems you've been quite busy since you left us. When we called in to ask our friend Sergeant Wilford if he'd seen you, we were shocked to hear he was dead. My! We couldn't believe what you'd been up to. And killing poor Karlib was near as bad," she scolded in a singsong tone, her stare unwavering.

Billie couldn't deny she was surprised Bland was so informed. She knew Wilford? Shit. Obviously she knew a few others as well for her to be so up to date about him and Karlib.

After their escape, Billie and the girls had followed the road right into Wilford's rundown, pathetic town. The Sergeant had shown his hospitality by throwing the girls in a cell on false charges. On learning of Billie's self-defence skills, he had then forced her to fight the local legend, a brawny aboriginal called Karlib. Both opponents had been armed with a spear tied to their wrists; it had been a vicious battle.

Again, Billie hid her feelings.

Bland continued. "The whole town is in mourning and is still very, very mad at you. What a pity we can't hand you back to them, to let them have their revenge." Bland smiled and shifted her weight, sitting back off the detective without altering the position of the pistol. "You know, they told us all about the fight . . . how you'd picked up some new injuries..."

The gun moved. In a slow drift, it traced down Billie's left arm, for a moment resting lightly on her wound. Bland watched for a reaction. When none came, she pressed harder. The detective couldn't stop herself wincing. Bland smiled and moved the gun on, tracking it downwards.

"You have to look after yourself now that you belong to the sheik. Maybe that little point slipped your mind. He is awfully anxious to have you back, you know."

The gun rested on her wounded thigh. It took all Billie's concentration to prevent herself reacting to the torment. When Bland pressed harder on her cut, she sucked in a slight breath.

The big woman smiled. "I'm afraid you've upset him though," she said, easing the pressure off the cop's leg. "Mm, very much so. You see, killing his girl near on shattered him, but, then again, I'm sure you'll be able to make it up to him."

In a blur, Bland lifted the pistol and rammed the butt hard into the cop's cut ribs. Billie cried out with an agonising groan. Rolling onto her side, she curled up with her eyes shut tight, every breath expelled in grunts as she fought against the excruciating pain threatening to make her pass out. The blow was hard enough without having a major cut across her ribs.

"Oooh, silly me," Bland said superficially. "I didn't realise you were so sore."

Billie didn't reply; she couldn't. She fought to keep Bland in focus.

Bland grunted a short laugh and stood up. With a contented sigh, she lifted her gaze and looked around the room. The innocent action set Billie's nerves off. Shit, the girls! Were they here too? As if on cue, a moan sounded. With Bland out of her face, Billie had a better vision of her surroundings. Sucking in short gasps, she lifted her head and looked around in a fleeting glance. Four walls surrounded her. The timber shack had been thrown together with odd-sized logs in their rough and raw state. It had no furniture or windows. The narrow gaps between the logs helped circulate the air against the heat.

The three girls were sprawled around the floor of the room, one at the foot of each wall. Even in the dull light and after days of travelling, their beauty shone through. It was clear why Bates had chosen them.

Sarah Jones lay opposite Billie, cuffed and secured with half a metre of chain attached to a large steel ring fixed to the floor. Only now did Billie realise she was secured in the same manner. The tallest of the group, Sarah's short black hair set off her attractive fine facial features.

To Billie's left, Casey Reynolds slept. Thick, cropped blonde hair fell just above her shoulders. The wild, untamed cut carried a natural wave. A lengthy fringe hung down around a lightly tanned face. Billie knew from the brief time they'd shared together that a smile from Casey sparked prominent dimples in her cheeks.

Jane Walker lay to her right. Jane's 'girl next door' image portrayed a subtle beauty to catch any man's eye. Thick, brown, shoulder-length hair enhanced her dainty face. The button nose and thin lips were complemented by a clean, fresh complexion. Long eyelashes protected her closed eyes.

Jones moaned again. Concern ate away at Billie. She lowered her head, panting hard while watching the girl stir.

Bland returned her gaze to the detective and sighed. "I would so enjoy going to town on you McCoy, but, unfortunately, I've had orders to lay off. After all, you're sold now, and the sheik wants you back in one piece. Pity."

Billie's fuzzy mind fought to overcome the torment hounding her. Bland's comment stirred her reserves, motivating her to find the strength she so desperately needed to override the pain.

Bland continued. "But as for this lot..." Turning, she ambled to Jones while keeping her gaze fixed on the cop. Billie tensed. She didn't like this at all.

A grin sprang to Bland's lips. "Well, it's open slather." Without a downward glance, she kicked Jones in the stomach. The girl cried out, curling up with short, sharp breaths.

Billie watched in horror. Jones was in big trouble. Bland was here strictly to cause misery, to throw her weight around, no matter who got hurt. Gritting her teeth, Billie rolled onto her knees. She gasped. A glance at Jones inspired her to keep going. With her cuffed hands supporting her tender ribs, she managed to sit up. Breathing hard, she leant forward to help ease the throbbing that came in waves. Somehow, she had to stop this bitch. Jones' life could depend on it.

Bland walked around Jones in slow steps, looking at her victim with a sour smile.

"W–what the hell d–do you w–want, Bland?" Billie gasped.

The big woman's attention returned to her. The smile broadened. "Why, whatever do you mean?" With her stare locked on the cop, she kicked Jones in her lower back. Jones yelped a sharp cry and arched her back in pain. Every breath rasped through her lips.

"Leave her a-alone," Billie demanded, terrified the bitch wasn't going to stop.

Bland's slow walk carried her around in front of Jones. She turned and faced Billie. The smile dropped. "Are you telling me what to do, McCoy?" she spat through clenched teeth. She kicked Jones in the ribs. The girl groaned again. She curled her knees up to protect herself.

Billie was at her wit's end. Her gaze shot from Jones to Bland, locking on the big woman's beady eyes in a challenge. The sneer was back on Bland's face, demanding an answer. Hatred washed through the detective. It gave her strength – not only strength but a clearer outlook to the problem at hand. This wasn't working; it wasn't the right approach. Bland only wanted her to beg her to stop. Until she heard that, she wouldn't let up on Jones. And this crazy woman could easily kill her if she wanted to. It was in her nature. Billie prayed the greedy side of Bland would hold her off – Jones wasn't worth anything to them dead.

"No," the cop quietly stated in response to the question, forcing her tone to remain calm. "Just let her be, okay? If you k-kill her, you've blown a few grand, right?"

Bland gave a slight, unconcerned shrug. "Sometimes sacrifices have to be made."

Billie tensed at the cold, calculating words. Had she left it too late to succumb to her wishes?

A wicked smile lit up Bland's face. After a drawn-out moment, the big woman sighed.

"Okay, McCoy, I'll let her off. But remember this, if you give me a hard time, just one little ounce of trouble, I won't stop next time." The dark eyes narrowed. "Do you understand?"

Billie nodded. "Yes."

"Good." With no more to say, Bland turned and strode out, slamming the door behind her. Billie watched her leave, her hatred boiling over. She glanced at Jones who was still gasping in pain. Her eyes were closed tight, her face twisted in agony. Her hands clasped her stomach in an effort to ease the suffering. Unable to help her, Billie turned her attention to Jane and Reynolds. Both were coming round. It was all the time she could give them. She couldn't hold back her own pain any longer. With Bland gone, the throbbing in her ribs consumed her, washing over her in persistent waves. Billie lowered her head onto the wooden floor and dropped onto her side. She closed her eyes and focused on her breathing, willing her body to relax.

Moments passed before Jane's quiet nervous voice broke the silence. "What's going on? Where are we?"

"I don't know," Reynolds said groggily, her tone just as strained.

Billie briefly opened her eyes. Both girls were sitting. Reynolds crawled as close to Jones as her chain would allow.

"Sarah? Sarah, what is it? What's wrong?" No answer met her. "Shit." Concern strained her voice. "McCoy? Can you hear me?"

"Yeah," Billie gasped, without opening her eyes.

"What happened to you two?"

"B–Bland."

An icy silence followed.

"Shit." Reynolds' voice was laced with fear.

"But . . . how? How did they find us?" Jane's voice shook with disbelief.

"I don't know, but they were definitely waiting for us. That truck was a setup. They put it there to get us to stop."

"But . . . how did Bates know we'd be coming along that road, at that time?"

"I don't know." Reynolds' voice turned to anguish. "Hell, we were almost out of here, almost home!"

Billie looked up at the girls. She could hear the hopelessness in their voices. "They knew–Wilford. The others filled them in. They'd been waiting–a few days for us beside the road."

Both girls stared wide-eyed.

"Shit." Reynolds sat back on her haunches and gripped her head with her cuffed hands, as if to stop the words sinking in. "Well, that's just great, isn't it. Damn it!"

Billie watched her, hearing her distress. There was no denying it was a big hurdle to get over but, hopefully, once the shock settled, she *would* get over it and then be free to think proactively. The cop rolled onto her knees and attempted to kneel. A cry escaped her lips. She sank back down onto her heels, riding the pain with short, shallow breaths.

"I take it Bland's still pretty upset with you," Jane stated.

Billie looked at her and then Jones who gasped from the pain.

"She knows she can't touch me. I'm already sold. That's why Jones copped it. It's Bland's sick way of getting at me." Billie returned her gaze to the two listening girls, delivering the rest of Bland's ultimatum. "If I play up, she takes it out on you three."

Except for Jones fighting to catch a breath, a heavy hush engulfed the room. Jane shook her head.

"Oh, really. Well, if she can't touch you, why are you in so much pain?" she questioned, a touch of anger creeping into her voice.

Before Billie could answer, Jones gasped from the floor, "McCoy? Was that B-Bland who c-caved my ribs in?"

Everyone turned to her. Her eyes were open, looking across at the detective. Billie gave a nod.

"Yes."

"Sarah, are you all right?" Reynolds anxiously asked. She looked her over, the worry painted across her strained features. Jones gingerly rolled onto her knees and sat up nursing her stomach. Her breath came fast and hard. She glanced at Reynolds and nodded.

"Yeah, I'll live." She dropped her gaze and stared at her cuffed wrists. "Shit, it's starting all over again." Her head shot up to meet Billie's gaze. Her brow tensed in a reflective frown.

It surprised Billie. What had she done to deserve such an accusing stare?

"You knew," Sarah said. "You knew something was wrong when we f-first stopped at the truck, didn't you?"

The words stunned Billie. That's what this was about? The uneasy feeling she'd had in the van before they'd been caught, warning her something wasn't right? At the time, it hadn't warranted enough significance, but now, it was an entirely different matter. Unsure if Jones was passing blame her way, Billie found herself on the defensive.

"I didn't know for sure."

"But–you–knew something wasn't right, didn't you?" Jones insisted through her torment.

Billie held her gaze, studying her resolute face plagued with twinges of pain. Jones wanted an answer right or wrong – not just an answer, but the truth. Blame wasn't the issue here. The detective glanced at Jane and Reynolds. They looked just as curious. She sighed and turned to Jones.

"Like I said, I had a bad feeling. I wasn't expecting anything like this."

"It doesn't matter. You still knew something was wrong," she maintained firmly. "Had we listened, maybe we could've prevented this."

Billie shrugged half-heartedly. Jones had a point but it was too late now. "Maybe, maybe not. Bates' trap was pretty much foolproof."

Jones nodded. "It still may have given us a better chance than we had, right?"

Billie struggled to understand where Jones was going with this. Her persistent questions seemed frivolous. "Jones, I really—"

"Yes or no?"

Billie hesitated and considered the question. She nodded. "Possibly, I guess, a small chance but I doubt if—"

"That's all I wanted to hear," she cut in over the top of her.

Billie stopped, watching her. It wasn't worth pushing. What was done was done.

Jones lowered her head.

Billie exhaled. Rolling off her knees, she dragged herself to the wall and leant against it, stretching her legs out in front of her. Resting her head on the rough timber logs, she closed her eyes and took the time to think. Hindsight could be a real guilt tripper all right. Was Jones right in what she'd said? Bates had set such a fail-safe trap. Who was to say she would have sprung it anyway. How could she have contended against a dart gun?

Reynolds sighed. "Bloody hell, they've really got us this time. No way will they let us out of their sight."

"Hey, come on. We've broken away before, we can do it again," Jane said, somewhat hesitantly.

"No, not this time. They'll be expecting it. We've got no chance."

"There's always a chance," Billie said quietly, casting her a glance. Reynolds' negativity was too strong for her liking. She badly needed her to keep her hopes up, to focus on how they were going to make it out of this mess.

"The hell there is. Even if we did get away, they're never going to give us up. Shit, they'll follow us again, all the way into George Street if they have to, just so we don't blab our story and blow Bates' cover."

Billie lifted her head off the wall and looked her in the eye. "We'll just have to be extra careful then, won't we. Come on, don't give up yet, you never know what's ahead. I thought you'd appreciate that by now after what we've been through."

"Ha!" Jones blurted, the sarcasm strong. "The cop's great philosophy."

Billie's gaze shot to her. Instantly, she recognised the bitter tone that so regularly reared its ugly head. Disappointed Jones had turned on her so readily, Billie watched her haul her bruised body across to the wall. Jones fell into it with a gasp. She closed her eyes against the pain, resting a hand on her ribs.

"Casey's right. They'll be on our backs the whole time."

Billie refused to give in to her rising scepticism. "So what then? We just give in and let them take us without a fight? There is always a way out if you look hard enough."

"Bullshit! Not this time," Jones snapped.

Before the detective could answer, the door opened. Billie dragged her gaze from Jones and rested her head against the wall, fighting her frustration. She *had* to keep the girls' spirits up or they would lose out. Once hope was gone, so was everything else. Billie watched as the visitors entered the room.

Bates, Smith and two men walked in. In his late fifties, Captain Bates carried the same confident air Bland had. Short and plump, his rounded, beach ball face was clean-shaven. A thin strip of grey-flecked hair ran around the lower part of his bald head from ear to ear. As usual, his clothes were bright and contrasting.

Smith wasn't as presentable. Encumbered with a large beer belly, a wild bushy beard and long oily hair accentuated his unkempt appearance. The two men standing behind him like dogs on a leash had to be the hired help. Scruffy looking with lean builds, their faded jeans and T-shirts were stained with dirt and grime. The stubble on their faces and lust in their eyes only added to their feral appearance.

The party stood inside the door looking the girls over. Bates cast a careless glance at his prisoners. A smile tugged on his lips.

Billie met his gaze with a blank expression, scarcely giving the other three a look. Her hatred was for the slave trader, and it had grown in intensity.

"Well, I hope we have all recovered." Bates said, his gaze roaming over the watching faces. It settled on Billie. "We outsmarted you this time, McCoy."

She fought down her disgust. "You're such a hero, Bates. It was a sick trick. Nothing short of what I'd expect from you."

Bates sniggered. He strolled closer and bent over her, positioning his face in front of hers. "You'd better believe it," he snarled with venom. "See, you *won't* be getting away from me this time, you hear me? I am taking you back one way or the other, by whatever means I have to. I've had enough of your games, and you've wasted enough of my time. If I have to keep you drugged the whole way, don't think I won't do it. If I have to sacrifice one of your companions to keep you in line, don't think I won't do that either. Are you hearing me, McCoy?"

Keeping her face blank, Billie's mind raced as she assessed how serious he was. Would he go to the extent of sacrificing the girls? Sacrificing his profits? It was hard to say.

Bates chuckled. He straightened.

The thought of Bates believing he was untouchable fired Billie's emotions – threat or no threat. As he turned away, she hooked her feet around his right ankle, the leg he'd put his weight on. Pulling hard with one foot, she pushed with the other. The leg was yanked from under him. The boss man plunged to the floor.

Her unforeseen actions instantly started a chain reaction. In the back of her mind, Billie knew she was in a lot of trouble, but that was the price she was willing to pay. She'd started this; now she had to finish it.

The instant Bates hit the hard floorboards, Billie slammed her heel into the side of his jaw. The impact threw him over on his stomach with a heavy thump, leaving him too dazed to move.

The two men with Smith jumped forward. Billie buried her foot into the closest guy's crotch, crippling him on the spot. He moaned and doubled over, sinking to his knees gripping his manhood. Using the heel of her sandal, she slammed him across the jaw, driving him into the floor. He was no more of a threat at the moment.

The other guy sidestepped his partner and threw a punch at her face. Billie ducked to the side. The fist flew past – straight into the wall behind.

"Arggh!" The thug jumped back, nursing his injured hand. Billie drove her foot into his knee. A dull crack sounded. He dropped to the floor with a cry. Brought down to her level, she smashed the same foot into his jaw. He rolled across Bates and landed on his back beside him without a movement.

Bates sat up and turned to Billie. Posing the closest threat, the cop struck out with her cuffed fists and slugged him in the nose. All her pent-up hate and anger were behind the punch. Bates dropped to the floor with a grunt, rolling away.

Too late, Billie caught a glimpse of Smith stepping towards her with a raised hand. He slapped her hard. She fell sideways onto her elbows, her cheek stinging. A sharp pain cut across her wounded ribs.

Smith reached down and grabbed her by the shirt, dragging her up to face him. Billie used the momentum he yanked her with and punched him in the face. The plump man staggered back with a grunt, blood gushing from his nose. Falling free of Smith's grasp, Billie started to get up. Once she was on her feet, she could end this quickly.

A gun cocked to the side of her.

"Damn it, McCoy, don't even think about it. Stay right where you are."

Halfway to her knees, the command pulled her to halt. She turned. Bates sat facing her, his Beretta aimed at her head. A savage glare twisted his chubby features, daring her to reject the order. His aim then dropped.

"You move another muscle, and I'll put a bullet in your leg, you hear me? I don't give a damn if I have to carry you out of here." His tone held a hard edge. Billie had no doubt he meant every word.

Back on his feet, the guy she'd kicked in the crotch lunged forward. Billie turned towards him – and met his fist full on. Her head rocked to the side. She'd had little time to ride it. The blow thumped her into the wall, almost toppling her over.

The thug grabbed her by the front of the shirt and hauled her up. He gave her no time to recover before following through with a second punch. A groan escaped her lips as she was flung backwards. Only the guy's strong grip on her shirt kept her upright. Her head spun wildly. All strength was zapped from her body. Now she was completely helpless.

Chapter Two

Jones caught her breath. Shit, what the hell was going on? McCoy had stirred up a hornet's nest which could see them all dead. What was she thinking? These bastards were crazy. How far would Bates go? It was all getting out of hand.

"That's enough," Bates snapped when Smith's man yanked Billie forward and raised his fist for a third hit. Billie hung in his grip giving no resistance. The slave trader altered his aim to the scruffy thug – a slight yet convincing action to strengthen his command. The guy paused, panting hard with his hand poised high.

The girls were on their knees strained against their chains. Jones yanked on her cuffs, but the steel ring holding the chain didn't budge. She couldn't do anything to help the cop. None of them could.

The thug looked around at Bates, his grimy face twisted in irritation.

Bates ignored the look. "She is not your property, so lay off."

The guy stared at Bates while contemplating the order. Slowly, he lowered his fist and let Billie go, shoving her into the wall. She slumped against the logs, her head tilted back with closed eyes. Her cheek was red. Blood smeared her lip.

Bates climbed to his feet and shoved the henchman out of the way with a scowl. He backed off, watching Bates with a cagey stare. Bates turned and leant over Billie. Taking her by the shirt, he yanked her off the wall and pulled her closer. The barrel of the gun pressed into her cheek. Billie hung like a rag doll in his hands showing no reaction to it. Her head fell back.

"You are walking a very thin line, McCoy, don't fall off it," he snarled in a bitter tone, his face only centimetres from hers. She made no response. He stared a moment longer and then shoved her into the wall none too gently. Straightening, he sucked in a deep breath and turned his gaze to his other three prisoners.

Jones' nervous stare darted from him to the cop. She couldn't believe McCoy's unexpected attack, particularly after Bates' threatening speech. It had scared her into behaving, so why hadn't it worked with McCoy? The cop had managed to hurt each of the men, not only physically but mentally, bruising their egos. On top of that, she'd almost taken control. Probably would have, if not for Bates bringing out the gun. Damn him. Jones glanced at the two thugs. The one who had slugged Billie was hauling his crippled partner up. He couldn't put weight on his leg.

Smith climbed to his feet and touched his bleeding nose. He pulled out a handkerchief and wiped the blood while gazing at Billie slumped against the wall. He suppressed a laugh.

"Huh, she doesn't give up, does she? No wonder she got the jump on you. She's full of surprises."

Bates glared at him. "Just pick one, okay? Anyone but McCoy," he said through clenched teeth. Smith looked at him and chuckled. Turning his attention to the prisoners, he strolled across to them.

Jones met his wicked gaze with a defiant stare.

Smith walked slowly from her to Reynolds and then Jane, giving each a close examination. He stepped back and folded his arms while he continued to assess each of them. "Hmm, it's a hard decision."

Bates exhaled a frustrated sigh.

Smith's gaze came to rest on Jane. "This one, I think."

Jane stiffened and stared up into his smiling face.

"Fine," Bates blurted.

Jane's panicky gaze shot to him, and then to Jones and Reynolds. Jones returned her look with a troubled expression. As worried as she was for Jane, there was nothing she could physically do.

"Hedley," Smith called. The thug let go of his partner and stepped to Jane. She struggled the instant he took hold of her. The fear shook her voice.

"No! Please, no!"

Hedley fought to keep her still while Smith leant down and undid the chain from her cuffs.

"What do you want? Let me go!" Jane fought against him.

Smith chuckled. "Now, now, behave."

"Leave her alone, you bastards," Jones spat. Desperation gripped her.

"No, not her! Don't take her!" Reynolds yelled over Jane's distressed cries. Neither of the men cast them a look. Finally freed from the chain, Jane was hauled to her feet. Hedley took her in a tight bear hug and stepped towards the door. She kicked and wriggled hard.

"Please, no! Let me go!"

Jones climbed to her feet, straining against the short chain securing her. She could only look on in horror and stunned disbelief. The other guy limped to the door and opened it for Smith. The boss man strode out. Hedley dragged his wriggling prisoner across the room.

"You bastard!" Jones shouted over Jane's anguished pleas.

"Let her go, you creep!" Reynolds yelled.

Hedley didn't stop. Almost at the door, Jane made her own efforts to save herself by throwing herself down in his arms and forcing him to carry all her weight. It had some effect in slowing him down, but it didn't stop him. Hedley growled. Heaving her up, he tightened his grip and hauled her forward. In three steps, he disappeared through the door, taking Jane out screaming in protest.

Hedley's partner sniggered. He cracked a disrespectful grin at Jones and Reynolds. Turning, he hobbled out. The two girls' protests died. They stared at the opened door in disbelief.

"What the hell are you going to do to her?" Reynolds demanded when Bates started after the departing party without offering any explanations.

The bald man halted and slowly turned to face her. Behind the rigid stare, he considered the question. His gaze turned to Jones. She returned it with a look of disgust. With a half turn of his head, he looked at Billie. Jones followed his gaze. The cop hadn't moved. She sat slumped against the wall with her head on her chest.

Bates turned to Reynolds. "Well, to tell you the truth, *I* won't be doing much at all to her," he replied smugly. "She is going to thank Mr Smith for his services to me." He smiled.

"You bastard," Jones spat. Jane's cries echoed in the background, fuelling her anger. "You sick, heartless bastard."

"Shut your mouth, girl, or you may be next," Bates snapped, pointing a stumpy finger at her. "You should be grateful he didn't pick you."

Jones held his irate stare. As much as she wanted to tell him where to go, she held her tongue. To be the subject of Bates' wrath was definitely not healthy.

The slave trader dropped his hand and went on in a calmer manner, looking from her to Reynolds.

"And while we're on the subject, let me tell you this. This is also a lesson to McCoy for not sticking by the rules. She wants to play games, then so will I. I warned her the fate of you three was in her hands, and she blew it." He raised his eyebrows in delight. His voice softened. His tone almost sounded compassionate. "I just hope Walker understands."

The statement was a cruel blow, driving home the serious trouble Jane was in. Jones stared numbly, unable to comment. Bates flashed a quick smile. He turned and walked out, pulling the door closed behind him.

"Damn him!" Reynolds yanked on her cuffs in frustration and dropped down to sit on the floor. She drew in her knees and hugged them tightly.

"He's a sick bastard, and I really hope he gets what's coming to him," Jones muttered, staring at the door. "Shit, why the hell couldn't Bates just pay Smith in dollars?"

"Poor Jane." Reynolds shook her head. "She doesn't deserve this. They won't go easy on her, you wait and see," she murmured, rocking gently back and forth on her heels.

Jones shot her a depressed look. She felt sick thinking of Jane. Staggered, she sat down, striving to ease the knots in her stomach.

"She'll be okay. She's strong," she said, forcing positivity into her tone.

Reynolds looked at her but couldn't answer.

Jones sensed what was on her mind simply by the look in her eye. "Come on, Bates won't let him hurt her too much. He needs her. She'll make it."

"Sarah, who are you trying to kid? You heard him say he's willing to sacrifice one of us."

Jones was lost for an answer. She stared hard at her. "She'll make it, okay?" she repeated, injecting more assurance into the words.

Reynolds maintained the piercing stare for a lingering moment before turning away shaking her head.

Jones dropped her gaze to the floor, retreating into her own thoughts under a strained silence.

Billie sucked in a breath and lifted her head, resting it against the wall. She kept her eyes closed while gathering her shattered wits. Her cheek pounded. A trickle of blood ran from her lip – the tender cut from previous blows reopened yet again.

"McCoy? You okay?" Despite Reynolds' harsh tone, concern laced her words.

"Fine," Billie murmured.

"What the hell were you trying to achieve?" Jones growled. "It didn't get you anywhere, other than a few more cuts and bruises."

Billie lifted her shoulders in a tired shrug. "Nothing I guess. I just didn't like seeing Bates act so smug."

"Well," Jones stumbled after a sudden hush. "You sure brought him down a peg, and the others." Her humble words carried more compassion, and possibly a touch of respect. Billie opened her eyes and met her stare.

"Yeah." Her voice was weak. "Pity it wasn't a bit more." Her gaze drifted to Jane's vacant spot. "Where's Jane?" She lowered her head and fingered her bruised cheek. Silence met her. She dropped her cuffed hands and looked up. Both girls stared with sombre faces.

"Bates said she was to pay Smith for his services," Reynolds glumly informed her.

Billie's stare locked on hers. "Pay?" The girls didn't need to elaborate. "Shit." Leaning her head back, she looked up at the roof. Her heart went out to Jane. She was in for a hard time. Damn them.

Jones intruded into her thoughts with a hesitant conclusion. "He also said it was to teach you a lesson for not sticking to the rules." Her tone hardened with each word.

Billie looked at her in surprise, stunned by the words, as well as the insinuation behind them. She glanced at Reynolds, who looked in the same frame of mind.

"You think it's because of me Jane's in trouble? Because I took them on? Is that what you're saying?"

A brief silence met her. The suspicion was definitely there but not so much the blame.

"You tell us," Jones said.

Again, silence engulfed them. Billie had to give them credit for not jumping in and accusing her straight out like they normally did. They were giving her a chance to defend herself. She lowered her head to collect her thoughts. It was a touchy situation and had to be handled carefully. Finally, she looked up. The girls waited patiently for an answer, watching her with guarded stares.

"If you really believe that, well, I guess that's your choice, and I can understand it, but let me tell you this – if you think I'd deliberately want to hurt any of you guys, you're wrong." She paused, taking the time to study their concentrated faces. "To tell you the truth, I doubt if my effort made any difference at all. It's no more than an excuse for Bates to throw his weight around. He's still pissed at me and is obviously trying to turn us against one another. He had every intention of taking Jane the moment he walked in here. That's why he came in the first place – to fix up Smith for his . . . services, right?"

The thought almost choked her. She turned away to contain the anguish gripping her. Damn Bates. Fear gripped her at the thought of Jane facing it alone. She prayed they'd bring her back in one piece. Billie fought to appear strong for the two girls with her. She had to. They needed to get through it together. Bravely, she forced herself to look at them.

"I didn't do anything to change his mind. He was simply killing two birds with one stone."

Jones and Reynolds considered the answer. They looked at each other. Faint smiles slipped to their lips. They seemed to relax.

"We knew that. We just wanted to hear it from you," Jones said.

Billie looked from one to the other and then lowered her head, gathering her thoughts and emotions. The girls had tried and tested her, and she'd come through on top. It meant they finally believed in her. Lifting her gaze, she returned their smiles. "Thanks."

Chapter Three

The quiet click of the door opening woke Billie.

Darkness had fallen a long while back. Light from an outside lantern filtered into the storeroom through the log walls, enough to soften the stark darkness. Since Jane had been taken from them, she and the girls had been left alone. No one had checked on them or bullied them. Neither food nor drink had been offered. Despite their worry for Jane, they'd fallen asleep.

The door gently closed. Lying still, Billie half opened her eyes to see who was sneaking in on them. To her surprise, it was the boy, the aboriginal boy at the truck with Smith who had assisted in their capture. The silhouette of his small frame in front of the door pinpointed his position accurately. What was he up to? Why would he come in here? Surely they'd be out of bounds to him.

He glanced at each of them. He didn't appear to be armed and didn't seem a threat. After a few moments, he took a step forward.

Billie slowly sat up to let him know she was awake. He stopped instantly – not only stopped but jumped back a step. The detective stiffened. Had she scared him off? He was obviously in two minds about being there.

The young boy peered intently at her through the semi-darkness, making no effort to retreat any further. Inwardly, Billie sighed, relieved he wasn't running away. Her curiosity stirred. Had he come as an ally or enemy? After meeting Smith, the boy was nothing more than a pawn, a hostage to his authority, a slave to his egotistical power – in short, an innocent party. Prepared to give him the benefit of the doubt, she had to gain his confidence. He'd come this far – he needed to know it hadn't been for nothing.

"Hi," she said softly.

He neither answered nor moved.

Reynolds and Jones woke to Billie's welcome, as quiet as it had been. Both sat up. Their attention was drawn towards the door. The boy shot them a look and took another step backwards. It carried him into the door with a bump. He jumped.

"Hey, it's okay. We're not going to hurt you," Reynolds gently said. "Besides, we can't go anywhere in these chains so you're pretty safe over there."

"Do you have a name?" Billie asked. He looked at her but still refused to say anything. "Mine's Billie."

His gaze swept across Reynolds and Jones. After a moment, he stepped forward.

"I'll set you free as long as you take me with you."

Billie contained her surprise, hardly believing what she was hearing. He'd come to free them? Despite his fears, he'd made a huge effort to contemplate a deal with them. She looked at the girls. Both shrugged, as caught off guard by his request as she was.

The cop turned to the boy. She smiled and nodded. "You've got yourself a deal."

"Promise?" he pressed. "You're not saying that just so I'll let you go?"

"Promise," she assured him.

"Cross your heart and hope to die?" His timid voice sounded panicky and frightened.

Slow and precisely, Billie crossed her heart with her cuffed hands. "Cross my heart and hope to die," she said in a quiet, sincere tone.

The boy relaxed a little and nodded. Hesitantly, he stepped forward, his hand digging into a pocket of his shorts. From it, he pulled out a key. He knelt in front of her. Billie held the cuffs up. Even in the subdued light, they stood out. The boy fumbled with the key in the lock.

"Good boy," she praised after the cuffs sprang open. "Thank you, very much."

"My name's Janda."

Billie checked the urge to hug him. The fact he'd willingly told her his name, and more than likely saved her life, stirred her emotions deeply. But it was too soon. She didn't want to put him off. Instead, she put out her hand.

"It's nice to meet you, Janda." She smiled. "Very nice indeed."

With some hesitancy, he took the offered hand. They exchanged a brief shake. Janda stood and moved to Jones. Billie climbed to her feet. Her body had stiffened up. A gasp left her lips. She paused, waiting for the sharp pain across her ribs to pass. Only the adrenaline pumping through her blood at the taste of freedom helped her get on top of it. Supporting her ribs with one hand, she walked to the door and opened it a fraction, peering out. There were no guards anywhere to be seen. Within a few moments, the others joined her.

"Your van's around to the left, out the back," Janda whispered.

"Okay, you lead the way," Billie said. He nodded. She turned to Jones and Reynolds. "I'm going to get Jane. I'll meet you there."

Both were taken by surprise.

"Wait a minute! We—!" Reynolds started but was drowned out by Jones' abrupt and negative objection.

"What? We need to get out while we—!"

The sudden attack from both girls raised Billie's guard. "I'm not leaving her!" she said in a harsh whisper, cutting them off. Jones looked confused, and maybe a little panicky. It was obvious she wanted to get out of here as fast as possible, which was understandable – but with or without Jane? "You go," she said to her, striving to control her irritation. "Get to the van and be ready to roll. I'll meet you there."

"Shit, McCoy—" Reynolds started.

"I'm not leaving without Jane."

"Hey, I'm not suggesting you do, but you don't have to go on your own," she protested. "We care about her, too, you know, and you've still got tender wounds in case you've forgotten."

Billie's anger suddenly fizzled. Put off by Jones' quick jump to run, on top of her worry for Jane, she'd failed to recognise Reynolds' concern. Her words touched her. She was actually considering *her* welfare before her own, or Jane's for that matter. So used to full-on attacks, insults and accusations from these girls, it caught her off guard.

She glanced at Jones. She failed to object or support Reynolds' reasoning. Was she still as eager to get out of here or was she regretting what she'd said? Ignoring her, the detective turned to Reynolds, forcing herself to stay composed. Her voice mellowed. "I'll be okay."

"Shit," Jones grumbled. "Damn it, I'll come with you then." Her harsh tone lacked commitment.

Billie noted the aggression and dread mixed with displeasure in the girl's tone. "No. There's no—"

"Shut it, McCoy. Casey is better off at the van. She may have to hotwire it. Besides, you could run into trouble. Who knows what they've done to Walker, and you're certainly not up to carrying her out if you need to."

Billie stared at her. They could dispute this all night. Every second was precious, and her worry for Jane consumed her. But could she put her trust in Jones? In the past, they'd clashed every time. Who was to say that wouldn't happen when they were alone? Could she rely on her if there was trouble? Her heart wasn't in it now so how would she cope if things went wrong?

Reynolds cut into her thoughts. "Damn it, neither of you are up to it."

Billie glanced at her and then turned to Jones. She stared back, unflinching. Billie relented.

"You want to come? Fine. We're wasting time so let's move." She looked at the boy and rested a hand on his shoulder. "Janda, do you know where they took our friend?"

He nodded. "She's in the third hut down to the right."

Billie smiled and squeezed his shoulder. "Thanks, you've been a great help. Oh, just one other thing. Can I borrow your key for the cuffs?"

Nodding, he dug it out of his pocket and handed it to her.

"Good boy," She looked at Reynolds. "Look after him. We'll be as fast as we can. Make sure you're ready to go."

"Hey, you don't have to worry about what I'll be ."

"Just be ready," Jones reinforced with an impatient assertion. Reynolds looked sharply at her. The hurt on her face was visible even under the semi-darkness.

Jones caught herself. "Just be ready," she said with less aggression in an apologetic tone.

"I will be. Just *you* be careful, damn it. I don't want to have to leave here without you."

Jones nodded. "You won't, I promise."

Reynolds looked at Billie. The detective nodded. Swinging open the door, she slipped out. Jones followed, and then Reynolds and the boy stepped through. Reynolds pulled the door quietly closed behind her. With a quick glance at the two girls, she rested an arm around Janda's shoulders and led him off to the left. Billie watched them disappear into the shadows. Catching Jones' gaze, they turned in the opposite direction.

Chapter Four

Thanks to Janda's directions, Billie and Jones easily found the third hut. After listening for any noises coming from within, the detective silently opened the door and peered in. Her gaze swept around the room. Jane was asleep on a bed. No one guarded her. Giving Jones a quick nod, the two slipped in. Closing the door behind them, they stopped, stunned.

Under the soft light thrown by the kerosene lantern on a corner table, their focus locked on Jane. She lay half-naked and bloody with long welts across her body. Her wrists were cuffed separately to the bedhead, rubbed almost raw. Billie had known Smith wouldn't be gentle but never imagined he'd go this far, never imagined Bates would *let* him go this far.

The detective shot Jones a glance. She returned it with a look of horror. Without a word, the cop moved across the room. Jones hesitantly followed. They went to opposite sides of the narrow bed, studying the battered girl more closely. Jane's face was bruised. Red welts stretched across her arms, stomach and thighs. Her shirt was torn, stained with her own blood. Her shorts hung off her hips with the fly gaping wide. It looked as if they'd been carelessly pulled on as an afterthought. There had been no clemency. Smith had abused her without rules or limitations. The only small comfort was Jane still lived.

Billie glanced across at Jones. She lifted her sombre gaze, unable to say anything. The detective reached up with the key and unlocked Jane's right cuff. It sprang open. Gently, she lowered Jane's hand and passed the key to Jones. Without a word, Jones took hold of Jane's left wrist and positioned the handcuff so she could see the lock more clearly. Before she could slide the key into the hole, Jane woke with a start. She immediately tensed and sat upright, pulling free from the hands holding her. She cowered against the bedhead whimpering.

Stark terror marked her face. Turning away, she dropped her head low and closed her eyes.

"No, please..." she sobbed.

Billie's stomach tightened. "Jane, it's okay. It's me, McCoy."

Jane tried to shrink away.

"Come on, it's over. Take it easy," Billie said in a tender voice. "Jones is here with me. We've come to get you out. How does that sound?"

Slowly, Jane lifted her head and focused on the face in front of her. Sitting without a movement, she stared with wet, wide eyes. They narrowed. A confused expression twisted her frightened features.

Recognising the beginnings of a responsive look, the detective kept up her comforting words. "It's me, Billie. We're getting you out of here." She reached out and took Jane's hand.

The girl jumped at her touch but didn't pull away. She looked harder at the face in front of her.

"Billie?" she whispered, focusing on the detective with an unwavering stare. "Billie?" Her voice held more strength.

"Yes, and Sarah." The cop smiled, nodding towards Jones. Jane slowly turned. Jones flashed a comforting smile, at the same time trying to hide her unease.

"Hi."

"Sarah?" Jane sobbed. A crooked smile pushed up her swollen lips. With a shaky hand, she reached out and grabbed her arm. "Please get me out of here." Tears filled her red eyes.

"Hey, that's why we came." Jones forced her voice to sound positive as she fought to hold back her tears. "Hell, you didn't think we'd leave you here, did you?"

Billie shot her a questioning look. Jones briefly met her gaze and flashed a faint smile. Guilt and regret washed it away. Billie's faith in Jones kicked in. Now her heart was in it.

Jane sobbed. She looked from one girl to the other as Jones and Billie kept up a quiet, positive chatter. She began to relax under their reassuring words. Jones sprang the cuff on her hand. Jane gave a sob and lowered her head. She rubbed her chafed wrists.

Billie took hold of her arm. "You okay?"

Jane looked up and nodded.

"Good. Do you think you can get up?"

Another nod. Billie smiled.

"Come on." As the detective started to help her up, Jane suddenly grabbed her. She pulled her in close and hugged her tight. She sobbed uncontrollably. Billie held her, letting her cry. It was the best way to get it out of her system. She spoke quiet, soothing words while stroking her hair.

Jones rested a hand on Jane's shoulder, doing her bit to comfort her.

After a few moments, the battered girl sat back and looked at the detective, and then Jones. She wiped her tearstained eyes with the back of her hand.

"You're doing fine," Jones encouraged, squeezing her shoulder.

Jane nodded. "Can we go?" Anxiousness tainted her voice. "I want to get out of here, before they come back." She spoke in a whisper, a scared whisper.

"You bet. I'll check the door," Jones offered, glancing at Billie. The detective gave a slight nod and turned to Jane. Now that she'd sat up, her clothes hung open. Gently she did up what buttons were left on the torn, bloodstained shirt. It barely covered her, but it would do for now; they had spares in the van.

As Jones walked off to the door, Jane briefly looked into the cop's concerned eyes before bowing her head. It was nothing more than a fleeting glance, but Billie was quick to catch the dismay in her look. Now that Jane had some control over her emotions, the horror of the ordeal was no doubt hitting her full on. It would take time to get over, and Jane would experience many feelings before she took control again, if ever she did. It wasn't going to be easy. To let her know she was there for her, Billie stroked her arm.

A thump and soft cry suddenly snatched her full attention. Billie's head shot around. Jones was rolling across the floor away from the opened door. Shock gripped the detective when Bland stepped into the room with an evil grin spread across her hard, sun-dried face.

Jane sucked in a breath.

Jones came to rest beside the wall, unconscious. She lay on her back. Blood ran from her nose.

Billie's gaze snapped to Bland. The big woman slowly closed the door. The beady, calculating eyes were fixed on the cop with a hateful stare, challenging, goading her to stop her if she dared. Billie knew she didn't have a choice. The only way they were leaving this room was through the big bitch.

She let go of Jane's arm. Jane immediately grabbed her forearm, tight. Billie shot her a look. On the verge of panic, Jane obviously didn't want to be left alone. Billie had to peel her fingers off to pull free.

"It's okay," the detective quietly assured her with a brief smile. It was all she had time for. Her attention returned to Bland. Billie stood off the bed and faced the big woman.

Bland's glare didn't alter. The piercing eyes followed her every move. "I told you you weren't getting away from me again, you bitch." The words fired like daggers.

Jane's frightened gasp drew the cop's attention to her. She cowered against the bedhead hugging her knees with her face buried behind them. Focusing on the problem at hand, Billie stepped forward to meet the approaching freak. The further she was away from Jane, the better. She didn't want her involved; she'd been through enough.

Bland raised a fist and swung a powerful punch the moment the detective was in range. The cop ducked under it and struck out, ramming Bland in the stomach and then in the face. The big woman staggered into the wall beside the bedside table.

Billie waited poised in a fighter's stance. Even though she'd got in quick, Bland had already recovered.

The big woman snatched the cracked china vase off the table beside her. Snarling, she charged, swinging her weapon in a wild swipe. Billie backed off, avoiding any contact by ducking. As fast as Bland attacked, she couldn't land a blow.

Jones moaned. Her head lolled slowly to the side and then settled. Billie couldn't expect any help from her. Returning her attention to Bland, she continued to weave and duck under each swing the big woman launched at her. The constant movement put pressure on her wound. The pain gradually increased, enough to slow her down.

Finally Bland got lucky. The vase clipped the detective across the forehead. She reeled into the wall. Somehow, she managed to stay on her feet. The room spun in front of her. Billie shook her head in an effort to clear it.

"NO!" Jane leapt off the bed and dived at Bland as the woman stepped towards the cop.

Bland turned and shot out a hand in an upward swing, backhanding Jane across the cheek while in mid-flight. She was swatted to the side like an annoying fly. She landed with a grunt in a sprawled, dazed heap beside Jones.

When the big woman turned to face the cop, Billie's foot slammed her in the face. She staggered backwards. Billie followed and kicked again and a third time with a speed Bland had no chance of contending with. Billie's fury fuelled her vigour. The bitch had hurt her friends one too many times. Focusing every ounce of energy into hurting the woman, her concentration engrossed on each kick, she directed the point of contact where it would do the most damage.

The cop jumped high and spun in the air, her right foot coming around and smashing into Bland's bleeding face. Landing and catching her balance, Billie kept up her relentless attack. Although her kicks landed hard, they only managed to stagger the big woman back a small step at a time. She could have been made of steel for all her staying power. With determination driving her on, the detective continued her assault.

Given no time to launch any attack of her own, Bland opted for defence. In a rash turnaround, she caught Billie's foot, preventing it from connecting a sixth time. Billie stood trapped, pivoted on one leg. Bland glared a vicious scowl.

Billie suddenly threw herself up and over, driving out her other foot to kick the surprised Bland in the nose before she could react. Involuntary, the big woman released the trapped foot and fell into the wall with a grunt. Billie landed on both feet and stumbled forward with a few shaky steps. She caught her balance and straightened, sucking in short breaths. A hand rested against her throbbing ribs to help support them. The pain was intense, but she couldn't stop.

Her gaze returned to Bland. The woman hadn't moved. She leant on the wall half-dazed, her head tilted back with closed eyes, her hands outstretched to keep her there. Her lip and cheek were cut open and bleeding. Blood ran from her swollen nose. Bruising had swollen her eye and jaw. It seemed her kicks had at last had some effect. The vase slipped from her grasp.

Billie moved in and punched Bland hard in the stomach and then kneed her in the face after she folded forward. The freak was powerless to offer any resistance. Her body went with the punches, taking every hit full on. Billie's antipathy drove her on regardless of her own agony. She'd waited for this moment far too long. Again, she punched Bland's bloodied face. The big woman groaned, unable to oppose any attack. Her head rocked to the side yet she refused to fall.

Breathing hard and swaying dangerously, Billie stopped her attack. She stepped back and looked at her victim. Bland clung to the wall dead on her feet, her battered and bloody face barely recognisable. Her head lolled back, the closed, puffy eyes unable to open.

Still, the detective wasn't satisfied, and wouldn't be – not until this woman had fully paid her dues. Ignoring the burning pain across her ribs, Billie dredged up her inner strength and kicked up one last time. Making it count, she smashed her foot into Bland's jaw with all the power she could muster. Bland crashed to the floor and lay still. It was over. Billie stood clasping her side and panting hard, watching her fallen opponent while letting her emotions bathe in the victorious, avenging moment. Bland wouldn't be getting up for a long while.

But victory came with a price. Now that it was over, her body screamed its complaints. She struggled to stay on her feet. Staggering to the side, she fell into the wall, taking her weight on her shoulder. Billie closed her eyes. She held her ribs to ease the pain engulfing her. Her shirt was wet and warm – blood. Desperately she strived to control her breathing, calling on her diminishing strength for added assistance. Unfortunately, her reserves were spent. She'd put everything into beating Bland and now had to pay the consequences. Slowly, she slid down the wall to her knees, gasping and lightheaded. She couldn't stop herself sinking lower onto her calves. Her head dropped down. She could do no more.

Hands took hold of her arm and gently pulled her around, leaning her against the wall. Billie didn't resist. She slid off her bent knees onto her rump, bringing her legs out from under her with some effort. She leant her head back and, with half opened eyes, looked at the two girls kneeling in front of her, unable to say anything to take the worried looks off their faces.

Jones pulled Billie's bloody hand away from her soaked shirt and looked at her wound. Shock widened her eyes. "Shit."

"Oh no," Jane breathed, the concern heavy in her tone.

"Oh, that's great," Jones growled. "You've probably busted open your stitches. You're supposed to be taking it easy, damn it. Don't you remember Todd telling you that?"

The cop lowered her head and closed her eyes, too weak to argue.

"What are you trying to do? Kill yourself?" Jones went on in a heated reprimand. "You shouldn't be fighting. Who knows what sort of mess you've made of your wound."

Billie lifted her head with an effort and rested it against the wall. She looked at Jones' livid face. "I didn't w-want her following us."

"Following us? You stopped her following us about six hits ago. She was dead on her feet, going nowhere, but *no-o-o*, you had to keep hammering her, didn't you. Hell. You won't even be able to walk out of here now. Just another problem to burden us with. Hell, we may as well stay until daylight with the time we've lost here."

"I h-had to make sure," Billie weakly defended herself. She closed her eyes to concentrate on studying her breathing and ride the pain.

"Shit. We've got enough problems without having to worry about stitching you up all the time."

"Maybe I sh-should have just let her take us." The detective forced her eyes open to look at Jones. The last thing she felt like was a lecture, especially after saving the girl's arse – again.

"Oh. So now you're going to be smart? Didn't I tell you we'd run into trouble? I knew Bland wouldn't give us up. I knew it."

"Hey, come on, lay off. McCoy is on our side, remember?" Jane interrupted, resting a hand on Jones' shoulder. Jones' head snapped around. The fiery eyes stared hard. About to blast her, Jane's sombre bruised features suddenly robbed her of any comment.

"We owe her quite a lot, don't you think?" Jane added in a shaky voice.

Jones sat stunned in a rigid pose.

"Can we please get going?" Jane persisted.

Relaxing a little, Jones glanced at Billie. Over her laboured breathing, the cop blinked hard, struggling to keep her eyes open and her attention focused.

Jones turned to Jane and nodded. "Good idea," she said without harshness, backing it with a flash of a smile. "I'm sorry. I guess I can get a little carried away sometimes."

Jane managed a feeble smile. Jones squeezed her arm. Standing, she helped Jane to her feet and then leant down and took Billie by the arm.

"Come on, McCoy, you can't sit here all night."

Billie looked up, surprised by Jones' sudden change of mood. "Funny, I th-thought you w-anted to s-stay."

"Shut up, or I'll leave you here with Bland." With a strong hand, she hauled the cop to her feet. Billie gasped and fell against the wall when a dizzy spell hit her. Caught off guard, Jones was pulled with her. She struggled to keep the cop on her feet. Jane jumped forward and helped.

Jones lifted Billie off the wall and threw the cop's arm around her shoulders, gripping her by the wrist to keep her upright. She slipped an arm around her waist as added support.

The detective gasped with every movement and had to lean into Jones. Being on her feet brought a new wave of torture. Jones staggered under her weight but held her upright. Billie's head sank low as she dealt with the agony across her wound. Rasping in shallow breaths, she lifted a hand to support her ribs.

"At least McCoy gave Bland what she deserved," Jane stated in a flat tone.

"Yeah, I guess she did," Jones said.

"Do you need help with her?"
"No, I'll manage."
"Yell if she gets too heavy, okay?"
"Sure."
Billie looked up. Jane, anxious, stood in front watching her.
"You okay?"
Behind the concerned question, the detective read the respect in her eyes. The troubled look on her battered face was strained, along with the twinges of pain she tried to hide. She guessed Jones had knocked back her help because of her injuries.
"Yeah, much better n-now, thanks," Billie answered, followed by a faint, appreciative smile. Jane returned it. "H-how about you?" the detective asked.
"Me? Just eager to get out of here."
"Well, I'm r-ready when you guys are."
Jane nodded and glanced at Jones. "I'll check the door."
"Hey," Jones cut in. "Stand to the side when you open it – just in case," she advised with a tired smile. "Doors and faces don't go together, believe me."
Jane cast a quick glance over her bruised cheek and bloodied nose. Meeting her eye again, she nodded. She hobbled to the door. Following Jones' 'opening' instructions, she peered out.
"It's all clear."
Billie winced the instant they moved off. Every step brought pain. All she could do was grit her teeth and push on. They had to get out of here. Who knew how long before Smith would visit again.
At a steady pace, the girls trudged towards the van. Jones half carried Billie. Too weak to fully take her own weight, the cop could do little to help. Jane hobbled ahead of them, casting nervous glances around and behind them for any signs of trouble. On the girls pushed, slow but surely, moving like the walking dead, edging their way to that wonderful world of freedom.

Chapter Five

The side door of the van slid open with a loud rattle. Both Reynolds and Janda jumped. Seated in the front, their heads snapped around. Relief momentarily swept across Reynolds' strained features before the irritation washed it away.

"Where the *hell* have you been? I was sure they must've caught you again, damn it!" she exploded in a harsh whisper.

"Yeah? Well, they almost did. We ran into Bland," Jones said, helping Billie in.

Exhausted from the walk, the detective collapsed on the thin mattress breathing hard. Jane climbed stiffly in with Jones' help. She crawled over the cop to the opposite wall.

"Bland?" Reynolds' voice held shock mixed with panic.

Jones jumped in and closed the door. "Just get us out of here."

Hesitating a moment to absorb the news, Reynolds faced the front and started the van. It kicked over in a healthy idle. The vehicle leapt forward with spinning wheels.

Jones watched out the back window tight-lipped. "Shit, they must know we've escaped. Lights are coming on in the huts."

"Don't worry, they won't catch us. We've had too much of a head start," Reynolds said confidently. "Besides, I did McCoy's trick and fiddled with the other vehicles. They won't get them going in a hurry, that's for sure."

Jones turned to her with raised eyebrows. "Really? That's . . . great. Good thinking."

"Yeah. I thought you'd like it."

"Yeah, I do, a lot."

The van rattled and shook as it raced over the gravel road through the shelter of the towering trees.

"So what happened to you guys back there?" Reynolds asked.

"McCoy took out Bland but I think she's busted open her stitches." Jones reached up and turned on the interior light.

"Shit, you guys look like you've been to hell and back," Reynolds gasped.

"No kidding."

The cabin's dim light revealed Jones' bloody and swollen nose and the darkening bruise on her cheek. Jane sat huddled along the wall with her knees pulled in tight covered in welts and bruises, her clothes torn and bloody. The cop lay breathing hard. Blood covered the front of her shirt.

Jones knelt over her and pulled the shirt up, revealing the bloodied bandage underneath. She carefully unwrapped it and took off the soaked dressing, at last exposing the wound.

"Bloody hell, McCoy, no wonder you're in so much pain. It looks inflamed." She leant closer and dabbed at it with the bandage to clear away the blood. "I don't believe it. The stitches are still intact, just stretched a little. Shit, Todd should've been a doctor." Her gaze lifted to meet Billie's. "You sure are lucky."

"Really? I don't feel so lucky," the detective gasped.

"Stop whinging. Typical bloody cop. Always has to find something to complain about."

Billie managed a faint smile and tried to relax. Jones used water and the first aid kit Todd had given them to clean the wound before strapping it up with a clean bandage and new dressing.

"There. Now, stay put, damn it. If I see you make one move, I'll lay you out myself."

Billie looked at her. "I'm not going anywhere, honest." The pain had eased considerably, allowing her to appreciate Jones' words of wisdom and assistance. Through all the trouble, the girl hadn't let her down. Without her, she wouldn't have made it out. "And, hey, thanks, for everything."

Jones returned her gaze thoughtfully. She nodded. "Sure." Flashing a smile, she glanced at Jane. Billie rolled her head to look at her. Jane hadn't moved. She sat staring at the opposite wall. The shock must have caught up with her. Jones crawled to her, dragging the first aid kit. Lightly, she touched her arm. Jane jumped, cringing. Jones was quick to reassure her.

"Hey, it's okay. I just want to clean you up a little, that's all."

Jane stared at her, almost coldly, distantly. Slowly, the glassy look faded from her eyes. She gave a hesitant nod.

"I'm sorry," she whispered.

Jones made no comment. She started cleaning the blood from her face. Jane stared blankly ahead. From the look on her face, Billie guessed the horror scenes were still haunting her. She was obviously trying to deal with it in her own way, any way. But rape came with a high price.

"Want to talk about it?" Jones asked.

"No." The answer was abrupt.

Jones took no offence. "Might help."

Jane looked hard at her. Her lips trembled. Words failed her. She looked at Billie lying calmly, watching. Jane's strained features betrayed her tumultuous emotions.

"It's not good to bottle things like this up," Billie said quietly. "You helped me a great deal by listening to my story, you know, about my parents and Digger. I carried that heartache for years on my own, but now, since opening up to you guys, for the first time, the pain has lifted somewhat. The loss is still raw yet, talking about it has given me a reprieve. Don't let the same thing happen to you. Let us help you."

Billie's parents had been cruelly shot down in front of her when she was twelve. She moved in with Digger, her grandfather, but over the years, they drifted apart. At seventeen, she left to pursue her career to give her the means to hunt down her parents' murderer.

Tears welled in Jane's eyes. She lowered her head to collect her thoughts. The girls gave her a moment. She looked up and nodded, her voice strained and broken.

"He used the whip on me, and his fists, and then he'd force himself on me. He didn't care if it hurt. I think it excited him more when I screamed. The pain was unbearable... and his stench... and the burning inside when he kept on with his..." She fought to hold back the tears. "After having a break and a smoke, he'd start it all over again. He never seemed to tire. And then Bland came to watch."

At the mention of Bland, Jones shot Billie a look. The cop was just as surprised to hear she'd been in on the act. No wonder Jane had been so terrified when the bitch had stepped into the room.

Jane kept on in a low monotone. "She must've got turned on by it because she started to help. She'd hit me... and touch me while Smith was doing his bit... getting off on it." Her voice faded. "She used the whip, making me jump and cry out to excite Smith. He kept urging her to do it..."

Suddenly, she burst into tears, burying her face in her hands. Billie went to get up but Jones lifted a hand and stopped her. She took Jane in her arms and pulled her close in a hug. Jane hung on tightly as the tears flowed. Her body shook, the effects of the shock gripping her in a merciless hold.

"Come on, it's over. Let it out," Jones comforted her.

Billie looked on, containing her surprise. This was a very different side to Jones, a gentle and caring side, one she hadn't seen before, not to this extreme. It was hard to believe it was the same girl. Billie relaxed, confident Jane was in good hands.

After some time, Jane's sobs died. She pulled free and sat back, her face tearstained. She seemed more serene and at peace with herself. Sheepishly, she looked at Jones.

"I'm sorry."

Jones reached up and brushed a strand of hair out of her red eyes. "Don't be. I didn't mind at all. As long as you feel better for it." She smiled.

Jane nodded, also managing a light smile. "I do, a lot, thanks." She glanced at Billie. The cop offered a supportive smile. Jane turned to Jones and shook her head. "How can I ever thank you guys for coming to get me out? I know you didn't have to."

"Of course, we did. We've made it this far as a team; we'll make it the whole way as a team, right?" Jones stated confidently. "Correct me if I'm wrong, but weren't those your words?"

Jane's smile strengthened. She nodded, stifling a sob. Billie related to her reaction. Right from the start, Jane had fought to keep them together, to work together. Huh. To merely put up with each other was a feat on its own. But her persistence had paid off. The four of them *were* a team, friends, looking out for one another.

"And McCoy sure got Bland back," Jones added. "That little work over should keep her out of the picture for a long while. It couldn't have happened to a nicer person. Ha! Bates will get the shock of his life when he finds our little surprise in the 'third hut'."

Jane suddenly tensed, staring fixedly at her with an alarmed look. Jones stiffened. Slowly, the smile faded from Jane's lips. Her gaze shifted to Billie.

"I really hope she's dead."

Billie studied her grim face, reading the mixed look of hate and hurt across her stressed features. Jane desperately needed some cheering up.

"It would be nice, but, unfortunately, she seems to be more machine than flesh. She's too thick skinned to die that easily, I'm afraid. Mind you, had I had a two by two, it might've been a different story," she said, ending on a weak smile.

Jones' head snapped around in surprise. Both she and Jane stared in a fixed trance, absorbing the words.

"Always full of excuses, aren't you, McCoy?" Jones finally said.

Billie looked at her and gave a laugh. She turned to Jane. "Shit, imagine the lecture she would've given me if I *had* killed her. I copped enough for knocking the bitch down to save her arse and take the heat off her."

The comment drew a short snort from Jane and a yelp of protest from Jones.

"You call that just 'knocking down'?" Jones challenged. "I didn't think you were going to stop."

"Well, she does tend to get me riled fairly easily, and you were just lying around – I had to be sure she wouldn't get up to come after us."

"Oh, of course! I was just . . . lying around," she mocked, throwing her hands in the air. Shaking her head, she glanced at the smiling Jane. "Can you believe the shit that comes out of her mouth?"

"I'm starting to." She glanced at Billie before turning to Jones. "Hey, can I fix up your nose?"

"Are you up to it?"

"Sure."

Jones nodded. "Be my guest." She sat against the wall and brought her knees up, resting her arms on top. Jane took a clean cloth from the first aid kit and began cleaning the blood from under her nose. Jones glanced at the cop.

"McCoy? I'm sorry for going off at you back there. I was way out of line."

Billie looked at her, a little surprised she'd brought the subject back up. "Forget it, we were all uptight."

"Yeah, I know, but it still didn't give me the right to take it out on you. I want to apologise."

"Apology accepted."

"Good." Her shoulders shifted down. She exhaled a tired breath. "Man, it sure has been a long night."

Jane sighed. "More like an eternity." Her hand dropped from Jones' face. A frown furrowed her brow. She looked from Jones to Billie. "Which reminds me, how did you guys get free?"

A smile lit up Jones' face. "We have Janda to thank for that."

On cue, the boy poked his head up over the front seat with a friendly smile. Jane stared in astonishment.

"Janda, meet Jane," Jones said.

"Hello," he answered shyly. Beneath his short, curly black hair, his placid face expressed only innocence.

Jane smiled. "Hi, Janda."

"Yes, he came to us with a key and an offer we couldn't refuse." Jones smiled at him. "A sure godsend."

"And in the nick of time," Reynolds added on a warm note.

"Definitely."

The boy nodded and ducked out of sight. Jane finished cleaning Jones's face.

"There you go. That looks better."

"Thanks. How about we get you out of that shirt," Jones suggested. Jane nodded.

"That would be good." She removed her shirt. Jones attended to the wounds across her body. All were superficial. Given time, they'd heal even though they'd most probably be uncomfortable for a few days. After doctoring her patient, Jones found Jane a clean shirt and pair of shorts. She passed Billie a shirt to change into as well. Luckily for them, Kym had thrown in a few spares.

Wrapped in conversation, and the wonderful sense of freedom, the kilometres rolled on beneath the girls with no sense of measure or distress.

Chapter Six

Jones woke with a start. The movement of the van rattling across the dirt track settled any anxious thoughts that sprang to mind. They were safe, away from Bates and on their way home, hopefully. She sat up. Everyone slept around her. She looked to Reynolds behind the wheel. She had to be tired. She hadn't stopped since they'd made their escape. Jones shuffled in close to the seat beside her.

"Hey, want a break?"

Reynolds jumped and cast a look over her shoulder. "Shit, don't do that."

Jones chuckled. "Sorry, I didn't mean to scare you." With everyone asleep, Casey wouldn't have expected a voice in her ear. "You've been driving for a while." She looked out the windscreen. Dawn was breaking. The early hours of the morning bathed the passing trees in soft, sunlit greys. "Man, all night by the looks of it."

"I didn't mind, but I think now I'd love a break." Reynolds pulled up and left the van idling while she climbed over into the back, allowing Jones room to slide into the front. Jones looked at the sleeping Janda slumped against the door.

"I think Janda would be more comfortable in the back with you guys."

"Good idea. Pass him over."

Jones sat him up. He woke and looked at her with sleepy eyes. She smiled.

"Hey, Janda, hop in the back, buddy. You'll be more comfortable."

He nodded and knelt up. She helped him slide over the seat to Reynolds who settled him on the mattress beside Billie. He closed his eyes and didn't move. Neither did the cop. Reynolds stretched out beside Janda, exhaling a grateful sigh.

"Home, James, and don't spare the horses."

"Ha. You'll have no argument there." Jones smiled. She turned and slipped in behind the wheel. As she drove off, movement to the side caught her attention. Jane gingerly climbed into the front seat beside her.

"Hey, shouldn't you try and sleep?" Jones asked, a little surprised.

"I have and I can't, so I may as well keep you awake," she said with a faint smile. Jones looked at her thoughtfully and nodded, returning the smile.

"Good. I hate driving alone. How are you doing anyway?"

"You mean up here?" she queried, touching her temple.

Jones nodded, momentarily taking her eyes from the road to look at her passenger. Jane dropped her hand and held her gaze with a pensive expression. She turned away, looking out at the road.

"Okay, I guess. I just feel so . . . used . . . and dirty. I wish I could take a shower."

"Yeah, I understand exactly where you're coming from." Jones sighed and glanced briefly at Jane, their gazes connecting.

"What do you mean?"

"It happened to me once and, believe me, it really shook me, which is crazy. I mean after all, that's what I do for a living," she said, throwing a hand up and shaking her head. "This time, it was different though. This guy, a real creep, hired me one night and tied me to the bed. He was crazy – mean and cruel, *and* he went against all the rules."

Her voice faded. She stared ahead as the memories came flooding back after so long. Pushing them aside, she continued.

"He used a knife on me. Not enough to, you know, maim, just enough to draw blood and cause a lot of discomfort. He got such a kick out of it. A bit like Smith. I couldn't get away. The mental torture of it was frightening. I've never been so scared – so helpless – well, not up until this little adventure anyway," she joked. A faint smile crept to Jane's lips in understanding. "But it's a different fear, a personal one that hits deeper, scars deeper. Anyway, I ended up in hospital for a few days, but it took me a long time to get over that bastard."

Jane sat frozen, a look of shock etched across her features as she stared at Jones. "Wow." Slowly, she turned away. She nodded. "I never dreamt it could be so terrifying. I felt so – defenceless."

"Hey, if it means anything, I think you're doing great."

Jane looked at her and smiled. "Thanks, it does."

Sarah changed the subject and spoke of nicer topics. Jane relaxed and engaged with her more freely. The kilometres rolled on. The strengthening daylight washed over the dimness, brightening the surroundings with its magic touch of freshness.

"Must be my turn to drive," Jane said with a renewed confidence after a few hours. "Pull over and we'll swap."

"Are you sure you're up to it? I mean you've been through—"

"Yes." There was no hesitation in her answer. "I'd like to. I need something to do."

Jones watched her for a moment and then obliged. She slowed to a halt, leaving the van idling. Casting Jane a smile, she reached for the door handle. About to open it, suddenly she paused. Her gaze shot past Jane to the scenery beyond.

"Well I'll be. Maybe you'll get your bath after all."

Jane turned and followed her gaze. Out to the left was a creek. Fresh clear water weaved through the trees, sparkling under the new rays of the morning. Jones flashed a cheeky grin when Jane looked back at her.

"I'm game if you are," she said with a daring glint in her eye.

Jane smiled. "I guess. As long as you promise no fighting this time."

At the last creek they'd stopped at to take a refreshing wash, Jones had jumped Billie on the excuse she'd needed to pay her back from an earlier fight. Ending up in the water, Reynolds had joined in, turning it into a biased and dangerous attack. In the end, with Jane's help, Billie had come out on top after putting the two girls in their place – with a respect that squashed all desires to take it up again.

Jones chuckled. "I promise. Mind you, I think I could pretty much handle McCoy at the moment."

Jane smiled. "Don't you believe it."

"Ha, you're probably right. Don't worry, I've learnt my lesson, especially after seeing the opponents she's defeated. I think I got off somewhat lightly."

Jane nodded. "That you did."

"Okay, rise and shine! Surf's up!"

A loud, rapid banging on the side of the door accompanied the call. Billie jumped to her elbows and groaned, forgetting about her wound in her haste. Reynolds and Janda sat up in fright. The cop sank back to the mattress, gasping and struggling to absorb the burning across her ribs.

"Hell, Sarah, what's with you? You scared the shit out of me," Reynolds said, rubbing her eyes.

Billie looked at her, just as confused by Jones' strange wake-up call. Why the urgency to get them up? Was something wrong? No, there couldn't be; Jones was in good spirits, more than she could say about herself at the moment. Her ribs ached. The dull throb came in waves, brought on by the sudden movement. On top of that, she was tired and drained.

"What's wrong? Why have we stopped?" She rolled onto an elbow. As slow and careful as she moved, a moan still slipped from her lips. She clasped her ribs.

Jones grinned. "Give me a break. Nothing's wrong. I just thought you all might like a bath," she said with an added cheeriness.

"A bath? Now? Here?" A strange look shot across Reynolds' face. "Are you taking something you haven't told me about?"

Jones laughed. "I wish."

"So, where are we supposed to take this bath?" her friend asked.

Jones half turned and pointed to the creek behind. All eyes followed her finger. Reynolds' mouth dropped open.

"You're kidding."

"All right," Janda exclaimed, crawling to the door with a wide grin.

Billie fell onto the mattress with a laugh and closed her eyes. Jones had caught her out again. The last thing she expected from this 'city girl' was a bath in a creek.

"Thatta boy, Janda," Jones said. Her voice became sober, directed at the girls. "Come on, it's for Walker's sake. She wants to wash. I thought it would help boost her spirits if we swam with her, you know, to let her know we don't think she's some kind of outcast."

Billie looked past Jones to Jane. She stood with folded arms down near the water.

"But in a creek?" Reynolds protested.

The cop turned to her. "It didn't stop you last time if I remember correctly," she said, drawing Reynolds' attention to her.

The girl smiled and pulled a face. "That's only because you were in there first."

A mischievous grin sprang to Jones' lips, but she didn't comment.

"I will! I always swim in creeks!" Janda cut in on a high-pitched squeal. Without any hesitation, he jumped out of the van and raced down to the water.

"Well, at least someone is excited about it." Jones smiled, watching him go.

"Okay, okay," Reynolds said. "Fine, we'll go for a swim." She looked at Billie and tapped her on the leg. "How about you, McCoy?"

"Sure." The detective rolled onto her elbow and sat up. Immediately, she winced. Reynolds and Jones watched her with a new concern.

"Er–maybe you'd better not," Reynolds said.

"No, I'm good. I'm just a little slow at warming up." Taking a grip on the sharp throbbing, she gazed out the door at Jane. She looked sad and alone. Billie wanted to be there for her, to help her get through this. The sight of her gave her the incentive she needed to override her suffering. Once she was up, she'd be fine. Jones' thoughtful participation also boosted her confidence. Her concern for Jane's welfare touched her. Maybe it was her way of making up for that moment of almost running out on her before they rescued her from Smith. Whatever it was, she'd well stepped up her loyalties.

Billie turned to her. "A swim sounds good – I mean, now that we're up."

Jones nodded and smiled. "Mad if you don't."

Reynolds chuckled. She climbed out, and then the two helped Billie. The cop was grateful for their assistance and, once she was on her feet, stood quite steadily. She'd stiffened up over the last few hours but had to admit she felt much better than last night.

"Thanks."

They nodded in acknowledgement with warm smiles. The three girls walked down to the creek. Already the day was warming up, and the water did look inviting. Billie approached Jane, who stared at the water in a daze. Billie could only imagine what was going through her mind. Left alone, even for such a short period, she'd already been caught in the trap of isolation and recurring horror. She wasn't even aware they'd stopped alongside her.

"Morning," Billie greeted.

Jane jumped and looked sharply at her. Her gaze darted to Jones and Reynolds on the far side of her. Both offered friendly smiles. Jane looked at Billie.

"Morning," she replied with a weak smile. "Sorry for waking you guys."

"Come on, it's the best time of the day."

"Besides, it wasn't you who woke us." Reynolds shot an accusing look at Jones.

"True," Jones admitted, "and it was fun."

"Fun, huh? Let's go feel the water, shall we?" She hooked Jones' arm in hers and led her closer to the creek.

A smile played about Billie's lips.

"Water can be a lot of fun, too, you know," Reynolds added.

"Get that evil glint out of your eye," Jones said.

Jane turned to Billie with an affectionate look. "So, how are the ribs holding up?"

"Not too bad." She cast her a quick glance before turning back to the creek. Janda jumped in with a delighted squeal after Reynolds chased him. "How about you?" she asked, returning her gaze to the girl by her side, at the same time assessing her condition.

Jane bit on her bottom lip and nodded. "Okay, I guess."

"Hey, I think you're doing great."

Jane met Billie's eye and then lowered her head to hide her distress. Billie tensed. The last thing she wanted was to upset her any more than she already was, and she sensed her very presence was doing just that. On top of her terrible ordeal with Smith, the fight with Bland would still be fresh on Jane's mind. Jane cared about her and would have been worried sick during it. It had come at a time when she'd least needed it. The wounds, both the physical and the emotional, had been raw. But time was a great healer, and Jane would work it out in her own way, with enough support. The detective left it at that for now. Jane was handling it quite well, within reason.

She'd accepted what had happened; now, she had to learn to live with it.

"Come on, let's hit the water." Billie took a step towards the creek. Jane's head shot up. Quickly, she grabbed the cop's arm. Billie stopped and looked at her. Jane stared with teary eyes.

"McCoy? Thanks so much for last night."

"You thanked me last night. You don't have to—"

"I know, but it just doesn't seem enough." She looked at Jones and Reynolds standing on the bank. "All of you. Thank you – so much."

Both looked around, meeting her watery gaze. They simply smiled. The four girls' stares danced from one to the other, expressing the sudden mutual understanding between one another.

Reynolds finally broke the silence. "Hell, you're a sorry-looking bunch."

Billie had to agree. After everything they'd suffered, none of them had escaped unscathed. One look at their battle-scarred faces told their story.

"Speak for yourself." Jones gave her an unexpected push – straight off the bank.

"Hey," Reynolds yelped, just before she disappeared into the water. The girls burst into laughter. Jones plunged in beside the submerged girl, taking away any threat of being pushed in herself.

Reynolds emerged spitting out water. The moment Jones surfaced, she lunged at her, pushing her under. Janda swam over to join in.

"Come on, Janda, give me a hand here," Reynolds said with a laugh when he reached her. He cracked a wide grin and eagerly helped.

Jane turned to Billie with a smile. "Can't let them have all the fun, can we?"

"No way."

"Just one thing. Don't go getting into any scuffles out there with them, okay?"

Billie smiled. "Okay. Today, I'll let them off."

"Good."

They stepped down the bank into waist deep water. Jane walked out deeper and sank under the surface. Billie remained by the bank, happy to watch rather than join in on the antics out in the middle. The cool water soothed her battered body. Jane soon joined her.

Both Jones and Reynolds gave Janda the time of his life. They tickled him, ducked him, splashed him, gave him rides on their shoulders, everything young boys loved to do. His contagious giggles never let up. For half an hour, they played, the girls enjoying it as much as he did. When the swimmers climbed out, everyone sat contentedly in the sun, letting the heat dry them off.

Janda beamed. "That was fun," he said, shaking his curls to flick the water out of them.

Reynolds ruffled his hair. "Sure was."

"Can we do it again?"

"Sure, maybe further down the track."

"Great!"

"Feel any better?" Jones asked Jane.

Jane, smiling at Janda, turned to her and nodded. "Much, thanks. You were right."

"*Occasionally* she gets things right," Reynolds teased, and then frowned. "What did you get right?" she said to Jones.

Her confused question drew chuckles from the group.

"My wisdom to take a bath turned out good for Jane."

Reynolds looked at the smiling Jane, who nodded. "That it did."

Jones changed Billie's bandage, and, after a light snack, the travellers were ready to get back on the road. Jane offered to drive. Looking from one to the other, she shook off all objections in a stubborn stand. The girls gave in.

They travelled for another few hours. Everyone was relaxed and in good spirits. The conversations came easy. Not until Jane unexpectedly pulled up did Billie take note of their surroundings. Over the quiet idle of the engine, she stared out the windscreen. They'd stopped on top of a ridge. Tall gums stood proud on either side, towering over a layer of crisp cover of long brown grass. To the right, a timber-slatted gate leant against a tree. It looked as if it hadn't been moved in a long time.

"What's wrong?" Jones asked, studying the surrounding bush.

Jane looked at her and sighed. "We're almost out of fuel, and there's a house down there in the valley. This must be the entrance."

"A house?" Jones crooked her neck, looking past her out the window. "Are you sure?"

"Yes. I saw it through the trees back up the track a bit."

"So, what's your point? We have no money to buy fuel anyway," Reynolds pointed out from behind her.

Jane turned to her. "I wasn't exactly thinking of . . . buying it."

"Oh." Reynolds' quiet answer confirmed she understood exactly what she meant.

"I'm sure they'd have fuel stored out here and wouldn't miss what we'd need," Jane said.

"Mm, good point." Reynolds looked at Billie with a curious glint in her eye.

The detective held her gaze, guessing what was on her mind. After all, she did represent the law, and stealing was a long way from it. Sensing the others' eyes on her, she shot a look at Jane and Jones in the front. Both girls watched her with querying looks.

"Hey! Did I say anything?" she yelped, lifting her hands in defence. "Times are tough, right? Out here, it's everyone for themselves."

After a lingering stare, Jones turned to Reynolds with a half smile. "I think we've got her bluffed."

"Definitely." Reynolds grinned. "We should make a note of this."

A laugh escaped Jane. Janda watched on in delight.

Billie gave a laugh and shrugged. "Come on, I'm as anxious to get home as you are, you know," she said, returning their smiles. "And, after everyone else we've met on this trip, I think it's wise *not* to introduce ourselves."

A brief silence met her. Everyone absorbed her reasoning with fixed, thoughtful stares.

"Yep, you could be right, Sarah." Reynolds nodded with a wide smile, "We've *definitely* got her bluffed."

Billie smiled and shook her head. Why did she always feel ganged up on, no matter what the situation? This mild attack came with a warm sense of acceptance and respect. She was happy to give in to their light teasing and playful mockery, knowing it was hopeless to argue anyway. She rested her head against the wall without any comeback.

Jones smiled at Reynolds. "Most times I am." She turned to the defeated cop with an air of victory. "Tell you what, McCoy. How about you stay here? I mean, we don't want you opening your wound up again, do we."

Billie held the challenging looks with a steady gaze, knowing this was their way of offering her a way out.

"Besides, you won't be much help to us anyway, not in your state."

The excuse brought a wider smile to the detective's lips. All bitterness had vanished from Jones' tone, replaced with a hidden, protective concern – a concern for a friend.

"It's nice to see you finally care," Billie said, happy to let the girls handle it. The less strain she put on her wound, the better, and, besides, this was more down their alley.

"Care? Who said anything about caring? You'd be lucky to *walk* down there let alone carry fuel back."

"Uh huh." Billie smiled, letting the matter drop unchallenged after glancing at the other two grinning girls. She turned to the boy. "Hey, Janda, want to keep me company?"

"Sure."

Everyone climbed out. Reynolds and Jones took the two empty jerry cans from the back. Reynolds turned to Jane. "Maybe you should stay here too."

She shook her head. "No, I'm feeling fine. Besides, the more of us there are to carry the jerries, the lighter they'll be and the quicker we'll get back, won't we."

The girls held her stare for a moment. Jones shrugged.

"Fine. We shouldn't be long," she said to Billie.

The detective nodded. "Be careful."

"We will."

They walked through the gate and followed the winding track down over the ridge out of sight. Billie sighed. If this place was anything like the others, the girls could find trouble. Hopefully, it wouldn't come to that. Pushing the thoughts to the side, she sat down with Janda in the open doorway on the side.

"So, how long have you been a slave, Janda?"

He looked at the ground and kicked away a stone. "As long as I can remember. They told me my mother sold me, that she was too poor to keep me."

Billie's stomach tightened. A likely story. They'd probably stolen him before his mother knew he was gone, lost forever and enslaved for life. Up here, it would be so easy to get away with. She slipped an arm around his shoulders and hugged him.

"Well, if I have anything to do with it, you won't ever be a slave again."

He looked up. His dark brown eyes seemed sad as he gazed into hers. But, then, backed by her promise, he smiled. Billie returned it and gave him another hug.

"You're a good kid, Janda. Don't ever forget that."

Chapter Seven

At first sight of the house, Jones motioned Reynolds and Jane down. They crouched low in the cover of the trees. Jones assessed the scene. It wasn't a big house, more of a shack than anything, with a covered verandah running along its front. A farm shed sat to its left thirty metres away, nestled under the gumtrees. The two buildings stood in the centre of a cleared section. Random piles of the felled trees lay between them and the house ready for burning. Thin saplings grew in amongst the dried logs – obviously they'd been sitting for a while.

Casting encouraging looks at one another, the girls crept out of the trees. Keeping low, they hurried down to a large log. Roughly halfway between the tree line and the house, and their last source of cover, it provided a good position to reassess their approach.

The visitors searched the grounds for any sign of movement or residents. All was quiet. Satisfied no one threatened them, they made their move and rushed down to the shed across the rough ground. They arrived safely without leaving any evidence of their presence. Slipping inside through a large open door, they studied the dark musty interior. Old pieces of machinery, bits of tractors, parts of vehicles and a heap of other useless items lay scattered over the dusty ground or stored on shelves. Most of it was covered in cobwebs and dust. The shed was no more than storage for junk. A battered Toyota Ute with a closed-in canopy was parked against a side wall.

"There." Jane pointed to three forty–four-gallon drums along the wall. Two had hand pumps fitted to the tops. The girls went over. Reynolds put her nose to one of the lids for a sniff.

"It's diesel."

"What?"

Jane and Jones stared in disbelief. Reynolds stepped to the next drum and leant close to the pump.

"Bingo."

"It's petrol?" Jane said with uncertainty.

"Sure is. Come on, give me a jerry."

Jane kept watch while Reynolds and Jones shared turns at pumping. As loud as the creaky mechanism squeaked and sucked, no one interrupted them. The slowest ten minutes for the girls gradually passed. At last, they were ready to leave with both jerries full.

The three formed a human chain to carry the laden jerries. Jones and Jane took the outside handles, leaving Reynolds in the middle gripping both to even out the weight. After checking to see it was safe for an exit, they walked side by side rather than in single file. They followed the shed wall to the back corner, keeping them safely out of sight of the house.

"It's clear. Let's go," Jones said. The three intruders stepped away from the shed and picked up the pace across the open ground. Step by step, they clambered up the hill. The trees grew larger as they closed the gap but the weight of the jerries and the steep incline began to take its toll, slowing them down.

A barking dog intruded into their rasping pants. The girls stopped and looked back towards the house, searching for it.

"Bloody hell. We hadn't counted on them having a dog," Reynolds gasped.

"Can you see it?" Jane asked, striving to control her shallow breaths.

"No."

"Let's move before it sees us. Come on." Jones stepped off at a faster pace, ignoring her aching arms and legs and breathless lungs.

The dog broke into a rapid, high-pitched barking.

At the sudden change of yapping, Jones glanced over her shoulder. A brindle bull terrier stood beside the house looking towards them, its bristles raised stiff on its back. Jones' concerns rose when it bounded forward and gave chase.

"Shit, it's coming after us." Despite the dangers of the attacking dog, Jones' attention was drawn beyond it to the two men stepping onto the verandah. She tensed when she realised they carried rifles. To her horror, both raised them and aimed at the fleeing girls.

"Get down!" She dived to the ground, breaking the rhythm of the chain. Her plunge dragged Reynolds and Jane down with her. The two girls crashed into the dirt with startled grunts. Reynolds turned to Jones with a confused look.

"What are you doing—"

The whistling bullets that lifted the dirt in front of her immediately answered her question.

"Shit! They're shooting at us." Reynolds looked towards the house.

Jones turned to her. "Crawl to the log."

The same log they'd used to screen themselves on their descent was only a few metres away. They wormed their way towards it amidst the bullets flying dangerously around them. In those terrorising moments, Jones came to a conclusion – either these guys were terrible shots, or they were merely playing with them. Refusing to leave the jerries behind, she helped the girls drag them along. The daring decision placed them in twice the danger. Bullets and fuel were a bad combination, but the petrol cans were their only lifeline home.

The girls reached the log and quickly heaved the jerries over the top before scuttling after them. They collapsed behind the dead tree's shelter, breathing hard; safe, for a few moments anyway.

The firing stopped. Jones peered over the log. The men stood on the verandah with their guns held at waist height, as yet making no sign of coming after them. Struggling to settle her shallow panting, she slumped down. Now they were trapped. The bush was another twenty metres or more up behind them. It was impossible to outrun a bullet that far.

Reynolds stole a look over the log and tensed. "Ah, shit. Here comes the dog."

Jones followed her gaze and sucked in a breath. It raced towards them, closing the gap fast. Reynolds looked around behind her, searching. She crawled forward and picked up a thick branch. It was all she had time for. The animal leapt on top of the log, its teeth bared, its snout pulled back in thick wrinkles adding savagery to the agitated growl. Saliva dripped from its gums and sharp, pointed teeth.

Jones gasped. It looked much more vicious this close.

Reynolds swung wildly with a loud grunt as if to give her courage. The branch slammed into the dog's nose. It let out a yelp and fell back. Within seconds, it was back. Instead of coming over the top, it charged around the end. Reynolds turned and faced it, swinging the branch. The dog skidded to a halt, growling a menacing snarl. Bristles stood high on its back as it danced from side to side to dodge the thick stick. Suddenly, it leapt forward. Reynolds swung hard.

"Get back, you mongrel," she spat through clenched teeth. Jones armed herself with another branch and helped hold it off.

"Here come the men," an anxious Jane said.

Jones shot a quick look down the hill. The two bushmen ambled towards them in no particular hurry, rifles held ready. They didn't have to hurry, not when the dog had them bailed up. They were sitting ducks.

"Run!" Jones yelled at her. "Make a break for the trees. They won't find you in there. Go!"

She and Reynolds swung at the dog vigorously, repeatedly, barely dodging its vicious jaws each time. The two parties were evenly matched with neither gaining any headway.

"What? No. I'm not leaving you." Jane's tone was mixed with shock and loyalty.

"Run, you crazy idiot. Go!" Jones said through gritted teeth.

"No, I'm not running out on you guys, no matter what." Jane crossed her arms and didn't move.

"Shit," Jones grumbled. She was mad – mad at the dog, mad at these gun-toting maniacs, mad at the way things had turned out and mad at Jane for not following a simple request.

* * *

When the first shots fired, Billie jumped to her feet and darted to the end of the van, looking down into the bush opposite. Although she couldn't see what was happening, her instincts warned her. Anything involving gunfire definitely had to be bad.

"Come on, Janda, they're in trouble."

He jumped down from the doorsill and climbed into the front. Billie slammed the sliding door shut and raced around to jump in behind the wheel. The van leapt to life. Billie reversed to enter through the gate and then sped down the track towards the house. The van bounced over the rough ground, throwing its occupants around with little mercy. Janda hung on tight without a word.

Breaking into the clearing, Billie searched for the girls. As she approached the dwellings, she caught sight of them to the left, pinned behind a log on the hill. Two armed men walked casually towards them. Now, she understood what had gone wrong. Swerving off the track, she steered the van across the cleared paddock.

"Get down, Janda," she ordered, fighting the wheel over the uneven ground. He slid to the floor and held on.

Billie jumped when bullets slammed into the side with sickening clunks. Hell, these guys were crazy. Ducking lower, she pushed on, guiding the vehicle towards her friends. In no time, she pulled up between them and the men, on the lower side of the log. The van's bulk offered the girls shelter from the gunfire and a chance to get in unharmed.

The detective shot a look over the seat and out the side window as Jane jumped on the log, hauling a jerry can with her. Reynolds and Jones kept the dog distracted, giving her time to get over safely.

Unfortunately, parking this way left Billie's side of the van exposed to the men. Two bullets ripped into the door forcing her to duck. She half expected them to bury into her. Thankfully, they didn't penetrate the metal. Too much distance separated them, but, with the men closing in, she couldn't lay her trust in the thin, double panelling of the door. She thanked the gods they weren't using high-powered rifles. To add to their troubles, the dog slowed them down.

Sitting up, Billie peered out at the men. They'd broken into a jog towards them. Shit. The side door opened, catching her attention. Jane jumped in, dragging the jerry with her. Reynolds clambered on the log with the other one. She tossed the jerry in before leaping after it. Jones made her dash after a final swing at the dog. Her branch caught the animal across its snout. It gave a yelp and jumped back. In a flying bound, Jones leapt onto the log and across the short distance into the van. As soon as she was in, Reynolds threw her weight behind the sliding door to close it. The dog was so close behind Jones, it crashed into it with a loud bang, bringing the door to a momentary halt. The sudden impact jarred Reynolds. Pushing hard, she almost had it shut when the dog's head appeared in the diminishing crack of the doorway. Wriggling and growling, it began forcing the door back open with the sheer power of its bulky snout.

Reynolds cursed and slammed the heel of her sandalled foot into its nose, twice. With a yelp it retreated – the door slammed shut.

"Okay, McCoy, go!" she yelled.

Billie turned to the front and planted her foot. She steered the van around the log and up across the paddock in the general direction towards the track, at times driving blind. She prayed there were no holes or stumps hidden in the grass. The gunfire never let up, pushing her to keep going. Bouncing at speed onto the track, the van rolled and rocked dangerously as it carried them up the hill. The firing stopped, and then they reached the safety of the trees. Billie kept up the pace to the main track. Easing up to drive through the gate, she swung the van in a skid, aligning it in the right direction before planting her foot again. The van responded and sped off. If the men followed, she wanted as much distance between them as possible.

"Shit, that was close," Jane said on a shaky breath.

"You guys okay?" Billie adjusted the rear-view mirror as Jane dropped onto the mattress.

"Just great," Jones answered irritably.

"That bloody dog." Reynolds frowned at Jane. "Shit, Walker, why the hell didn't you go when we told you to? You could've at least saved yourself."

Jane sat up and looked at the perturbed Reynolds. "I wasn't going to leave you. Besides, it wouldn't have done any good anyway."

"The hell it wouldn't. You could've made a break and got away, especially if those two had caught us."

"But they didn't, did they? Besides, how far do you think I would have gone anyway? They would've caught me, that's if they hadn't shot me first. They only had to send that mongrel dog after me. It would have run me down in no time."

"You don't know that. Hell, it's crazy for all of us to be caught when there's a chance for someone to escape."

"Casey's right. If one of us can make a break, we should take it," Jones said. "Shit, you're getting as bad as McCoy."

Billie smiled. As yet, she'd offered no input, purposely holding off while they thrashed it out between them, giving them time to release some of the built-up tension. She looked at Jane in the rear-view mirror.

"Take that as a compliment, Jane, that's as good as it comes."

All three girls turned to her, their heated conversation temporarily forgotten. A laugh slipped through Jane's lips as she met Billie's eye. The other two also gave light chuckles.

"Speaking of which," Jones said, smiling at the detective, "what the hell kept you, McCoy?"

Now, it was Billie's turn to laugh. Jones was the one who had told her she wouldn't be much use to them in her condition, to let *them* handle it. Jones knew she'd saved their necks but wasn't quite ready to admit it.

Billie turned to the smiling boy beside her. "Well, that's gratitude for you, Janda. They don't appreciate anything we do for them."

He shook his head, his eyes alive with pleasure. With a wide grin, he looked around at the girls.

Billie smiled into the mirror, catching glimpses of the three watching faces. "It just goes to show, crime doesn't pay."

"Hey, we got the fuel, didn't we?" Reynolds said, her tone laced with mischief. "After we lugged the jerries up that steep hill, fought off that savage beast, and dodged flying bullets. I mean, we could've just left it there in all the excitement."

Billie's smile widened. "Well, yeah, I guess that is something."

Jones gave a grunt. "Too right it is. And don't you forget it."

With cheerfulness calming their tense nerves, the girls relaxed. Once again, they'd somehow scraped through another tight situation, together pulling one another out of trouble. Billie drove for another twenty minutes before pulling up to refuel. The girls emptied both jerries into the tank. Though they didn't fill it, the gauge looked much healthier when the detective turned on the ignition. On she drove. Unfortunately, after Bates had captured them, he'd taken them a fair distance out of their way. Janda had guided them over what ground he knew, but this area was all new to him. Well off Todd's mud map, the inconvenience had cost them time and fuel. Focusing on the positive side, they still had their freedom, and that's what mattered.

Chapter Eight

Close to dusk, Billie drove into what was once a town. Many of the buildings looked as if they were about to collapse. Loose timber hung off walls. Windows were smashed and doors broken. The gravel road was littered with patches of tar, the only remnants of the bitumen that had once covered it. Long grass had taken hold in cracks in the compacted street and along the footpaths and edges of buildings. The van crawled along the rough, overgrown street.

Reynolds stared out the front over Billie's shoulder. "It looks like a ghost town."

"Looks like a good place to hide and rest," Jones said, reserved.

Jane turned to her in bewilderment. "You think so?"

Jones broke her scrutiny and looked at her. "Why not? We can hide the van and find a room, stretch out and have a good rest."

"You've got to be kidding, right?"

"Sounds like a good idea," Billie idly said.

Jones glanced at her with raised eyebrows. She turned to the other two. "See? Even the cop thinks so."

Billie smiled, making no comment. She returned her concentration to searching for a hiding place big enough to conceal the van.

"I don't know," Reynolds said. "I'm with Jane on this one. I am not overly keen about the idea of sleeping in a dusty, probably cockroach, and spider, not to mention mice and rat infested room."

"Exactly," Jane backed her.

"It'll be fine," Billie said. "It won't hurt to check it out." She turned into an alley.

Jane sighed. "Great."

Billie followed the alley around to the back of a two-storey building and turned off the ignition. They were out of sight of the street and, hopefully, to anyone who might come looking. The weary travellers climbed out and looked around. Silence greeted them. It hung heavy, eerily. There wasn't even a bird call. The shadows stretched long, intensified by the sinking sun. A light breeze added its own ghostly flavour to the scene by rolling a few spinifexes down the alley towards them.

The girls did their best to ignore the gloomy conditions. Nothing out of the ordinary caught their eye. Behind them, the laneway continued in the opposite direction, crossing the way they'd come in and disappearing around a corner further down. A few rusted drums, stacks of timber and crates littered it.

Janda and the girls warily entered an unlocked door into the building they'd sheltered behind. It led them to a large open room. After a quick look around, they concluded it had once been a hotel. A raw timber bar top ran along one side of the spacious room. Shelves and remnants of cracked mirrors sat behind it. A few broken chairs lay on the floor. The double front doors were boarded up and secured with a padlock. There was a door behind the bar and another on the wall opposite to the one they'd come in by. A staircase ran up along the wall, no doubt leading to what had once been guest rooms upstairs.

"What a dump," Reynolds whined. Cobwebs clung in corners and from the ceilings, unappealingly decorating the fittings and what was left of the furniture. The room held a distant smell of sweat and stale beer no doubt soaked into the bar. She caught Jane's gaze.

"Just what we suspected – terrible."

"It'll do to camp in," Billie said, walking over to check behind the bar. She guessed the town had probably been a mining town, going by the clues of different tools and photos left lying around. Maybe the mines ran dry, explaining why everyone had left.

Jones opened a couple of the side windows to allow fresh air to filter in. The visitors didn't bother checking what was upstairs or through the other doors. It had been a long day. All they wanted was a good night's sleep, and there was ample room for that. They set about cleaning an area to bed down on.

Jane sat back on her knees after sweeping away some dirt with a rag and looked at the others. "Hey. Why don't we bring in the mattress from the van? That way at least a couple of us could have a decent sleep."

"Oh, that's good. But exactly which 'couple of us' would be lucky enough to score it, may I ask?" Jones queried, a touch of a challenge in her tone.

Jane looked at her, considering the question. And then she smiled.

"Tell you what. Seeing how it was my idea, I'll help carry it in – which means I get to sleep on it. You guys can fight over who wants the other half."

The three dubious faces stared in contemplative silence.

"How did I know you were going to say that?" Jones said.

"Must be intuition," Jane replied with a flash of a cheeky grin.

"Hey, that's not such a bad idea," Reynolds said, the dimples in her cheeks emphasising the warm smile.

"Told you." Jane smugly nodded at Jones.

"No, I mean, we could draw straws. Do it fairly."

"What?" Jane yelped, looking sharply back at her.

"No offence; it's a great idea but knowing our luck, McCoy would be the one to worm her way onto it so it's only fair we do it properly."

Reynolds' calm and matter-of-fact delivery of her reasoning caught everyone out, particularly Billie. All eyes turned her way. Smiles crept to the three girls' lips as the cop looked uncomfortably from one to the next.

"Hey, don't go—" Billie started in defence of this unjust call, well aware no one would be willing to side with her. As she suspected, she was cut off before she could begin.

"See, already she's at it," Reynolds said, turning to Jane and Jones. Jane blurted a laugh and cast a warm look at Billie. Reynolds gave the defeated cop no chance to say anything. "The mattress isn't heavy so it's nothing to get out. I reckon straws are the go. Who's for it?"

The girls looked at her with amused expressions while thinking it over. Billie didn't bother answering. They already had her singled out and one word from her would only bring on another attack. Inwardly she smiled. These light insults and accusations were their way of showing they'd indeed accepted her. Happy with this, she was willing to go along with their game, particularly after seeing how much Jane was enjoying it.

Jones shrugged. "Sure, whatever. I'm easy."

Reynolds nodded and looked at Billie and Jane in anticipation of their answer. Jane wasn't convinced.

"What is it you have about straws? Every time we come to a situation that needs a decision, you always want to draw straws."

"What are you talking about? I just think it's a fair way of doing things. What's wrong with that?"

"Huh, it *was* my idea, you know. Doesn't that entitle me to automatically get a—"

"No!" Jones and Reynolds answered together. Billie smiled and lowered her head, refusing to join in. At least she wasn't the target now, but silence hadn't saved her the previous time. They'd probably deny her the chance of even drawing a straw let alone sleeping on the soft mattress. Yes, this was better handled by these three, and these three alone. She'd accept whatever they decided.

"Okay, I just thought I'd ask," Jane defensively said. "Man, you guys are so toey."

The two girls smiled and turned to the detective.

"I'm in," she hastily announced before they could ask.

Jones slowly nodded. "Good," she said somewhat hesitantly, watching the cop under a curious stare. "Okay, then, it's settled. We draw straws for the mattress."

"Next point," Jane said, looking from one to the other. "What do we use for these straws?"

"Ahh. Now *that* I can help with." Billie smiled. Halfway to her feet she stopped and glanced at the girls with a cautious look. "That is, if you want to hear it. I mean I know how hard it is for you to listen to me, to a cop in particular, and I'll understand if you don't want to. I just thought it was the best—"

"McCoy, can you get to the point?" Jones said on an impatient breath without any hint of aggression in her tone.

Billie looked at her and then the other two. Jane offered an inspiring smile. Even Reynolds couldn't hold hers in.

Billie nodded, raising her hands in surrender. "That's what I was doing." She stood and walked to the bar, remembering having seen some old cane mats under its shelves when she'd checked it out earlier. She lifted one out and held it up to the watching girls.

"If we break this up, we'll have our straws." Pulled apart, the thick fibres of cane would suffice as the straws. Long and sturdy, they'd easily break into the lengths they needed.

"Well, I guess that'll do." Jones smiled a resigned smile and glanced at the two girls.

"S'pose so. I guess a cop comes in handy for some things – at times," Reynolds said, drawing Billie's gaze her way. The girls chuckled.

Billie shook her head and returned their smiles. "It's a good thing you brought me along then, isn't it."

"Too right. We knew we'd need a straw breaker somewhere along the way."

Again, chuckles warmed the air. Jones and Reynolds returned to wiping the floor. Jane's gaze lingered on Billie a moment, her silent message expressing her pleasure. Turning away, she continued helping the girls. Billie turned her attention to the mat. As she started parting it, she became conscious of something, or rather someone, missing. Yes, Janda. She looked around. He was nowhere in sight.

"Has anyone seen Janda?"

The girls stopped and looked up. They gazed around the room, unfazed by his absence.

"He'll be okay. He's probably checking the place out like any normal kid," Jones said. "You know, it's called *exploring*. Boys do that."

"Yeah, give the kid a break. He hasn't had any freedom in a long time," Reynolds commented, turning back and sweeping away the persistent dust with her piece of rag.

"Hey, I only asked if—"

Janda's distant yet piercing scream cut Billie off. The girls froze. All stared at a door leading into the room behind them. Billie reacted first. She dropped the mat and raced towards the door. The others were close on her heels. Charging through into the adjoining room, they skidded to a halt, looking frantically around. The small room was empty. Only one other door led out so they took it. They entered a room with two doors. It, too, was empty.

"Janda?" Billie called, suppressing her concern.

"Billie?" His muffled call sounded frightened.

"This way." She guided the girls through the left door. They found themselves in a long narrow room. Quite cluttered, it ran along the back of the pub. Shelves lined the walls storing empty kegs and bottles. Crates and cupboards filled in the gaps between the shelves. A set of stairs led up to a floor above. Another door was visible at the other end of the room.

"Janda, where are you?" Jane called, looking around.

"Down here! Help me!" His voice was louder, closer, anxious. Billie hurried towards the end door with the girls in tow. As she drew closer, her gaze was drawn to the floor a few metres before it, to a hole, a square hole. A trapdoor. The lid was flipped back flat on the floorboards. It was barely half a metre in diameter – just wide enough for a young boy to fit through.

She crouched down and peered in. Only blackness met her.

"Janda?"

"I'm here." His shaky voice echoed up from the darkness. Billie's stomach knotted. Hell, what was he doing down there? The girls dropped down around her, looking in. Billie bowed lower but still couldn't see a thing.

"Billie?" Janda called. "I'm scared."

"Are you all right, Janda? Are you hurt?"

"No, but I'm caught by my shirt. I'm so sorry."

"Okay, you're doing fine. We're going to get you out of there."

"Just hold on, Janda, we're coming," Reynolds assured him. "How did you get down there anyway?"

"I found the trapdoor and wanted to see where it went."

"In the dark?" Jones asked.

"Exploring, remember? Boys do that," Billie said.

Jones' head shot up with a look of surprise across her features. Reynolds and Jane also looked up. Billie flashed a brief smile. These were Jones' words and, at the time, didn't seem to hold any significance. Before the girls could comment, Janda's trembling voice distracted them.

"I went and got a torch from the van. When I was climbing down, the ladder broke away. I fell into this post and got hooked on the wall. Sorry, but I dropped the torch. I didn't hear it hit the bottom. I'm scared, Sarah. I don't like it here."

Jones leaned over the hole. "Hang in there, buddy, we'll get you out very soon."

"How can there be a hole like this in the middle of a building?" Reynolds growled.

"It looks like a mineshaft," Billie said. Her guess about the town being an old mining town was pretty much on target – she just hadn't speculated they'd mined right underneath it. "I think we're in a mining town. This must have been an exit tunnel, probably used for emergencies only."

"Great." Concern weighed heavily in Jane's tone. "You think they would have sealed it up."

"I'll go see if we have another torch." Reynolds jumped to her feet and broke into a jog back the way they'd come.

"And some rope," Jones called.

The girls comforted Janda with calm words until Reynolds returned carrying a torch and a rope coiled over her shoulder. She shone the torch into the shaft, revealing the situation. It was a little wider than the trapdoor. The boy squinted against the light as he looked up at them. His shirt was bunched up under his arms exposing his thin stomach. It was hooked on something behind him. A rusty bolt stuck out of the timber beside him. Billie guessed one similar was what held him. These would have been supporting the ladder that broke away. Janda clung to one of the four thick timber beams which cornered the shaft. The remainder of the wooden ladder stretched down below him, fixed to the beam he gripped. The broken piece lay jammed across the shaft lower down.

"Uh-oh. I don't like this," Jones murmured. "That shirt could let go any minute."

Reynolds shone the light down into the depths, only to see it merge into the blackness. "Shit, it could be hundreds of metres deep."

"All the more reason to get him out of there," Billie said as she tied a loop in an end of the rope. "Janda, this rope has a loop in it. I'm going to drop it down to you. Do you think you can slip it over your shoulders so it's under your arms?"

"I'll try."

"Good boy. Just one hand at a time, okay?"

"Okay."

He was directly beneath them. Billie lowered the rope till the loop hung in front of his face. Reynolds moved to the opposite side of the trapdoor to keep the light on him. Jones and Jane remained crouched beside Billie, the rope ready in their hands to haul him up.

Carefully, Janda lifted a hand and took the rope. He slipped the loop over his head and fed an arm through.

"That's it. Now the other one," Billie encouraged.

He nodded and lifted his other hand, squeezing it through the loop. He looked up and smiled. "I did it."

And then his shirt ripped. The tearing material seemed amplified in the shaft. Janda squealed and dropped off the wall.

"Shit! Hold him," Billie yelled. She gasped as the sudden weight put pressure on her wound. Jane and Jones instantly jumped in behind her and took up the tension, easing the strain. Billie looked down. Janda slowly circled in a gentle swing, the rope under his arms holding him. He'd fallen another two metres.

"Janda, are you okay?" Reynolds asked.

"Yes." Fear thinned his voice.

Billie and the girls stood up. The cop shot a glance over her shoulder at them. "Okay, let's get him out of there."

"We're ready," Jones said.

"Hey, McCoy? How about you take the torch and I'll help lift him," Reynolds suggested. "I mean with your wound and everything."

Billie looked at her across the trapdoor. "Thanks, but it's okay. He's not that heavy with the three of us lifting."

"Fair enough, but let me know if it gets too bad."

"I will. Thanks." She nodded at Jones and Jane. "Together. Go."

All three pulled — and the floor under Billie suddenly gave way with a sickening crack. Unable to save herself, she fell through the splintering floorboards into the shaft. As if in slow motion, she could see the horrified look on Janda's face as he dropped with her.

"NO!" Jane's anxious yell was filled with shock and disbelief.

"Hold them!" Reynolds screamed.

The shaft darkened the further Billie fell. The torch light bounced around the trapdoor above. Reynolds must have dropped it to help Jane and Jones. Billie could imagine the girls trying to get a grip on the runaway rope but being nylon, it would be slippery and hot in their hands from the friction. Hell, would they get a hold before it ran out? Too late now to wish they tied the other end to something. Plummeting towards the black abyss with Janda, all seemed lost.

Chapter Nine

Desperately, Billie let go of the rope with one hand and reached out. Though the walls passing by her were a blur, she remembered the ladder, her last hope. She caught a rung in her descent, and instantly jerked to a halt, the force slamming her into it. A grunt shot through her lips. A sharp pain cut across her ribs almost causing her to lose her grip. Instantly a powerful yank tugged through her as Janda's abrupt halt beneath caught up with her, jarring her arm and putting more pressure on her hold of the rung.

"McCoy!" Jane yelled. Before Billie could reassure her she was okay, the rung snapped, the wood as rotten as the floor above. She dropped, and managed to grab the next rung. It, too, snapped from the jerk of Janda's weight, unable to support both of them. She fell to the next. It held. The pressure on the rope suddenly eased as the girls took up the weight from above. Panting hard, Billie swung her legs in. The comfort of a rung under her feet boosted her confidence. She stood, taking the strain off her arm. Janda whimpered below in the darkness.

"McCoy, are you all right?" Jane's voice was laced with panic.

"McCoy?" Reynolds sounded just as alarmed.

"I'm okay. It's all good," Billie gasped, catching her breath.

"Are you sure?" Jane wasn't convinced.

"Yeah."

"What about Janda?" Jones called.

The torch light flickered around above before shooting down the shaft and lighting it up. Billie glanced at Janda hanging below her. "Janda?"

"I'm okay," he stammered.

"Good boy." Billie looked up at the three anxious faces poking out from the floor.

"What the hell are you doing to us?" Jones snapped. "That was crazy."

"You should have tried it from this end."

"Sit tight. We'll haul you up," Jane called.

"I was hoping you'd say that. Any time would be good. In fact, the sooner the better."

"Stop grumbling. Bloody cops." Apprehension rushed Jones' words. "You're not exactly light, you know. Wait, I've got an idea." She disappeared beyond the edge. Noises and thumps sounded above. To calm her tense nerves, Billie looked down at Janda. He watched her with wide frightened eyes, gripping the rope tight while it gently swung in a slow circle.

"You're doing great, Janda."

He simply nodded. Billie glanced upwards again. The girls still hadn't started to pull them up.

"You guys are intending to haul us out today, aren't you?"

"Of course we are. Just hang ten a minute."

"Oh, that's easy. We're definitely hanging ten, don't you think, Janda?"

"Yes." His answer was barely a whisper.

Jones reappeared. "Okay, here we go. McCoy, are you going to be able to hang onto the rope?"

"As long as you don't take too long, I should be able to."

"Don't worry, I've got that sorted."

"I'm just putting the torch down," Reynolds said. "It might get a little dark again."

"That's fine." Billie took the rope in both hands and hung on tight. The rope tugged upwards. Pulled free of the ladder, she swung out into the middle with Janda. Quickly she wrapped her feet around the rope to give her more support. The girls disappeared from sight, and then in a smooth action, she rose towards the top. Jane was there to drag her up onto solid ground. She rolled away from the edge, relaxing her aching body and struggling to settle her breathing. Janda's head popped up. Jane hauled him out and laid him down beside Billie. Jones and Reynolds knelt with them. Everyone was short of breath. Billie pushed up onto an elbow and looked at them.

"Thanks, guys, that was a close one."

Reynolds exhaled a shaky sigh. "Shit, McCoy, you scared the crap out of us."

"You and me both." She sat up and looked at the broken floor. The snapped boards and joist underneath looked damp. She pressed a thumb against the joist, and easily pushed through the timber. "Dry rot. I didn't see that coming."

Janda knelt up and threw his arms around her, almost knocking her over. "Thank you so much."

Billie hugged him. "You were so brave."

"I'm never, ever going near a trapdoor again."

"At least not one where you can't see the bottom."

"Not even that." He pulled back and looked around the girls. "Thank you, all of you."

"Hey, we owed you one, remember?" Reynolds said with a smile, ruffling his hair.

He nodded and shot a grim look at the hole. Billie followed his gaze. Only now did she notice a rounded, six-inch steel pipe laying across the edge of the rotted boards. Yes, she remembered climbing over it. About two metres long, its ends were jammed against the feet of the cupboards either side, cupboards that were stacked with the same pipes. She turned behind her and followed the rope. It fed around a second pipe standing upright, tied to the corner of a set of shelves with the other end of the rope. That explained how she was lifted so quickly. Pulling the rope from the trapdoor using the pipes as a pulley system, it had made it much easier to haul her and Janda up. Not only that, the one over the trapdoor took the pressure off the rotten floor, taking full support of the rope. She had to admit, she was impressed. She turned to Jones.

"This was your idea?"

Jones smiled. "Yeah. Pretty cool, huh."

Billie glanced at the smiling Jane and Reynolds before turning back to Jones. A smile touched her lips. "Very cool. I don't know how you came up with it, but it worked exceptionally well."

"As do all my plans." She grinned. Reynolds stood, watching Jones affectionately.

"Come on. Let's get out of here before your head swells too big to fit through the door."

Sarah chuckled. "Jealous, are we?"

Reynolds hauled her up. "Only a little."

Jane smiled and helped Billie up. A little sore, the cop rested a hand against her wound. Janda jumped up with her. She slipped a hand around his shoulders and gently squeezed.

"You okay?"

He nodded. "I am now."

"Good boy."

Jane flipped the door over, closing the trapdoor. With some of the floor missing, it left a gap along one edge.

"Let's hope no one else falls down there."

"I wouldn't worry too much about it. I don't think too many people pass by this way," Reynolds said.

Jane caught her eye. "You never know."

Jones looked at her. "It's not our problem." She flashed a smile and walked off.

"Good point," Jane said, glancing at Reynolds. Reynolds smiled and caught up to Jones. Jane, Billie, and Janda followed. Once back in the hotel room. Billie sank onto a rickety stool beside the bar. Jane sat beside her. Reynolds and Janda settled on the clean swept floor intended for their beds, leaning against the wall facing the girls. It was close to dark outside. The room was already in semi-darkness.

"I'll go and get the water bottle out of the van," Jones said. "All that pulling has made me thirsty." She strolled across to the door.

"Bring in the picnic basket while you're there," Reynolds joked with a cheeky grin.

"And don't forget the wine," Jane added with a smile.

Jones stopped and slowly turned, looking back with a dubious frown. Her gaze darted from one to the other, meeting their mischievous expressions. "What, you don't want the caviar?"

"Naw, not tonight." Reynolds grinned and shook her head.

"Hey, though," Jane said, "you could bring in the mattress while you're there."

Jones looked at her. "Sorry, but I seemed to remember *you* offering to do that little job."

"Yes, but that was only on the condition I slept on it, remember?"

"True, but I'm so worn out from coming up with all the great ideas, I'm plumb out of energy, so I guess you're committed, aren't you." She smiled.

"Great ideas? What great ideas?" Jane teased.

"You know damn well my pulley idea worked to a tee. Had McCoy and Janda out of that shaft in no time."

Jane had no comeback, other than a smile. Jones nodded. A victorious look washed across her relaxed features. She glanced at Billie sitting watching with a faint smile on her lips. The detective refused to come into it. She was indeed thankful to the girls for getting her, and Janda, out of the shaft so was prepared to let them have their moment of glory.

Jones looked at Jane expectantly. When silence met her, she raised her arms and said in a high-pitched, mocking voice, "Sorry,

Sarah, you're right! I'd love to get the mattress for you! *You* deserve to sleep on it! *You* had the best idea! It's the least I can do for you!"

Janda and the girls burst into laughter. Any delayed tension from the shaft episode was totally gone. Jane nodded, taking the hint. She giggled.

"Get out of here before you make me sick."

Grinning, Jones turned on her heel and walked out.

Happy everyone was safe after their little venture down below, Jones sighed contentedly. It could have gone very wrong, very wrong indeed. Proud of herself for staying level-headed under such intense circumstances and that she and the girls had worked together and saved their friends' lives, she admitted they were undeniably a powerful team. They could conquer any enemy who tried to stop them.

"Shove that up your arse, Bates," she mused to herself.

By the time she reached the van, she found herself coming around to Jane's line of reasoning. Maybe she would take the mattress in for her; after all, it wasn't heavy and she was already here. Hell, she seemed to be giving into things far too easily these days, *and* far too often.

With a chuckle, she slid open the van's side door – and gave a gasp. She froze. Every hair on her neck stood high. The smile instantly dropped off her lips. She stared down the barrel of a rifle only centimetres from her face. Her gaze lifted to the man holding it. His sun-hardened face was shadowed with a bristle of dark whiskers. Matching his leathery, tanned skin were his well-worn and faded clothes. His eyes were alive, dancing with glee, like the hunter trapping the hunted. He cracked a broad grin.

Another click sounded behind her – another hammer cocking. Jones turned, just enough to view the new danger. A second rifle stared her in the face. The guy holding it was short, shorter than her, but that didn't make him any less dangerous. His jeans and shirt were as faded and filthy as his partner's. He wore a cropped beard and shoulder-length greasy hair. The leer on his weathered face did little to ease Jones' stunned mind. He gave her a wink, and then a smile lit up his features, an unfriendly and cold smile. She cringed. Her blood ran cold. Who the hell were these guys? What did they want?

"Well, if it isn't one of our petrol thieves," the guy in the van drawled with a raspy voice.

Her attention snapped to him. Everything fell into place. Shit, they'd followed them all this way? For what? Petrol?

"Why don't we go in and meet your friends," he said with a smile that sent goose bumps skittering along her skin. The nozzle of the other gun pressed against her back. She couldn't stop the fear chilling her bones. The girls were now in danger and she couldn't think of anything to help them, not when she had two guns threatening her. Her stomach tightened as despair and helplessness returned. Now where was her cockiness? Huh, bring on the enemies. Well they were here all right, and she was about to lead them straight to her friends. A surge of anxiety sickened her. Hell, would it ever end?

"I mean now," the bushman growled when Jones failed to move.

She focused on his piercing stare. She couldn't answer, couldn't tell him to shove it, couldn't say she didn't want to or to leave them out of it.

His grin slowly vanished. He frowned. She read the warning signs. Hesitantly, she turned. Forcing one foot in front of the other, she walked towards the building with her escort in tow.

Chapter Ten

Billie sat relaxed on the stool. Her and the girls' smiles still lingered after Jones' little show.

Jane looked at her. "How's your wound? You took a rough fall down that shaft."

"Yeah, what lousy luck, huh?" Billie turned to Reynolds sitting with Janda against the wall opposite. "What a pity I didn't take up your offer to hold the torch. That way I wouldn't have fallen and my ribs wouldn't be sore now."

Reynolds' face lit up in surprise. "You think? Somehow I feel the outcome would have been a lot different if I'd been swinging on that rope. A lot different, and I mean bad different." She held Billie's gaze with a sober look. The cop glanced at Janda and then Jane. They, too, sat with grim looks staring steadfast at her in the wake of Reynolds' words. Billie returned her attention to Reynolds.

"You don't know that for sure."

"Yes, I do. I'm very grateful you knocked me back. Believe me, I couldn't have done what you did." She looked at Janda and slipped an arm around his shoulders before turning to the cop tight-lipped and struggling with her emotions.

Billie nodded. It was obvious Reynolds believed she would not only have lost her life but Janda's as well.

"So," Jane interrupted. "Your ribs are sore? Mind if I check?"

Billie turned to her. "You don't have to—"

"I want to, okay?" She smiled.

"Fine." Billie allowed Jane to pull up her shirt to look at the bandage. A calm contentment washed through her. Jane cared about her. They'd at last built a friendship based on respect and thoughtfulness, and it felt good.

"There's no blood," Jane said. "And while there's no blood, I think we'll leave the bandage in place. No point disturbing it when we don't have to."

"Well, thank you, doctor." Billie smiled. Jane looked up and returned the smile. She dropped the shirt down.

"Careful, I could remind you how sore it can get."

"Ha, I'm sure you could. Okay, point taken."

"I can't believe you didn't open the stitches again. You fell a fair way down that shaft."

"Oh, you noticed?"

"Hey, I was the one who had to watch, remember?"

"Oh, of course. You *watched* me fall."

"Damn right I did, and I want you to know you scared the hell out of me."

Billie flashed a smile and nodded. "Well, next time, I'll try and avoid it, for my sake *and* yours. Unless, of course, you can get your arse into gear faster and catch me before I drop."

Jane's mouth dropped open. "Get my...! You think...! Did you hit your head on the way down as well? You disappeared so fast, we barely saw you go."

Billie's smile widened. Jane stared wide-eyed. And then she relaxed, aware the cop was teasing her. A smile crept to her lips.

"You're so funny, McCoy. I don't know why we bothered pulling you out. You're just lucky Janda was on the other end."

"What. What did I say?"

"Everything okay, Sarah?" Reynolds asked with a hint of concern, cutting into their conversation.

Billie and Jane turned to her. Reynolds and Janda stared across the room straight-faced. Following their gazes, Billie was surprised to see Jones standing in the doorway. She looked rigid, as if she were carved of stone. She made no attempt to enter the room or make conversation. Despite the fact she'd gone out to the van for water, her hands were as empty as the blank expression on her face.

"No, not really," Jones finally answered, quiet and strained. On cue, two armed men strode in from behind and stood on either side of her.

"Nobody move."

Billie tensed. The tall guy shoved Jones forward, following her deeper into the room. One rifle rested against her ribs, the other aimed loosely at the girls. Billie took in their grotty appearance, at a loss to who they were. She stood slowly, not taking her attention off the two wild looking bushmen.

Reynolds jumped to her feet with Janda. "What do you want?"

The gun swung her way. "We'll ask the questions, understand?" the taller of the two snarled. His gaze wandered over the girls. "What are you lot doing here?"

"Camping," Billie said, taking a slow step away from Jane. Jane shot her an anxious 'what are you doing' glance. Billie made no reaction to it.

The men looked at the cop.

"Camping, eh?" the tall guy scoffed. He directed a dubious look at his partner before turning back to Billie. "Sure you are. How much money have you got on you?"

"If we had money, we wouldn't have taken your petrol," Jones spat.

Now it fell into place. Jane blurted Billie's thoughts.

"That was your property?" she said in astonishment. "Aren't you rather a long way from home?"

"Well, you see, you made us quite mad nickin' our fuel so we decided to come and take it back, with interest." He smiled.

"What? That's crazy."

"Crazy, but well worth it." He grinned in a way that sent shivers of unease down Billie's spine. His green, hungry eyes narrowed as he ogled Jane's figure.

"But how did you find us?" Reynolds asked.

He shrugged. "Pretty easy. We figured you'd be headin' for the coast, which meant you'd have to pass by this way. We pulled into camp for the night, as well as to check this little ole town out to see if you were hiding here. And guess what? You were."

Billie couldn't believe their luck. Didn't these guys have better things to do other than drive all over the countryside looking for them merely for the sake of two jerry cans of fuel? It didn't add up. There had to be more to it.

"Hey Marty? Isn't that Smith's kid?" the shorter guy queried. Marty turned his attention to the boy standing beside Reynolds. Janda shrank into her.

"Sure looks like it, Ronny boy." Spinning to Jones, Marty grabbed her by the hair and shoved the gun under her chin. She exerted a startled cry. "What's the kid doing with you?" When she didn't answer, he shoved the gun in harder. Jones winced.

"He likes us," she gasped.

Marty's high-pitched giggle echoed in the room. "Uh-uh. Wrong answer."

"Maybe he was sick of being a slave," Billie said calmly, taking another slow step forward. It took her further away from Jane and closer to the men. Marty looked at her. Without releasing Jones' hair, he dropped the gun from her neck and aimed it towards the detective. She stopped.

"A slave? Ha! What is it with you lot? Do you like playing with death?"

"It's true," Billie said.

"You expect me to believe that?"

"It is the truth, you thick bastard," Jones gasped, trying to break free.

Marty turned to her and yanked hard on her hair, drawing a cry from her lips. His face was only inches from hers as he glared into her eyes. Jones stopped struggling and stood tense under his grip, returning his glowering stare through half-opened eyes. Marty's face relaxed. He smiled. It was a cold, impatient smile, one that displayed no compassion. He let her go. Jones staggered forward. She caught her balance and straightened before glancing at him. He raised his eyebrows in a questioning innocence, and then rammed the butt of the rifle hard into her stomach.

"Ofh!" she cried, folding over. Struggling to inhale, she dropped to her knees. Marty reached down and grabbed her by the back of her collar when she sank lower. He yanked her up, holding her tight. She slumped into his leg fighting to breathe. The gun rested behind her head, pressing against her skull.

Billie tensed. Jane and Reynolds gasped. They could do nothing to help Jones.

"We pulled the boy out," Billie said in a bid to take his attention off Jones. "Smith has held him as a slave for years." It took great effort to force herself to stay calm.

Marty looked at her. "Smith isn't a slave trader."

"No, not a trader. He uses them. Uses young boys to satisfy his own sick needs by terrorising and threatening them with beatings and other sadistic acts. Much the same way I'm sure your sick mind would work."

Her quiet words cut deep. Marty stared icily, contemplating her bold challenge. Sensing Reynolds and Jane's eyes on her, the slandering words no doubt catching them out, Billie deliberately ignored their shocked looks and returned Marty's calculative stare with a composed and confident demeanour.

Marty's gaze didn't waver. He gave a grunt and shoved Jones to the floor. She groaned and pulled in her knees, gasping. The bushman stepped toward Billie. Stopping in front of her, he raised the rifle and aimed it between her eyes. His face expressed only irritation.

"One thing I hate is a smartarse." He cocked the hammer. Jane gasped. Billie held the bushman's gaze. After a lingering moment, the tension suddenly drained from Marty's features. He tilted his head slightly to the side, still studying Billie thoughtfully.

The detective seemed unruffled. She had to. Any small move or show of fear could prove fatal.

A smile curled the thug's lips. "A slave boy, you say?"

"Yeah, it happens."

Stepping closer, he rested the rifle barrel against her brow. His gaze jumped to Jane standing beside them.

"You, get over there with the other two." He jerked his head towards Reynolds and Janda.

Hesitating a moment, Jane slowly stepped forward. Billie caught her worried look and gave a slight nod. Jane crossed to Reynolds. The two exchanged anxious glances before Jane turned to the dangerous scene threatening the detective.

Marty pushed on the rifle, forcing Billie backwards towards the bar. Only when she'd backed into it, did he take the pressure off. He withdrew the rifle barrel from her brow, leaving it in a position where she couldn't argue with him.

Billie watched him with a guarded eye, making no effort to question his actions. Marty's gaze dropped to her shirt half hanging out. The smile returned. He took hold of the hem to lift it. Billie instantly went to grab his hand.

"Uh-uh! Don't try it," he said, looking up into her eyes.

She held his challenging stare. The gun pressed against her temple again. Slowly, she lowered her hand, succumbing to the order.

A grin sprang to Marty's lips. He pulled the rifle back and continued lifting the shirt without shifting his eyes. Not until it was above Billie's shorts did he drop his gaze. His eyes lit up in surprise at the sight of the bandage. He nodded and dropped the shirt down.

"You know, now that you mention it, I've heard some stories going around about slavery." With no warning, he rammed a fist directly into her wound. Billie cried out and doubled over. Her legs buckled, dropping her into the bar. Slowly, she slid down, sinking to her knees hugging her stomach.

Jane and Reynolds jumped forward, only to be targeted with both rifles.

"Come on, try it," Marty snarled a bitter warning.

Scared for them, Billie glanced up through her distress. Held at gunpoint, the girls looked frightened. She guessed it was more for her than themselves.

Janda rushed forward and kicked Marty in the leg. "Leave her alone!"

Marty laughed and shoved him to the side. Jane grabbed him, holding him tight.

Billie lowered her head to ride the pain.

"You bastard. What do you want?" Reynolds asked, her voice strained.

"Want?" Marty took hold of the cop's arm and hauled her to her feet. He shoved her into the bar none too gently. Billie groaned. She had little strength but, now that she was up, wanted to stay there. With great effort, she grabbed the bar top with one hand and leant into it for support. The other hand she used to clasp her pulsating wound. Her shirt was soaked in a warm wetness. She sank forward. Her eyes closed against the pain. Sucking in raspy gulps of air, she stood resolute, refusing to give in to the agony engulfing her.

Her hand was roughly pushed aside from her ribs and her shirt pulled up.

Marty chuckled. "Oh, now look what I've gone and done. I've made it bleed. Still a little tender, I see."

"You bastard. Leave her be," Jane snarled.

"Shut up." He yanked Billie's head up by the hair. She winced. "Not so cocky now, are you?" No answer met him. "See, we heard there's a reward out for four criminals, wanted pretty bad. One has a cut to her ribs. Now, I'm asking you nicely, do you know anything about it?"

Gritting her teeth against the pain across her head and ribs, Billie opened her eyes. Now she knew the real reason why they came after them. She met his glare with a defiant look. "It's all lies," she gasped.

"Well, looking at you, I find that a little hard to believe."

"We're n-not criminals. We w-were kidnapped and brought here to be s-sold as slaves."

He smiled while pondering over her answer.

"She's telling you the truth," Jane said, drawing his gaze to her.

"Hmm – doesn't really matter. Just thought I'd ask anyway." He looked at Billie. "You see, the reward for turning you in is too good to pass up, so I don't really give a shit who's in the right here. As far as I'm concerned, you lot are one big bag of money to us. Thank you for coming."

He released his grip. Billie slumped against the bar, gasping. She glanced at Jane and Reynolds. They looked scared – scared for her because of the risk she'd taken and scared of what he'd told them. Marty's words painted a gloomy picture. The creeps were intent on giving them to Bates, and they weren't in any position to stop them.

Billie tore her gaze from the girls' distressed looks and dropped her head, concentrating on catching her breath and controlling her pounding ribs.

Marty stepped back and faced the others. "The problem is though, before we turn you in, we do have the matter of the petrol you stole. Seeing as we can't take it back, now that you've gone and used it all, we'll have to be paid in some other way. Now, fair's fair, right?"

A silence lingered after his announcement. Billie glanced at her friends. Their stares clearly expressed their loathing, including Jones. She sat on her knees, rubbing her bruised ribs.

Marty looked from one to the other and chuckled. "You're all good-looking girls, we're good-looking boys…" He let the sentence hang, his intentions apparent. Jane turned to Reynolds, catching her eye with a look of alarm.

"I'd just like to know one thing," Marty continued when they faced him again. A childish cackle slipped through his lips, highlighting his animated face. "Who's going to be the lucky first?"

Chapter Eleven

Ronny guffawed at his mate's question. Marty looked at him, sharing his amusement with a crooked grin and a wink. He turned to Jane and Reynolds.

"Now, come on, there's no use fighting this, and, besides, you might even enjoy it."

"What makes you think you're man enough to satisfy one of us let alone all of us?" Billie gasped from behind.

He spun angrily around to her. As she'd hoped, challenging his manhood was the perfect way to demoralise him, *and* the fastest. She rammed a knee into his crotch before he could register she'd tricked him. Marty froze with an anguished groan, as if he'd run into a wall – a wall of knives.

Ripping the rifle from his now loose grip, Billie flipped it around towards Ronny. Everything happened so fast. Panic washed across Ronny's features as he fumbled to bring up his rifle.

Holding on to the pain-stricken Marty and using him as a shield, Billie fired from under his arm – a fraction before Ronny's rifle discharged. A bullet ripped into Marty's back, driving him forward. The force propelled him and the cop into the bar. Over Marty's shoulder, Billie watched Ronny stagger backwards. Blood stained his chest. Shock widened his eyes in disbelief. A flash of panic shot through the detective when he began to raise the rifle, not at her but towards Jane and Reynolds.

And then Jones dived at him. She wrapped her arms around his knees and tackled him to the floor. Jane and Reynolds rushed forward.

That's all Billie had time for. Unable to support Marty's dead weight, she collapsed under him in an uncontrolled fall. The thug's dead weight knocked the breath out of her when they landed on the hard floorboards. A sharp pain shot across her already aching wound.

Sucking in short breaths and closing her eyes tight, she strived to get on top of the agony gripping her. In the background, grunts and squeals sounded as the wrestle with the bushman continued.

Marty's weight suddenly lifted off her.

"Billie?"

Jane's anxious call came from a long way off, rolling in over the waves of the painful breathlessness entrapping her.

"Oh no. Has she been hit?" Concern thinned Jane's voice. Billie forced open her eyes. Jane was beside her frantically searching for any new wounds down her body. Janda knelt with her. Jones and Reynolds stood behind, observing intently over their shoulders. With the throbbing easing, the cop looked up at their concerned faces. So caught up in checking her over, Jane failed to notice.

Reynolds rested a hand on her shoulder. "Jane. It's okay, it's okay. She hasn't been hit. Just winded by the looks."

Jane's distraught face turned to meet Billie's gaze, just before her eyes closed again.

"Thank goodness," Jane cried in relief.

Still too winded to speak, Billie let her aching body relax. The relief the girls were okay washed through her.

"She sure is lucky. That's all I can say," Jones said.

Reynolds blew out a tense breath. "Well, with crazy stunts like that, she needs to be." She frowned and glanced at Marty. "Shit, this bastard's bleeding everywhere. Let's get her away from this mess."

The girls lifted Billie and dragged her across to the adjacent wall, sitting her against the stained timber. She gasped. Moving did her no favours. The throbbing across her wound reignited. She sucked in shallow breaths to deal with it. Amidst her suffering, she glanced at Marty lying in a pool of blood, understanding why the girls had moved her. Ronny lay in the middle of the room beside an overturned stool, also covered in blood. Thankfully they'd overpowered him before he'd shot one of them. Giving in to her hurts, she lowered her head and closed her eyes. She lifted a hand to her tortured ribs.

"C-can't you guys be g-gentle?" she stammered.

"We *are* being gentle. Hell, McCoy, couldn't you have given us some warning about what you intended doing?" Reynolds grumbled rather harshly, pulling the cop's hand away from her wound. Billie flinched as she and Jane started unwinding her bandage.

"Are you crazy, trying a stupid stunt like that?" Jones snapped. A mixture of frustration, guilt and anger tainted the words. "You could've been killed, you damn cop."

"It w-was the quickest w-way out." Attempting to sit up straighter, she winced. Any little move made everything ache. Even the simple procedure of undoing the bandage brought pain. Keyed up over the stressful situation, Jane and Reynolds worked faster than necessary, which in turn, created unnecessary knocks against her sore side.

"Not to mention the most dangerous," Jones countered Billie's response. "Shit. And what was the idea of taking the heat off me, huh? Another crazy notion?"

Billie rested her head on the wall and looked at her. "Y-you didn't look like you w-were having all that much fun."

"Don't start getting cocky with me, damn it. It was a dangerous thing to do."

"I had to do s-something to stop you from taking a bullet."

"What? What the hell are you talking about? What bullet?"

"You were pushing him too f-far. H-he would have p-pulled the trigger if you'd kept going."

"That's bullshit."

"Really? The way your mouth w-was shooting off, you're lucky he only h-hit you. "

"McCoy, you don't know shit about what you're talking about."

"No?"

"No."

The cop didn't answer. She didn't have the energy to argue. Besides, she wasn't getting anywhere anyway. Instead, she closed her eyes, concentrating on dealing with her hurts.

Frustration and fear oozed from Jones. "You don't get it, do you? If this hadn't have worked, you'd be dead, we would've been raped and then handed over to Bates to become sex slaves for the rest of our days."

Billie forced open her eyes. Jones' livid features twitched under the emotions manipulating her.

"But it did work, didn't it, so drop it."

"Drop it?" The girl shook her head. "Hell, McCoy, I can't work you out. How come it's all right for you to stand up to them and not us, huh? Who put you in charge? What, do you like pain? Is that it? Talk about me taking risks? You never seem to stop. Are all cops this mad? Wait, I can answer that. No. No one is this crazy, no one."

"I can't agree more. Damned if I know how you pulled it off without killing yourself," Reynolds said, failing to conceal her anxiety. The cop's gaze drifted to her. She'd given these girls a good scare, and it was only natural for them to be angry at her.

Reynolds turned to Janda sitting beside Billie with a strained look on his face. "Janda, run and get the water bottle and the first aid kit out of the van."

"Is she okay?" he asked, his worry heavy. His fixed stare stayed on the detective.

Watching him for a lingering moment, Reynolds' hardened frown relaxed – marginally. "Just go, please," she said with more courtesy.

He looked at her and nodded. Shooting the detective another quick glance, he jumped up and raced off.

Billie flinched when Jane and Reynolds pulled the last of the bandage off to reveal the wound underneath. Both examined the stitches. Jane wiped away the blood.

"A couple of them have busted, but the rest look intact."

"Shit, McCoy, if you keep this up, you'll never make it home," Reynolds said, her tone still heated.

Billie looked at her. Reynolds' strained features revealed her concerns, just like Jane and Jones'. These girls had been through a lot and needed some relief.

"So, at last you b-believe we're going to make it. It's about time."

Reynolds looked up sharply. The other two were also caught out. Jones gave a grunt.

"Don't start, okay? Sit there quietly while we fix you up – again. Understand?"

Billie's gaze fell on hers. "Sure." The cop sensed Jones' anger had ebbed from the tone of her voice.

"Bloody cops. They never know when to stop," Jones added without the harshness.

Billie didn't comment. While the going was good, it was better to leave it be.

Janda raced in with the first aid box and passed it to Jane. She started cleaning the wound. He watched on with a troubled stare. Reynolds flashed Billie a comforting smile. Squeezing her shoulder, she stood and moved back to give Jane more room.

"I think I'll check around the place, just to make sure no one else is lurking around."

"I'll come with you," Jones said, standing with her. "Besides, I need some fresh air. These close calls are not good for the heart."

"Take a rifle with you, just in case," Billie suggested.

Jones nodded. The two girls walked to Ronny and stared at him.

"He doesn't look good. Maybe I hit him too hard with the stool," Reynolds said.

"It stopped him, didn't it?" There was no empathy in her tone.

"Yeah, it did." Reynolds crouched beside him and felt his neck for a pulse. "Hell, he's dead," she said, a little strained. She looked up at Jones with a blank expression.

Jones sighed. "I don't think it was the whack on the head that killed him. He couldn't have survived that wound." Her focus drifted to the cop. Billie met her questioning gaze, and then watched Reynolds stand and look her way. The cop shrugged.

"I figured it'd be too much of a problem if we had to nurse him."

Jones nodded, her implication confirmed. She tilted her head as she pondered a thought.

"Tell me if I'm wrong but you had it planned right from the start, right from when you stepped away from Jane on their arrival."

"Yes, I knew you were up to something," Jane backed her.

Billie glanced at her and then contemplated Jones' assumption under a lingering silence. She sighed. "I wouldn't say I had it planned. It just worked out that way. They made the rules by playing hard so I followed."

Jones' intent stare bore into the detective while ciphering the answer. "You know, I'm actually happy to say – I'm glad to have you on our side. Whether on purpose or by luck, your crazy stunt did save our necks." A flicker of a smile followed the words.

Billie held in her surprise. Jones was admitting she was grateful to her? The shock almost choked her reply. "Thanks," was all she could get out.

Reynolds tapped her friend on the shoulder. "Come on."

Breaking her stare from the cop, Jones nodded. She picked up Ronny's rifle and the two walked out.

Billie looked at Jane. She sat frozen, watching her. Despite the small respite Jones had offered, she seemed anxious and uptight. Jane dropped her gaze to the wound. Billie had a fair idea what was bothering her.

"I'm sorry for scaring you guys, but I had to act fast."

Jane glanced up. "Does it show that much?"

Billie smiled. "Yeah."

Jane exhaled a long sigh and returned her attention to cleaning the wound. "Well, you're right. You did scare the crap out of me. When you moved away from me, I knew you were planning some kind of attack but it didn't come close to what you pulled off. So, yes, I have to admit, I was scared . . . a lot, more so when he laid into you." She lifted her gaze to the cop's. "Sarah was right on one thing. You took a big risk doing what you did. It could've gone terribly wrong." A touch of anger hardened her tone.

"Maybe – but the way I looked at it – if I didn't do something, the consequences would've been much the same in the end had I not pulled it off. They weren't going to give us up, not with a reward on our heads."

"I know that, but..." She stopped, staring hard at Billie. Exhaling a tired breath, she lowered her head to collect her thoughts. Finally, she looked up at the detective and offered a thin smile. "I guess there's no point in going on about it, is there?"

"I guess not. What's done is done, and we won. Remember that."

Jane nodded. "Thanks to you. Don't get me wrong, I'm extremely grateful and glad you did it – now – or will be when I get over the shock – I think."

By the time she'd stumbled over the words, Billie was smiling. "Sure. I think I know what you're saying."

"Yes – a very big thank you."

Billie nodded. Jane breathed a shaky breath.

"Boy, you sure took those creeps by surprise though." She chuckled.

"That *was* the whole idea."

"I think you did great," Janda said from beside Jane.

The girls looked at him. He'd been so quiet, they'd forgotten he was there.

"You stay out of this," Jane warned.

"Ignore her, Janda. I need all the support I can get."

A wide grin lit up his features, his admiration evident in his gaze.

Jane shook her head. "Poor kid's been brainwashed," she joked, directing her comment to Billie.

"No way." The cop flashed him a smile. "He's just a smart kid."

His face was alive with merriment.

"Too smart." Jane grinned. She finished strapping her patient up. "There, how's that?"

"Good, thanks."

Nodding, Jane lightly tapped Billie on the leg. "Right, now stay put, okay? Don't move a muscle." As she stood, the two girls walked in, their arms laden with tins of food and cans of beer.

"Look what we found in their truck," Reynolds exclaimed, dumping her armful on the bar. Jones unloaded hers beside it.

"My goodness." Jane walked over with Janda, looking at the pile in awe. "Baked beans, spaghetti, peaches, pears, stews – they must have been planning to stay on the road for quite a while."

"Sure looks that way," Reynolds said, studying their find more closely.

"The reward must be big," Billie commented from the floor. Everyone turned to her with fixed stares. Their smiles faded.

"Hell. Not only will we have to dodge Bates, but, with him spreading the word, every man and his dog will be on our trail to cash in on the reward," Jones growled. "Great."

"Well, in McCoy's words – we'll simply have to be more careful, won't we," Reynolds said matter-of-factly.

The girls looked at her. Smiles relaxed their troubled looks.

"Definitely."

"How about we worry about our stomachs for the moment and not fret about what's ahead," the detective suggested, regaining everyone's attention.

"I guess that's all we can do – for the moment," Jones said.

"Yeah, I'm starving," Janda announced.

"The boss has spoken." Jane laughed.

Janda grinned at each of them, nodding.

Jones pointed at the dead men. "Let's drag these two out, get cleaned up, and then eat."

"You could throw them down the shaft," Janda offered as a proposal.

The girls fell silent, staring solemnly at his serious face. They turned to one another, lost for words. Jones shrugged.

"I guess it beats burying them." She smiled and looked at Janda.

"Good thinking, Janda," Reynolds said. He nodded. A touch of a smile played on his lips. Reynolds and Jones picked Ronny up and carried him out.

Chapter Twelve

After the bodies were removed, the girls changed rooms. The bloodstained floor reminded them of the horror they'd survived. They moved into another at the back, out of view of the road and anyone else who might be in the vicinity. Slightly smaller, it had a table and a few chairs. In no time, they had it cleaned up. The campers laid out blankets on the floor and dragged the mattress in. Billie changed her bloodied shirt and after freshening up with water borrowed from Marty's truck, the gang finally satisfied their starved appetites. They now sat undisturbed around the rickety table under the light of a gas lantern, again compliments of Marty.

Reynolds sat back and stretched. "I don't think I could fit one more thing in." She sighed and relaxed in the chair.

"Me neither," Janda agreed, blowing out his cheeks. "I am so full."

Jones relaxed back, nodding and rubbing her full stomach. "Sure feels good though."

"You guys will have to roll out of here," Billie said, finishing a tin of peaches.

Reynolds looked at her with raised eyebrows. "You can talk. How many tins have you had? Three, four?"

"Hey, I have to build up my strength," she yelped.

"Oh, of course." She smiled.

"Speaking of which, I can't help wonder if it's going to be safe staying here," Jane said. The girls turned to her with questioning looks. "I mean, what if someone else comes nosing around looking for us? Anything's possible now that there's a reward out on us."

A brief silence fell upon the party while they thought it over.

"Well, I for one sure would like a good night's rest." Jones looked around at the faces. "And here seems the best place on offer to stretch out."

"Wouldn't we all, but Jane has a point," Reynolds argued. "Is it worth the risk? Who knows how many more creeps like our boys today are keen to catch up with us."

Jane turned to Billie. "So what does our cop think about it?"

Billie read the mischievous glint in her eye. Placing the empty peach tin on the table, she leant back and glanced across at Jones and Reynolds. "What, my opinion counts now?"

"No, not really. We're merely curious to hear what you have to say," Jones informed her. "I mean, it's never stopped you before."

"Yeah, so don't go getting a big head over it," Reynolds said with a cheeky grin.

Billie nodded with a faint smile playing on her lips. "Okay then – just for the record," she directed at Jones, "I don't think anyone will bother us, at least not tonight. It's too hard to search in the dark, plus we're well hidden. But, on the off chance someone does come around, we are armed, and they'll have trouble getting in here now that we've locked up – that's if you choose to stay."

The girls stared at her, dubious, absorbing the answer.

Jones grunted. "Typical cop answer – can't understand a word of it."

Billie simply shrugged, smiling.

"Well, maybe we are better off staying." Reynolds sighed. "I mean to catch up on some sleep."

Jane looked at her and nodded. "Yeah. Besides, McCoy needs rest after her eventful afternoon."

"Hey, I'm fine. If you want to go, that's okay by me," Billie said.

The girls turned to one another.

"Of course she'd say that, she isn't up to driving," Jones said, which invited a chuckle from Jane and Reynolds.

"Don't you believe it," Billie contested. "I'm feeling a lot better."

Everyone turned to her while considering her assurance. Reynolds sighed and looked at Jones and Jane.

"It *is* harder finding our way in the dark I suppose."

They nodded.

"I don't like it here," Janda said in a quiet voice, drawing everyone's attention his way. Jane leant over and slipped an arm around his waist.

"Janda, this room is locked up tight. No one can get in. The thing is, we're all pretty tired and could do with a break."

He returned her gaze with a sober yet sympathetic expression. Slowly, he nodded.

"*And* we have to nursemaid McCoy," Reynolds added.

Billie instantly jumped to her defence. "I've told you, you don't have to stay because of me. I'm up to travelling."

Reynolds turned to her. "Forget about arguing, McCoy, we've made up our minds. We're staying, okay?"

"I'm only—"

"*We're . . . staying*," she repeated over the top of Billie. "Shit. Have you ever had this much trouble with a cop before?" she asked Jones.

Jones blurted a compressed laugh. Her gaze shot to Billie. "Are you kidding? I've *never* spent this much time with one let alone experienced the trouble she's dragged us through."

"What do you mean dragged *you* through?" Billie queried.

Ignoring both the question and her stunned expression, Jones smiled at Jane. "How about you, Jane?"

Jane shook her head and grinned at Billie. "Same for me." Her gaze dropped to the boy beside her. "Janda?"

He glanced around at the girls' faces, his look quite serious. His gaze rested on Billie. She watched him expectantly, her last chance for backup.

Finally, he turned from her and looked at the others. "I don't like cops," he said, lifting his tiny shoulders in a defensive yet innocent shrug.

The three girls burst out laughing. Billie dropped her head back on the chair and closed her eyes. He'd betrayed her, turned her down for the enemy. Now, she knew exactly where she stood. Looking up, she met the four mischievous faces smiling victoriously at her. She could only smile with them, happy to let them have their fun.

"Great. I don't know why you just don't leave me here."

The response set off more giggles.

"Don't tempt us," Jones said, struggling to control her laughs.

Billie picked up her beer. "Okay, time out. I'd like to make a toast," she said on a more serious note. The gang stopped their tomfoolery and looked at her.

"A toast?" Jane asked, surprise raising her eyebrows.

"Sure, why not? We've got good reason, don't you think?"

The girls met her gaze with remnants of their smiles. Hesitantly, they turned to one another.

"A toast? Why not?" Reynolds' smile emphasised her dimples. "How can we argue? She has a good point."

"Indeed." Jones nodded.

They picked up their beers. Janda reached for his can of coke. Billie looked around the table at the relaxed faces and nodded.

"A toast to you guys, for the times you've pulled me out of trouble *and* for putting up with me for this long." She smiled. "I know how much of a strain that has been on some of us," she added, her gaze shooting to Jones. The girl smiled.

"Shouldn't that be our toast – to you?" Jane asked.

Billie met her eye. "Ha, maybe, but it doesn't matter. I want you to know I think you guys are all right – more than all right. I really had my doubts there for a long while, but you're not that bad after all. My point is, I couldn't have made it without you."

Silence engulfed them, wiping away all smiles. Billie knew her words had hit hard, harder than she expected. Suddenly, she felt she'd said enough. There was no point in pushing it, or spoiling it for that matter. "Anyway, I'd like to toast all of you in appreciation. Cheers."

"Cheers," they said in staggered unison.

Everyone took a swig from their cans after clinking them together.

"To tell you the truth, I didn't want anything to do with a cop..." Reynolds started, directing a sincere look across the table at the detective.

"Yeah, I did pick up on that," Billie cut in, drawing a chuckle from Jane and Jones.

Reynolds flashed a warm smile and continued. "The fact you kept sticking your neck out for us, taking crazy risks and – well, everything else you did for us – I guess we found it harder and harder to leave you behind."

"Mm. It's like you've – grown on us," Jones admitted with a nod, looking intently at Billie. "After what we've been through, I could almost forget you're a cop."

Swathed in the girl's sudden earnestness, the detective's smile faded. Behind the light insult, Jones seemed very genuine.

Jones didn't stop. "It doesn't matter now. Cop or no cop, you *have* proven yourself. You've stood up for us, you've fought for us, and you've certainly known how to set us straight when we've been out of line."

Reynolds and Jane nodded. Faint smiles touched their lips. Billie could hardly believe what she was hearing. After all the conflicts they'd shared, Jones was full of sincerity, honesty, and respect. They all were. In their own way, they were telling her they liked her – a lot – and had accepted her as a friend.

"I can't say I've ever met anyone like you before," Jones continued. "And as much as I hate to admit it, I'm glad to have you around."

A brief silence fell upon the table, choking any further input. The girls sat speechless, staring at one another in a numb stupor. It was the first time they'd discussed the topic openly.

Billie couldn't ignore the rush of contentment warming her veins. She sat up and leant forward, resting her elbows on the table with her hands nursing the beer can out in front. Looking around the watching faces, she was still at a loss. She hadn't expected anything like this, especially from Jones. Her little speech was overwhelming yet very welcome.

"Tell you what. If – I mean *when*," Billie quickly corrected herself, "we do get out of this nightmare, and if it's not too much of a strain on your reputations, I'd really like to buy you guys a drink."

The three girls smiled.

"Maybe we'll take you up on that." A warm smile lit Jane's features. Reynolds and Jones nodded.

"I guess we could risk it," Reynolds said, turning to her friend.

Jones met her gaze with a mischievous look. "Yeah. We could pick a place pretty inconspicuous where no one knows us, just to be sure." A smile bloomed on her lips as she turned to the cop.

Billie blurted a laugh. "Fine." She was happy with the answer, as long-winded as it was. She didn't care where they met. The fact they'd agreed to socialise with her was all that mattered. She sat back and took another swig, feeling exceptionally satisfied. They'd become friends, good friends. Never in a million years did she believe it would happen.

The girls smiled and joined her with their drinks, engaging in jovial conversation. The amber liquid was helping them all to relax and ease their misgivings of this unfavourable trip.

Half an hour later, Janda was ready for bed. As hard as he tried, he couldn't keep his eyes open any longer. Everyone bade him good night and watched him lay on his blanket. The girls continued their talks around the table, relaxed and sipping on their beers. The night aged gracefully, slipping by the distracted girls unnoticed, until their drinking splurge began to catch up with them. Billie was first to call it a night. Like Janda, the strain and events of the day seemed to hit her all at once, particularly after the beers.

"Well, guys, I'm bushed. I need to get some sleep." She lifted her weary body out of the chair.

"Hey, take the mattress," Jane said. The cop looked at her. They hadn't got around to drawing straws or resolving who was going to sleep on it.

"No, it's okay. I'm so tired, I could sleep on a bed of nails."

"McCoy, quit arguing and do as you're told," Jones instructed.

Billie looked at her.

Reynolds nodded. "Take it while the offer's hot."

Still Billie hesitated, looking from one to the other. She hadn't expected this, and didn't deserve it any more than they did, but, after studying their unyielding faces, knew it would upset them if she refused. She nodded and smiled, appreciating the considerate offer. "Fine, I'll take it, thanks. Night, guys."

"Night," they chorused.

Jane smiled. "We won't be far behind you."

"Okay. Remember to turn out the lights," she joked.

"Huh, don't worry, we'll lock up and do everything – as usual," Reynolds retorted.

"I was hoping you'd say that." Billie stretched out on the mattress and closed her eyes. It was good to lie down. Even without a pillow, the mattress's softness soothed her weary body.

"Don't you want a rifle?" Jones asked.

Billie lifted her head, casting her a look. "I thought you guys might feel safer with them."

"Safer? Huh, I hate guns," Jane promptly stated. "I'd be more likely to shoot my foot off."

"Which way do you hold it again?" Reynolds asked Jones with a furrowed brow.

Jones gave a laugh. Billie and Jane looked at her and chuckled. The cop nodded, well aware the girls were uncomfortable sleeping with a gun. To her, it was second nature. She pushed up onto an elbow.

"Well, maybe you better throw one over here then."

"Sure." Jane smiled. Picking a rifle up off the floor, she tossed it to her. Billie deftly caught it and laid it beside her. She smiled at Jane.

"Feel better?"

"Much."

"Good. You two can fight over the other one," she said to Jones and Reynolds.

Jones nodded. "You're so kind."

"I've got it! It's the end with the wood, right?" Reynolds said brightly, answering her own question. Her playfulness brought more chuckles from the girls.

Jones groaned, shaking her head. "Put a sock in it, will you?"

"Sarah, make sure you take the rifle," Jane said, grinning at Reynolds. Billie smiled and lay back. She closed her eyes and relaxed. This time no one disturbed her.

"One more before we turn in," Jones said.

Reynolds sighed. "That'll do it."

The sounds of three opening cans was the last thing Billie registered.

The time lazily drifted by, just like the table talk. Relaxed in their chairs, the girls could have been guests in one of their living rooms. Beneath the serene mood, Jane sat staring at her half-emptied beer can, toying with it while listening to Jones and Reynolds' easy conversation. She looked up in the lingering silence that followed with a faint smile.

"It sure is funny how danger can bring people together."

"You mean like us?" Reynolds asked.

Before Jane could answer, Jones cut in. "Or maybe you mean like us and McCoy?"

Jane's gaze shot to hers. "Well, yeah. We're complete opposites. She's a cop and we're . . . you know, on the other side of the law. It really is weird, don't you think? Any other time, there would have been no way in the world we would've been friends. Even maybe us three. Yet look at us, working together as a team. We're looking out for one another and jumping into danger without a second thought. Well, maybe a second thought, but, hell, we've achieved the impossible, both in friendship and the fight for our freedom."

Jones and Reynolds remained silent.

Undeterred by their solemn faces and lack of input, Jane carried on. "I really like you guys, and admire you."

"Admire?" Jones scoffed and sat up straighter. "How can you admire us after the way we first treated you?"

"That was then. I've seen past that to the real you, to what's underneath. And I'm sure Billie has too. Besides, why else would Casey stand by you for so long?"

The girls stared, momentarily speechless. Jane glanced over at Billie. The cop looked peaceful and relaxed in her sleep.

"In a way, I'm glad this has happened. Mind you, I'll be even gladder once we make it out." She smiled at the girls, inviting smiles from them. "But honestly, I mean about meeting you three. I'm so glad we were given the chance, regardless of the problems. Maybe I'm crazy, but I've never in my life had anyone do what you three have done for me. No one has ever stuck by me so loyally." She shook her head and looked down at the table. "Hell, I don't know, call me . . . mad, foolish." She lifted her gaze and shrugged. "I just needed to tell you that. I don't expect you to understand but thanks for listening anyway."

"No, it's not foolish. I can actually see where you're coming from," Jones said. "I can be a real bitch, right, Case?"

Reynolds gave a laugh. "That's an understatement."

Jane and Jones smiled.

"Nobody, other than Casey, has ever given me the benefit of the doubt, or stood by me, not like McCoy, or you. I guess it's because she's a cop I give her such a hard time, and yet, she perseveres with me. Maybe what you say is true. Maybe there is some good to come out of this."

"I'm sure of it," Jane replied. "I just know I'm glad I've got to know you."

The three stared at one another. A sudden rush of blood warmed Jane's heart. For the first time, she felt as one with these women, a connection unlike any she'd had with anyone else.

Jones nodded. "Come on, I think we've had enough philosophy for one night. Let's call it a night."

Reynolds pushed to her feet. "Good idea, I'm bushed."

"So," Jones said, looking at the empty spot beside Billie, "who gets the mattress with the cop?"

The two girls followed her gaze.

"I guess seeing it was Jane's idea in the first place, it's only right she does," Reynolds said, glancing at her.

Jane was caught out. "What? No. I was only joking when I said that. Honestly, I'm happy to take the floor."

Jones looked at Reynolds. "Here's another one who wants to argue."

"Man, they never let up, do they? Tarred with the same brush, her and McCoy."

"Cut it out you two, I mean it. I—"

"Jane, take the mattress, okay? And we don't want to hear one more word out of you."

Jane stared at them, lost for words.

Reynolds chuckled and turned to Jones. "Didn't I tell you McCoy would end up worming her way onto it?"

A laugh sprang from Jane. Jones grinned.

Reynolds looked at Jane. "It worked for the cop so you may as well make the most of it too."

Jane shook her head. Her smile widened. "You guys . . . thanks."

Taking up their offer, she lay down beside Billie. Jones and Reynolds bedded down next to her, continuing to grumble about the hard floor, turning out the lights, locking up, the cop getting her way and anything else they could bring to mind.

Chapter Thirteen

The gang ate a hearty breakfast the following morning. Refreshed and rested, they took turns at the wheel throughout the day. As the kilometres rolled by, the bushland thinned into grassy plains. Gone were the clear creeks and rivers. What isolated streams they crossed were small and muddy. The heat hung heavy and thick, more so without the protection of the trees. Paddocks emerged dotted with cattle, their fences running endlessly away over the grassy horizon. It drew excited comments from the girls. At last there was a sign of people, farmers, which, in turn, meant there must be towns with communications to the real world.

Late afternoon found Reynolds at the wheel. Billie sat beside her, leaning against the passenger door half turned with her feet on the seat so she could face Jane and Jones in the back. The talk was casual, binding their friendship more so as they joked and laughed together. Over the last two days, they'd found out a lot about one another. In a way, the long drives had been beneficial to all of them.

"Uh-oh," Reynolds quietly said, slowing down. Billie glanced at her. Her attention was fixed on the road ahead. The cop's smile weakened. Turning, she followed Reynolds' gaze out the front.

"What's up?" Jones asked.

"Take a look."

Janda and the two girls crawled to the seat and looked out. On the side of the road, two men struggled with a girl, attempting to drag her into their Ute. From the resistance she put up, she obviously didn't want to go with them. A battered trail bike lay beside the road.

"Do we stop?" Reynolds asked, a little apprehensive.

"She sure looks like she could use a hand," Billie said, her gaze set on the scene ahead.

"I'm starting to feel like a real goody-goody," Jones mumbled.

Jane gave a light chuckle. "Yeah, the cop's a bad influence on us crims."

Billie glanced at their grinning faces and had to smile.

Reynolds blew out a sigh. "Shit, here we go again." She pulled up alongside the grappling trio. The two men were so engrossed in their struggle they failed to see them stop.

"What seems to be the problem here?" Billie asked nonchalantly from her open window.

The men paused long enough to shoot her a quick look. Their captive glanced at the strangers, surprised. In the sudden distraction of their arrival, she yanked an arm free from her assailants' slackened grip, but they were quick to take a firm hold again.

Billie assessed the girl. Panting hard, she looked frightened. Perhaps a little younger than the detective, the woman was flushed from the struggle. Wearing a collared, sleeveless shirt and jeans, some of her long auburn hair had escaped her ponytail. Her tanned face and arms bespoke the amount of time she spent outside. Her wide-brimmed hat lay upside down in the dirt near the bike.

The men weren't much older. Their faded jeans and T-shirts gave them the appearance of stepping straight out of a western, right down to their cowboy hats and boots. Both had short hair and a distinct similarity between them – the same build, the same facial features – like brothers. The taller one had a moustache, the only difference between the two. He curled his lips in a snarl.

"Get lost and mind your own business."

Billie ignored the harsh attitude and kept her voice calm. "I think you should let her loose. It's quite obvious she doesn't like you."

"Butt out, okay? This has nothing to do with you. We're only treatin' her the way her farmer family deserves to be treated – like shit."

The girl kicked at him, drawing a curse from his lips. He fought to hold onto her. For her wiry build, she had a lot of strength.

"Seems to me you and your mate are more like the shit, so why don't you call it even and quit while you're ahead." Billie's tone hardened.

The side door slid open. Jones sat with Marty's rifle aimed at them.

"Hey, creep, when we say leave her be, we mean it."

The men's eyes widened at the sight of the rifle. In a cowardly retreat, they shoved the struggling girl in front of them, using her as a shield. The taller, skinny cowboy's gaze jumped to Billie.

"Who the hell are you? This has nothing to do with you."

"It does now," Billie said. "Let her loose."

He looked from her to the rifle beside her, considering the alternatives. He glanced at his partner. Reluctantly, they released the farm girl, who stepped to the side. Turning, she adjusted her clothes without taking her eyes from her attackers.

"You won't get away with this," the guy with the moustache threatened, straightening his hat. He glared at the women with a mixed blend of agitation and embarrassment.

"We already have. Now, beat it," Jones ordered, cocking the rifle for emphasis. "And thank your lucky stars we aren't turning you in to the local law." Her voice dropped to a mumble only the girls could hear. "Ha. If only he knew the half of it."

The cowboys begrudgingly stepped to the Ute and climbed in, all the while keeping a wary eye on the strangers.

"You'll be sorry, you hear me?" the driver spat after starting the engine. He threw the gear stick forward and sped off in a cloud of dust.

"Ha, run, you yellow bastards," Jones jeered after them. "Woo!"

Billie returned her attention to the girl. She stood like a statue – tense and apprehensive, staring at her rescuers. The detective climbed out and strolled towards her. "You okay?"

The girl nodded and took a backwards step, her gaze drifting over the cop's bruised face. No doubt Billie's beat up appearance added to her apprehension. The cop stopped. Her hands lifted in a sign of submission. The last thing she wanted was to appear threatening.

"We're not going to hurt you," she assured her.

The girl's gaze darted from her to the van. Guessing what was upsetting her, Billie half turned, throwing a look over her shoulder. Jones met her eye – and the message in them. Only then did she realise she still held the rifle aimed towards the girl.

"Oh." She placed it inside the van. Flashing the cop a quick smile, she looked at the farm girl.

Billie faced her again. She failed to relax even with the threat of the rifle removed. "It's all right. We didn't like what those guys were up to." Receiving no response, Billie kept on in a soothing tone. "What's your name?"

The girl's nervous gaze jumped from her to the others in the van. "Kate. Kate Cauldron," she answered in a timid response.

"Hi, Kate, I'm Billie McCoy. Can we give you a lift home? Just in case those creeps come back."

Kate shook her head. "No, you don't have to do that."

Jane climbed out and crossed to Billie, stopping beside her and watching the stranger with interest. Kate's attention drifted her way, for a minute focusing on her marked face.

"Hi, Kate, my name's Jane Walker. Maybe you can help *us* out. You see, we're a little lost and we'd really appreciate some directions."

"You can trust them, Kate. They won't hurt you," Janda said, poking his head out the doorway.

Kate stared at him while considering his advice. She looked at Billie. The cop stood calm, waiting. Her patient and un-pressured expression had its effect. The farm girl relaxed a little.

"If you follow this road, you'll come to a town called Willowbank."

Billie glanced in the direction the two men had taken. Obviously, the girl didn't want any more help but was happy to get them on their way as a token of appreciation.

"Okay, thanks. Are you sure you'll be okay?" Billie asked, turning to her.

"I'll be fine. I've got my bike." She pointed to the Yamaha trail bike lying on the edge of the road.

Billie nodded, casting it a casual glance. And then something caught her attention. She studied the bike harder. Standing closer to it than Kate, she was in a better position to see the split in the petrol tank. For a moment, she thought she was seeing things but the constant leaking onto the ground confirmed her scrutiny. She glanced at Jane. From the look on her face, Billie knew she'd seen it as well. They walked over and crouched beside it. The smell of petrol was strong.

Kate's brow furrowed in puzzlement as she knelt on the topside opposite the girls, keeping her distance without being too far away. She leant forward and examined the Yammy. Everything was wet under and around the tank where fuel had leaked from the split in the seam on the bottom side.

"Doesn't look like you're going anywhere on that," Billie said. Kate's gaze shot upwards. Billie read the uneasiness in her eyes.

"Our offer still stands. We can drop you home. It's no trouble."

Kate stared in a fixed gaze, unable to answer. Her attention dropped to the immobilised trail bike while she considered the offer. Lifting her gaze to the watching girls, she nodded. "I live down that road about ten k's." She pointed behind her. The dirt road ran over a grid and disappeared across grassy plains lightly scattered with trees.

Billie nodded. "Fine. Come on, climb in," she said with a smile.

A faint, shy smile crept to Kate's lips. She gave a curt nod and stood with the girls. "Wait." Leaning down, she lifted the bike onto its wheels and pushed it further off the road, laying it beside the fence. Picking up her discarded hat, she dusted it off and walked with her rescuers to the van. Following Jane into the back, she cast Jones and Janda an uneasy look as she sat down.

Jones held out a hand. "Hi. I'm Sarah, Sarah Jones."

Kate hesitantly took the offered hand and shook it.

Jones smiled and dropped her hand. "This is Janda, and that's Casey in the driver's seat."

Kate nodded. Uncertainty reflected across her features.

"Don't worry, she's been practising driving most of the day and she's getting pretty good at it."

Kate's head shot around. She stared at Jones in horror.

"It's all right, Kate, I haven't hit anything yet," Reynolds teased, picking up Jones' cue. The farm girl looked at her, failing to shake the look of dread from her strained face. She cast a nervous glance around the smiling faces. A faint smile formed on her lips. She nodded.

"Well, I'm glad to hear that."

Billie jumped to her defence while pulling the door closed. "Ignore them, Kate. They'll try and throw their weight around, but, underneath, they're like little mice."

"Little mice, huh? That's not what you would've said a week or so ago," Reynolds said.

"Ah, but it's not a week ago, is it? Now, I know you better."

Reynolds smiled and started the van. Steering it over the rattly grid, she picked up speed down the dusty track.

Chapter Fourteen

"Who were those guys?" Billie asked.

"Jack and Tony Riley. They're brothers," Kate said, confirming Billie's theory. "Their family more or less runs Willowbank. They're the unofficial law, and they use bullying tactics to get their way."

For some reason, the news didn't surprise the detective, not after what they'd left behind. As Todd and Kym had pointed out, there was very little law up this way. Anyone with enough money and muscle was in their element.

"So what did that guy have against your family being farmers?" Jane asked.

"My family don't run cattle. Out here in this country, that's sacrilege," Kate said. "Like a lot of people around here, they don't like us being different. Because we have sheep and horses, they deem us as outcasts. It's probably also because my father tends to stand up to them and refuses to do what they want."

"What creeps."

Kate soon relaxed in the girls' company and was happy to answer their questions. In no time, Reynolds pulled up in front of her house. Quite large, it was built out of timber and set two feet off the ground. A wide verandah stretched along the front. Large windows, open to capture any passing breeze, lined almost the full length of it. A couple of tables and chairs sat up one end, offering a relaxing corner under the shade of the overlapping roof. A few trees grew close to the house helping to provide protection against the long, hot summer sun.

A high shed stood opposite the house a good forty metres away. Its two big doors hung open. Billie could make out a tractor, a Ute, and bales of hay. A reasonable-sized set of yards butted up against one side of the shed. A few more trees provided shade within the yards, one sheltering a water trough beside a tap. A windmill towered over a galvanised tank on the far side. This was the farm's water supply, the vital necessity for survival in such harsh conditions.

Kate looked at the girls. "Well, this is my home. Would you like to come in for a drink – and maybe stay for dinner?"

"I don't know. We don't want to impose," Billie said distractedly, looking over the house.

"It's not imposing. Call it repaying, for the lift out here."

Kate's statement drew the cop's gaze around to her. Kate's stare was fixed on her. Billie sensed the strong plea in her expectant look. A little undecided, she glanced at the others.

Jones, breaking her gaze, turned to Kate. "Sure, we'd love to. Thanks, Kate." She smiled and glanced at the detective, who smiled in turn.

The door of the house swung open. A solid man in his late fifties stepped out onto the verandah with a shotgun aimed in their direction. Wiry and fit, he obviously worked the farm. His wide brimmed hat, shaped by long years of sweat and wear, barely contained his dark grey hair. A bushy beard jutted out from his chin as if in defiance.

"Shit." Jones reached for the rifle.

"Wait! That's my father," Kate hastily said, her tone anxious. Billie looked over her shoulder, watching Kate drop a hand on Jones' arm to stop her picking up the gun. Billie appreciated why Jones wanted to arm herself. Seeing a man coming at them with a shotgun put them all on edge.

"He doesn't know I'm in here," Kate said. "It'll be okay."

Jones nodded and released the rifle. The farm girl slid open the door and jumped out. She strode forward to meet her father. The farmer stopped in his tracks, surprise washing across his features.

Kate didn't hesitate. "It's all right, Pa. They just gave me a ride home."

He stared from her to the four girls climbing out of the van. "Kate, what on earth are you doing riding with strangers?" His deep voice boomed. "Don't you remember what I've told you about that?" His aim didn't alter from the girls even after they joined his daughter.

"They saved me from the Riley brothers."

"What? Saved you?"

"Yes. They chased them off."

Hesitating, he frowned. "You know I don't like strangers, especially on the property. You were wrong to bring them here."

The front door of the house creaked. A plump woman pushed open the screen door and stepped out. Her faded dress hung to her knees, the apron tied over the top of it dropping halfway to her ankles. A bright yellow scarf around her head kept the hair out of her eyes. She stopped on the edge of the verandah cautiously looking out. Shock lit up her face.

"Kate, who are these girls?" she called a little anxiously.

"They helped me, Mum," Kate answered, stepping towards her. "And gave me a lift home."

"You don't know them," her father said, his unfriendly gaze set on the four strangers with mistrust.

Billie waited, tense, studying the farmer and his wife.

Kate turned to him. "Pa, the Riley's were..." She suddenly stopped, recalculating her words. "Were hassling me. Billie and the girls stood up to them and made them leave."

Billie glanced at her when she altered her story but didn't question it. It didn't really matter. The big man wasn't interested in excuses anyway. The concern for his daughter overrode any truths she had to offer. Not wanting to cause any unnecessary trouble, she needed to end it before it got out of hand. Kate had tried, and, for that, she was grateful. In the same respect, she couldn't blame her parents either. She'd probably react the same way.

"It's okay, Kate. We should be moving on anyway."

Kate looked at her, flustered. "But you don't even know where you are."

Billie held her gaze. Before she could answer, Janda caught her attention when he jumped out of the van and stepped to Jane. Jane rested her arm over his shoulders. He glanced at Billie and then looked at the two new strangers. Billie followed his gaze.

Kate's father merely glanced at him, more interested in the girls, particularly their marked and bruised faces.

Kate's mother stared at Janda with motherly compassion. "You poor child. John, we could at least feed them for bringing Kate home," she said, studying the girls with more interest.

John's gaze shot to her. "What?"

"Please, Pa," Kate said. "They didn't have to help me."

He turned to her, meeting her beseeching eyes. His attention returned to the girls and Janda. Under a contemplative stare, he reconsidered the argument. A resigned sigh slipped through his lips.

"Well, I guess if Kate thinks you're all right, you can't be too bad," he said without aggressiveness. Lowering the shotgun, he hooked it in the crook of his arm and cleared his throat. "The name's John Cauldron. This is my wife, Eve."

For a second time, the screen door opened on a scratchy squeal. Three youths stepped out and stood beside their mother against the railing. John looked at them and smiled.

"And this is Julie, Mary, and Tom."

They smiled, bobbing their heads as they were introduced. The two teen girls were younger than Kate. Mary stood taller than her mother. Of slim build, a pink ribbon tied her hair back, a contrast to the old jeans and T-shirt she wore. Freckles sprinkled across Julie's nose and cheeks. Tom looked to be about Janda's age. Like his father, he had a strong build. Short-cropped, reddish hair enhanced his mischievous look.

Billie stepped forward and introduced herself and then the others. Eve walked down the four steps of the wide staircase and stood with John, taking a closer look at the strangers.

"What on earth have you girls been up to?" she asked, studying the bruised faces and ragged looks.

"It's a long story," Reynolds said.

"Yeah, too long," Jane added with a tired sigh.

"Are you in some kind of trouble?" John asked warily.

"Not now," Billie said. She really didn't see the point in explaining.

John's brow furrowed. "Not now?"

"Come on in," Eve said, silencing her husband. "We have plenty of food, all home grown." She smiled.

John looked sharply at her. His frown deepened, but he didn't argue.

"As a matter of fact," Eve went on, "I have a fresh pot of stew on the stove, ready and waiting."

"Thank you, that sounds great." Billie glanced at her friends. They returned her look with approving smiles.

"Come on," Kate urged with a wave of her hand, stepping off with her mother. "Mum's a great cook."

The girls followed their hosts onto the verandah. The three siblings hurried in ahead. They seemed excited about having guests for dinner. The front door of the Cauldron's residence opened into a large lounge room, virtually running the length of the verandah. Clean and tidy, it had ample seating. Bereft of TV or any other electronic appliances, the room contained only the bare essentials. Walking through to the next room, Billie failed to see a phone, radio or computer, in fact, any means of communication.

Eve led them into the kitchen. There wasn't even a radio in here. The distinct homely smell of a wooden combustion stove lingered in the air. Nestled in the corner, its blackened flue disappeared into the ceiling. A large, covered pot sat on top of one of the four plates – the stew. The aroma drifted to her nose, stirring her appetite.

Cupboards and a sink lined the walls on two sides. An old fridge stood alone along another beside a second door. In the middle of the room was a long, wooden table with eight chairs tucked under it. The guests were ushered to their seats. They sank into them, expressing their thanks.

"Have you hurt yourself, Billie? You seem to be moving a little stiffly," Eve asked.

The detective looked up to find Eve watching her. Caught out by the question, Billie hesitated. The family had enough issues without adding theirs. She gave a flicker of a smile. "Oh, it's nothing. I'm just mending a little slower than I'd like."

"It looks more than nothing to me."

As Billie was about to reply, Kate distracted her by placing a bowl of stew in front of her. Her two sisters did the same with each of their other guests. Billie nodded her thanks before answering Eve, who waited patiently. "I'm fine, thanks. It's nothing to worry about."

"Where's Tom and Janda gone?" Kate asked, changing the subject. She placed a bowl in front of Janda's empty chair and looked around the room.

"Maybe Tom's showing him his room," Julie said.

"Probably. Can you bring them back?"

With a nod, Julie dashed out in search of them. Eve and John sat down opposite the girls. Now that they'd finished their waitressing duties, Kate and Mary stood to the side leaning against the sink watching their guests.

"So, do the Riley's trouble you much?" Jones asked, swallowing a mouthful of stew. Her eyes widened. "Oh wow, this is so good." She took another mouthful.

"I'll say." Casey shook her head. "It's the best I've ever tasted."

Eve smiled. "Thank you. We try to stay out of their way as much as possible," she said to Sarah, answering her question. "There are five of them."

"They have the town running scared," John spat with distaste. "Everyone is too gutless to band together to squash them. The town would be a much better place without them."

"They only think they run it. I'm not scared of them," Kate said, spitting the words out in a mimic of her father.

"Kate, the more you fight them, the more they'll provoke you," Eve warned.

"They were certainly doing more than that today," Billie said, glancing at Kate.

Eve shot her a look and then turned to Kate. "Why? What happened today?"

"Nothing happened, Mum. They . . . seemed a little pushier than usual, that's all. These guys arrived in time to move them on. Honestly, I'm fine."

The girls looked at one another. Kate's watered down version certainly lessened the threat she'd faced, but no one questioned it.

Eve shook her head. "They are such horrible boys. I really wish someone could stop them."

"If the townsfolk would stand together, we *would* beat them," John said. "They're nothing but a bunch of cowards."

Billie looked at him, her thoughts churning. She could understand his irritation. Nobody deserved to be dominated like that, and, if nobody was prepared to stand up to them, then it would never end. She turned to the girls and was surprised to find them watching her. They'd paused in their eating, their sober looks expressing a clear message – stay out of it. It was as if they knew what she was thinking. What, were they mind readers?

Jones gave a slight shake of her head to reinforce their point. Taking the subtle hint, Billie dropped her head and took a mouthful of stew to calm her rising concerns.

"What's the town called again?" Reynolds asked, changing the subject.

"Willowbank. It's about forty k's from here."

"Is there a phone there?" Billie asked.

John looked at her curiously, suspiciously.

"Well . . . yes," Eve said. "Trouble is, you have to go through the exchange which is usually screened by the Rileys. You may be lucky enough to get through without any hassle, or you may not."

"Come on," Jane exclaimed in disbelief.

"It's true, unfortunately. The Rileys govern everything, including the one public phone."

Julie returned with the two boys. "Would you believe I found them playing on the woodheap?"

Eve smiled. "Tom, you can play after Janda has eaten."

"Sure, Mum. Sorry."

Janda slipped into his chair and picked up his spoon. He shovelled the stew in with barely a breath.

John sat back against his chair, studying each of the visitors in turn. "So why are four good-looking girls like yourselves trekking around this type of country with a boy, and lost at that? And don't tell me you haven't run into trouble." Slowly, he folded his arms and rested them on his chest. His head tilted to the side in a patient expectancy.

Billie stopped eating. Something about his tone and inquisitiveness set her on edge. She believed the topic had been buried, but now he was digging. Would it be to their advantage to tell the truth? Or was their story too bizarre to believe? She glanced at her friends before answering. "Like Reynolds said earlier, it's a long story."

"I know why," Tom brazenly spoke up from beside Janda. "Janda was a slave boy, and they saved him."

Everyone looked at him. A shocked silence filled the room.

"What did you say?" Eve asked. "A slave boy?"

Tom nodded. His gaze darted around the room of stunned faces.

"Janda, I thought we agreed not to tell anyone," Jones rebuked, glaring at him.

He cowered. "I'm sorry, Sarah. Tom asked me so I told him. It's the truth, and, besides, you didn't do anything bad."

"Is it true?" John put to Jones somewhat harshly. When she hesitated, he turned to Billie. His eyes narrowed, enforcing his question.

She returned his stare with a steady gaze. "We found him with a guy called Smith, a sick bastard who liked to abuse him."

"How did you know what he was doing with him?" His voice was mistrustful.

"John..." Eve cautioned her husband.

"How?" he barked, ignoring his wife's warning. He sat forward, his stare fixed on Billie silently demanding an answer.

"They were captured by him too," Tom exclaimed.

Billie sighed. Like Jones, she'd hoped Janda had kept their story to himself, but kids rarely kept secrets, especially if they could brag about their adventures and impress potential new friends. Under her gaze, Janda shrank lower in his seat and gave her a feeble smile.

"This gets better and better," John muttered through clenched teeth. "Who exactly are you?"

Billie glanced at the girls before looking back at him. Obviously, he expected an answer, and she couldn't blame him for being so guarded. He was only concerned for the welfare of his family. Would he believe their story? Maybe. Maybe not.

"Okay, maybe we should start at the beginning."

"That sounds like a good idea to me." The harshness weighed heavy in his tone. Billie ignored his unfriendliness. Remaining calm, she went on to explain.

"We're all from Sydney. I'm a detective—"

"A detective?" He stared in astonishment. His gaze roamed over the other three. "Are you all cops?"

Billie gave a laugh and glanced at the girls.

"Er, not quite," Reynolds replied hesitantly. "We're sort of – just out of jail." She cast a nervous look at her friends. The girls' solemn faces readied for the outburst that was sure to come.

"Great." John threw his hands up. He glanced at Eve and then Kate with an 'I told you so' look. They didn't dispute it. Disgruntled, he turned to the watching girls. He blew a heavy sigh through his tightened lips. "Okay, at least you're being honest with me. Go on."

The girls told their story, keeping it brief without going into the details. When they'd finished, silence filled the room for a drawn out moment. Disbelief smothered the suspicion and tension within the Cauldron family.

"You're lucky to be alive," Eve claimed. "I'd really like to see where you were cut, Billie."

"Honest, it's not that bad."

"I insist. I used to be a nurse, and a good one at that."

"Yeah, she patches us up enough," John said and smiled. "You are better off giving into her rather than arguing, believe me."

Jane looked at Billie. "It wouldn't hurt to have it cleaned properly."

Before Billie could argue, Eve stood and slapped her palms down on the tabletop. "That's it then, come on."

Billie looked at her and then Jane.

"Come," Eve insisted.

The detective shrugged. "Fine." She pushed out of the chair and stood, slow and stiff.

"I'll come with you," Jane said, standing with her.

Eve looked at her daughter. "Kate, could you please get me a bowl of warm water, clean cloths, and the kit bag."

"Sure, Mum." She exited through the door beside the fridge. Eve turned to Billie.

"Follow me." She led her through the same door with Jane accompanying. They entered a bedroom at the back of the house. Eve sat the detective down on one of the two single beds. Jane stood protectively beside her. Neat and clean, the room was large. A chest of drawers separated the beds with a tall, matching timber wardrobe at the foot of the beds. Beside it, a stool was tucked under a narrow desk. Eve grabbed the stool and placed it in front of her patient, settling herself on it.

Billie pulled up her shirt and held it while Eve undid the bandage. She flinched when Eve tugged on the very end to free it and the dressing from a patch of dried blood.

"My goodness," Eve gasped. "No wonder you're moving so stiffly. You should be resting until this heals properly," she said, examining it closely. "It looks like you've reopened it at some stage."

"Yeah, maybe a couple of times."

"A couple?"

"More like three or four times," Jane corrected. She flashed a smile when Billie glanced at her. Eve continued her examination without a shift of her head.

"Yes, it certainly looks that way. These stitches are well stretched."

Kate carried in the water, cloths and the bag Eve had asked for and placed them beside her mother on the chest of drawers. Eve began cleaning the wound. Billie winced even though she was gentle.

"It's a little infected, but it should be okay. This cream will help," Eve said, smearing it across the wound after dabbing it dry.

Billie jumped. "Hell, what is that stuff?" Already the pain had lost its edge as a numbness set in.

"Don't be a wimp, McCoy," Jane teased with a smile. Before the detective could answer her, Jane turned to Kate. "She'll try anything for sympathy."

Kate smiled at Billie. Amusement danced in her eyes. Shaking her head, Billie gave in and smiled with them.

Eve finished strapping her up with a fresh bandage. "There." She searched for other wounds. Her gaze rested on the strip of plaster on her arm. "What's this?"

Billie dropped her shirt and looked at it. "Oh, that's healing fine."

"I'll be the judge of that." Taking hold of the strip, she ripped it off before the cop could object.

Billie sucked in a gasp. Removing the plaster so abruptly disturbed the tender wound, causing it to sting. She looked at the woman in front of her. Eve was too busy studying the cut to meet her gaze.

"Did you retire from nursing or did they throw you out?" she queried.

Her question drew a giggle from Kate and Jane. Eve cast her a quick glance with a touch of a smile.

"For your information, young lady," she said in a flat, stern tone, her attention returning to the half-healed cut, "they threw me a big party when I *retired*."

"Ah huh."

Eve's lips twitched. Merriment washed across her face. "Mm, I can clean it up and give it a new dressing."

"You should check the one on her leg as well," Jane told her, smiling at Billie when she shot her a look. Eve caught Jane's gaze. She turned to Billie with a mischievous smile.

"Yes, I will. Thank you, Jane."

The detective looked at her, offering a faint smile. As usual, the numbers were against her.

"Fine, feel free."

Eve sat back after cleaning her arm and thigh. "There, all done. Any others you haven't told me about?"

"No, you've got them all covered. You've done enough, really."

"Nonsense, I've hardly done anything. Those ribs need frequent cleaning and rest. I insist you stay for a couple of days."

The invitation caught the cop by surprise. She stared at Eve while her mind raced. Stay? They couldn't stay. Not with Bates on their tail. "Thanks for the offer, but—"

Eve remained adamant. "You need the rest. A couple more days won't hurt you."

"Eve, I appreciate what you're saying but it's not quite that easy. We have—"

"I can make it *very* easy for you. I will tie you here if need be. You need to rest these wounds or you could end up with big problems."

"We already have big problems and staying here could make them much bigger."

Eve smiled. It was a cool smile laced with an unyielding caveat. "Let me put it to you this way. Your wound is infected and, at the moment, bearable. Within hours, it could flare up and make you so sick you wouldn't know who or where you are. Now, I'll ask you again – are you going to stay?"

The cop considered her offer. Eve had a good point. The wound had become increasingly sore, a new pain to what she'd been used to, and it didn't seem to want to go away. Added to that, she well knew they could all do with a rest. The farm was isolated, and Bates would have trouble finding them in the middle of nowhere, but she wasn't prepared to make the decision alone. Her focus settled on the problem in front of her. Eve waited patiently for an answer.

Billie smiled. "You *do* have a mean streak in you, don't you."

"You haven't seen anything yet. What's your answer, or do you need more convincing?"

The detective sighed and glanced at Jane. She merely smiled and shrugged, a sign she was happy to go along with whatever she decided – or maybe preferably to stay. Billie looked at Eve.

"All right, but only on the condition the others agree, okay?"

Eve smiled. It held a definite challenge. "Oh, don't worry, they will."

From her tone, Billie had no doubt she would persuade Jones and Reynolds. Pity those who should try and dispute it. They'd definitely met their match here. Billie nodded with an appreciative smile.

"I guess it wouldn't hurt," Jane said.

"It's settled then. Let's go spread the news." Eve grinned and helped Billie up.

They rejoined the others where Eve put the idea to the girls very persuasively, leaving little room for compromise. After discussing it and throwing the blame on Billie for again holding them up, Reynolds and Jones finally agreed.

"With such good company and great food, I guess we could hang out here for a while," Reynolds said.

"Yeah. It's definitely worth the risk." Jones smiled at Eve and John. "Looks like you've got yourselves some boarders."

Eve grinned. "Good."

Chapter Fifteen

The following day found Billie confined either to the bed or the long chair on the verandah. She opted for the latter more frequently, particularly when the others sat out there. Under Eve's watchful eye, she had little choice. Eve insisted she needed total rest and was determined to see her get it. In the end, Billie gave up arguing and simply took her advice, using the time to catch up on some sleep. At last her ribs had the chance to heal.

The other three weren't about to miss such an opportunity either. They spent their time catnapping throughout the day replenishing their reserves, enjoying the carefree mood enveloping them.

Billie hardly saw the two boys. Janda and Tom got on like a house on fire and spent most of their time outside.

The days lazily rolled by. Kate looked after her guests, getting to know them and enjoying their company immensely. The girls gradually regained their strength. In appreciation and exchange for their board, they began doing odd jobs for John and Eve. By the third day, Billie became anxious to use a phone. Kate put her mind at rest by offering to drive her into town, giving the excuse she needed to pick up a few supplies.

The three girls stood beside the Ute as Billie and Kate climbed in. Jane closed the door for the cop, watching her pull the seatbelt across her shoulder and click it in place.

"Are you sure you don't want one of us to come with you?" she said through the open window.

"No, I'll be fine. Straight in and out," the detective assured her with a smile.

"But what if Bates has his scouts out?"

Billie lifted a wide brimmed hat and a pair of sunglasses Kate had loaned her off the seat. "I have these to help disguise me, remember?"

She dropped the hat on the seat and slipped on the sunglasses. "Besides, they'll be looking for four girls, not one. I shouldn't stand out on my own so stop worrying. We'll be back before you know it."

Jane stared thoughtfully and then nodded. Billie could tell she was uncomfortable about the idea of her going alone. Offering a faint smile, she made an effort to reassure her.

"This is the best chance we've had. I can't afford not to take it. A phone call will get us out of here once and for all. We won't have to drive blindly, worrying if Bates is right behind us or waiting in hiding to ambush us. My squad will move fast to get us out of here. We'll be home free."

Jane nodded. She bit on her bottom lip, drumming her fingers on the top of the door. "I know. I'm sorry. Just be careful."

Warmth filled Billie. Jane was concerned, more than she cared to admit. "I will, thanks."

Nodding, Jane stepped back and stood with Reynolds and Jones. Billie looked at them. Even they seemed a little uneasy. After being together for so long and pulling through as a team, the girls were worried that if she did get into trouble, they wouldn't be there to help her – very different from when they'd first met.

Billie flashed a smile and lifted her hand in a wave as Kate pulled out. The girls returned it.

***

Thirty minutes later, Kate drove into Willowbank. A variety of shops lined either side. Houses nestled behind and beyond the quiet stores. Blacks and whites mingled in the street, lounging around doing nothing in particular. The scene seemed all too familiar to Billie, jolting her memory of Wilford's 'warm' township. The only difference was, Willowbank appeared slightly more modern and cleaner.

"Well, this is Willowbank." Kate sighed and looked out the window at the near empty street.

"It's an improvement on where we've been," Billie said.

"I'll bet." Kate pulled up in front of a convenience store. She pointed across the road to a phone box. All that was left of it was the frame. The glass had been either smashed or removed. "There's the phone. How about you make your call while I get my supplies."

The cop nodded. "Sure." She pulled on the hat and tucked her hair up underneath to hide it. She looked at Kate.

"Nice," Kate said. "It's amazing what a hat and sunglasses can do. It doesn't even look like you."

Billie smiled. "Good. Let's do it."

The girls climbed out.

"Good luck," Kate said across the roof of the Ute.

Shutting the door, Billie smiled. "Yeah, thanks."

Kate disappeared into the store. Billie turned and crossed the street, her gaze fixed on the phone box. Her nerves tightened the closer she got to it. A lot was riding on this one link to the outside world. Here was the first opportunity to finally get her out of this mess. She stepped into the booth and breathed out. Picking up the handpiece, she inserted the money John had lent her. A woman's voice sounded, rude and abrupt.

"What number do you want?"

Only for the fact the Cauldrons had explained the procedure for reaching an outside number was Billie able to keep her surprise under control. In a calm manner, she rattled off her boss' mobile number. Immediately the operator began to complain; how much effort it was, how she didn't get paid enough, how long her hours were. All the while Billie forced herself to remain calm. In the back of her mind, she wondered whether it was merely a stall to alert the Rileys. Was she secretly contacting them to come and check who was in the phone booth? Did they have that much power? Or maybe she knew Bates.

Her fears were unfounded. Finally, there was a ringing – a familiar voice answered.

"Edwards."

The operator babbled over the top of him, asking if he'd accept reverse charges.

"Dave?" Billie managed to get in before the woman told her to be quiet.

"Billie?"

The operator grew aggressive. "Do you accept the charges or do I terminate this call right—"

"Yes, yes!" Dave answered. "I accept!" There was a click and then she was gone. "Billie?"

"I'm here, Dave," she said, gripping the phone tight, fighting to control her stirred emotions. Just hearing his voice filled her with a renewed assurance. Though Dave was her boss, he was also a father figure to her. He'd been her father's best friend and had taken her under his wing after his death, in some ways, caring about her as if she were his own.

"Shit, Billie, we have been going crazy here. We couldn't find any leads to track you down. Everywhere we turned led to a dead end. Where are you? Are you all right? Can you talk?"

"Yes, and yes I'm fine. I'm in a town called Willowbank, in north Queensland."

"North Queensland?"

"Before I met with the gun-runners, I went to help a girl two thugs were attempting to abduct."

"Yeah, Jane Walker. We've got her details and assumed she was somehow tied up with your disappearance because of her trashed room. Unfortunately, the room was clean when it came to finding any leads."

"I'm not surprised. I'm so sorry, Dave. Things sort of turned on me and the next thing I knew, I was caught up in a slave trade run by none other than Joseph Bates."

"Bates? Captain Bates? Chief of Missing Persons Bates?" His voice filled with disbelief.

"Yes, the very same."

"Don't tell me he's tied up with the 'Lonely Hearts Club'."

"You got it. All those prostitutes and other women who've been disappearing over the last three years – Bates was responsible for every one of them. He's selling them as sex slaves to buyers both here and overseas. He's still on my tail and has contacts everywhere. This is the first chance I've had to use a phone since I escaped."

"Bates – a slave trader? I don't believe it. Hell, I've met the guy a few times. I never would have guessed."

"Same here."

"Shit, no wonder there were no leads. He would've had everything covered."

"Yeah. He flew us out of Sydney to somewhere out west and, from there, trucked seven of us north along dirt roads well inland away from the highways."

"Damn it. We found out the bastard was on leave when we checked with Missing Persons, and it still didn't click."

"You had no reason to connect him to any of this. He hid his tracks perfectly."

"So true. I'm guessing Sarah Jones and Casey Reynolds were amongst the girls taken?"

"Yeah. They are with me and so is Jane. Good to see you worked out a few details."

"Only the bare ones, and nothing to lead us to you. All we have are names, and that the girls went missing pretty close to each other." A pause. "Bloody hell. Bates a crook? Geez, he would have had all the information he needed to set up each girl without leaving any trace."

"Exactly, and he only chose the best. They're all attractive, a good selling point, no doubt."

"What a bastard."

"Believe me, he has it well planned. If it wasn't for the girls helping me, I'd probably be in Egypt about now."

Dave hesitated, taken back by the comment. "Are you safe where you are? I can possibly be there by early tomorrow morning."

"Yeah, we're on a farm owned by a John Cauldron, about forty k's northwest of here."

"Don't worry, I'll find it."

"I also have a boy with me."

"A boy?"

"He's another one I owe my life to. I'll fill you in later."

"Sure, no problem. I'll be there as soon as I can."

"Man, it's so good to hear your voice," she breathed.

"Same here, babe. Mark and Johnny are going to be so relieved when I tell them you're okay."

Detectives Mark Burrows and Johnny Karle were her partners, and close friends. They'd been her backup on the day she'd disappeared.

"Say 'hi' to them for me."

"I will, now, take care. I'll see you in the morning."

"We'll be waiting." Reluctantly, she hung up. She rested her forehead on the phone and closed her eyes, letting the excitement wash through her. It was almost over. For once, she had good news to tell the girls. They were going home – home, back to the life they'd so rudely been plucked from. The tables had turned. Bates would be the hunted and the one on the run, and there was no way she would let him get away.

She stepped out of the booth and inhaled deeply. For the first time, the fresh country air tasted good. She cast a casual glance across the street, searching for a sign of Kate. She'd said she didn't have much to get. Billie froze. Her heart skipped a beat with the sight that met her. Kate was in clear view — and clearly in trouble.

Even as the thought registered, Billie watched two men ram her into the passenger door of the Ute and pin her against it. Kate struggled but couldn't break their hold. The detective's anger stirred. These were the guys who were hassling her the other day, the Riley brothers. A third guy, almost the spitting image of his comrades, watched from the side wearing a wide grin. With the same arrogant attitude and looks, no one could mistake them for anything but siblings. Disregarding her own safety, Billie strode across to them.

"We've got some unfinished business, Katy girl," Jack Riley sneered, his face inches from hers.

"Let me go, you creep," Kate spat, fighting against him.

"That's no way to talk to my brother," Tony said, jabbing her in the side. Kate gasped and bowed forward.

"It's okay, Tony, I'm sure she didn't mean it," Jack said with a grin, pushing her up so he could look her in the eye.

"The hell I didn't." She kicked at him. He easily dodged the foot and laughed.

"Come on, bros, let's give her a good time, one she won't forget in a long while." His big hand clasped her arm and yanked her off the Ute. He dragged her along the street towards his Ute four parks away. Kate fought him, trying to pry open his strong fingers with her free hand. When that failed, she resisted by pulling away from him in an endeavour to slow him down. Jack chuckled at her feeble efforts and yanked her forward with little effort. His two brothers followed, eager and ready to be of assistance.

"The only good time she'd get from you would be to watch you get your arse kicked," Billie said from behind.

The three brothers jerked to a halt and spun around to the stranger wearing a hat and sunglasses. Arms folded, Billie watched them.

Kate stared at her, her concern clearly etched on her strained features.

"Who the hell are you?" Jack asked, studying Billie.

"Piss off," Tony growled.

Relief washed through the detective. So, her disguise was working. They didn't recognise her under the hat and sunglasses.

"Is she with you, Katy?" Jack asked without taking his eyes off the intruder.

"Why would she be with me, you slimy bastard? Maybe she can see how much of a jerk you are. Now, let me go." She gave a sharp yank and almost pulled free.

The third brother ambled towards Billie, his hungry stare running over her body. "Ooh eeh! What does it matter? She can come with us as well. Keep Kate company."

"Now that's a good idea, Chet," Tony said. "The more the merrier."

Chet reached out to grab her arm. Billie knocked the hand to the side and stepped forward, smashing him across the jaw with her elbow. He fell backwards into the stunned Tony's arms. Tony caught his brother, only because he happened to be standing within reach. Half-dazed, Chet sank heavily against him.

"You bitch," Tony yelped. Dumping his brother on the ground, he charged at Billie in a reckless attack. She struck out with a sudden snap kick. Tony landed on the ground beside his brother.

"What the...!" Jack stared at his fallen siblings. Grunting, he shoved Kate to the side. The uncontrolled lurch reeled her in a helpless plunge towards the footpath. She tripped on the low step with no chance of saving herself. Robbed of balance, she went down, hitting the concrete floor hard. Jack didn't give her a second glance.

Billie ducked under his fist and threw her own, ramming a powerful punch to his solar plexus. The blow folded him forward. He staggered back, struggling for a breath. Billie kicked up and out, slamming him in the nose. He reeled into the door of his Ute and slowly slid down. In a desperate effort to stay upright, he half turned and clasped the open window.

Chet was back on his feet and moved in. Billie drove her foot into his nose. The impact knocked him to the ground. Blood gushed over his mouth and chin. He landed spreadeagled and didn't move.

Jack pushed off the door and lunged her way. She spun around, kicking him in the ribs, showing no mercy. She hated what these men stood for – mean and big-headed bullies who gained everything by enforcing a lawless power to create fear. She could understand John's hatred towards them. It was time they were given some of their own back.

Jack folded over in pain. Billie punched him in the nose, lifting him upright. He staggered backwards into the Ute. There he stood on wobbly legs, staring blankly, making no effort to attack. His eyes were glazed over, his arms hanging limp beside him.

With fist raised and ready, Billie paused, watching him. It was finished. Jack toppled forward without any further resistance, crumbling at her feet. She glanced around at the other two. They hadn't moved. Lowering her stinging fist, she shook it to help ease the pain. Her gaze returned to Jack stretched out on the road unconscious. He was no more of a threat.

Kate grabbed her arm and pulled her after her. "Come on, let's get out of here," she said, casting nervous glances around. Billie looked at her but didn't argue. Kate guided her around the brothers and over to her Ute. She yanked open the door. Billie climbed in, sinking slowly into the seat to keep the niggling pain in her ribs at bay. Grabbing the seat belt, she pulled it across her. Kate raced around the front and into the driver's seat. Starting the Ute, she threw the gear stick into reverse. The wheels spun furiously as she backed out. She pounded the gear stick into first. The Ute leapt forward when the farm girl released the clutch and planted her foot. Spitting up stones and dust in her exit, Kate sped out of town.

She let out a squeal of delight. A wide grin lit up her face. "Hell, I'm so happy and scared at the same time! For so long I've wanted to see those creeps get smashed. They deserve every bit of it, and more. Man, I only wish I could have given it to them."

She glanced at her passenger. Billie met her gaze with a smile, doing her best to ignore the dull ache across her ribs.

"Hey, are you okay?" Kate asked.

"Fine. How about you?"

"Me? Oh, just great." She turned to the road, shaking her head. "Where on earth did you learn to fight like that? I mean, I knew you must have been able to look after yourself after what you told us, but watching you in action..." Awed silence filled the car for a moment. "You were great. The Rileys didn't know what hit them."

Billie smiled out at the road. Hard training had perfected her skills, but she didn't like to make a big deal about it. "Oh, I've picked up a few tricks over the years." She pulled off the hat and shook out her hair.

"Hell, when I saw you just standing there, not a care in the world, my heart jumped to my throat. They're mean bastards, and, for one crazy minute, I thought we were both in for it." Her voice held respect. "I've never seen anything like it and have *never* seen the Rileys take such a hiding."

Billie turned to her. "Do they always hassle you like that?"

Kate's smile faded a little. Shaking her head, she turned to the road. "It's never been this frequent and never so heavy. Usually, they only tease me about being a farmer, you know, the usual childish things that seem to amuse such small minds. But, now, I'm guessing they want more."

"Well, I suggest you always have someone with you from now on, preferably your father."

Kate looked at her and nodded.

"I will. I'm just glad you were with me today. And they didn't recognise you, which is even better."

"Yeah."

"Hey, how'd you go with your phone call?"

Billie's face lit up. "Help's on the way."

"That's great."

Chapter Sixteen

The Ute pulled up close in front of the farmhouse. John and the girls sat at the table on the verandah splicing ropes, an activity John had promised to teach them. Billie guessed it'd helped take their mind off her while she was in town. Jones, Reynolds and Jane dropped their ropes and stood up. John stood with them. The girls walked down the steps to the Ute. John stopped at the top and leant on the post with folded arms, watching Billie and Kate climb out.

"Hi, guys," Billie said with a smile, pushing the door closed.

"Hi. Everything okay?" Jane asked, looking pleased to see her back safe and sound.

"Sure." Her gaze ran over the expectant faces. It wasn't hard to see they were dying to know her news, to know whether they were going home.

"Well?" Jones asked when Billie failed to bring the topic up.

"Well, what?"

"McCoy, don't get smart at a time like this."

"At a time like what? What are you talking about?"

"Did you or did you not make contact with Sydney?"

"Oh, that," she said, as if suddenly remembering.

Jones' fixed stare didn't alter. "Yes that. You know, that *is* why you went into town in the first place – to phone Edwards."

"Yeah, it was." She shook her head. "Man, I have never had such a crazy experience dealing with the rude operator to—"

"McCoy, did you talk to Edwards or not?" Jones pressed, her frustration loud. Billie held her gaze. Impatience flared Jones' eyes. Billie turned to Jane and Reynolds. They looked as if they were ready to pounce on her if she didn't put them out of their misery. Tempted to keep them in suspense for a few moments longer, she thought better of it. She smiled. "We're out of here as of tomorrow."

"You got through?" Jane exclaimed, staring with widened eyes.

Reynolds and Jones shrieked excited squeals and hugged each other, spinning around in a circle. Jane grabbed Billie and hugged her tight. The girls regained their composure and stood apart, looking from one to the other in delight. Billie gave them a short version of the phone call.

"I can't wait," Reynolds squealed, almost dancing on the spot.

"Says a lot for our hospitality, don't it, Kate," John said with a smile from the verandah. Kate glanced at him and grinned.

"Sure does, Pa, and after all we've done for them."

The comment jolted her guests back to reality. They turned to Kate and John.

"Come on, you know that's not what we meant," Jane said, looking from one to the other.

"We didn't mean anything against you." Reynolds promptly backed her.

John chuckled. "Hey, we understand completely." He pushed off the post and descended the steps. Slipping an arm around Kate's shoulders, he looked at his guests. "After what you guys have been through, you deserve to get home. I'm glad it's worked out for you at last."

Kate's enthusiasm echoed in her voice. "Me too. I'm very happy for you."

"Thanks, guys. We do appreciate everything you've done for us," Jones said. "Truly."

The girls nodded.

"Very much," Reynolds added.

"You're very welcome," John replied.

"It's been such a pleasure having you here," Kate said with sincerity. She turned to Billie and smiled. Her eyes suddenly widened, as if remembering something. She looked around the faces. "Oh, you'll never guess what else happened in town."

Billie picked up on what she was about to say. "Kate, maybe it's better not to—"

"No, it's okay, Billie." She looked at the gang. "We ran into the Rileys and they started getting pretty pushy."

John's face instantly hardened. He dropped his hand off his daughter's shoulder. Reynolds, Jones and Jane looked at her in surprise.

"What?" John growled. He turned her towards him, staring in shock. "Did they touch you? Boy, if they laid one hand—"

"Pa, I'm all right. They tried to but Billie put them in their place. She dropped the three of them flat on the ground before they knew what hit them. She was amazing."

All eyes turned to Billie. Not sure how this was going to go down, she waited quietly. Judging by her friends' stunned features, it didn't look good.

"Dropped the three of them?" John's astonishment thinned his tone.

"Are you crazy?" Jones cut in on him, directing the question at Billie in a high-pitched voice.

"You're supposed to be resting," Jane said. "Do you want to bust open your stitches again?"

"We're supposed to be lying low." Jones' disapproving growl overrode Jane's compassionate perspective. "Like, inconspicuously. Now everyone will know you're here."

"I knew we shouldn't have let her go alone," Reynolds said, staring intently at the detective. "Damn it, this could mean big trouble."

Billie understood their argument. Being such a small town, everyone knew Kate, and everyone would have seen they were together, clearly stating, 'the newcomer is staying with the Cauldrons'. Then again, maybe not. Really, they weren't together, not when the Rileys first attacked. Anyone watching would have seen her come to Kate's rescue. The fact she left with her didn't mean she went home with her. Either way, she didn't regret her call. Nodding, she lifted her hands in defence. "I know what you're saying but I didn't have a choice."

"The hell you didn't," Jones snapped.

Billie's gaze locked on hers. "Well, next time they try and force Kate into their car I'll just turn my back and let them take her."

"Don't pull that on us. No one's supposed to know we're here, remember? Or didn't that little fact occur to you? 'Stay out of trouble.' Remember those little words?"

"It couldn't be avoided."

"No?"

"No. What, do you think I purposely went looking for trouble?" Billie asked.

With eyes aglow, Jones' face hardened in her frustration. "Shit. You might as well have posted Bates a letter to tell him where we are because now you're going to stick out in the minds of everyone who saw you."

"No I won't. The Rileys didn't pick me with my disguise, and no one else had a clear look at me. It all happened pretty quick, and we were straight out of there."

"But you still left with Kate."

"Wait a minute here," Kate interrupted. "This is *my* fault, not Billie's. *I* was the one in trouble. She came to help *me*."

Jones glared at her. "You don't seem to understand what we're saying here."

John stepped in between the girls. "Hold it! Hold it!" he barked, silencing the argument with his booming voice.

Jones glared at him. Angry energy billowed off her in waves, but, instead of blasting him, she stepped back and folded her arms, scowling.

John gave her a short, grateful nod. He looked at Jane and Reynolds. They watched on tight-lipped, holding their comments. He faced Billie. She stood wary and somewhat on edge.

"Now, did I hear right? You brought the three Riley boys down on your own?"

The detective glanced at the others before arguing her defence. "They were dragging Kate off, so I—"

"That's not what I asked you," he said quite calmly.

She stopped, confused. His question didn't seem significant under the circumstances. So what if she'd brought them down? Her gaze darted to the girls. Jane looked more compassionate but not Jones and Reynolds. Their fiery glares clearly expressed their thoughts.

"She did, Pa," Kate answered for her, admiration strong in her voice.

"You were supposed to go straight in and out." Reynolds flew in, taking up the dispute again. "Just *one* phone call, *one* little call was all you had to make. Nothing more."

Billie looked at her. "I know that, but—"

Jones slapped her thighs. "It was a simple exercise. Go to town, make the call, and come back. Not—"

"Okay, lay off!" John boomed.

The two girls fell silent. John turned from them to Jane, ready to challenge any attack from her. None came.

"Good." He breathed a little calmer. "Now, I can see you're all worried. You think if Bates is in town, one question in the right ear and bingo – he'll know you're here."

"You've got it in one," Jones said, the annoyance obvious in her voice. She cast an irritated glance at Billie.

The detective ignored it and concentrated on their immediate problem. "Look, maybe we should—"

John put up a hand and silenced her. His intent gaze filled with admiration. "The way I see it, you saved my girl. I'm indebted to you. Anybody comes snooping around here – they'll have me to deal with."

"No, it's not that easy. Bates is extremely dangerous and ruthless."

"So am I."

Billie shook her head, refusing to take his casual attitude lightly. John and his family could be in danger if the slave trader did happen to find them. "John, I appreciate what you're offering, but—"

"Forget it, Billie. While you are my guest and staying under my roof, I refuse to let you leave on the chance some guy might find you here, and that's a pretty strong 'might'. No one recognised you and no one knows for sure Kate brought you here. The fact it was only you and not the four of you also lessens the suspicion to anyone who might, and I say *might*, have been on the lookout. Hell, there's a good chance Bates isn't in the area at all. He could be miles away."

"He is too shrewd to underestimate. You have to give him the benefit of the doubt and assume he is close behind us. The more I think about it, the more I think we should—"

"No." He stepped closer to her. "You are not leaving based on an assumption, simple as that. Together we can stand up to him – if we have to."

"It's never that easy. He always plays dirty."

"I don't care. You've stuck up for Kate twice now, so I'm prepared to stick up for you."

"Even at the risk of your family getting hurt?"

He paused for only a second. "Yes."

Billie fell silent. He was willing to stand by them no matter what. He saw them as part of his family, wanting to protect them as his family. At a loss, she sighed and turned to the girls. Their anger had subsided. They watched with an air of uncertainty, hesitant to offer any support.

Kate stepped to Billie. "Pa's right. You only have to stay one more night anyway. Besides, isn't this where you told your boss to find you?"

"Yes, but—"

"Then it's settled. One more night." She smiled. "If Bates was going to find you, wouldn't he have done it by now? I mean, you've been here two nights already, what's one more?"

Billie gazed at her thoughtfully, still uneasy about the idea. A lot of fears and assumptions had been raised after thrashing through this. A lot of it could simply be speculation. She looked over the faces around her. Without any input from the girls, she assumed they were leaving the decision to her. She also assumed they must want to stay or they would have objected by now. Frustrated, she ran a hand back through her hair, pushing it off her face.

"I'm sorry, I can't risk it. We really need to be somewhere else tonight. We can come back tomorrow to meet up with Dave. The van is comfortable enough to sleep in; we've done it enough times. I'm sure there are plenty of places we could hide." She looked around the watching faces. The silence was heavy. It obviously wasn't the answer they expected.

"Shit." Jones sighed.

Unless she was mistaken, Jones seemed a little deflated, as if the point of her arguing had caught up with her and dumped the severity of their situation on her shoulders.

"Are you that worried?" Jane asked Billie. Concern filtered into her voice.

The cop looked at her. "I just think it's better to be safe than sorry. John may be right; Bates could be a few days behind us, or he could be an hour away. The thing is if he does come snooping around, we can't afford to be here, not only for our sake but for John and the family."

A heavy silence met her. Her words left an impression. Reynolds broke it.

"Okay, fine, I see your point." She looked at Jones and Jane. "It's only for a night. It's no big deal."

Jones nodded. "Yep. Let's do it. I don't trust Bates one bit and we certainly can't afford to underestimate him."

"Hang on a minute," John cut in. "Before you go rushing off, I may have a better solution."

"John, it's okay. We will—"

"Sarah, I'm not disagreeing with you. I think it's a good idea, now that Billie has so clearly pointed out all the disturbing facts." He cast her a glance. She flashed a faint smile. He looked around the listening girls. "What I am saying is, rather than trek all over the countryside, I may have the perfect hideaway." His gaze rested on Billie. "There's a shed across the farm over on the far boundary, well away from here. It's not all that flash but it's clean and much more comfortable than the van. It already has stretchers set up and you can take food. When your lieutenant arrives tomorrow, we'll come and get you."

Billie thought it over, a little tempted. Way across the farm could be as good, or maybe better, than hiding somewhere random. "How far is it?"

"From here? Oh, probably about twenty minutes."

"Twenty minutes? Your property is that big?"

"Yeah. And you won't find the shed without someone showing you. That's how well hidden it is."

"How come you have a shed over there?" Jane asked.

"We camp in it when we're mustering on that side of the property. Saves driving back here every night."

Billie turned to the girls with a questioning look.

Reynolds shrugged. "Sounds good to me. It's nowhere near here and yet it's not too far to go."

"I agree," Jane said. "And it would be much better than being cramped in the van."

Billie's gaze drifted to Jones.

The girl shrugged. "Yeah, I'm happy to do it."

Billie considered it.

"I can take you there," Kate offered. "I'd love to," she added when Billie turned to her.

The cop nodded and faced John. "Looks like you've got yourself a deal. Thanks." She flashed a smile.

"Good. We'll get you packed and moved over there straight away, just in case."

"Good idea." She glanced at the girls. They seemed a little more relaxed with the decision.

John chuckled. "Boy, you must have hurt those Riley boys' egos when you dropped them. One lonely girl putting down three hefty men."

Billie shot him a look, caught out by the change of subject. A faint smile drifted to her lips. She shrugged. "What do they say? The bigger they are, the harder they fall."

"Ha! They've had it coming for a long time. I wish I'd seen it."

"Don't say that. We've seen enough for a lifetime." Jane glanced at Billie with respect. "She's scared the hell out of us too many times with some of the people she's taken on."

"Amen," Reynolds agreed.

Billie flashed them a brief smile but made no comment. She was just happy to see them lighten up.

"Come on," Kate said. "Let's get organised. Who wants a coffee? I think I need one." She exhaled a shaky breath and walked to the steps.

"Me, too," Reynolds said.

Everyone filed into the house. Billie was glad the girls had settled. She didn't want their last few hours with the Cauldrons spoilt with hostilities between them. One thing she did know – they were going to miss this wonderful caring family. Pushing all pessimistic thoughts from her mind, she concentrated on a welcoming coffee.

Chapter Seventeen

An hour later, the van was packed with food, drink, and other small necessities to make the night more comfortable. Except for Kate, everyone gathered in front of the van ready to say goodbye.

John pulled the rear door closed and stepped to the group. "Okay, looks like you're all set."

Billie met his eye with a smile. "Yeah. Thanks again, John, for everything."

"It's no trouble. And try to relax over there. It's only for a night."

"Sure, and you keep an eye out, too, just in case Bates does happen to show."

"Don't worry about us. If he turns up here, which I very much doubt he will, his quarrel is with you, not us. It's you who needs to be careful. We'll be fine."

"That's all well and good, but you're missing the point. He'll do anything to get what he wants."

"It won't come to that, not if I cooperate with him. I'll admit you were here and tell him you moved on after the fight today, which is basically true. Only I just might give him the wrong directions." He smiled.

Billie held his eye, considering his words. Hopefully, it would be that easy. Before she could answer, the screen door squeaked. Billie turned, surprised to see Kate stepping down off the verandah carrying an overnight bag.

"Kate, what are you doing?" she asked, already guessing her intentions.

"What's it look like? I'm staying over with you guys."

"You said you were driving us over, not staying."

"I changed my mind. It's not a problem, is it? I'd like to spend the last night with you. I'm so going to miss you when you're gone."

Billie inwardly flinched. Kate's unexpected compassionate reasons caught her out. She couldn't deny she was going to miss her too. She glanced at John. He stood relaxed with a half-smile warming his features. It was obvious he wasn't concerned about Kate staying the night. Eve had a tear in her eye but didn't comment. It seemed she was already missing them. Billie turned to Kate.

"It's not that we don't want you to stay, but you're probably better off being here."

Kate brushed her off. "Why? I'm taking you there so I may as well stay. Honestly, it's no big deal."

Jane couldn't contain her enthusiasm. "I think it's a great idea. It'll be nice having you, Kate."

Billie looked at her. "Jane, don't encourage her."

"Come on, relax. What's the big deal with Kate staying?"

Reynolds backed her. "It'll be sweet." She turned to Kate. "Did you pack any cards? We'll need something to help pass the time."

Kate smiled. "I did, and a few wines."

"Nice."

Kate tossed her bag into the back of the van through the side door. It landed on top of the stacked boxes. "Right, then, let's get going."

She gave her parents and siblings a quick hug and then jumped into the passenger seat. Closing the door, she cast the girls a challenging look. "Are we good?"

Billie blew out a sigh and gazed at John and Eve. John slipped an arm around Eve's shoulders and chuckled.

"Don't even bother arguing, Billie."

Before the cop could comment, Reynolds cut into the conversation. "Yeah, McCoy, relax. Come on, Janda, in you get."

Janda waved to Tom standing beside Eve. "Bye, Tom."

"See you tomorrow, Janda."

He and Reynolds clambered into the back. Jones and Jane followed after a quick wave at the family.

"Move over, guys," Jones said. "Man, I'm glad we're not going too far. It's a bit of a tight squeeze with all this gear."

"Why, because you can't lie down?" Jane teased.

"I can't help it if I like to stretch out."

Billie shook her head. She smiled at John and Eve.

"It's going to be a fun night. See you tomorrow."

"As soon as Dave arrives, I'll bring him over."

"Looking forward to it. Remember to stay alert at all times."

"We will. Stop worrying. Enjoy your time together."

She nodded and walked around to the driver's side and climbed in behind the wheel. As she pulled out, everyone yelled goodbyes to the family and returned their waves. Kate guided Billie along a rough dirt track across the open paddock. Sheep and horses grazed in the distance. They stopped a few times to open gates before continuing on. An occasional fork split the track. Billie followed Kate's directions whenever they encountered one. Eventually the paddocks evolved into thicker scrub. Billie found herself in a valley winding around a few low hills.

"Man, this is a bit like the roads we travelled on up north," Jones said from the back.

"Yeah, rough and never-ending," Reynolds stated. "Is it much further, Kate?"

The farm girl cast a smile over her shoulder. "Maybe five minutes."

Billie chuckled. "You guys are getting soft."

"Hey, we are pretty cramped back here," Jones grumbled. "Not to mention sitting on a hard floor."

Billie turned to Kate. "Like I said, getting soft."

Kate and Jane giggled.

"You're so funny, McCoy," Reynolds said with a laugh. "How about you concentrate on the road and try to miss a few more of the bumps."

Billie smiled. "What bumps? Maybe I should aim for the holes."

"You are so sitting in the back on the return trip," Jones said.

At last, they reached their destination. The shed appeared quite suddenly through the scrub.

"Here we are," Kate said.

"Finally," Reynolds called from the back.

Billie pulled up in front and turned off the van, studying their accommodation. It was much like the shed at the house. Made out of corrugated iron, many of the sheets were rusty. Two wide entry doors faced them, locked with a chain. The bush had been cleared around it, leaving a grassy area as a boundary. A few rusty implements were scattered across the dry lawn.

Kate jumped out and walked to the doors while digging for the key in her jeans pocket. The side door of the van scraped back. Billie shot a look over her shoulder. Everyone was exiting, moaning as they stretched their cramped bodies.

"Aah, it's so good to stand," Reynolds said, rubbing her behind.

"I think I've got more bruises now than before," Jones said. "I can see why John doesn't use this shed too often."

Billie climbed out and looked around. John was right; it was well hidden. A loud creaking filled the air as Janda and Kate pushed the shed doors open with a heave. The girls strolled over and filed inside. The interior was fairly empty. On one wall, a few tools and rolls of wire were neatly stacked. Six stretcher beds took up the back wall. The rest of the floor was empty.

"This is good, Kate," Reynolds said brightly.

Jane looked around. "Yeah, it's nice and cosy."

Kate slapped her thighs. "Right then, let's unload." She smiled at Billie.

The cop smiled back. "The sooner, the better."

With everyone pitching in, the shed transformed into a living room in no time. The girls unfolded a camping table and chairs ready for dinner. They placed the esky and a couple of boxes with lights and other necessities to the side of it.

"Right, who's for a game of Five Hundred?" Reynolds asked, looking at the girls lounging on the stretchers.

"You don't muck around, do you," Kate said.

A grin lit up her face. "Uh-uh. We've got to win back our reputation from McCoy and Jane."

Billie grinned. They'd started playing Five Handed Five Hundred a couple of days ago, and she and Jane had beaten Reynolds, Jones and Kate six games to three.

"Reputation? You never had one to start with."

"Oh really? Come on, hotshot, put your money where your mouth is." Reynolds jumped up and rummaged through one of the boxes, digging out the pack of cards. She faced Billie and held them up. "You up for it?"

Billie glanced at Jane and then Jones before turning to Reynolds. "Yeah. We're ready to whip your arse again."

Giggles broke out.

"I'm in," Jones said, pushing off the stretcher. "Come on, Kate, let's bury them."

"Definitely."

The girls settled around the table. Reynolds was already dealing. Janda moved in to watch. Laughter and jokes soon circled the table, fed on by the light rivalry prompted from the game and possibly the couple of beers the girls consumed. Time passed quickly. Janda nominated himself to hang the lanterns when it began to get dark. By the time the game finished, the girls were relying on the soft light from the camping lanterns.

Billie sat back, smiling in victory. "Now that we've whipped you again, I think it's time we ate."

Reynolds pulled a face. "That was just luck."

"I'm with Billie. I can't put that lamb stew off any longer," Jane said.

Janda grinned. "Me either."

While the girls got busy heating up the stew on a small gas cooker, Billie walked to the doors and looked out into the darkness. Only a silence met her. She couldn't entirely smother her anxiety regarding Bates, but they had raised the odds of him finding them before Dave arrived. She'd just be glad when tomorrow arrived and they were on their way home. A smile touched her lips. It was a nice feeling knowing they'd somehow survived this nightmare.

The wafting odour of the heating stew reached out to entice her back. She pulled closed the doors and strolled to the table to help the girls.

Under a pleasant atmosphere, the group savoured the meal with a few bottles of wine, and a Lemonade for Janda. Added with cheerful stories, the shed bubbled with laughter. It was so relaxed and carefree it could have been a get-together with long-lost friends.

After the meal, the diners sat for a while finishing their wines and exchanging tales. Janda yawned. Billie looked at him. His eyelids drooped.

"Hey, Janda, I think it's time you hit the sack."

All eyes turned to him. He gave a tired smile.

"Maybe I will."

"I'll have to speak with Tom. He wears you out too much," Kate said with a smile.

Janda returned it. "He does, but it's so much fun."

"Don't we know it. Go on, get into bed," Jones said. "We'll let you off the washing up tonight."

He chuckled at her joke. "Thanks. Night, everyone."

"Night, Janda."

He stood and then stopped. His gaze rested on the cop. "Billie, Bates won't find us here, will he?"

The question caught her out. Bates hadn't been mentioned since they'd arrived even though it no doubt played on everyone's mind.

"Let's hope not, Janda." She flashed a smile. "Hey, remember what I said? I won't let anything happen to you, no matter what."

Slowly, he nodded. "Okay. Night." He turned and walked to his bed, falling onto it belly down. Billie turned from him to find the girls watching her. Her words seemed to have an effect on them more so than Janda. She smiled, making light of their questioning stares. "Stay positive, remember?"

"We were, until now," Jane said somewhat soberly.

Billie glanced at Jones and Reynolds. Her advice failed to fade their grim looks.

"Come on, guys, we are going home tomorrow. That's all you have to think about."

After a moment, Jane broke the silence. "You're right. But can we not mention the 'B' word. It's too depressing." She smiled and took a swig of her wine.

"I'll drink to that," Reynolds said and swallowed a large mouthful.

Billie chuckled. "Keep that up and you won't even see tomorrow."

Reynolds shot a grin at Jones. "Now, there's a plan."

"Yeah, I like it," Jones said with a nod.

"Right, who's for another game of Five Hundred?" Kate asked, smiling around the group.

Jane nodded. "Yeah, why not?"

"Sarah, it's your deal." Kate slid the pack to her.

"Right then, let's put these two down," Jones said, shooting a look at Billie and Jane.

For two hours, the girls battled it out. At the end of the game, Jones stood up and stretched.

"I need a quick walk. Anyone want to join me?"

"I will," Jane said, pushing back her chair. "I'm busting."

"The torch is beside the box," Billie offered. She'd been out not too long ago. Drinking beer and wine meant regular trips outside.

"I'll deal the next hand," Reynolds said, scooping up the cards.

"Good on you," Jones said. "It *is* your turn, you know."

Reynolds pulled a face. "All the more reason for me to do it then, isn't it."

Jones shook her head with a grin and walked off, pushing open one of the doors wide enough to allow her and Jane to slip through.

Kate sighed and leant back in the chair. "I know I've said it before, but I am really going to miss you guys." She looked from Reynolds to Billie. "You are such great company. I don't have any close friends, other than my sisters."

Billie nodded. "We will miss you too. If it wasn't for you, we'd still be on the road, lost."

"I'll say," Reynolds added. "You were our lifesaver, Kate, and we are very grateful."

"And, you know, there's nothing stopping you from visiting the big smoke. You're welcome to stay with me," Billie said. "Come for a week, or more if you want."

Kate bit on her bottom lip. Her eyes watered. "I would love to do that. Thank you."

"Good."

"Have you ever been south, Kate?" Reynolds asked, finishing her dealing.

"Never. Hell, I've only been to the coast a couple of times. Sometimes I get the urge to pack up and travel, find a job doing something else, but then I feel I'm walking out on Mum and Pa. It's a hard life here but rewarding, so I'm torn between both."

"Yeah, it's a tough one, but sometimes you have to do what your heart wants," Billie quietly said.

"I know, and that's the hard part." She smiled. "I will definitely make the effort, though, to come and visit you guys. Maybe visiting Sydney will help open up my eyes."

"Ooh, yeah, it's good at doing that," Reynolds said with a chuckle. "Sydney has a lot to offer, and it's very, very different to here, not that I'm saying here is bad. I'm just saying it's different."

"I know where you're coming from. It'll be exciting, a whole new world for me."

"Yeah, definitely, and it's going to be a whole new world for Sarah and Jane if they don't hurry it up." She looked at the door and yelled, "Are you two planning on coming back any time soon?" She turned to Billie. "What's the score? Five to four? It's time to even it up."

A familiar voice from the doorway intruded upon them, leaving an icy chill in the air.

"Is this who you're waiting on?"

Billie shot a look towards the opened door. Her blood turned cold. Instantly, she, Reynolds and Kate jumped out of their chairs. Kate gasped and took a step forward. Billie grabbed her arm, preventing her from going any further.

Bates stood with a rifle aimed at them one-handed from his waist. A polite smile lifted his lips. His other hand gripped a terrified Eve by the arm. She stared wide-eyed, her tear-stained face etched with fear looking from Kate to Billie and Reynolds.

The big doors swung fully open. Four men filed in behind him and stood to the side. Billie recognised two – Jack and Tony Riley. Noting the similarity of the other two, she guessed them to be their other brothers. Jane and Jones' unconscious bodies were slung over Jack and Tony's shoulders, their heads and arms hanging limply behind the men's backs. With scornful smiles, the brothers dropped their shoulders and dumped their bundles at their feet. The girls didn't respond to the hard landing in the dirt. Both were tied.

All of the brothers carried rifles. With five guns pointing their way, the girls were denied any chances of escape or argument.

Billie stood tense, fully aware how dangerous these men were, especially with Bates leading them. Damn him. He'd recruited the Rileys? That reinforced his squad tenfold. Not only was she worried for everyone here, she appreciated just how grim her own predicament had become. Not for a minute did she trust Bates, not one little bit.

Chapter Eighteen

Billie held Bates' gaze without conveying any of the concern eating at her. Pleasure and victory danced in his eyes. She strived to come to terms with his presence, to the fact he'd found them. Shit. He'd forced Eve to guide him here, but under what conditions? Her stomach knotted at the thought he'd done something horrible to John and his family. Emotions strangled her. She couldn't speak.

Bates turned his attention to Kate while he addressed Eve. "Ahh, Mrs. Cauldron, this must be your daughter. Kate, I believe," he said with a curt nod. "The brothers have told me all about you."

"You leave her alone," Eve snarled.

Panic shook Kate's voice. "Mum, what's going on? Where's Pa? Is he all right? Are the others okay?"

Tears trickled down Eve's cheeks. She focused on Billie. "I'm so sorry. I had no choice but to bring them here. They shot John in the shoulder and beat him, and then when they were going to start on the kids, I had to do what they wanted. I'm so sorry, so sorry. Please forgive me."

Billie held her stare tight-lipped. Before she could comment, Bates cut in.

"Come on, Mrs. Cauldron, had you cooperated right from the start, no such violence would have been necessary. Despite the fact I explained to you and your husband how these four were wanted by the law and that it was my duty to arrest them, you still chose to hinder my investigation and feed me lies." Bates chuckled at her strained expression. His gaze swung to Billie. "You almost outsmarted me, McCoy. Almost. The Cauldrons put up a good act. They had me believing you'd taken off." Another chuckle shook him. "Lucky for me my new cohorts here were with me."

Billie glanced at the Rileys listening with smug smiles. Her gaze returned to Bates when he continued.

"As they know the family better than I do, they suspected Cauldron was lying, only for the fact Kate was missing. The boys thought it was a bit strange she wasn't at home. Where else could she be? See, that got me thinking. It was a little too coincidental how she and you and your friends were all gone together, which led me to believe, maybe you hadn't gone that far after all, if you know what I mean." He lifted an eyebrow in amusement. "And let me tell you, your disguise in the street was good. These guys didn't connect you to Kate, at least not until I prodded them with a few questions. And then it seemed to fall into place, including when you rescued her the other day. Anyway, with Kate missing from the good family home, we figured she was probably with you." A wide smile cracked his lips. "After that, it was simply a matter of an elimination procedure, with added persuasion at times."

Sickened by his story, Billie shot Kate a glance. She stared at Bates with guilt haunting her strained features. Slowly she turned to Billie. Forgiveness saturated her eyes. Billie's stomach clenched. It was probably hitting Kate harder because she'd gone against her wishes to stay at the house. But who would have known the Rileys would be with Bates when he rocked up at the farm? Last time they'd seen him, he'd had his own men.

"Huh. That old bastard is a tough cookie," Bates went on, drawing the cop's gaze to him. "He wasn't prepared to give you up so I had to change my tactics." He tilted his head towards Eve with a shallow smile. "It's amazing what a mother will do to protect her husband, and her children."

"Oh no," Kate gasped.

"They're okay, Kate," Eve sobbed. "Everyone's okay."

"Yes, you have your mother to thank for that," Bates said with a smile. "So far, she has held up her part of the deal." His gaze drifted to Janda asleep on the stretcher.

The gesture jolted Billie's concern. Damn it, where did Janda fit in this? Would Bates involve him?

As if hearing her thoughts, Bates mumbled to himself, "Hmm. If we were going back via Smith's village, I'd probably do him a favour and give him back his kid. It's a pity we're in such a rush."

Billie inwardly sighed. Hopefully, that meant Janda was safe. Bates turned to the detective.

"Right. You four are officially under arrest and will be coming with me. I do have a schedule to stick to." He smiled at the detective. "The sheik is pressed for time."

Billie easily recognised the subtle message; the sheik who had bought her was eager to take possession. She tried not to dwell on the horrible thought. "Give it up, Bates. The Cauldrons know the whole story about what you're involved in."

His smile widened. "Oh, and what story's that?" The innocent question was laced with cynicism. "It's your word against mine."

"There are five of us," she reminded him.

"Ha! What, three criminals and a black kid? That is weak grounds to support you," he mocked, "particularly around these parts."

"And that's a typical answer I'd expect from you, but it doesn't change the truth," she spat with distaste.

"I'm afraid the truth is on my side so I suggest you keep your mouth shut."

He shoved Eve forward. She stumbled and almost fell. Kate caught her and hugged her tight. Bates smiled.

"Isn't that sweet." He looked at Billie. "Be aware I may walk away from here without leaving any witnesses should you decide to do anything rash."

His cold stare held a challenge. Though he'd delivered the threat calmly, it held a dangerous overtone. Billie didn't push it. She couldn't afford to risk her friends' lives. Bates nodded.

"Now, I want you and Reynolds to move your arses over here," he said, firing a scornful glare.

"Please, don't do this," Eve pleaded. Billie looked at her, watching her take a step away from Kate towards Bates with outstretched hands. "Please, this isn't fair."

Billie empathised with her. Hell, what a mess it was. Guilt slammed her in the chest. Because of her decision to come here and not move on, the Cauldrons were in grave danger. But what if they had taken off? Would Bates have believed John even with Kate at home? He could still have terrorised them to get the answers he wanted. Torn, whichever way she looked at it, whether they'd stayed or left, Billie was convinced Bates would've caught up with them tonight. Hopefully, she could prevent him from hurting anyone else. Cooperation was possibly their only saviour, just as Eve had used at the farmhouse to save her family.

"I'm waiting, McCoy," the fat man cooed, cutting into her thoughts.

Her attention snapped to him. She met his calculating stare. He'd brushed Eve's pleas aside without any show of emotion. That alone stated how serious he was. Billie glanced at Reynolds. The apprehension was back in her eyes. Her solemn, depressed look was mixed with fear, the fear of going with these people and knowing what awaited them. Billie inwardly cringed. She hated the thought of involving her, or anyone, yet she couldn't stop it. She took a reluctant step towards Bates.

Bates' gun followed the detective. Reynolds hesitantly followed alongside her.

A truck engine grew louder from beyond the doors, beyond the darkness. Within seconds, it appeared out of the shadows, charging into the soft illumination projected between the two large doors. Turning sharply away from the shed, it straightened and stopped, almost disappearing back into the darkness it had come from.

Billie stopped, recognising it. It was the same truck they'd been transported in before. On a clunk of gears, it reversed to the opened doors of the shed. Its bulk almost blocked the whole exit. For a few lingering moments, the shed echoed with its rattling idle. The driver killed the diesel motor.

"You won't get away with this." Eve's faltering voice was mixed with fear and loathing.

Bates chuckled. "I already have, thanks to you."

The distressed Eve glanced at Billie. Accountability shone in her eyes. Billie flashed a smile, hoping to ease it.

"Aw shit," Reynolds mumbled in a scared and unbelieving breath from beside her, yet intense enough to alert the detective. Breaking her stare from Eve, she turned to her. A look of horror froze Reynolds' features. Billie followed her gaze towards the truck. Her stomach instantly tightened.

Bland limped towards them in an awkward gait. How could this be? She looked like death warmed up. Her badly bruised face was pushed out of proportion due to the swelling. Cuts on her lip and cheeks marred her already ugly, butch looks. One eye only half opened, leaving a thin slit for her to see through, if she had any vision at all. Although she tried to hide it, she looked in pain, wincing with every step. Her piercing glare locked on Billie. She strode to her tight-lipped, stopping two paces in front. The two stared at each other without a word, their dislike evident.

With Bland came one of the brothers, falling casually in behind her on the way past. He stopped beside her in a protective guard, watching the prisoner with a wary eye. Billie glanced at him. The only significant difference between him and his brothers was his short-cropped beard.

"I'm not sure if you've met this brother," Bates said. "Paul Riley, meet McCoy."

Paul Riley flashed her a fake smile and then stepped around behind her. The rifle barrel rested against the back of her neck. Obviously, he'd been warned about her, no doubt by his brothers as well as his new employers.

Billie ignored him. She stared into Bland's eyes. Hate rose in her at the sight of the woman, and, from the look in Bland's cold, dark glare, the feeling was mutual.

"Give me one reason, just one tiny, little ounce of a reason, and you're history," Bland growled in a low, vicious tone.

"I should have killed you," Billie said quietly.

The big woman stepped a pace closer with a sneer twisting her features. "Yes, you should have." She struck out, fast and hard, driving an uppercut into Billie's face. Having only a fraction of a second to see it coming, the cop rode it as best she could. Her head rocked to the side. Before she could control her spinning mind or gather her wits, Bland rammed her other fist hard into the wound on her ribs.

"Aggh!" The cop folded forward and dropped to her knees, her hands clasping her tortured ribs. Short, raspy breaths ripped from her throat. The pain doubled her over further. She dropped onto an elbow, the other hand wrapped around her stomach. Her head sank low while she battled to deal with the torture. Winded and gasping, every intake came with a groan. Although her wound had healed considerably, it wasn't up to this. Desperately, she fought to ride out the severe agony racing through her body.

"Leave her alone," Eve demanded through clenched teeth.

"Stay where you are, Mrs Cauldron," Bates barked.

Billie glanced up through her agony. Blood ran from her nose. Eve stood closer to her. Bates had obviously stopped her with the threat of the rifle.

Eve glared at him for only a second before turning her wrath on Bland. "Don't you dare lay another finger on her, you hear me?" The big woman simply sneered at her. Eve turned to Bates. "Tell her to back off."

"You are in no position to give orders." The calm threat held an evil intention. Frantic, Eve looked at Billie. Too winded, the cop couldn't offer her any words to ease her stress.

"She needs help. Let me go to her, please," Eve begged Bates.

"She is out of bounds to you and anyone else here, understand? Now stand back."

"No, I won't stand back." Ignoring his warning, Eve stepped forward.

"You take one more step, Mrs Cauldron, and I'll make you regret it."

The rifle swung towards Kate. The girl gasped in fright.

Billie attempted to get up, worried Eve would do something stupid. She groaned and fell onto her side. She didn't have the strength. She curled up, hoping to ease the biting pain crippling her.

"You are spineless, just like Billie said," Eve spat fiercely.

"Ha, you'll need more than words to upset me, I'm afraid." Bates chuckled. "Now I suggest you keep your mouth shut or it could turn bad for your daughter."

No argument came.

"Okay, Mrs Bland."

The simple statement hung ominously in the air. Billie looked up, her apprehension strong. She glanced at the Riley brothers standing with Bates. The three held their rifles aimed at a chosen victim, ready to fire if the need arose. Kate watched on with terrified eyes, too afraid to move. Billie's stomach churned. These innocent women weren't used to violence, particularly anything this evil and frightening. Damn Bates. She caught the slave trader's eye when he looked at her. Panting hard and feeding off the concern for the others, she rolled onto her knees. The effort instantly drained her energy. She could go no further.

Bates' gaze lifted to Reynolds standing beside the detective. Billie's heart went out to her. She was left to face Bates on her own. And with Bland standing so close and Paul Riley beside her armed with a rifle, Reynolds was helpless to do anything other than watch.

"Can't you just leave us alone?" Eve appealed, her voice breaking under the strain.

"We'll be out of your hair in no time, Mrs Cauldron," Bates assured her in a calming tone, "providing you give us your full cooperation, of course." A quick smile flashed across his face. "And to assure me that you will be on your best behaviour, we have something to show you, something we don't want you to forget in a long while, something to guarantee the cooperation I expect from each of you. In other words, this is a lesson for everyone, not just McCoy. Go ahead, Mrs Bland."

"Pick her up, boys," Bland ordered.

Billie knew she was in trouble. Bland wanted her blood and now was in a position to take it. Acting on the loathing rushing through her veins, the cop pushed up off her knees – only to stop when the sharp burning across her ribs cruelly gripped her. She groaned and sank down.

Jack and Paul Riley dragged Billie to her feet, supporting her by the arms between them. She sagged in their hands, leaning forward in an effort to ease the hurting. Her ribs were on fire.

"Please don't hurt her anymore," Eve cried in a desperate plea. "She's had enough. Can't you see that?"

"When I think she's had enough, I will leave her be. Now you keep your mouth shut, or I'll give her twice as much, do you hear me?" The words scraped through the air, leaving a cold silence in their wake.

Billie made the effort to look up. Across from her, Eve glared defiantly at Bates.

"No, it's not fair. She doesn't deserve this. Please let her be."

"Weren't you told to shut your mouth?" Bland answered for him. "Maybe I'll come and do it for you."

"I'd take heed of the warning if I were you," Bates said. "Especially with the mood she's in." He smiled. "Like I said, this is a warning to everyone. That includes your daughter. Be quiet or Mrs Bland may not stop. Do you understand what I'm saying?"

Eve stared in silence.

When no comment came, Bland turned to the cop. "Now, where were we?" she said, directing a disdainful look at the detective. "Shit, McCoy, you don't look too good. Silly me, I should have remembered about your cut ribs," the big woman purred. "I'll be more careful next time."

Bland's belittling tone was enough for Billie to drag up some inner strength. Eve's extended intervention had given her a brief chance to renew her reserves, and the sight of the derisive expression across the bitch's face fuelled her. She might not be in a position to do much, but she hated seeing Bland have it all her way. Gritting her teeth and mastering the pain, she let the men take her full weight. Both feet smashed into Bland's already bruised ribs. Taken by surprise, the woman doubled over with a gurgling cry, momentarily winded. Bland couldn't stop the next kick smashing into her face. With a groan, she crashed over backwards to the ground, gasping hard with blood pouring from her nose.

Billie stood back on her feet, struggling to break the brothers' tight grip. Reynolds suddenly jumped forward towards Bland, intending to take advantage while she was immobilised.

"Get back," Paul Riley snapped at her. Without loosening his grip on the detective, he thrust his rifle against Reynolds' ribs. She jerked to a halt, eyeing him with a cautious look.

The detective caught her gaze and gave a slight shake of her head. Now that the men had overcome their surprise, it was too risky for her to get involved. Reynolds stepped back from Riley, taking the cop's advice. On a nod from Bates, Tony stepped in behind her. He grabbed her by the arm and jabbed his rifle in her side to keep her from making any other moves.

Giving up her struggle against the brothers, Billie sank in their hands, concentrating on rebuilding her strength, appreciating she'd tightened the noose hanging over her. Bland always stirred her deepest aversions, propelling her into uncontrollable acts, but any punishment she could afflict on the woman was worth the price.

The two Rileys tightened their grip on her. Without dropping their rifles, awkwardly they supported her weight one-handed.

Billie looked at Bland. The big woman rolled onto her knees rubbing her ribs and fighting to catch a breath. She glanced up, catching the cop's gaze. Giving a grunt, she staggered to her feet, groaning with the effort. She stumbled forward, straight at her foe. Face hard-set, she ripped the baton from her waistband.

Billie stood up off the brothers. Her focus didn't falter from the advancing woman. "Come on, Bland – just you and me," she gasped, grappling against the Rileys to free herself. Paul shoved the barrel of his rifle into her side but it did little to deter her. Her loathing was too strong.

Bland's cold stare hardened. "Oh, don't worry. It already is just you and me."

Jack suddenly lifted his rifle and drove it down hard, smashing the butt into the side of Billie's knee.

"Agh!" She dropped in their hands, fighting against the new pain. Desperately, she tried to regain her feet but her leg wouldn't support her, not yet. She sank down. The brothers were forced to take her weight. Denied strength, time was now against her. Bland swung the baton. It caught the trapped girl across the mouth. Billie groaned and slumped in the men's grip. She hung helplessly in their arms with her head on her chest, striving to control the spinning in her pounding head.

"You, bitch. Why can't you fight her fairly, you yellow pile of shit," Reynolds spat.

"Keep your mouth shut, or you'll be next," Bland bellowed, her exasperation obvious. She paused for a moment. "Now, there's a thought. Maybe I should do it anyway, just to get at McCoy. I'm sure she'd like to see you all black and blue."

Reynolds sucked in a fearful gasp as Bland took a step towards her.

Billie lifted her head at the words. They drifted in from a long way off, but she heard them loud and clear. Her concerns shot to Reynolds. Now, she was under fire. Not for a moment did she have any doubt Bland would follow through with her threat. Without a second thought, she lunged forward in an effort to stop her. It was so unexpected she almost broke free from the Rileys' grip. The cop thrust out her left leg in a high kick at Bland. Unfortunately, the two brothers recovered from their surprise in time to pull her back, robbing her of the millimetres she needed to make full contact with Bland. Her foot grazed her jaw rather than burying into her face.

Bland's head rocked to the side, and although the blow failed to knock her down, it staggered her back a couple of steps with a gasp. Catching her balance, she turned and glared at the cop. Raising her hand slowly, she touched a finger to her bleeding lip. Her piercing gaze overflowed with annoyance and agitation, boring into her enemy.

Billie struggled against her captors. So badly did she want to get at Bland to finish this, but as hard as she tried, she was robbed of the opportunity. The brothers kept her restrained and away from the big woman.

Bates and the fourth Riley brother raised their guns to reinforce their command when Eve took a step forward to help the detective. She stopped, glaring at him. Reynolds struggled with Tony to break free. All she achieved was having the rifle barrel shoved in her neck. With a gasp, she was forced to stand still.

"Damn you, Bland. Why won't you fight me?" Billie spat. "Are you scared I'll whip your arse again?"

The big woman looked at the blood running from Billie's busted lip and nose. It made her smile. "You whip my arse? No, you've got it wrong, McCoy. It's me who'll do all the whipping." She moved in.

"No. Leave her alone," Reynolds demanded, wriggling to break free.

Billie fought against her captives, regardless of the guns pressing into her side. Her efforts did little to help. Bland struck out with the baton, whacking the detective above the eye. Billie groaned and collapsed in the Rileys' arms. Her head fell forward, sinking low on her chest.

Silence filled the room.

Bland gripped Billie by the hair and pulled her head up. Barely conscious, blood ran from a cut over her eye.

"That's only a taste of what you're going to get, cop," Bland said through clenched teeth. In her unsettled rage, she lashed out again. As her large fist made contact with the cop's cheek, she let go of her hair with the other. The blow knocked Billie almost senseless. Her limp body crumbled. Her head dropped onto her chest. The two brothers released her. She fell onto her side, struggling to stop herself sinking into oblivion.

A foot kicked her hard in the ribs. Billie groaned and curled up in pain. Robbed of what strength she'd had, she drifted over the brink of consciousness.

Chapter Nineteen

"You, bastard," Reynolds snarled, writhing to break free from Tony in a frantic struggle. She glared at Jack Riley standing beside the cop. She couldn't believe he'd kicked her so cruelly. "Leave her alone." Her gaze dropped to Billie's still form lying beaten on the floor. Her raspy breaths had fallen silent. She'd passed out.

"Don't tell me what to do, you cheap piece of crap," Jack snarled, stepping over Billie towards her.

Reynolds' head shot up. "You spineless bastard. What, are you too afraid to take her on alone? You need to kick her when she's down and can't fight back, you creep."

Bland scowled and lunged forward, intercepting Jack. With one hand, she shoved him aside; with the other, she turned and backhanded Reynolds with a force that knocked the startled girl into Tony.

"Stop it. Please don't hurt them anymore," Eve begged in a choked voice.

"Very well, Mrs Cauldron. For now, you can have your wish," Bates said.

At his words, Bland stepped back from Reynolds and cast a casual look over at the Cauldrons.

"You call yourself a policeman? It's you who should be locked away," Eve said with disgust.

Bates expressed shock. "I'm simply doing my job. They are wanted criminals. All I'm doing is upholding the law."

"You lying scum," Reynolds spat.

"Shut up, Reynolds," Bland warned, raising the baton. Reynolds cringed, bracing herself for the attack. It didn't eventuate.

"Not now, Mrs Bland, not now," Bates calmly said, his gaze resting on Reynolds. Bland's hand stopped in mid-air. She stared hard at the girl. Reynolds looked from her to Bates, the anxiety so intense it hurt.

Bland barked a short laugh. Slowly, she lowered her hand. "Certainly, Mr Bates. Not now," she said with a sinister smile. The words gave the clear impression the matter would definitely be taken up later. Bland's gaze drifted past Bates to Kate standing behind. On edge, the farm girl's nervous stare darted from Bland to Bates. The big woman hobbled towards her. Kate bravely faced up to her as she drew nearer.

Stopping two feet in front of her, Bland stared with a pensive attentiveness. Her gaze dropped, running down over the girl's slim figure in a careful investigative manner.

"Hmm, maybe we should take you with us as well for harbouring and abetting wanted criminals."

Bates strolled across to Bland. His calculating stare rested on Kate. She watched him nervously.

"You know, that's not such a bad idea, Mrs Bland." He studied Kate's looks and build. "I'm sure she'd love to come with us." He finished his examination and looked her in the eye. He smiled.

Kate's solemn features didn't alter. She held his gaze with apprehension and dread.

"No. Not Kate. You are *not* taking Kate, you hear me," Eve said through clenched teeth, striding forward with tightened fists.

Bland placed a hand on her chest and shoved her back. "Stay put."

Promptly regaining her balance, Eve stepped forward again. Bland blocked her, squaring her shoulders and glaring in a warning not to push her.

Eve looked at Bates. "Please, don't do this. She hasn't done anything wrong. She is not a criminal. You can't just take her away for no reason. That's against the law. You of all people must realise that."

Bates turned his back on her, ignoring her pleas. His gaze ran over Kate.

Reynolds watched. The anguish in Eve's voice tore her apart, not to mention the fate hanging over Kate's head. "You bastard, Bates, you don't need her."

Both Bates and Bland slowly turned to her. Annoyed looks furrowed their heartless faces.

"Careful, Reynolds, insubordination is not a strong point in my books. May I remind you, you have no say in the matter so keep your nose out of it."

Reynolds stood defiant. "McCoy has been in touch with Edwards. She told him all about you. Your game's blown. It's all over so why don't you run while you can. Edwards is already on his way here so you aren't going to get far anyway."

He stared intently, thinking over her warning. He cast a complacent look at Bland, meeting her curious gaze. Turning, Bates walked to Reynolds, showing no concern at her words.

Reynolds cringed back. Trapped in Tony's grasp, the man gave her a sharp shake as a reminder to keep still. Bates' piercing stare bore into her.

"Too bad he's going to be too late, isn't it," he said in a cold voice, throwing the warning back in her face.

"He'll follow you. He won't give McCoy up."

"And neither will I so don't worry your little head about it, okay? Any more smart comments out of you, and I'll let Mrs Bland give you a taste of what she gave the cop. Understand? Obviously the little lesson didn't sink in deep enough."

Despite his misinterpretation and validity of the 'little lesson', his words did have some effect, enough to make her hesitate. Lost for words, Reynolds stared at him.

Bates nodded. He turned to his new recruits. "Get them in the truck and let's get out of here. Geoff, open up the back."

The Rileys jumped to his command. Geoff, the last brother, unlocked the large rear doors. He swung them open and climbed up inside. Jack and Paul carried Jane and Jones to the truck, roughly tossing them in. Geoff dragged them to the front out of the way.

Bates looked around at Kate. "Come on, Cauldron, don't be shy. That includes you," he said with a cold smile. "Seems I've got nothing to lose now so I might as well get what I can. You will bring in a good price."

"What? No! You can't," Eve sobbed.

Kate stood rigid. She glanced at her mother with a confused look twisting her frightened features. Tears flooded Eve's eyes.

Bates cocked his gun and aimed it at Eve while addressing Kate. "If you want me to shoot your mother, you're on the right track."

Kate's attention snapped to him.

"Move, girl," Bland growled from beside her. "We haven't got all night."

Kate glanced at the big woman. Hesitantly, she stepped towards the truck.

"No." Darting forward around Bland, Eve intercepted her daughter and grabbed her in a hug. Kate fell into her arms, unable to control her sobs. "No. Not you, Kate," Eve cried. "Not you."

Stepping forward, Bland yanked them apart. Maintaining a strong hold on Kate, she shoved Eve back with such force it dumped her on the ground.

"Move it," she said to Kate, giving her a hardy shove towards the truck, "or I swear I'll start on the kid on the bed."

Kate stumbled a few steps before catching her balance. She spun and faced Bland with a watery stare.

Reynolds looked over at Janda. Shit, she'd forgotten about him. He hadn't stirred. He slept on regardless, unaware of the dangers lurking so close. That was probably a good thing. She prayed Bland would leave him be. She glanced at Kate. The farm girl returned her look with a fearful gaze.

Eve sat up, her features laden with sadness.

Bland stepped forward and gave the farm girl another shove. Kate staggered backwards, falling into the back of the truck. "Get in there now."

Tears streamed down Eve's cheeks as her daughter climbed into the crate. Kate shot her a final depressed look and then Geoff shoved her towards the front. She disappeared into the shadowy depth of the cabin.

Bates turned to Tony holding Reynolds and gave a nod. Tony forced his prisoner forward. Reynolds, suddenly gripped by fear and panic, was impelled into a frantic attack. She struggled against him, fighting every inch of the way.

"Maybe Jack could take up where he left off with McCoy," Bates said.

Reynolds stopped and glared at him. Tony, acting on her sudden compliance, shoved her to the truck without further resistance. Geoff grabbed her and hauled her up out of his hands. As soon as Reynolds stepped onto the floor of the cabin, she was catapulted forward to join the others deeper inside. Kate reached out and grabbed her, pulling her up before she crashed into the wall. Regaining her balance, Reynolds glanced at her. Wet-eyed and looking scared, the farm girl met her eye bravely. Reynolds managed a faint smile in appreciation before looking at Geoff. He jumped down out of the truck. Her attention dropped to Jane and Sarah at her feet. They hadn't woken. She knelt down and looked them over, searching for any new wounds. Under the reflected light sifting in through the opened doors, all she could find was a new bruise on each girl's jaw.

Paul and Jack lifted Billie. Blood covered the front of her shirt and the side of her face. Her lip and nose were bleeding. The two brothers showed no consideration for her condition. They dragged her between them to the truck and dumped her in.

Reynolds stood up, glaring at the brothers. "Damn it, go easy on her."

"Why, what are you going to do, sweetheart, call the cops?" Jack jeered.

Reynolds' fists clenched in anger. With every bit of willpower, she fought to ignore the remark. Kate grabbed her arm. The touch startled her, *and* rekindled her common sense. She couldn't win this. Somehow, she stayed where she was.

The two brothers laughed, mocking her, Kate's firm hold acted as a reminder it wasn't worth the problems, or the pain.

The Rileys stood back from the tailgate. Each took hold of a large door and swung them inwards. They slammed closed with a loud metallic clang. The familiar sound of the locks slid into place. Reynolds stared at the doors, struggling to come to terms with being trapped in the confines of this horrible box. Enough light filtered in through the mesh windows along the top of the walls to give her visibility. Kate released her hold on her and fell against the wall. Reynolds glanced at her. The farm girl's distressed look revealed how hard it was hitting her. She rested a comforting hand on her shoulder.

"Are you okay?"

Kate nodded. It carried little conviction. Reynolds squeezed her shoulder. The fact Kate couldn't answer warned her she was in shock.

"Come on, it's okay, we're going to get through this."

Another nod.

Reynolds returned it, convincing herself as well as Kate. She couldn't think of anything else to say to help ease the girl's worry. They were in a bad situation, a very bad one, and she had strong doubts they would be lucky enough to get out of it this time. One good thing washed across her dismal thoughts: if they'd closed the doors, they weren't bringing Janda. He really was no use to them, so it made sense. But what was his fate?

She could hear Bates talking to Eve. Though it was a little muffled, it was clear enough to understand.

"We'll be off now, Mrs Cauldron. Tell me, do you know how to change a tyre?"

"A tyre? Yes. Why?" she asked in between her sobs.

"Because you will need to change one on the van out there before you can use it to get you home. Sorry, but I don't want you getting back too quickly, if you know what I mean. I must say, you have done the right thing by cooperating."

"Then you won't hurt my family anymore?"

A silence lingered before Bates continued. "That you will find out when you get there."

"What? No. You said you wouldn't hurt them if I brought you here. Please. Leave them alone."

A pause.

"Let me remind you where you stand, Mrs Cauldron. You have a choice. It's either Kate or your family. Should I let your family be and then find out you are following us, there won't be much of your girl left to bring home."

"No. You can't do this. I did everything you asked. Leave Kate and we won't do anything, I promise."

Bates continued as if she hadn't spoken. "Her life depends entirely on you, but so does your family. Should I hear you've called the cops in on this, or that Edwards is on my tail, you won't *have* a daughter to bring home. It doesn't bother me if I have to make the sacrifice to get my point across. She is simply a bonus after all, one I can live without. Do you understand what I'm saying?"

"Yes." Eve's answer was barely audible.

"Good. Shall we depart, Mrs Bland?"

"Immediately," she responded.

The diesel motor soon fired up. After a couple of revs, the big six wheeler noisily pulled out.

Reynolds and Kate rocked with the motion of the truck as it picked up speed. Reynolds flashed Kate a smile.

"How about you untie the guys. I want to check McCoy."

"Sure."

Reynolds dropped her hand and offered a faint smile. She reached up above them and flicked on the dull light bulb. A soft glow bathed the interior. Sighing, she crossed to Billie.

Chapter Twenty

Billie lay with closed eyes, breathing raspy breaths. The touch of a hand on her arm stirred her awareness.

"Come on, McCoy, take it easy," an anxious Reynolds said. "Damn Bates. Damn him!"

"I-I'll b-be okay," Billie gasped.

"Oh, sure you will."

The detective opened her eyes and made the effort to roll her head and look at her. Reynolds' distressed face said it all – she was scared and had lost all hope. As much as Billie wanted to console her, she didn't have the strength, or the breath. Her gaze drifted to the girl kneeling beside her. Surprise gripped her.

"Kate..." What was she doing here? Shit, Bates just didn't stop. Why did he have to involve her? She could imagine the frantic state it would have left Eve in. She didn't need this.

"I'm okay, Billie. Just worry about yourself." Her shaky tone carried apprehension, and fear. Both girls looked worried. Billie sensed most of it was for her.

"Me? I'm g-good." To prove it, she attempted to sit up. The effort made her wince and her head throb severely. Reynolds pushed her down none too gently. A cry escaped Billie's lips. She closed her eyes against the pain.

"Stay put, damn it, or I'll lay you out myself, I swear. Moving around won't do you any good."

The cop didn't argue. She was too weak and sore.

"Shit, McCoy, Bland didn't want you walking away this time," Reynolds growled.

"She j-just got l-lucky." Her voice was fading.

"Lucky? She has got us exactly where she wants us and don't deny it."

"The h-hell she has," was all she managed to get out. Her head lolled towards the floor, and her body relaxed as she sank into the comforting darkness.

Reynolds stared at the cop. Billie's collapse took her by surprise, and increased her worry. How bad *was* she? Could she have internal injuries from the kick and was worse than she thought? Checking the panic threatening to overcome her, she touched two fingers to the detective's neck. To her relief, her pulse was quite strong. The confirmation helped alleviate her rising negative assumptions; it did little to ease her inner rage.

"Shit." McCoy had left her on her own to cope with everything. With the cop hurt and out of action, she felt pressured into the head position, one she definitely didn't want. It carried too heavy a responsibility.

"What's wrong? Is she okay?" Kate asked in an anxious tone, lifting her gaze off Billie.

Reynolds inwardly cursed, realising what she'd done. Voicing her frustrated comment straight after feeling McCoy's pulse would lead Kate to assume the worst. The girl was scared – for McCoy, for her, for all of them. She had no idea the amount of trouble they were in so hadn't yet tasted the rage, the burning fury born only from fear and anxiety. That would come in time, along with the hate. How Reynolds wished she could protect her from all this. She cast her no more than a glance before looking at the detective. She still wasn't ready to face her – or was she? Something unexpectedly snapped inside, igniting a renewed strength. Who was she kidding? She *did* have a responsibility now. She couldn't expect Kate to look after everything on her own. Innocent and naïve to such violent circumstances, it would affect her hard. Yes, if anything, she had to be strong for her. Settling her emotions as best she could, Reynolds nodded, softening her voice.

"Yes, she's fine. She's passed out, that's all."

Kate stared at her for a long moment absorbing the words. Nodding, she dropped her gaze to Billie. "It just hurts to see her like this. I can't get that scene of Bland beating her out of my head. The woman scares me so much."

"You're not alone there. She's a cruel, callous bitch riding on way too much authority."

"And a coward. Billie showed only class and style with the fight in the street against the Rileys. Bland used a spineless, dirty attack on her, knowing she couldn't lose. Billie didn't stand a chance, and yet she still fought back knowing she was going down."

"Yeah, she has a bad habit of doing that. She did hurt Bland though, *and* saved me from a severe beating."

"I hope I never have to watch anything like it again."

"Me too."

Sighing, Kate looked over Billie's bleeding face. "Maybe it's for the better she's out to it. She was in some pain."

"Yeah."

"She will be all right, won't she?"

Reynolds sucked in a breath and forced herself to look up. Meeting her eye, she was unable to say anything. But Kate's expression begged for the truth. Reynolds felt trapped. She couldn't lie to her, no matter how bad the facts were. Kate had a right to know, now that she'd been dragged into it.

"She's worth too much to them to let die," she murmured, gazing down at Billie's still form. "Bates sold her to a sheik before we escaped. He obviously wants her back. Despite that, I think she's in for a pretty rough time. Bland's carrying a heavy grudge."

Kate sat horrified, staring at Reynolds with wide eyes. She gave a weak nod. "Yeah, I noticed." She looked at Billie with a sober and strained expression. "This is so . . . unbelievable, and terrifying."

"Yeah." Reynolds offered a weak smile but had no more to say. She'd said enough. The two girls sat in silence, adjusting to their predicament in the comfort of their own minds.

Jones moaned. In a slow roll, she fell onto her back. Her eyes flickered open. Reynolds' worried face sharpened into focus, staring down at her.

"What happened?" Jones asked, her voice weak.

"Judging by the bruise on your jaw, I'd say you were slugged pretty hard," Reynolds said.

"Slugged? Yeah... someone stepped in front of us... but it was dark. I don't remember what happened," she stammered, trying to piece it together.

"Let me help you. Bates found us is what happened, and now we're going back to his slave camp," Reynolds explained in a blunt tone.

Jones froze, staring in horror. "Bates? Yes, we were walking back and were attacked," she said as if in a trance. She rubbed her bruised jaw.

"Are you okay?" Reynolds asked.

"Yeah, I think so."

Reynolds took hold of her arm and helped her sit up. Jones winced. She fingered her tender jaw. Her eyes widened in surprise when her gaze settled on the farm girl.

"Shit, not you too, Kate. Why did they bring you? You had nothing to do with this."

"He said it was for helping you guys out." Fear tainted her voice.

"The bastard. Who the hell does he think he is?"

Jane groaned beside them. Her head rolled to the side as she sluggishly came around. The girls moved in closer, placing themselves around her.

"Take it easy," Reynolds said after her eyes opened.

Jane glanced from her to Jones and Kate.

"How are you doing?" Reynolds asked.

Jane's attention shot to her. She nodded. "Okay, I think." She gasped and lifted a hand to her jaw the moment she spoke. "Hell, did someone hit..." She stopped, thinking.

Reynolds helped her sit up and calmly filled her in. Jane's face paled. Slowly, she shook her head.

"Oh no," she breathed. "I don't think I can do this again." She lowered her head. Reynolds slipped an arm around her.

Jones could understand her distress. She'd already been down this road. The despair was a killer, and to add to their misery, Bates wouldn't be giving them any slack – not after losing them twice already. They were history, lost forever.

Jane suddenly looked up, anxious. "Where's Billie? Why isn't she with us?"

"She is," Reynolds quietly stated.

Jane stared at her for a moment and then looked around. Jones followed her gaze. Her stomach knotted at the sight of the cop lying motionless beside the rear doors. So distracted by the shock of their capture, she'd momentarily forgotten about McCoy.

"What's wrong with her?" Jane gasped.

Reynolds didn't answer. She didn't have to answer. She glanced at Jones. The expression on her strained face said it all. Jane pushed past and crawled to the detective. Jones tore her gaze from Reynolds and followed. The girls knelt around the cop. Gently, Jane rolled the unconscious girl onto her back, examining her condition more carefully.

Jones studied her in awe. "Shit. Who did this to her?"

Reynolds looked at her, and then Jane, her expression apprehensive. When she finally spoke, her voice was quiet and strained. "Bland's with them."

"What?" Jane said in barely a whisper.

Jones stared in disbelief. How could Bland be here after the beating McCoy gave her? She'd left her half dead – three quarters dead. "But–McCoy smashed her into the floor," she stammered, struggling to comprehend how Bland could have recovered from such a brutal beating so fast.

Reynolds nodded. "Yeah, so you said. Don't worry, she's definitely still suffering from it but believe me, McCoy didn't do a good enough job on her, and now the bitch is mad, mad as hell. She went straight at her and laid into her. I've never seen her so worked up. What made it worse, the cop gave some back, particularly when Bland started for me. Hell, it just made the bitch retaliate more."

Jane and Jones sat stunned, unable to comment as the words sank in.

"I thought she was going to kill her," Kate whispered, gazing at the detective.

"Had it not been for the 'sold tag' hanging over her head, Bland probably would have," Reynolds said.

"But how did they know we were there?" Jane asked, confused. "How did they find us? I mean, how did they find the shed? It was so well hidden."

"I'm so sorry but Mum brought them," Kate said, her tone laden with guilt. "They forced her to by threatening Pa and my brother and sisters. They shot Pa in the shoulder and were going to start on the kids." Her eyes watered. She shook her head. "She didn't have an option."

Jane held her gaze and nodded. She gently squeezed her shoulder in a comforting gesture. "She did the right thing."

Kate nodded. She looked at Jones who flashed a faint smile and then Reynolds.

"You're right," Reynolds said. "Eve didn't have an option."

"No." There was little strength in Kate's answer.

Jane sighed and leant over to examine Billie's forehead. An egg-shaped bruise had raised the cut. "She could have a concussion with this."

"She was talking to us before she passed out. I'm more worried about her wound," Reynolds said with little expression. "That Jack bastard kicked her pretty hard after Bland knocked her down. She could have bruised or even cracked ribs as well."

Jane's gaze drifted to Billie's bloodied shirt. "He kicked her on her wound? Is that why it's bleeding?" she asked, glancing up at her friend. Reynolds shrugged a tired shrug.

"Maybe. Bland also punched her hard on it. It could've been either of them – or both. Hell, you guys got out of it lightly not having to watch what went on in the shed."

"I'll say," Kate said. "It was so horrible."

"Yeah, I can imagine," Jane breathed.

Jones sat frozen, hardly listening to the conversation. She stared, absorbed, her mind racing. "Did you say Jack? As in Jack Riley?" she asked in a quiet yet perturbed voice.

Reynolds looked at her, surprised. She nodded. "Him and three of his brothers are with Bates."

Jones sat back. She looked at Reynolds and Jane's puzzled expressions with a hardening gaze. An angry breath hissed through her lips. "Damn it. I knew this would happen. I just *knew* it. Didn't I tell you this could happen?"

"What are you talking about?" Jane probed.

"When McCoy took on those brothers in the street today, it was a dead giveaway."

Kate looked up sharply from Billie, staring hard. "No, please. You know she only did that to help me," she defended her. "Please don't blame her."

"Kate's right," Jane said. "Bates would've found us anyway. He must've been closer on our tail than we assumed. Who's to say he didn't pay off the phone operator to keep him informed? Or what about the contract out on us? Anyone could have dobbed us in. It could have been any number of reasons. We don't know for sure it was because of the fight."

"It wasn't—" Reynolds started, only to be ignored.

Jones glared at Jane. "Well, of course, you'd say that, but it still leads back to someone seeing her, and the only time it could've been was when she went into town and got into that fight in the street. Why else are the bloody Rileys here, huh? To get even, that's why."

"Guys—" Reynolds cut in. Still no one listened.

"You can't blame McCoy. Not this time," Jane argued.

"Hey. You're forgetting one small point," Jones snarled. "We were out of here tomorrow, remember? A few more hours and we would've been gone, departed, on our way home to Sydney and out of this godforsaken, desolate piece of earth."

"Okay cool it, come on," Reynolds said over the top of them.

"It's the truth, isn't it?" Jones threw at her.

"Not entirely. Bates told us the Rileys didn't recognise McCoy in the street today. They had no idea it was her."

Jones and Jane stared at her, taken aback. Jones shook off her surprise. She wasn't convinced.

"Oh really, then how else could they have found us?"

Reynolds hesitated. She glanced at Kate. The girl tightened her lips.

"It was my fault," she muttered.

"No, Kate, it wasn't," Reynolds said firmly. "It was not your fault, you hear me? Blame it on bad luck, nothing more."

Jones looked from one to the other. "What are you talking about?"

Kate shrugged. "Bates worked it out I was with you guys after he barged in on my family. He'd believed Pa when he told them you'd left, but then the Rileys thought it was strange I wasn't there. After a few questions between them, they put two and two together. That's how they knew you guys were still in the area because they knew I wouldn't have gone far from home."

"Oh, Kate, I'm so sorry," Jane said. "But Reynolds is right. You can't carry the blame for this. It was purely bad luck that the brothers happened to be with Bates."

"Exactly," Reynolds said. "Without the Rileys, Bates wouldn't have been any the wiser." She looked away, thinking. "None of us saw that coming. Shit, why are they even with him anyway? He had his own men."

Jones blew out a frustrated breath. "It still leads back to McCoy being involved with them in the street, doesn't it. Why else did they lead Bates to the Cauldron's house, huh? How did they know we'd be there? I'll tell you why, because someone must have seen her leave with Kate after the fight, who no doubt passed it onto the Rileys. They would have still been pissed at her, which is why they're helping Bates."

"How can you even think like that? It's crazy," Jane growled.

"Is it? Then why else did they arrive at Kate's house."

"Maybe they linked her to us when we first helped her on the side of the road. It wouldn't take Bates much to put two and two together after talking to the Rileys, would it."

Before Jones could answer, Billie moaned and rolled her head. All eyes dropped to her, the quarrel, for the moment, suspended. Jones glanced at Jane with an irritated scowl. Jane returned it with a cold stare. Jones met Reynolds' eye but was too uptight to justify her actions. She looked away.

"Take it easy."

Jane's soothing voice lured Billie's eyes open. She looked up at her worried face. It was a relief to see she was all right. She glanced at the others. Jones was with them as well. They all looked miserable, no doubt struggling to come to terms with this. She went to lift her head and winced. Resting it back, she closed her eyes. The sudden pounding sent her head into turmoil.

"Come on, relax," Jane insisted.

"You s-should speak for y-yourself." The answer was weak.

"How do you feel?"

A faint smile flashed across Billie's sore lips. She looked up into the dark brown eyes. "Terrific."

Jane failed to share in her fabricated enthusiasm and sat tight-lipped.

"How the hell are we going to get out of this? Damn it." Jones jumped to her feet and started pacing. Suddenly, she turned and kicked the side of the truck with a growl.

"There must be a way. We just haven't thought of it yet," Reynolds said, watching her.

Jones spun and faced her. "Oh, really? Like what? Wait, I know." She lifted a hand with her palm facing the girls. "We can shoot them with our fingers. That'll fix 'em."

The girls watched on in bewilderment, surprised by her uncalled-for behaviour.

Billie lay quietly. Her vigour stirred after listening to Jones' gloomy ranting. Her pessimism fed the detective's stamina, rebuilding her drive, motivating her. She needed to throw the effects of the beating off fast, before the girls lost all hope. They needed reassurance. They needed to hear encouraging optimism to help them see a clearer picture and develop positive energy for another escape. She wasn't kidding herself, though. It wasn't going to be easy, but she couldn't give up, not yet. First, she needed to regain her strength. Then she could show them some sanguinity, even if it was to prove Jones wrong, if *only* to prove Jones wrong.

"Sarah, calm down. This is getting us nowhere," Reynolds said.

Jones' stare burned into hers. "This time Bates has us exactly where he wants us. *You* know that and *I* know that so he's not about to give us the slightest chance to make an escape."

Jane shook her head. "We still can't give in to them. We should work on a plan, something at least."

"Stop dreaming," Jones snapped. She took up her pacing across the front end of the crate.

With more control over her hurts, Billie rolled onto an elbow. Her head throbbed, and her ribs ached, but some of her strength had returned, and now she had good reason to get on her feet as fast as possible. The girls were rapidly sinking into a state of depression. They couldn't afford to lose that spark of hope.

"McCoy, what the hell are you doing?" Jane said the instant she moved.

"I thought that was obvious," Billie gasped. She looked up at her. "You know, I'd really appreciate a hand."

Jane sat frozen, staring under a deep frown. "What's the point? You've just taken a beating. What can you do, huh?"

In the brief silence that followed, Kate leant forward and took Billie by the arm, offering her assistance.

"Damn it," Jane growled, casting the farm girl an irritated look. Kate glanced at her but didn't stop. Giving in with a frustrated sigh, Jane grabbed Billie's other arm and together, they sat her up.

Billie gasped. Even with the girls' help, moving proved painful. Everything started spinning, threatening to topple her over. Lowering her head, she closed her eyes to deal with it.

"You are not up to this," Jane said, maintaining her hold.

"Just g-give me a minute."

"We'll lean her against the wall, okay?" Jane said to Kate, her voice still harsh.

Without answering, Kate helped Jane drag Billie across the metre of floor space to the wall and lean her against it. The detective winced and rested her head back with eyes closed tight, sucking in short, shallow breaths, gritting her teeth against the sudden piercing stab across her ribs. Her hand rested on them to help ease the throbbing.

"Are you happy now?" Jane said none too gently.

"Elated," Billie whispered, refusing to accept her 'I told you so' attitude. She opened her eyes. Ignoring Jane's reprimanding stare, she looked past her to Jones pacing the floor.

Reynolds stood and walked to her. Grabbing her by the arm, she stopped her in mid-stride. "Listen up, okay? Together we can come up with something, like we have every other time."

"Do you think Bates is stupid? After escaping from him twice already, he is *not* going to give us any rein at all." She yanked her arm free.

Reynolds stared at her silently. Jones stepped away.

"Reynolds is right. It'll be the last t-thing they'll expect," Billie stammered.

Jones' glare shot her way. "Don't start, McCoy. I don't want to hear it. You can't tell me you're up to it, not this time."

"Maybe not on my own, but together—"

"Wait a minute, wait a minute." An overwrought Jones strode to Billie. "Have you forgotten they've just worked you over? Hell, I wouldn't be surprised if they don't do it again, purely to stop you from getting any ideas. You're sold, remember? Paid in full. They may not kill you, but they can certainly keep you down."

Billie wasn't deterred by Jones' attitude. "Listen to me. I may be down, but you four are in good shape. Working as a team—"

"Shut it. I don't want to hear it, okay? We're badly outnumbered, especially without you, so face the facts."

"Okay, ease up," Jane said, glaring at Jones. "Jumping down each other's throats won't get us anywhere."

Jones met her eye. "What, you don't like the truth?"

"Billie is making sense. Together we can—"

"Are you so blind? We are beaten so accept it. Bates has us where he wants us, and there is no getting out of it."

A brief silence filled the room. All eyes were on Jones. A curtain of doom draped over them, smothering them.

Reynolds turned to the three girls on the floor. "She's right. We're kidding ourselves. They do outnumber us, big time. We can't take on that many."

Billie gritted her teeth and pushed up the wall with her hand supporting her ribs. Unsteadily, she gained her feet. Surprised by her actions, Jane and Kate stood with her and took hold of her arms to help support her.

Gasping from her efforts, Billie focused hard on Reynolds. "You're wrong, you hear me? Once you give up, once you lose that last bit of hope, you may as well lie down and die. We've defied Bates in the past, and we can do it again. He only thinks he has us beaten. You think it's over but it's not, not by a long shot. At the moment, you're in shock. He's put you in a state of depression only because he happened to catch us at a crucial time, a time when we had our rescue in our hands and the certainty of going home in our sights. Okay, he took that from us. I can understand how you're feeling, but you have to realise *that* is what has knocked you the most, the actual timing of this whole mess more so than our capture. We don't have to keep it that way. Bates badly underestimates us. He thinks by putting me down he'll have more control and we'll have less chance of making any escape. Well, he's wrong. We *can* do this. Together we can beat him, and the sooner, the better."

No one answered.

After a brief pause, Jones stepped forward, glaring at Billie. "That's a nice little speech, McCoy, but as far as I'm concerned, you're full of bullshit."

"You can think what you like about me but don't put yourselves down."

"Get real. We can't take him on without you, and you can't do a thing for us. In case you've forgotten, you're flat out moving. Do you need reminding of that little point? Maybe another workover might help it sink in."

"Come on, Sarah, let it go," Reynolds said, taking her by the arm. Jones yanked free. Her piercing stare remained on Billie.

"Face it. You've finally been beaten. It's all over. Bates has won so there's no point in beating around the bush."

"No, he hasn't. He only thinks he has."

"How the hell can you say that? Accept it. We have no chance, especially with Bland back on duty and ready to knock you down at the drop of a hat."

"It doesn't matter. We still have to try."

"Bullshit. I've had it with trying and the sooner you learn to accept it's over, the better. Hell, maybe I could do Bland a favour and take up where she left off? Knock some sense into you. How does that sound, huh?"

"Oh, and that'll help our cause, won't it."

"It will for me. Because of you, the Rileys led Bates straight to us, damn it."

Billie's next line of attack suddenly caught in her throat. She stared at Jones in surprise – and understanding. "Is that what this is about? You're blaming me for this?"

"You bet I am."

"Lay off, Jones," Jane said.

Jones ignored her. Her focus never faltered from the detective. "I told you this would happen right from the start but would you believe me? No...o! And now it's too late, damn it. Well I may not be able to pay out on Bates, but hell, there's nothing stopping me from taking it out on you. And you know the best part about it? You're in no position to stop me."

"Damn it, Sarah, cut it out." Reynolds, her impatience blown, took Jones' arm in an attempt to pull her back but Jones shook her off. Jane grabbed her other arm and turned her to face her the moment she pulled free from Reynolds.

"Jones, what the hell are you talking about? You lay one finger on her and I swear you'll have me to answer to."

Jones' eyes narrowed. "You stay out of this, Walker." She yanked her arm free.

"The hell I will."

"Come on, calm down," Billie said. This was snowballing. It needed to be stopped – quickly. "This is not solving anything."

"I don't want to hear one more word come out of your mouth, McCoy. Do you hear me?" Jones spat.

The words might have been water off a duck's back for Billie, but for Jane it was a different matter. She let go of the cop and took hold of Jones intending to push her out of Billie's face. At her touch, Jones' bottled emotions exploded. She shoved Jane off her and threw her hard into the truck wall. Raising a fist, she stepped forward. Instantly, Billie reacted. Jones had gone too far and needed pulling into line. Ripping her arm free of Kate's hold, her hand shot up, catching Jones' fist in mid-flight before it could make contact with Jane.

With her hand trapped, Jones' glare shot to Billie, the fury in her eyes clearly visible. And then almost instantaneously, the cop's grip slackened. Billie gasped in pain and sank forward, her attack forgotten. The sudden movement had caught her out. Lifting her arm so fast only invited a sharp pain across her ribs, severe enough to make her unwillingly pause for a vital second and lose every advantage.

It was all Jones needed. She jabbed a fist into the cop's ribs. Billie cried out and folded forward. With an excruciating pain tearing across her ribs, she sank to her knees clasping her stomach.

Grabbing Billie by the front of the shirt, Jones yanked her up and held her in a firm grip to stop her slipping to the floor. Gasping, and helpless to defend herself, the cop knelt at Jones' feet hanging in her grasp. Jones could now pay her back big time, and there wasn't a thing she could do to stop her.

Chapter Twenty-One

Jones stood with her knotted fist raised in readiness to lay another punch into the cop – and suddenly she paused. In that split second, at a time when she knew she could finish it so easily, something held her back. Shit. What was she doing? Fighting McCoy wasn't the answer. All the grudges that had possessed and driven her on earlier in the trip weren't there anymore. She had no reason to want to hurt her – not after everything they'd been through.

As the realisation raced through her head, Jane growled a savage grunt and leapt off the wall in a dive.

"You bitch."

The force of Jane's tackle ripped Jones' grip from Billie's shirt, knocking the cop to the floor. The two girls crashed beside her. The attack snapped Jones out of her culpability. Her survival instinct kicked in, and she took Jane on with the same ferocity. Both flung vicious punches, wanting to hurt the other as much as possible.

Reynolds leapt after them as they rolled around the floor. "Stop it!" she yelled, trying to pull them apart. "Stop it, you idiots! Stop it, you hear me!" Grabbing Jane by the back of the shirt, she hauled her off Jones and shoved her to the side. Jane hit the wall and rebounded to the floor. She sat up, shaky and disorientated. Despite the sudden 'time out', she glared at Jones.

Reynolds stood between the two, looking from one to the other. Jones climbed to her feet with a livid glare, dishevelled and panting, eyeing Jane with ill-feeling as she stood up. Both had traces of blood under their noses.

"Cut it out, you hear me?" Reynolds said. "Damn it, the last thing we need is to be fighting among ourselves. This is crazy."

"Please don't fight any more. Please," Kate pleaded. Jones' gaze shot from Jane to her. The farm girl knelt beside Billie with an arm protectively around her. The cop knelt hunched over with her head down, gasping short breaths. The anguish across Kate's face invited some compassion from Jones, enough to hold back any further attack.

The girls' stressed cries filtered into Billie's pounding mind. Her breaths were coming easier and the burning in her ribs was lessening. She looked up. Only now was she aware the girls had been fighting. Jones thrust an accusing finger her way.

"If you think you're up to making a plan, go for it, but you're kidding yourself. This time there's no way out." She backed off. Casting a sweeping glance at Jane and Reynolds, she spun on her heel and retreated to the front corner, dropping down on her rump. Drawing in her knees, she buried her head behind her folded elbows resting on top.

"What sort of attitude is that?" Jane questioned in a heated reaction. She stepped forward. "Damn it, Jones. Why the hell won't you—"

Reynolds intercepted her and shoved her back. "Just leave it, okay? Leave it."

"Leave it?" Disbelief widened Jane's eyes. "We need to work together, not—"

"I said, leave it," Reynolds enforced, cutting her off a second time. Jane turned from her resolute expression and glanced at Jones. Her head was still buried in her arms. Jane threw her hands up in frustration and looked at Reynolds.

"Fine. Whatever you say. I *will* leave it. Thanks so much for your support."

Reynolds stared hard at her, tight-lipped. She glanced at Billie. The detective returned her look but had nothing to say. All respect and reliance the girls had built up lay buried. They were once again divided, in a world they believed held no future. Reynolds turned and sat with Jones.

Jane shook her head. Exhaling a heavy sigh, she joined Kate and Billie, kneeling with them. Billie slowly sat up and leant against the wall. Catching Jane's look, it wasn't hard to see the concern in her eyes, and it wasn't hard to guess it was for her.

"I'm okay," she told her, appreciating she'd attacked Jones on her behalf.

Jane nodded a curt nod. "Sure you are." The words shot out harshly, the dismay and disappointment driving them. Billie rested a hand on her leg and looked her in the eye.

"Thanks anyway."

Jane's stare was steady and considerate. Her shoulders slumped as she relaxed. She gave another nod, backed with a weak smile. Her gaze drifted over the cop's bloodied face. The sight mellowed her mood. "You don't look so good."

"Oh, you noticed."

Jane's gaze met hers. "I hear Bland came along on this lovely trip." Her voice had turned icy and irritable.

Billie considered the words behind a pensive look. So, Jane knew about Bland. No wonder she was so on edge. The detective appreciated how the news would have affected her. Bland had caused her a lot of pain and torment that night with Smith, something she wouldn't forget in a long while, if ever. She herself was living proof the woman was here for revenge, her wrath stronger than ever and directed at her prisoners. For Jane, the knowledge carried a terrifying bearing.

"Yeah. You missed a great party."

"Shit, McCoy, you should have killed her when you had the chance." Her tone was laced with resentment, somewhat accusing.

Billie choked a laugh and rested her head back. "Funny, Bland said the same thing."

"Really? Well I don't find anything funny about it."

Again, a faint smile touched the cop's lips but it came without any comment. Jane watched her a moment before exhaling a shaky breath. Billie glanced at Kate. The farm girl sat wide-eyed, listening. Jane huffed another heavy sigh. "Looking at you, I'm glad I missed it," she said, drawing Billie's attention to her.

"It was horrible. I wish I had," Kate mumbled.

"Yeah, well that's typical Bates. He makes sure we all pay." Turning to the detective, Jane looked her in the eye. Her tone softened. "McCoy, do me a favour. Next time you take Bland on – make sure she doesn't get up, okay? And I mean never."

Billie gave a weak laugh. "I'll try and keep that in mind."

"Good." Jane flashed a light smile. She looked at Kate. "You heard that Kate, she's committed."

"I hope she never has to face her again," she replied in a quiet, strained voice.

Billie rolled her head and looked at her. "Now there's a thought. I could just let Jane do it."

Jane's eyebrows lifted. "And end up looking like you? No way."

Kate glanced at her and then Billie, her worry obvious. Jane rested a hand on her thigh and squeezed it in a gesture of support. Kate could only return a feeble smile. Jane turned to the cop, studying her face again.

"Hmm, maybe that first aid kit's still up the front. I'll check."

Billie nodded. "Sure, that'd be great." A sense of relief washed through her. At least she'd taken Jane's mind off Jones and eased some of her tension. Jane smiled and started to get up, and abruptly stopped. She sank back down.

"I guess there's one good thing that's come out of this."

"There is?"

"Janda. At least he's safe."

Billie looked in earnest at her. In all the commotion and anguish, she'd forgotten about him. "Yeah, you're right." She sighed. "It *is* one thing. I was worried Bates would bring him."

Jane nodded. On a fading smile, she stood. Billie glanced at Jones and Reynolds. Both watched them. The mention of Janda had drawn their attention across to them. Obviously they'd forgotten about him too.

Jones dropped her head onto her elbows. Reynolds momentarily held the cop's gaze before looking away. Billie now knew where she stood with these girls. Disappointed, her focus drifted to Jane walking to the cupboard on the front wall. Jane ignored the two girls sitting in the corner beside it, keeping her attention on the cupboard. With more force than necessary, she yanked open the door. Taking what she needed, she returned to Billie and cleaned her face.

Time passed slowly. All was quiet as the truck rolled on through the night. The girls eventually lay down to catch up on some sleep. With her mind crowding with thoughts, Billie tried to look to the future with some optimism. She had to. The girls needed someone to remind them to keep their faith alive, to tell them they were going to make it. Impossible as it seemed, she couldn't afford to give up.

One minor thought comforted her through the dismal situation – Dave was on his way. With a general direction where to look, he wouldn't stop until he found her. The only thing against him was time. Could he find them before they were shipped out?

Somehow she'd have to stall, do something, anything, to give him time to catch up. It was their only chance.

Chapter Twenty-Two

Billie stirred from her doze. The rough road gently rocked her as the truck continued its trek north in a relentless push against time. She glanced at the high glassless window running the length of the wall. It was light outside. Great. That meant kilometres separated them from Kate's farm, and more importantly, Dave.

Trying not to dwell on it, she measured her health. The injuries on her face and ribs had eased. Her vitality was gradually returning, giving her energy level a boost. Tired of lying down, she sat up. Although stiff and sore, the pain had lessened considerably. She slid backwards in a smooth, careful move and leant against the wall.

The girls lay around her, stretched out on the thin mattresses. Jones and Reynolds remained isolated in the front corner. Billie wondered how long it would last. Would they get over it and join forces, give their support to fight this? Or would they simply revert to the girls she'd first met and want to do it their way, if at all. It was hard to say. Just when she thought she knew them, they pull a stunt like this, tossing all her conclusions in the air. They were scared. Billie knew it. They hated this whole nightmare, but didn't they all? Disappointment welled up inside of her. They'd shut themselves off at a time when she could really do with their help.

The detective gazed down at Jane and Kate's sleeping forms. A faint smile touched her lips. She could definitely count on them. They'd do anything for her. Then she tensed as a horrible thought gripped her. What if they didn't make it out of this? What if she couldn't help them escape? The worry of not getting them out hit hard. She hated the thought of something terrible happening to them. If she failed, that very threat awaited them at the end of this road.

Shunting the horrid thoughts to the back of her mind, Billie rested her head back and closed her eyes. With her hurts quite bearable, she was able to think more clearly, and it wasn't hard to work out they were in a bad spot, a very bad spot. No opportunities of escape had been offered, and until she could determine how many brothers had remained with Bates, it was hard to put a plan together. Had all the Rileys come? Maybe Bates didn't think he needed them now that they were underway. Maybe he didn't plan to let his prisoners out until they reached his camp. They'd been in here for this long so who's to say it wasn't going to be like this all the way.

Thinking about it only frustrated Billie more. To take her mind off it, she let her thoughts drift to Dave. Hopefully he'd get them out of this, come to their rescue and give Bates what he deserved. It sounded comforting and helped relieve her stress for a brief second, until reality cut in, robbing her of all confidence. Who was she trying to kid? He'd only be arriving at John's now. There was no way he could catch them in time – they had too much of a head start. No, it was on her shoulders and hers alone.

After some time, the truck slowed to a halt. The engine died soon after. The girls stirred, woken by the silence and lack of motion. They sat up, weary and stiff, glancing at one another with apprehensive looks. One thing calmed Billie's nerves. They couldn't have reached Bates' village yet; they hadn't been on the road long enough.

The rear doors yanked open. Bright sunlight lit up the dim enclosure. Bland glowered at them. Jack and Tony stood armed beside her, watching with mocking grins.

Billie studied them. With the opened doors came some answers to her questions. So, Bates had brought them along. She had to admit, she wasn't surprised. Still, all wasn't lost. Two brothers were here and unless the other two were with Bates, which she doubted, the odds were beginning to favour them significantly.

"Right. Two at a time for the call of nature," Bland growled. Her gaze rested on Billie. "You're last, McCoy."

Billie made no comment. She simply returned her stare in a calm, unfazed manner, ignoring the sinister leer on Bland's battered face.

"What, not in the mood for talking? Hmm, I can imagine you must be a little sore this morning." Bland snickered. "I had so much fun last night beating the shit out of you. We should do it again – soon."

Billie refused to fall for her taunting tactics. Still she didn't reply. Her silence only inspired a victorious snigger from Bland. She turned to the others.

"Okay you lot, move," she barked. "Walker, you and Cauldron can go first."

An uneasiness settled on Billie. What was going on? Why did they need a toilet stop when they had their own private toilet on board? This hadn't happened on the first trip. Doing her best to appear calm, she met Jane's eye. The girl looked scared; not for herself but for her. Bland's threat of another beating had its effect. The detective nodded, encouraging her to do as she was told. It could prove much worse if she didn't.

Reluctantly Jane and Kate climbed to their feet and crossed to the opened doorway, jumping lightly down off the truck. Bland pulled out her baton. A cold smile appeared on her swollen face as she met the nervous stares of the two prisoners. She indicated with her head to walk up the track behind her.

The truck had parked in a clearing alongside the narrow road. They were back in the rainforest. The thick and dense foliage limited their view. Large trees towered above the six wheeler, providing ample shade.

The two girls hesitantly moved off in the direction Bland had designated. The big woman fell in behind, directing them into the bushes further along. Once off the track, the party couldn't be seen from the truck.

Billie glanced at Jones and Reynolds where they sat watching the now empty track, reading the defeat and despair on their glum faces. They'd sunk to the lowest of lows without any sign of revival in sight. They seemed set in their minds this was indeed the end. Jones hadn't offered any apology for her actions last night and neither of them had asked for her advice or ideas. They'd shut her out altogether, just like their hope, declining into an isolated and lonely battle to cope with it on their own.

Billie returned her attention outside. Quickly she assessed how they stood. She'd still only seen the two Riley brothers. Both stood at the back of the truck guarding them. Without their brothers, it meant there were only the four of them all up, including Bates – four against five – not counting the guns, if Jones and Reynolds joined them.

Her concentration focused on Jack and Tony. Both were quite casual about their duty. They stood slouched with rifles hanging loose, their attention wandering all around except where it was supposed to be – on the prisoners. The fact the two brothers were new at this 'hired thugs' game could very much be to her advantage and could prove to be the loophole to take the initiative.

"Taking a last look at freedom, McCoy?" Reynolds asked.

Billie turned to her, considering whether to keep her plans to herself or not. There wouldn't be much point in expressing any opinion, not with the mood these girls were in. Her gaze darted to Jones as she turned her way. The air of defeat and denial hung around her like a dark miasma. Nothing had changed. The detective looked at Reynolds.

"No. I'm just determining the best avenue to take."

"Ha," Jones scoffed. Shaking her head in a disapproving nod, she rested it against the wall. "You're contemplating an escape? As hurt as you are? You're crazy."

Billie's gaze shot to hers. She ignored the ridicule. It came as no surprise. Huh, maybe she did know these girls better than she thought. Letting it go, she turned her attention outside, concentrating on bringing her plan together.

Bland brought her prisoners back. As the two girls climbed into the truck, the big woman nodded at Jones and Reynolds. "Okay, you two, let's go."

The girls did as they were told without argument and climbed down off the truck. Expressing no urgency, they ambled up the track with Bland on their heels.

Billie turned to Jane and Kate. They settled beside her. She wanted to be sure they hadn't been hurt. Jane met her eye and flashed a brief smile before resting her head against the wall. Exhaling a long breath, she rolled her head and gazed at the girls disappearing up the track.

The detective looked at Kate on the other side of Jane. She sat with her head resting on bent knees.

"Kate, you okay?"

The girl looked up and nodded. "Sure." Her answer lacked conviction.

A smile flickered across Billie's lips. "Hey, you're doing great."

"You think so? I just want to go home," she said, dropping her gaze.

Billie nodded. "Just keep believing that."

Jane looked around at her. The cop glanced from one to the other but didn't elaborate. Turning from their scrutinising stares, she rested her head on the wall, a sign she had no more to say.

Five minutes later, Jones and Reynolds emerged from the scrub and strolled back to the truck. They seemed a little more relaxed now that their walk was almost over. Bland followed a couple of steps behind. Reaching the truck, Jones went to step up into it. Bland suddenly struck out with the baton, catching her across the kidneys.

The surprised girl exhaled a muffled cry and fell forward into the tailgate clasping her lower back.

Reynolds spun and faced Bland. On impulse, she tensed in a fighter's stance with fists clenched. Bland lifted the baton in response, backed by an evil and daring glare.

"Come on, try it."

At the first sign of trouble, both Tony and Jack snapped to attention. They lifted their rifles to cover Jones and Reynolds.

Billie also jumped to full alert. Sitting with a tight stomach, the cop had no idea what had provoked the attack – and didn't like it one bit. What was Bland doing? Why pick on Reynolds and Jones and not Jane and Kate? It didn't make sense. Inwardly, she prayed Reynolds wouldn't do anything stupid in support of Jones.

"You bitch," Reynolds spat at Bland. After a lingering moment, she unclenched her fists and straightened, a sign of surrender. It was what Bland was waiting for. She swung the baton in a swift arc, smacking Reynolds across the cheek – not with full power but enough to knock her to the ground.

Bland chuckled. "Seems now's a good time to take up from last night, don't you think, Reynolds?"

Blurting an irritated growl, Jones pushed off the truck and swung at Bland. The baton rammed her in the abdomen, halting her instantly. She gasped and folded forward hugging her stomach. Smiling, Bland raised the baton.

"Always trying to throw your weight around, aren't you, Bland," Billie threw at her from inside.

Bland's arm poised in mid-air. Her gaze shot to the cop, her eyes glowering with hate. Billie held the fierce look in a challenge, daring her to take it up with her and not the two girls.

"Oh, shit," Jane murmured fearfully beside the detective. "Here we go again."

Appreciating Jane and Kate's apprehension was generated by her call, Billie kept her focus on Bland. The big woman slowly dropped her hand and shoved Jones back.

"Get in the truck, now," she barked.

Breathing hard and rubbing her stomach, Jones looked up at the enraged face guardedly.

"Come on, move it," Bland said impatiently.

Jones stepped to Reynolds and helped her up. A little dazed, she was quite steady on her feet. With Jones' help, she climbed into the truck. Jones followed. Both girls maintained a wary watch on Bland, afraid to turn their backs on her. Nursing their injuries, they hobbled to their mattresses and sat down. Billie watched them. Regardless of their attitude towards her, she didn't like to see them hurt. Jones, still having trouble breathing, rubbed her stomach. Reynolds rested her head on the wall. Already a red bruise darkened her cheek. She caught the detective's eye and gave a slight nod, her eyes thankful for her intervening.

"Okay, hotshot, it's your turn," Bland said. Billie looked at her. The cold eyes bore into her.

"Hell, Billie, watch her," Jane whispered.

Billie glanced at her. The concern crossing Jane's strained features touched her. Stiffly, she climbed to her feet. With a hand supporting her ribs, she stepped towards the opened doors. It was the first time she'd been on her feet since her beating. To her surprise, her muscles ached less than she expected. Determined to prevent Bland from seeing her in distress, she walked with a steady confidence. Climbing down the tailgate, she did her best to hide any tell-tale signs of soreness from the effort. She looked Bland in the eye.

The big woman's icy gaze took in the fresh cuts and bruises on the cop's face. She smiled as best she could. "You know the way."

As Billie turned, Jack winked at Tony and tossed his rifle to him. Billie caught the lustful grin he cast her.

"Move it," Bland said, shoving her forward. Billie looked at her, reading the challenge embedded in her derisive stare. She glanced at Jack and then walked off without a word. Her two escorts fell in behind.

"Uh-oh. How come he's going with them?" Kate asked.

"I don't like it," Jane said quietly.

Jones glanced at the two girls staring out at the track. They looked anxious. She turned and watched McCoy and her escorts disappear into the scrub. The fact Bland had taken the cop on her own was a clear indication she had something in mind, not to mention why Jack was allowed to accompany them. Knowing how much of a handful McCoy could be, he was either going along as a backup for Bland, which would be a logical explanation, or he could be part of another of Bland's sick plans to unleash on the detective. A sexual attack was not out of the question.

"Damn it, what is Bland up to now?" Reynolds murmured.

"What the hell do you care?" Jane said in a harsh whisper.

Reynolds looked sharply at her. "What, you think I don't care?"

"After last night? Yeah, that's exactly what I think. You let her down badly, you bloody turncoats."

Jones looked at her, drawing Jane's fiery glare her way. Jones knew the words were intended just as much for her, in fact, probably more so for her. She didn't respond. For once she was prepared to take the blame. She felt bad about attacking McCoy last night. It'd been in a heated moment, one she'd had no control over, and the guilt ate away at her with a relentless taunting.

Jane didn't let up. "I'm damned if I know why she keeps sticking up for your two worthless arses. As usual, she's in big trouble because of it."

"She was in trouble well before she stepped in to help us, may I remind you, so back off," Reynolds said.

"That may be so but now it's come at her again well before it's due. The least you two can do is make it up to her – again. We have to do something, together, and fast," Jane said in an urgent low tone.

"Like what? What can we do?" Like Jane, Jones didn't want anything to happen to the cop, not after everything they'd been through. Despite all their disputes and disagreements, they *were* friends, and that was what hurt. But what made it worse, McCoy had taken the heat off her just now. She had no doubt in her mind Bland would have given her a stern bashing had the cop not intervened. She also knew she was helpless to stop the big bitch doing the same to McCoy.

Determination hardened Jane's features. "Something. I don't know, but we can't just sit here and leave it all up to McCoy."

Jones held her stare intently yet couldn't give her an answer.

Jane looked from her to Reynolds. "Damn, you two. Hasn't she stuck her neck out enough for us? Surely there must be something we can do."

"Well, we're all ears," Jones growled.

Jane stared at her. She opened her mouth to speak but nothing came out. Exhaling an aggravated grunt, she threw her hands up in frustration. "Damn you. Why do I feel like I'm all alone on this?"

* * *

Bland pulled Billie up once they were off the track. "This'll do, McCoy."

Billie stopped. She turned and faced them, calm and relaxed. Jack stood beside Bland, leering with a hungry glint in his eye.

"You're lucky. You get a bonus." He grinned, running his gaze up and down her body.

"How's that?" She glanced at Bland watching with a smug look.

"I'm going to give you the time of your life." No sooner had the words left his mouth, he stepped towards her. From his belt, he pulled a pistol and held it at waist height aimed at her.

"Huh," Billie scoffed, ignoring the gun. "You've tried before, remember? You're no more of a man than I am."

Jack stopped in his tracks. His face twisted in resentment at the insult.

Bland chuckled. "Oh, this is going to be fun."

"You little bitch. I'll show you how much of a man I am." Jack spat the words out like daggers. Striding forward, he swung the gun at her head. Ducking low under it, Billie swivelled on one foot and smashed the other hard into his knee. Jack squealed and started sinking to the ground.

From the corner of her eye, Billie saw Bland react. As dangerous as the situation was, the cop couldn't afford to lose even a second. She stepped forward. Grabbing Jack's pistol and shoving a finger behind his on the trigger to prevent him from firing it, she whipped her other arm around and smashed her elbow into his nose. He reeled backwards. With little effort, she yanked the gun free in his involuntary descent to the ground.

Bland moved fast for her condition, faster than Billie anticipated. The big woman swung the baton, bringing it down on the cop's hand just as she turned the gun and positioned her finger around the trigger. The impact fired the pistol before she could aim it, and then it was gone, knocked from her grasp and flung to the side. Backing off and shaking her aching hand, the detective faced Bland.

The big woman wore a sinister grin, unfazed by the bold attack. It was as if she'd expected it.

"Ooh, you shouldn't have done that, cop. It seems I'll have to teach you some manners, again." She stepped towards her prisoner.

Chapter Twenty-Three

Jones sat fuming. Her anger deflected any ideas, blocking her mind to any rational thoughts, which in turn, failed to inspire any kind of plan to help Billie. Jane, as yet, hadn't offered any ideas either. Kate sat tense beside her. She hadn't spoken a word throughout the argument, no doubt in shock trying to absorb this terrible nightmare.

Bates stepped into view. He stopped beside Tony, not even bothering to look into the truck.

"Aren't they finished yet?" he asked impatiently, looking at his watch.

"Nope." Tony's blunt tone lacked respect.

"Where's your brother?"

A shot boomed loud and hollow from beyond the trees, echoing across the thick bush. Both men instantly turned and stared up the track.

"Shit," Bates growled. "Who's out?" He looked in the truck. "McCoy. Who else." Irritation hardened his tone. He turned to Tony. "Lock them up, and we'll take a look. Hurry!"

On hearing the shot, the girls' attention snapped to the direction it had come. Surprise and shock froze them in their seats. Jones fought against thinking the worst. McCoy didn't have a gun, and the one shot sounded too final. A gun in Bland's hands or Jack Riley's meant big trouble. The cop's sale to the sheik would hold Bland off from killing her, surely – but what about Jack? What if he'd lost control and fired before thinking, against Bland's orders? Shit.

Tony started to swing the big door closed. Jane suddenly jumped to her feet and charged at the door, smashing into it with a dropped shoulder. The large steel door shot outwards and caught Tony full on, hitting him with a sickening thud. He catapulted backwards onto his back with blood gushing from his nose.

Bates turned towards the truck with a bewildered look. Before he could react, Jane leapt at him with a scream – a scream mixed with fear and purpose. She landed on his chest. He staggered backwards but failed to fall. Jane clung to him, her legs wrapped around his waist, her hands hanging onto the back of his head. In a frantic assault, she threw one-handed punches at his face, doing her best to hurt him. No matter how hard he tried, he couldn't peel her off.

Surprised and confused at Jane's daring attack, Jones cottoned onto what she was up to. Surprise was indeed a beneficial factor in any attack. This they'd learnt from McCoy. Right now, Jane's plan seemed a good idea, as long as she didn't think about how wrong it could go. Her adrenalin pumped at the smell of freedom. Now was a good time to launch an attack, while the enemies' numbers were down and while they least expected it. She glanced at Reynolds and then Kate. As if reading her mind, the three jumped to their feet simultaneously and followed close on Jane's heels.

Jones leapt from the truck and threw herself onto Jane and Bates, bringing the struggling pair crashing down. With flying leaps, Kate and Reynolds leapt off the truck at the dazed Tony. He'd only just rolled to his knees. The girls tackled him hard, forcing him to faceplant into the ground.

* * *

Bland swung at Billie as she backed off. The attack was fast and fierce. The detective stumbled over the rough ground. There wasn't a lot of room in the small clearing and the protruding tree roots and vines slowed her retreat. Not only did she have to dodge Bland's swings, but she also had to watch her footing.

Bland growled in frustration and leapt forward when she was unable to hit her target. She swung harder and more recklessly. The tip of the baton caught Billie across the mouth, rocking her head to the side. Bland swung the baton in a quick, backhanded action, catching Billie on the cheek. The impact dumped her on her back with a moan.

Through her spinning vision, Billie watched Bland loom threateningly above her. The familiar sneer twisted her swollen features. Bland stared down at the stunned cop for a moment and then sniggered. She leant forward and raised the baton. Dredging up her inner strength, the detective kicked up from the ground. Her foot smashed into Bland's face, reeling her backwards off balance with a grunt. Out of control, she tripped on a root and landed hard on her back. She lay groaning with each raspy breath.

Billie rolled her sluggish body over and gasped. All her hurts came alive at once, adding to her throbbing head. She forced herself on and staggered to her feet. Standing on unsteady legs, she concentrated on staying upright. Blood ran from her cut lip. A fresh graze marred her cheek. She breathed through the pain for a few seconds and then focused on Bland. The big woman had rolled over and was getting up. It inspired the detective to move. Striding somewhat shakily over to her, Billie drove her foot into Bland's face before she could reach her feet. There was no point in giving her any fair advantage, and the sooner this was over, the better. The impact flipped Bland onto her side. In her helpless plight, she lost her grip on the baton. Billie stood on wobbly legs watching her attempt to get up. Again she moved in.

Regardless of her weakening condition, Bland unexpectedly struck out with her right leg. Her shin slammed in behind Billie's knees, knocking her off her feet. Bland dived on the cop the moment she hit the ground, punching out hard. Billie fought back, throwing everything she had into it.

Bland outweighed the detective and easily took the advantage. The two rolled over and over, punching whenever possible, oblivious to everything but each other. They drove their skills and physical stamina to the limit.

For a few crazy minutes, all Billie wanted to do was hurt Bland. So intense was her dislike for the woman, all training and discipline flew out the window, pushing her into a frenzied assault that emerged with animal savagery way out of control. Unfortunately, with weight and strength heavy in Bland's favour, she fought a losing battle, and when Bland pinned her down beneath her, too late she realised she was in for a hiding.

Sanity slowly crept back into the cop's pain-wracked mind, screaming at her to get off the ground. Grabbing Bland's left breast, the detective squeezed hard. Bland jumped, distracted by the new pain. She gripped the hand and tried ripping it off. Billie refused to let go. The pressure made Bland squirm, enough to momentarily lose her concentration. Taking advantage, the cop drove a punch up into her nose with her other hand, sending her foe crashing to the side.

Now free, Billie rolled in the opposite direction and stumbled to her feet, sucking in short rasping breaths. Everything started to spin. Weak and exhausted, she staggered backwards, falling against a tree. Leaning into it, she half turned and wrapped an arm around it, the only way to stop from sliding down. She closed her eyes, struggling to maintain some strength and stay on her feet. With her other hand she held her throbbing ribs, the familiar ache restarted from the strain of the fight. Desperately she fought to gain control of her breathing.

Billie opened her eyes. Bland was on her feet – not only on her feet but approaching her. Almost on top of her. The detective pushed off the tree with barely enough time to defend herself. Bland threw a punch. Billie deflected it and jabbed Bland in the solar plexus beneath her raised arm. The big woman gasped and stepped back as the wind shot from her lungs.

That was her first mistake.

Billie kicked the woman in the face, in the ribs, on the leg, anywhere, as long as she hurt the bitch. Each kick knocked Bland back but, like a sponge, she absorbed every blow, and just like in Smith's hut, refused to fall.

Finally, Billie had to let up. She staggered back, panting hard. She stood on trembling legs, watching her bloodied opponent warily. Bland simply stared at her, swaying.

On the last dregs of her strength, Billie raced forward. Leaping high with a leg outstretched in front of her, her foot strategically positioned to form a deadly missile, she smashed it into Bland's neck. A faint crack sounded and then a sickening grunt. The 'freak' reeled backwards, crashing into a large knotted tree. As if in slow motion, she slid to the ground. Her wide eyes stared ahead unfocused as the life drained from her beaten body.

On landing, Billie caught her balance. Staggering forward, she almost toppled over but somehow stayed upright. Standing on wobbly legs, she fought to ignore the exhaustion descending upon her. A roaring haze clouded her mind as she stood staring at Bland. Even in death, Bland refused to fall. She sat at the base of the tree, her head angled in an abnormal position on her shoulders.

"That was for Jane," Billie said in between gasps. Covered in dirt, she carried bruises and abrasions all over her body. Her clothes were torn and bloodstained and clung to her battered body. She'd taken a beating but had won.

A noise distracted her. She glanced to the side. Jack was stirring. Through her numbed brain, an alarm sounded. Billie knew she had to do something with him, and fast. If he got to his feet, she wouldn't be able to hold him off, not now. Stepping to Bland, she searched her pockets and found what she wanted – a pair of handcuffs. Bland always carried them on her. Stumbling across to Jack, she pulled his unresisting hands above his head and cuffed him around a solid root jutting out from the ground. No sooner had she clicked them shut, his eyes opened. Billie gave him no time to question or dispute her intentions. She punched him hard, knocking him out cold. The last thing she wanted was any unnecessary noise.

Satisfied he was secure, she stood . . . and stumbled backwards a step. A severe dizzy spell hit her. Catching her balance, she closed her eyes, fighting the urge to lie down and give in to her aching body. If only.

Regaining some control, she opened her eyes and looked around for the gun. She hobbled to where she'd dropped it and, after a quick search, spotted it beside a raised root. With great effort, she leant down and picked it up. The touch of the weapon's cold metal boosted her confidence. This was her bargaining power. Now she could end this once and for all.

**

Jane and Jones pinned Bates to the ground. In a mad struggle, he drove a brutal punch at Jane. She fell back with a grunt. Jones threw a punch before Bates could strike at her. His head rolled to the side under the impact of her bony fist but he seemed otherwise unaffected by the blow. He came back quite quickly, catching her by surprise. Using his body, he rolled with a sharp jolt, tossing her off him and onto her back. In a blur, he jumped to his knees and straddled her, pinning her beneath him with his weight. Jones was now aware they might have bitten off more than they could chew. Just when she believed they had him beaten, he was on top again.

Jane jumped on Bates' back. Instantly he shot out an elbow in a backward jab, catching her in the ribs. With a stifled gasp, she slid off him clasping her stomach, struggling to catch a breath. Bates turned to Jones. Grimacing, he raised his fist to strike.

Jones looked up into his enraged face. He'd almost lost control, which could prove dangerous for her. But she wasn't ready to give up yet. Grabbing a handful of dirt, she flung it into his face. He yelped and dropped his hand to his eyes, trying to rub them clean.

Jones grabbed her chance and lashed out, punching him in the nose with all the force she could muster. He rolled off her to the side with a grunt. She climbed to her knees, intending to follow and take him while he was encumbered with his tormenting discomfort. She watched him come out of the roll and sit up, rubbing at his eyes one-handed. Then she froze. Bates held a gun in his other hand. A gun. A small deadly pistol. He must have pulled it from his belt in the roll. Hell, she should have known he'd be armed. This was Bates she was dealing with, the cunning and shrewd cop who defied the laws of humanity. How could she have underestimated him?

Even though Bates was having trouble seeing her, he aimed the pistol in her general direction. Its evil one-eyed black hole stared ominously towards her. Before she could do anything, or fully register the danger she was in, Bates fired blindly. The booming blast was loud and piercing. The bullet ripped into Jones' shoulder, throwing her to the ground.

"No!"

Jane's cry penetrated Jones' whirling mind. Gritting her teeth against the searing pain shooting through her shoulder, she opened her eyes. Bates still sat beside her but he'd twisted around to face Jane. She stood frozen, her unwavering stare locked on Bates. Wiping at his watery eyes, his pistol was aimed directly at her head, which could only mean one thing – his momentary blindness must have cleared. He was back in control, armed and dangerous, and very pissed off.

Bates climbed to his feet. The gun didn't alter from its target.

Fear shone in Jane's eyes. Would Bates shoot her? Dread and disbelief gripped Jones. She tried to get up. Too weak, she gasped and fell back, panting hard. "N–no! L–leave her!"

"I've had it with you," Bates said, his tone laced with cold venom.

To Jones' horror, Bates' knuckle whitened as it tightened on the trigger. Jane caught her breath. Shock etched deep across her features.

A cold shiver ran down Jones' spine. Bates really was going to shoot. This was how it was going to end for Jane, at the hands of this callous slave trader. And there wasn't a thing she could do to stop him.

Jane closed her eyes just before the gun fired.

Chapter Twenty-Four

The seconds passed, seeming like hours. Jane warily opened her eyes. Bates stood in front of her staring blankly. His gun sank down by his side. A thin line of blood trickled from the small hole between his eyes. Slowly, he crumbled to his knees. For a lingering moment his lifeless gaze stared ahead, absorbing nothing in the vacant expression. And then, quite unhurried, he toppled forward to the ground.

Shock held Jane frozen. She stared at his crumpled body without a sound or movement. Unaware she'd been holding her breath, she expelled it with a shaky gasp. She'd braced for the bullet's impact, expected it, but it hadn't eventuated. By some miracle it was Bates who had taken the bullet, it was him who was dead. Dead. Not a breath left in him. But how? Slowly she turned, looking behind her, in the direction where the bullet had come. Tears welled in her eyes.

"Billie," she sobbed. Her breaths came in short gasps, stifled from the shock gripping her. And then a warm sense of relief and respect washed through her, mixed with total disbelief. McCoy had come to her aid. Against all odds, she'd somehow escaped Bland to help her. It was almost too much to comprehend. She stared at the detective where she stood twenty metres up the track, her right arm outstretched in front of her, the gun aimed at where Bates had stood only seconds before. Cherishing the blissful moment, Jane used it to calm her stressed nerves.

Billie unhurriedly lowered the gun. She stared at Jane, savouring the emotions of seeing her safe. In painful and stiff steps, she hobbled towards her. Her gaze drifted over the scene. Jones lay alongside Bates. Beyond them, Reynolds and Kate knelt beside an unconscious Tony with their stares fixed on her.

Striving to hold in her sobs of relief, Jane walked forward to meet the battered detective. Her face lit up in a shaky smile. As she drew closer, she quickened her pace. Billie stopped, casting her a weak smile. Without slowing, Jane grabbed the cop and hugged her.

"Damn it, Billie, I thought you were dead."

Billie feebly returned her hug, sharing her heart-warmed feelings. "You mean I'm not?"

Jane choked on a short laugh. She stood back, her hands gripping her friend's arms in a firm hold. She looked into the cop's eyes, shaking her head, speechless.

Despite being covered in blood and grit and wanting to sleep for a few years, a sense of calm washed over Billie.

"Shit, look at you," Jane breathed, finding her voice, which was full of concern. "It must have been some fight."

Billie sighed. "Yeah, you could say that."

"What about Bland? Can she...?"

Billie shook her head. The look in her eyes said it all.

"The bitch is dead?" Jane's shaky tone lacked confidence.

"Totally."

Jane's hands started to tremble. She stared hard at the detective. "I wish I could've been there to see it."

Billie gently pulled free from her grip and squeezed her arm, fully understanding the meaning behind her words and her reignited anguish. "She won't be hurting anyone any more, that's for sure."

Jane nodded. "I don't believe it."

"Believe it. Besides, you did tell me to make sure she wouldn't get up next time we got together."

Jane stiffened, surprised. "What? Well yes, but . . . I didn't really mean . . . I wasn't implying that you should..." Words failed her. "Damn it, McCoy, I was only kidding. I never expected you'd actually have to do it."

"Huh. You should've told Bland that."

Jane gave a laugh, or was it a sob? Her cheerful expression faded. "I wish I could have told her she was no match for you, that she never came close."

The cop chuckled. "She wouldn't have believed you, even if you'd told her when the last breath was leaving her lips."

"Hmm, maybe. The point is she got what she deserved. Bloody hell, I can't believe it. Bland and Bates dead. We don't have to run anymore."

Billie smiled tiredly. "Sure is a nice feeling, don't you think?"

Jane shook her head in awe. "It's indescribable." Her smile suddenly faded, washed by a sober expression. "Thank you, so much." Her words were filled with sincerity.

"You're welcome."

Kate rushed towards them. The farm girl embraced Billie in a warm hug.

"I knew you weren't dead, I knew it."

"What, and leave you guys out here to defend yourselves all alone?" Billie tried to sound stronger than she was. Kate let her go and stood back with a wide smile on her lips. And then her elation began to fade after studying Billie's cut and bloodied face.

"Come on, let's get you cleaned up," Jane said to Billie. Taking the detective by the arm, she urged her forward, leading her towards the truck.

Kate fell in beside them. Billie stumbled after a few steps. Now that she'd slowed down, her body was following suit. The effects of the fight were seriously settling in. Jane steadied her. Kate took a firm grip of her other arm. Billie appreciated their support and let them help her towards the truck. She gasped. Each step brought a stab of pain. She found herself leaning on Jane more than intended. Her focus drifted to Reynolds kneeling over Jones.

"What's wrong with Jones?"

"Hell, I'd forgotten about her," Jane said. "Bates shot her."

Billie looked sharply at her. Yes. She suddenly recalled hearing a gunshot moments before she'd stepped onto the track. Everything had happened so fast after that she hadn't had time to consider if anyone had been hit. Her stomach tightened. After all they'd been through, she didn't want to lose anyone now, including Jones. Aware they had their differences, added to the hurtful argument only a few hours before, Billie couldn't hold it against her. These girls were her friends, friends she wanted to go home with.

"Bad?" she asked, a little anxious, not taking her eyes off Jones' still form.

"In the shoulder."

As they reached the girls, Reynolds looked up at Billie with a solemn face, the worry for her friend heavy in her eyes. Jane and Kate helped the detective kneel beside Jones opposite her. Reynolds' focus remained fixed on Billie. Looking as if she was about to say something, she stared at the cop behind the stunned stupor entrapping her.

Jones opened her eyes.

"McCoy," she gasped, surprise and relief strong in her voice. She reached up and grabbed the detective by the front of her shirt with her right arm – the other lay useless beside her. "Damn you. We thought you were dead."

Billie exerted a light laugh and shook her head. Jones' tone gave away her emotions. Up until now, she'd remained hidden behind her tough image, using it to throw the blame her way. But this time it was different. This time she openly expressed her concern and couldn't stop her feelings seeping through.

"Not quite. You can't get rid of me that easily."

Jones smiled. Her hand fell away from her shirt. She held Billie's gaze with respect. Her voice softened. "I'm glad. You scared the hell out of us when we heard that shot."

Billie stared at her, surprised by the comment. For a minute, she thought she referred to the shot that had killed Bates and wondered what she meant. And then she remembered the incident when Bland had knocked the gun from her hand, accidentally firing it. Up until now, she hadn't given it any thought, yet that one shot must have sounded extremely ominous to her friends, explaining why they all thought she'd died. They knew how much Bland hated her, and with her in charge, would have assumed Billie was the victim. All in all, she appreciated what Jones was telling her. In her own way, she'd genuinely been worried for her.

Breaking the connection, Billie glanced at Reynolds. She stared with a touch of guilt nibbling at her strained features. The girl tensed under the cop's gaze. Though no words were spoken, Billie guessed what she and Jones were thinking just from the looks on their faces. The remorse from last night's attack was obvious. Their recapture had been a big strain, a huge shock, so their behaviour was understandable. Not one for holding grudges, she blurted a weak laugh and looked down at Jones.

"You're not about to give me another one of your lectures, are you?"

"If I had the strength, you would've copped it by now," she gasped.

Billie nodded on a half-smile. "Don't I know it."

"Damn it, McCoy, you had no right–to make us worry like t-that."

If Billie hadn't been so tired, she would have laughed. Instead it came out in a heavy huff. "Forgive me. I'll try and remember that in the future."

"Good."

Managing a stronger smile, the detective leant forward and gently opened Jones' shirt to examine the wound. The bullet had passed straight through, leaving her bleeding from both sides.

Reynolds had acted quickly and placed a towel from the truck on it. One end was tucked in under her shirt, the other under her shoulder. The thick material helped slow the blood flow.

Jones studied Billie's battered and bloodied face. "Hey, you don't look so good."

Billie shot her a glance before returning her scrutiny to the wound. She lifted the towel to peer beneath it. "Huh, I was about to say the same about you."

"It's not so bad. I'm okay," she said bravely. "What about Bland?"

Billie looked up into her eyes, and then glanced at Reynolds. "She's dead." Bitterness laced her quiet voice.

Jones and Reynolds stared hard at her, letting the words sink in.

"Dead?" Reynolds asked in a thin voice.

Billie nodded. "Yeah."

A slight hush engulfed them.

"Good," Jones breathed. She closed her eyes. "That's real good."

Reynolds shook her head and gave a heavy sigh. "They're the sweetest words I've heard yet."

Dropping her gaze to Jones, Billie nodded. "And here I was thinking I'd started to educate you two."

It brought smiles to the girls' faces.

"Far from it." Opening her eyes, Jones looked up and focused on Jane. "Jane. Shit, I thought Bates had killed you. I couldn't watch. I heard the shot. And then I think I passed out."

"It's okay—"

"I tried to stop him."

"Sarah, it's okay. I'm fine."

"Where is he? What happened?"

"Well," Jane said, flashing a faint smile. "Like you, I thought I was dead. I really did." She shuddered, suddenly hesitating. With a strained breath, she continued, her voice filling with respect. "Our cop here turned up in the nick of time and saved the day. Put a bullet right between his eyes."

Jones stared intensely, absorbing the story. Her gaze drifted to Billie, awash with reverent admiration. "What, you weren't satisfied after battling it out with Bland? You wanted more excitement?"

Billie smiled and sighed. "Well, I had nothing better to do."

Her words drew light smiles to the girls, and then they faded. Billie glanced at each of them, sensing the tension gripping them. Her words obviously hit them harder than she'd intended. It seemed the shock of everything was catching up with them.

"Lucky for us," Jones said. Her gaze swung to Jane and Kate sitting either side of the cop. Jane brushed a strand of hair off Jones' face.

"Just take it easy. I'll go and see if I can find something in the first aid box to clean you two up." She turned to Billie and rested a hand on her shoulder.

The detective nodded. "Sounds good. A strong shot of Scotch wouldn't go astray either."

"Ha! That, my girl, you'll have to wait for."

"Too right," Reynolds cut in. "You offered to have it with us so don't even think about reneging, only now when you buy us that drink, I'm going to order a double – one after the other."

The girls smiled.

Billie looked around at their relaxing faces. "You guys are so pushy."

"You haven't seen anything yet," Jones said with a weak sigh.

"Hmm, that's what worries me."

Jane stood up. "How about you guys go easy on one another for a minute. I won't be long."

"I'll give you a hand," Kate offered, standing with her.

The two girls walked to the truck. Sensing Reynolds' eyes on her, Billie met her gaze. The girl watched her with a thoughtful, solemn expression. The smile had disappeared, replaced by a worried look. The small bout of light heartedness had passed, allowing the seriousness of the matter to take precedence.

"Sarah's right. You don't look so good. You should lie down," Reynolds said quietly.

"As long as I don't sit here for too long, I'll be okay." She looked at Jones and rested a hand on her shoulder. "Just hang in there; we'll get you home as soon as possible."

Jones nodded. Billie went to get up. The instant she kneeled, she stopped and winced. Maybe she had sat for too long. Sinking down, she rested a hand against her bloodied ribs to ease the throbbing. She couldn't stay here; there was too much to do. Again she tried to stand. The growing pain in her ribs brought her to a halt. She gasped and slowly sank down, momentarily giving in. Her head dropped. She leant forward with closed eyes to help gain control.

Reynolds stepped over Jones and knelt beside her. She slipped an arm around her shoulders, supporting her. Using a firm hand, she eased Billie's off her ribs and then lifted her shirt above her bandage.

"I think you might have busted your stitches yet again," Reynolds said, trying not to sound too worried. "When are you going to learn? You have to stop picking fights until you're completely healed."

Billie nodded, giving a laugh. She opened her eyes to see the bandage was stained in fresh blood. Lifting her head, she looked Reynolds in the eye. "Cute. Very cute."

The girl nodded. "Yeah. Come on, let me help you seeing you're so determined to get up."

Standing, she took hold of Billie's arm. The support made a big difference, taking the strain off the detective's ribs as she knelt up. Jones suddenly reached out and grabbed Billie's wrist.

"McCoy?"

Reynolds let her down. Billie focused on Jones' steady gaze. For a moment, silence engulfed them.

Finally, Jones spoke. "Billie . . . thank you, for everything."

It was short and sincere but it was enough. Billie was touched, deeply. She didn't expect this of Jones. And Jones wasn't finished.

"I want you to know . . . I'm so sorry for last night . . . for hitting you. It was a cowardly thing to do, and I apologise. I lost it there for a while. I'm truly sorry."

Billie stared for a long few seconds. Here was a rare moment indeed, and she treasured it. The heartfelt apology from Jones made up for all the trouble she'd had with her. She nodded and smiled.

"Apology accepted. Just don't die on me now, okay?"

"Deal." She let her go.

Reynolds smiled. "Okay cop, time you were out of here." She hauled Billie to her feet in a gentle lift. Billie gasped and swayed. Reynolds tightened her hold, steadying her. Jane and Kate joined them, both casting Billie worried glances.

Jane frowned. "There's not a lot here. We'll just have to make do." She lifted her hands displaying all she had: a bottle of antiseptic, a few cloths and bandages.

"It'll do till we get to Kate's place," Billie said with a glance, overcoming her dizzy spell.

"Hmm, going back to Kate's. What a lovely thought." Jane's smile suddenly disappeared. Her gaze snapped around. She stared up the track with a locked concentration. "Can you hear that?" Her voice was barely a whisper yet it contained anxious urgency.

Everyone turned to her, surprised, and then looked up the track where it disappeared around a corner. Billie stood rigid, straining her ears. And then she heard it. A faint drone sounded from beyond the trees, gradually growing louder.

"It's a vehicle," Kate said. "Coming this way."

Jane turned to Billie. "Should we get into cover?"

The detective glanced at her before returning her scrutiny up the track. She shook her head. "From the way he's moving, we won't have time." She turned to Jane and nodded at Bates. "Grab Bates' gun, just in case."

Jane stared behind a numb gaze. It was obvious she hated the idea of resorting to firearms but after studying the cop's serious face, hurried to Bates to retrieve his weapon.

Kate picked up the borrowed pistol Billie had used. She'd left it on the ground beside Jones. Billie took it from her offered hand, thanking her with a nod. She glanced at the two rifles over near Tony Riley.

"How about you and Casey grab the rifles," she said, looking at Kate.

Reynolds shook her head, cutting in before Kate could answer. "It'd be a waste of time. I wouldn't use it."

"I'm not asking you to fire it. All you have to do is point it."

Reynolds stared with a blank expression, thinking it over. "Fine."

Kate nodded and quickly retrieved the rifles, passing one to Reynolds. The girls stepped around Jones, positioning her behind them. There wasn't time to move her so they used themselves as a human shield. There they stood in a tight bunch, facing the corner with grim looks of determination, ready to deal with whatever danger closed in on them.

Within seconds, the vehicle shot around the corner into view, charging towards them over the rough track.

Chapter Twenty-Five

Billie didn't recognise the white Toyota Troop Carrier when it bounded into view. It flew towards them over the narrow track, bouncing from side to side before skidding to a halt ten metres from the grouped girls.

Two figures sat in the shadow of the cabin. Another was in the back. The passenger door swung open before the Troopy had fully stopped. A man leapt out.

"Pa!" Kate cried in astonishment.

John caught his balance. A shoulder sling supported his wounded shoulder. He hurried towards his daughter. Kate put down her rifle and leapt forward to meet him. With arms outstretched, she jumped into his. He held her tight, lifting her up and spinning her around one-handed, kissing her feverishly. Both cried tears of joy.

"Oh, Kate. Kate. You're all right. I don't believe it."

Turning from them, Billie's gaze was drawn to the Toyota. Two men strode towards them. Her smile broadened when she recognised their familiar faces. A wave of delight washed through her.

One was middle aged. Clean-shaven, his handsome angular face held concern. His short dark hair was flecked with streaks of grey, adding a sophisticated look to his features. Broad shoulders supported a slim build, enhancing a firm and wiry form.

"Dave," Billie breathed, hardly believing her eyes.

The man accompanying him was much younger. In his early thirties, Detective Mark Burrows had a thick crop of long blond wavy hair. His well-toned physique that only a disciplined workout could achieve, suggested strength and endurance. Like the man at his side, his tanned handsome rugged face was clean-shaven.

Their jeans and casual shirts stripped them of any connection to the law. They rushed towards Billie. She dropped the pistol and stepped towards them. Her heart pounded hard, her emotions in turmoil at the sight of them.

Tight-lipped and with strained features, Dave grabbed her and hugged her tight. Mark threw his arms around her as well, resting his head against hers. No words were spoken. The men finally released her and stood back. Grins of relief helped filter the heavy stress from their faces. As elation washed over them, the two officers took the time to study her condition. Slowly, the smiles faded. The tension returned to their faces.

"Billie, look at you." Dave's grave voice matched the anguish in his eyes.

"Hey, speak for yourself."

He looked tired. Concern and strain etched a path across his features. Mark was in no better shape. Both looked as if they'd seen a ghost. Maybe she was to them. For the past few weeks, they would have believed her lost forever, or dead, and the shock of finding her hit them hard. But for her it was different. Seeing them again and having them by her side lifted the trauma from her weary shoulders. Her stamina was returning merely with the presence of these two men who always stood by her. She couldn't believe they were here. Such was her trust in them she knew the ordeal was over. She had all faith in them to get her home safely.

"Dave, I'm fine," she assured him, looking him in the eye when he didn't answer.

The lieutenant reached out and caressed her bloodied face with a gentle touch. His hand shook. Billie cupped hers over his, holding it tight. She offered him a smile. He returned it. Her gaze drifted to Mark. The fact he hadn't said anything was a sure sign of his anguish. She dropped her hand from Dave, pulling his from her cheek and stepped to Mark, embracing him in a grateful hug.

"Hell, Mark, it's sure good to see your face."

"Huh, I'll bet there's a lot more wrinkles on it now. You certainly know how to age a guy," he said, holding her tight. Though they were workmates, everyone in the squad was close, looking out for one another whenever they could. Being the only girl on the squad, the guys tended to be overprotective, regardless of how well she could look after herself.

Dave looked on, stroking Billie's hair while she was in Mark's arms. Billie glanced at the lieutenant after Mark released her. Smiling, Dave's attention drifted to the company with her. Jane and Casey gave him uncertain smiles.

Stepping forward, he held out a hand, "Hi. Lieutenant Edwards at your service. I've come to take you home."

"Hi. Jane Walker, and this is Casey Reynolds. We've heard a lot about you," Jane said somewhat hesitantly, shaking the offered hand.

"All good, I hope." He shook Casey's hand.

She watched him behind a dubious look. "If you've come to take us home, then it's definitely all good."

"Ha! And may I say it's nice to finally meet you guys. Your disappearances have certainly given us major headaches."

"Yeah, sorry about that."

Mark stepped forward, casting an admiring glance at the two girls. Their dirty clothes and scruffy, tired looks failed to disguise their attractiveness. "Excuse Billie for being so rude. I'm Detective Mark Burrows." He held out his hand to Jane.

"Trust you to want to meet the girls," Billie teased.

Jane and Casey smiled. Both shook his hand, eyeing him with approving stares.

John and Kate joined them. With his arm around his daughter, the farmer stared at the cop in awe.

"Billie, thank goodness you're okay," he said with concern. Slipping out of Kate's arms, he hugged her. "We were so worried about you guys. Believe me when I say how sorry I am that we had to give up your hideout. We had no choice. You were spot on about Bates. He was very forceful."

Billie stepped out of his embrace. "John, I don't blame you at all. It was just bad luck he hired the Riley brothers and they picked up on Kate's absence. Hell, it was just as much my fault as yours for not moving right away."

"The hell it was."

"Come on, don't beat yourself up. It's over."

He sighed. "Yeah, you're right." He looked at Jane and Casey and then gave them a hug. "I'm so glad you guys are okay."

"Well we are now," Casey said, stepping out of his arms. "I wouldn't recommend this trip to anyone."

"I'll bet." A sober expression washed across him. His gaze drifted to Billie, focusing on her bleeding face. "Eve filled us in on what happened in the shed, after she finally got home that is, including the bashing Bland gave you."

"Yeah, it was a little intense but I'm okay."

"Oh really? By the looks of you, you've had another beating. Did Bland do that to you? Where is she? I'll give her some of her own back. We'll see how she likes it," he growled, looking around.

Billie couldn't help but smile. "John, it's okay. It's all taken care of."

His gaze returned to her. "It is?"

"Yeah."

"Who is Bland?" Dave asked, looking from one to the other.

"Bates' partner," Billie replied.

"Someone you don't want to meet in your worst nightmare," John added, spitting out the words. Dave and Mark stared straight faced. With each piece of the girls' horrid situation falling into place, their anxieties swelled, feeding their already distraught nerves.

Billie rested a hand on John's arm and flashed a smile. "You know, deep down, I think she really liked me," she said in an effort to ease the guys' tension. The shock was only just beginning to touch them now that they'd had time to study the condition of everyone.

"Billie's right, Pa, you're too late. She fixed her real good. Bland's dead. Billie killed her in a fight." Respect rang in Kate's voice.

John looked at his daughter, stunned by her announcement. He turned to Billie.

"Killed?" A look of mixed surprise and shock played on his features. He sighed. "Good, she deserves nothing less." His eyes suddenly widened after realising what he'd said in the company of cops. He turned to Dave. "Respectfully of course," he added, correcting himself. "I have no doubts it was in self-defence on Billie's part."

The girls smiled. Dave struggled to contain his grin. He nodded. "Yes, respectfully of course."

"Speaking of which," Billie interrupted. She turned and nodded up the dirt road. "She's up the track a little, off to the right. Jack Riley is with her, cuffed to a tree."

"You mean you didn't kill him?" Casey said with a look of surprise. "What the hell were you doin', gal?" she exclaimed in a southern drawl. All eyes swung her way. Casey flashed a cheeky smile at her watching audience before she looked at Billie, meeting her questioning eye with a smile.

Billie returned it, sharing in her small tension reliever. Dave nodded and rested an arm around Billie's shoulders.

"Don't take any notice of her," he said, casting a smile at Casey. He shot a passing implicative glance at John. "And don't worry about Bland either. We'll take care of it."

Billie met Casey's eye. "Hey, I don't intend to start taking notice of her now, especially when I have backup on hand," she said with a playful tone.

Casey choked a laugh. "Careful, McCoy, you know what happens when you get too cocky."

"Too cocky? When do I get too cocky?"

"Just count the bashings we've had to give you. Maybe that'll jog your memory."

"So," Mark cut in with a smile. "It seems to me like you've finally met your match here, detective."

Billie shot him a look. "What? That's crazy. I have them right under my thumb in case you haven't noticed."

He grinned. "Oh really? Casey just said they've had to keep you in line. No, my girl, from what I can see, they've got you outnumbered and on your toes." He looked at Casey. "Good to see. Make sure you keep her there."

"Sure, Mark, happy to." She gave the cop a victorious smile.

Billie chuckled and shook her head. Backing off, she was too tired to pursue it. "Great." She turned to Mark. "You're loving this, aren't you."

He shrugged. "Just stating the facts."

"If I were you, I'd quit while you're ahead," Jane said to the detective, cutting in before she could answer.

"That sounds like a good idea," Dave said. "By the looks of you, you need to lie down for a while, take a break." He lifted a hand to silence her when she went to answer. "A *big* break."

Holding his gaze, Billie nodded. "Fine, I might just do that, like for a month."

"Good. Take as long as you like."

Billie smiled. "You could be sorry you said that, I have witnesses," she said, looking at the girls. Dave followed her gaze.

"True, but how reliable are they?"

She cast him a glance before returning her focus to the girls. They watched on with mischievous expressions. Billie nodded. "I'm sure I can convince them."

Casey laughed. "Ha, it'd have to be good."

"Don't worry, it would be, at least on my part." Ignoring the puckish face Casey pulled, a thought suddenly struck her. She turned to her boss. "Dave? Tell me. How did you find us so fast? You weren't supposed to arrive until this morning. You must've travelled all night to catch us up so quickly," she said, a little confused after thinking about it.

His smile lit up with an affectionate glow. "I got things moving faster than expected. In fact, we haven't stopped since I spoke to you yesterday. We flew out of Cairns to the nearest strip at Willowbank and hired this four-wheel drive, arriving at John's place, would you believe, about an hour after Bates dragged you off." He lightly touched her tender face. "Hell, that almost destroyed us. We thought we were too late."

"Sounds like you were on the same wavelength as us." Casey sighed. "I was sure it was all over this time."

Dave looked at her and smiled. "I bet you did." He nodded at John. "Thanks to John, we had a rough idea which direction Bates would be heading. After hearing your story about the way you'd come, he traced a route on a map and we took a gamble. Thankfully it was the right one." His gaze jumped to the big man beside him. "He offered to guide us regardless of his condition and, well, here we are," he said, turning to Billie. "Lucky for us we had a lighter vehicle. We made up some time."

"Lucky?" Billie questioned. "If you'd arrived here fifteen minutes earlier, I wouldn't have had to fight Bland, and Sarah probably wouldn't have been shot." She knew all too well Dave had done exceptionally well to get there when he had. Everyone smiled. It was easy to laugh now, now that it was over and the danger had passed.

Mark reached out and brushed a strand of hair off her face. "Never happy, are you?"

"And don't think you're off the hook either," Billie said. "If you had lifted your game and caught Bates in Sydney, I wouldn't have been put through all this shit."

"And let me remind you, Detective McCoy, we were there to watch gunrunners, not slave traders, so had you kept to your assignment, you would never have come on this little adventure."

She smiled, taking the light reprimand in a carefree manner. "Blame Jane for that."

Jane's face lit up in surprise. "What? Hey, I never asked you to jump in and rescue me. I mean, I'm very grateful you did, but that's beside the point. I didn't even know who you were so don't go dragging me into this."

"Gee, thanks for the support," Billie teased.

"Anytime," the girl said, brusque and serious. Her smile returned in a flash.

"Like I said, met your match," Mark said to Billie, smiling. She went to argue but he was quick to cut her off. "As usual, it falls back on your shoulders. You messed up big time."

"Come on, I busted a big slave racket, didn't I? That's got to be worth some compensation."

"Yeah, a little I guess. We didn't get our gun shipments but then again, you did get Bates. That throws a little weight your way, I suppose."

"Too right it does, now back off."

Mark grinned. "I can see you need a holiday."

Jane and Casey chuckled, relaxing in the company of these strangers, these law enforcers. Billie looked at them and smiled. "Now there's a thought." She exhaled a tired breath and dropped her gaze. It drifted to Sarah. She lay still, her head slumped to the side.

"Dave, Sarah's wound needs to be cleaned up. The bullet went straight through."

"Like I said, I'll take care of it. As for you, I want you to sit your butt down, okay?"

Jane stepped forward and took her by the arm. "That, I can look after." She started pulling the cop towards the truck. Casey came around the other side and helped support her. The sight of Dave and Mark had kept Billie going. Now she was slowing down, fast. Tiredness descended upon her. Grateful for the girls' help, she walked with them to the truck. They sat her in the shade against the back tyre. The two girls settled with her. Jane examined her cut and bruised face. The detective could tell from her worried expression she didn't like what she saw.

"Hey, the worst of it's over. Cheer up."

Jane's gaze snapped to Billie's. "Does Bland look this bad?"

Billie gave a faint chuckle. "I don't think so."

"Huh. I'd lay bets she does," Casey said with a respectful smile.

The detective flashed a weak smile and rested her head back, closing her eyes. It was good to relax, to step down out of the driver's seat. With Dave and Mark taking charge, she had nothing to worry about, other than conquering her injuries.

Jane started cleaning her face. As gentle as she wiped away the drying blood, Billie winced when she touched her lip.

"Sorry." Jane smiled.

"I'll go and see if Dave needs a hand." Casey squeezed Jane's shoulder and crossed to Dave and Mark where they knelt over Sarah.

"I hope Sarah will be okay," Jane said, watching her.

"I'm sure she will. Casey stopped the bleeding pretty well, and Dave will give her some shots to ease the pain."

"Good."

John and Kate joined the girls.

"Seeing you and Sarah are in good hands, we'll go and check on Riley," John said.

Billie nodded. "Good idea. Thanks."

The two turned and strolled up the track. After doing what he could for Sarah, Dave returned to Billie with the first aid kit and knelt beside her. Mark ambled up the track to assist John and Kate.

"How's Sarah?" Billie asked.

"Fine. We've strapped her up and given her a sedative. Now what about you?"

Jane had cleaned her up fairly well.

"I'm fine."

"Really." Dave wasn't convinced. He added a few butterfly clips to the cut on her forehead and wrapped a clean bandage around her ribs with a new dressing. When he saw the wound, he prompted her for an explanation. Billie gave him a brief account of the fight with Karlib, keeping it basic, not wanting to worry him any more than what he already was. It failed. He fell quiet and seemed tense while he strapped her up.

Placing a blanket beside her, he and Jane helped her lie down. Even with their help, Billie gasped while stretching out on it. She lay panting with closed eyes, trying to overcome the increasing aches. Getting on top of it, she opened her eyes to see Dave pull a syringe and bottle from his kit. He pushed the needle in through the top and turned the bottle upside down, allowing the liquid to run into the syringe as he slid the plunger back. It wasn't the first time she'd watched him prepare a sedative.

"Dave, I don't need that."

Other than a quick glance, his concentration remained fixed on the bottle and needle in his hands. Extracting the exact amount he needed, he spoke in a quiet voice without stopping his actions.

"Well, I think you do and seeing as how I'm now in charge," he paused and looked at her, "you're overruled."

"Come on, Dave, that's not fair."

Pulling free the full needle, he returned the bottle to the first aid kit. He opened a swab and wiped her arm. "Billie, you've suffered enough so quit arguing. It's a long rough trip home, one you don't need to know about."

"He's right, Billie, you need rest," Jane said.

Billie's gaze jumped to hers. "Fine, I'll rest, but I don't need – ouch!" She looked down, watching the last of the injection disappear under her skin.

Dave flashed a smile. "Sorry, babe, but it's for your own good. Just relax. I'll take care of everything."

She looked up at him. "Looks like you'll have to now."

"Sleep well." He smiled, caressing her hair.

The detective looked at Jane. "Watch him, Jane, he can get pretty bossy."

The girl smiled a little apprehensively. "I will."

Billie's eyes closed. The drug was already kicking in.

"Don't worry about anything, okay? We'll be back at Kate's in no time," Jane said.

"Sure."

"Eve will be so pleased to see us, but, hell, she'll probably go off at you. There's no hiding your injuries this time, and when she learns you've opened your stitches again – hmm, maybe this *is* a good idea. She may have calmed down by the time you wake."

"I'm–sure you'll–explain..." Her words faded. Her breathing slowed. Her head lolled to the side as the sedative took effect.

Twenty minutes later, the group was ready to leave. Bates and Bland, wrapped in blankets, lay in the back of the truck with the two secured Riley brothers.

"Right," Kate said, "I'm happy to drive us girls back in the Toyota."

The lieutenant looked at her. "Kate, there is no need for you to drive."

"Dave's right," Mark said. "It's a tiring trip and you've been through enough."

"Please, I want to. It'll help take my mind off this little episode, plus it's a good opportunity to give us girls some time alone, you know, to come to terms with what we've been through, well, me anyway. It's no big deal, honest. I drive all the time at home. Ask Pa."

Dave stared at her thoughtfully. He turned to Mark and then John. The big farmer shrugged.

"If you think you can change her mind, go for it." He smiled.

Sighing, Dave looked at Kate. "Fine, but the moment you get tired, you let us know."

She nodded. "Promise."

Mark turned the truck around and took the lead. Kate followed, lingering on the edge of their dust cloud. Jane sat beside her, Casey by the window. Billie and Sarah lay asleep on the padded seats along the walls in the back, strapped in so there was no risk of them falling off.

"I can't believe it's really over. No more Bates, no more Bland. Man, it's like . . . the world's been lifted off my shoulders," Jane stammered in amazement.

"Amen," Casey murmured. The wind from her open window ruffled her hair. The scents from the rain forest drifted pleasurably to her nose, a small treat they'd been denied on their last trip while travelling this road.

Kate glanced at them, shaking her head in awe. "I honestly don't know how you guys ever got through this horrible nightmare. The last bit was enough for me, I'll tell you," she said in a shaky breath, looking out to the road. "I've never been so scared, so terrified in all my life."

Casey stared at the truck as it swayed and bounced over the narrow road in front of them. She inwardly shuddered. The thought of how close she'd come to losing the rest of her life left a terrible taste in her mouth.

Jane sighed. "Yeah, it sure was bad. If it wasn't for Billie, I doubt if we would have made it out, and I'm talking well back down the track. I've lost count of how many times she risked her life for us. She pulled us out of some pretty tight predicaments."

"Yeah, like with Bland and Jack Riley," Kate said. "I can't begin to imagine how she did that, you know, after taking such a beating last night. She was hurt yet still managed to beat them."

"Huh, it wasn't the first time. We were lucky we didn't have to sit through it this time. Watching all the others just about killed us from the anxiety and worry, especially the one with Karlib."

"McCoy definitely has some talents we'll never come close to matching, that's for sure," Casey said. "The problem with her is she never wants to give up."

"Ain't that the truth, and I for one am very grateful for it. If she'd turned up a second later when Bates had that gun on me, I'd be history now," Jane said in a strained voice. "Yes, that bullet definitely had my name on it. We pushed him a little too hard." She stared at the truck ahead with Bates' lifeless body in it. "He really was pissed off. I'll never forget that look in his eyes, not until the day I die. Billie couldn't have timed it better if she'd tried. The fact she even turned up is a big thing on its own. Man, I owe her so much."

Casey sat stunned, studying her solemn face, letting the words sink in. Bates had given Jane a big scare, one she found hard to deal with, which was understandable. Hell, *she'd* been scared, and she hadn't been in the line of fire. What Jane said had some truth in it, a lot of truth in fact. Bates *had* lost it. Would he have aimed to kill Sarah rather than wound her had his vision been clearer? It was hard to say. She was grateful the decision hadn't been offered. The scary part was Bates might not have stopped at just killing Jane. It could have been disastrous for all of them.

As if reading her mind, Jane met her gaze. In eerie silence, they held each other's stares, comforting one another while locked in their reminiscent gazes. Casey faced the front, numb. Slowly, she nodded.

"You know, you're pretty much right. We all owe her so much." She exhaled a heavy sigh. Her stomach knotted. She felt crushed, weighed down by a sudden guilt. "I am such a jerk. I was only thinking of myself last night, and today. I couldn't even help her. Let 'em down Casey, that's me."

Jane rested a hand on her arm. "Come on, don't be so hard on yourself. It was a frightening time . . . times," she added as an afterthought. "The thing is, Billie wasn't put off by it."

"That's no excuse. I still let her down."

"Casey, it's all behind you so cheer up," Kate said. "And it's definitely something to be cheery about, don't you think? It's all over, finished for good. Bates and Bland are dead, and you are going home."

The girls looked at her, staring. As good as it sounded, Casey failed to shake the guilt needling her. Kate chuckled, ignoring their glum faces.

"Cheery, remember?"

Jane slowly smiled and looked at Casey, encouraging her to do the same. Relaxing, Casey smiled with her. Kate was right, it was time to move on.

"Okay, I'm cheery," she said with little confidence.

"Good." Kate didn't push it. She focused on driving. A silence fell upon them, leaving each to withdraw into their own thoughts. After a while, Kate broke it.

"So, tell me, do you think you guys will stay friends after you get home?"

Both girls looked at her, surprised by the unexpected question. Casey considered it. She hadn't thought that far ahead, at least not about whether they'd remain friends.

"I don't know," Jane said, somewhat hesitantly. She looked at Casey. "I'd like to think so," she added with a touch of hope.

Casey shrugged. "We sure lead different lifestyles." It was one thing to assume they would, and to hope they would – it was totally a different matter once they arrived home and were immersed into the reality of it all. She looked over her shoulder at the two sleeping forms in the back and sighed. "Maybe it'll be too hard. How can we stay friends with a cop?" she asked, facing Jane and Kate again. "For a start, three of us are on the wrong side of the law."

Kate shook her head but maintained a positive look on her face. "No, you were. Now you're not. You've done your time for what you did wrong. You all told me you'd been recently released from jail, which means you are no longer charged, correct?"

Jane glanced at Casey, who shrugged. "Maybe," she said to Kate.

Kate continued. "And are you forgetting you've helped the cops bring these criminals to justice? You've helped Billie all along the way, right? That means you've helped the law all the way, does it not?" Before either girl could comment or argue, Kate kept on. "Besides, with the bonds you four have formed, it may be easier than you think."

"Oh, an expert on this subject, are we?" Casey teased with a smile. Kate's answer was so encouraging her heart skipped a beat. She couldn't think of anything better than to see the four of them remain friends. But, refusing to get her hopes up, she chose to cover her true feelings. "Do you read the future as well?"

Kate gave a laugh. "Hey, it's not that hard to see, especially from someone on the outside looking in," she said, glancing at Jane and Casey. "You four belong together, believe me."

"How can you say that?" Casey asked. "You saw the way we fight and argue with each other, especially with McCoy. Shit, we didn't even have the guts to back her when she needed us the most."

"But you did in the end. And you've been there for her on other occasions, haven't you?"

"Yes, but—"

"She cares a lot for you guys, I can see that so plainly."

"But all we do is jump on her."

"That's just part of the raw material. You guys have a bond that will hold you and keep you together. You may not be able to see it yet, but, to me, it's so obvious." She flashed them a reassuring smile before returning her attention to the track. "Billie frightens you a little because she's always there for you, always sticking up for you and always looking out for you. This is something new and that's why it scares you. All of you are used to looking after yourselves, being alone and never having anyone watching over you. Am I right?" Giving them no chance to answer, she continued. "Whether you like it or not, you've got yourselves a cop for a friend, and I mean a good one."

When neither Jane nor Casey commented, Kate glanced at them. Casey caught her gaze, overcome by the same tantalising sense of hope as before. It danced in front of her like a carrot on a stick. She badly wanted to believe Kate, but it seemed way beyond her hopes, and control. The farm girl had opened a can of worms, sending her mind into chaos. She couldn't think of anything better than to continue their friendships, especially with McCoy. She'd changed their world, their attitudes to themselves and others, and their whole outlook on life. They owed her so much. So used to being with her now, even under such grim circumstances, life would be empty without her in it.

Kate smiled. "I know I'm right. You four have come through some dangerous times, which, mixed together, are solid ingredients for a true and everlasting friendship."

Jane turned to Casey. "Think Dave will take her up in the truck?"

Casey laughed. Her gaze drifted from Jane to Kate. "I hope so. I've heard enough of her psychological lectures for one day, that's for sure."

Kate grinned. She turned to the front. "Fine. You don't want to believe me; that's okay but I know I'm right, and you'll come to realise it, mark my words."

"Just drive," Jane said with a smile.

Chapter Twenty-Six

It was dark when the travellers arrived at the Cauldron farm. Eve raced down the stairs to the Toyota as Kate pulled up. Dragging her daughter out, she hugged her tight. The tears flowed uncontrollably. Kate sobbed with her, assuring her mother she was all right.

Mary, Julie, and the two boys were close behind Eve. The two sisters threw their arms around Kate and their mother. Tom squeezed in underneath them.

Janda jumped into Casey and Jane's arms and hugged them tight. "Thank goodness you're okay. I've been so worried," he cried.

"We're fine," Jane said.

"Yeah. We're just so glad you didn't get hauled off with us."

Eve stood back, looking at Kate, touching her face. And then she broke into a rain of sobs and hugged her again.

"Mum, I'm fine, honest."

"I know, but I can't help it. I've been so sick with worry." Taking her daughter's arm in hers, she led her around the front of the Toyota to Casey and Jane standing with a smiling Janda between them. Slipping from her daughter's arms, she hugged each of them. When she stood back, her eyes were watery, her tears on the verge of spilling over. "It is so good to have you home."

Casey smiled. "It's good to be back, I'll tell you."

Eve looked at her, her affection visible in her eyes. "Promise me you'll never do that again."

"That's a definite promise, believe me."

Eve smiled. "Good."

John, Dave, and Mark strolled towards them from the truck parked by the yards. Eve glanced at them. Frowning, she turned to the girls.

"Where are Billie and Sarah? Are they all right?" she asked anxiously. "They are here, aren't they? I mean, they haven't—"

"They're fine. Or they will be," Casey said. "Sarah was shot through the shoulder, and Billie's beat up pretty bad. She and Bland locked horns again."

"Again? Oh, no." Anguish weighted her tone. "Where are they? Let me see."

"Eve, they're fine. Dave looked after them. He was great. I think he should've been a doctor."

"I'd still like to see them. You can't tell me it hasn't been a long drive. That alone would wear them out."

"It would have only Dave put them under with a sedative so they'd miss the rough trip." She turned to Jane with a playful look. "We should have done the same."

Jane smiled. "Now you think of it."

"And miss my wonderful talks?" Kate jumped in with, eyeing them with raised eyebrows. They looked at her blankly, thinking.

"Okay, I guess she has a point," Jane stammered. "I mean, some of her talks made sense, I think."

"You know they did," Kate said with a smile. "And don't deny it."

The guys joined them, breaking the conversation. Eve stepped forward and fell into John's arms, overcome with emotion.

"You did it. Thank you."

John hugged her. "Didn't I tell you I'd bring them home?"

"I can't believe it." After a moment, and without leaving her husband's arms, Eve half turned and looked at Dave and Mark with regained composure. "Thank you. Thank you for bringing Kate back to me."

"It was a pleasure but, to tell you the truth, they were all ready to come home on their own before we found them."

"What?"

"Yeah, Dave's right," John said. "Billie managed to get the jump on Bates and his crew. The girls had everything under control before we got there. All we did was patch them up and bring them back."

"Billie did? But..." She looked at Casey. "I thought you said she'd had another clash with Bland and was beaten up?"

"I did. Don't get me wrong, she is pretty beat up but this time she flattened her – fatally."

Eve's face trembled. "Fatally? Bland is dead?"

"I've never seen her looking better," John muttered.

Eve looked into his eyes and stared hard, unable to answer.

"We'd better get the girls in," Dave said as a distraction. "They'll need some attention. I gave them both a second sedative not too long ago."

Eve snapped out of her stupor and pulled out of John's grasp. "Yes, of course."

John looked at her. "Tell you what. You do what you can for them. I'll race and get the doctor."

Eve nodded. "Go, I'll be fine."

As John hurried to the Ute, Dave and Mark climbed into the back of the Troopy. They emerged with Billie and Sarah in their arms. The men carried them into the house. Jane and Casey stayed by their sides. Once settled, Mark drove the prisoners into town after arranging with the Cairns police to pick them up.

Within the hour, John and the doctor arrived. An elderly man, his wavy grey hair was brushed back over the top of his head and held in place with thick gel. Thin-rimmed spectacles balanced on a crooked nose. The white collared shirt beneath his grey suit coat hung half out of the baggy trousers, relying on a few buttons to hold it together. He carried a battered and bulging briefcase. It looked in no better condition than its owner.

Casey gave him a curious look in passing. The only thing that settled her uneasiness regarding his dishevelled appearance was John and Eve's trust in him.

"If you could all wait in the other room, that would be good," the doctor said.

Hesitantly, everyone filed out of the bedroom. Only Eve remained to assist him.

The group settled in the lounge room. John sent Mary, Julie, and the two boys off to bed. Casey found conversation easy with Dave. The well-mannered law enforcer didn't pry into hers or Jane and Sarah's backgrounds, or ask why they'd been in prison. Dave explained how the case of the missing girls had been going on for years and that they should be proud to have been part of cleaning it up. No one had ever come close.

"Huh, we didn't do that much. Billie was the instigator behind it all. She was the one who pulled it off," Jane pointed out.

"Yeah. I'm sure we hindered her more than we helped," Casey added.

"Really? Well, I'm sure when I ask her, she'll tell me differently," Dave said, his quiet tone laced with reverence.

The girls stared, meeting the low-key challenge.

Casey smiled. "She's a good liar."

The lieutenant chuckled. He turned to the farm girl. "What do you think, Kate? You were there for the last part."

Surprised, Kate's gaze darted from him to her friends before looking back at the lieutenant. "Huh, as far as I'm concerned, they're heroes in my eyes – all of them." She smiled and looked at the two girls.

Casey's bottom lip dropped. Her eyes widened. She glanced at Jane. The girl sat frozen. She turned to Casey, shaking her head in awe.

Dave nodded. "I rest my case." He slumped back in the chair.

"Kate, you don't know what you're saying," Casey stammered.

"The hell I don't. The lieutenant's right. You guys should be proud of yourselves."

Casey turned to Jane. "I don't believe this."

"I don't either. Are they blind?"

Dave smiled and winked at Kate.

John laughed. Sitting forward, he slapped a hand on his lap. "So, who's for coffee?"

Casey appreciated his subtle move to change the subject. She nodded. "Sounds good."

"Make mine a double," Jane said, curling her legs up under her and resting her head on the chair.

"Done." He looked at Dave and Kate. Both nodded.

"Just black for me," Dave said.

"Milk and one sugar for me," Casey added.

"Milk and no sugar," Jane said.

"Right." Climbing to his feet, John ambled into the kitchen quietly repeating everyone's order.

They'd almost finished their coffees when Eve and the doctor emerged from the bedroom. Everyone jumped to their feet.

"Well," the doctor started, answering their unasked questions, "Billie needs complete rest. The wound on her ribs is a little infected and will have to be cleaned regularly. Her face should heal without scarring. Her other hurts are superficial. She'll be stiff and sore for a while, but rest is important."

"She's taken a lot on," Jane quietly said.

"Yes. Sarah will also need rest for a few days. I've had to do a little bit of operating and stitching but there's no serious or permanent damage to her shoulder and it should heal nicely. Eve knows how to clean and dress it without me so I will leave Sarah and Billie in her capable hands. I've given them another sedative to give them a good night's sleep."

"That sure is good to hear." Casey sighed, casting a quick relieved smile at Jane, who nodded.

"Definitely."

"What about you two?" the doctor asked, scrutinising Jane and Casey's faces. "I think I should look you both over."

"We're fine, really. Now that it's over, I'm sure we'll heal a lot faster," Jane said after shooting a glance at Casey. She nodded.

The doctor stepped closer and examined Jane's marked face. "Hmm. Very well. I've left some cream with Eve that will help heal those cuts and soften those bruises. I suggest you two catch up on some sleep, too. You look bushed."

Casey gave him a confident smile. "Oh, don't worry, we intend to."

"Good."

John stepped forward. "Come on, Doc, I'll drive you home. I'll bring Mark back," he said to the lieutenant.

"No, you won't. I'll take him," Dave said. "You need to rest that shoulder."

"Honest, Lieutenant, I'm fine."

Dave glanced at the doctor, who shrugged. The lieutenant turned to John.

"Are you up to it? You've already had a long trip."

John nodded. "The Doc plugged me up pretty good. Besides, I'm too hyped up to sleep."

"How about I come with you then."

"Fine. Suit yourself."

Dave looked at the girls. "Have a good rest, guys. You'll feel better in the morning."

"Thanks again for coming to get us today," Casey said, flashing a smile.

"Forget it. I should be thanking you. You did a great job."

Eve turned to Casey and Jane after the men departed. "Right, you two, now's as good a time as any to start following doctor's orders. I think you deserve a good night's sleep. Your beds are waiting."

"To tell you the truth, I can't think of a better place I'd rather be," Casey said with a tired sigh.

The weary travellers followed Eve and Kate into Kate's bedroom. A single bed sat beside an old bedside table. It had been pushed up against the wall to make room for the two stretcher beds beside it. Casey recognised them from the room Sarah and Billie were in. Originally, the four girls had shared the same room during their stay over the previous few nights, but now the girls needed privacy to recuperate.

Jane sank onto the edge of the stretcher against the wall. Eve and Kate sat on the single bed. Casey threw herself on the middle stretcher with a grateful sigh and stretched.

"I can't believe you're all back safe and sound," Eve said, slipping an arm around Kate and hugging her. She followed it with a kiss to her cheek.

Kate glanced at her with a quick smile, and then it faded. She squeezed her mother's hand in hers. "It sure is good to be home. It was terrible, Mum. I was so scared."

"Hey, don't take all the credit, we all were," Casey said with a comforting smile.

Kate gazed at her and nodded. "I think the worst part was when we heard that shot, after Bland had taken Billie into the bushes. I thought they'd shot her. I really thought they'd killed her. I was so terrified."

"Yeah," Jane said with an empty tone. "You weren't alone there."

Casey met Kate's eye. "Just because we didn't show it, believe me, we all thought she was gone." She propped herself on an elbow. "It sure must've been some fight." She shook her head and dropped her gaze to the floor trying to imagine it. A brief silence fell upon the room. Casey looked up and over her shoulder at Jane. "You know, Billie was planning an escape when you two were with Bland. As usual, all Sarah and I did was knock her for it, telling her how crazy she was. Hell, she was beat up and had no help from us, yet she was prepared to take on Bland and Bates." Letting out a long, disheartened breath, she fell back on the bed and stared up at the ceiling. "All we ever do is put her down. I don't know why she doesn't tell us to go to hell. It's not as if we don't deserve it." The guilt was setting in yet again. When Billie had needed them, they'd failed to support her.

Jane shook her head. "You were scared. We all were. I think Billie is more used to these sorts of things. She works with danger in her job, remember? She's around it all the time, which probably helps her tackle it with a clearer mind. For us, it's like a mountain crashing down around us."

Casey appreciated her words of comfort. They did make some sense. She nodded even though her spirits failed to rise.

"Anyway, *I* feel worse. I owe her my life. How do I thank her for that?" Jane asked.

"Come on, guys, cheer up," Kate put in. "Remember what I said in the Toyota?"

They looked at her. Casey couldn't shake her doubt.

"I don't know. I think this time we've hurt her too much. We've let her down once too often. Why would she want to stay our friend?"

"She wouldn't have done what she did if she didn't care," Eve said.

"Maybe," Casey mumbled, glancing at her. "The thing is, no one has ever stuck their neck out for me to this extent. No one. It just seems so, I don't know, strange. I feel so . . . so grateful I guess, yet, lost as to how to thank her properly."

Jane shot her a look, her eyebrows raised in surprise. "You, too? I can't ever remember meeting anyone like her."

"Listen," Eve cut in. "You're all tired. Right now, it's too overwhelming. The shock of being captured and then freed, this time for good, has knocked you around. You've had a frightening experience. Just the bit I saw was frightening enough. It'll be different in the morning after a good night's sleep, so how about you take a shower and turn in."

Jane went to stand. "First, I'd like to check—"

Eve beat her to her feet and put out a hand to stop her rising any further. "*I* will look after Billie and Sarah. *You*, shower and then bed," she ordered in a stern tone. Jane sank down on the bed.

"Okay, I guess you're right."

"Of course, I'm right. Just ask Kate."

Casey smiled with Jane. She glanced at the nodding Kate. Jane gave a laugh when she answered.

"Believe me, she's *always* right. Even when she's wrong, no one's ever game enough to tell her."

Chapter Twenty-Seven

Billie woke slowly. The morning sun shone in through the open window, throwing a soft light across her bed. She recognised the room as Julie and Mary's, where they'd slept the last few nights. The room looked bigger without the two stretchers. Across in the other bed, Sarah slept peacefully. Her shoulder was bandaged, supported with her arm in a sling. An IV was secured into her wrist, held up with a make-do stand beside the bedhead. Billie lay watching her, thinking, running things through her mind to clarify everything had ended happily, that it was over with Bates and she hadn't just dreamt it. A contentedness gripped her. It was such a pleasurable feeling knowing they'd beaten him, and Bland.

Satisfied it wasn't a dream, she rolled from her side onto her back. Suddenly, her happy thoughts washed from her mind. Even though she'd moved slowly, she couldn't hold in a moan. She seemed to have seized up altogether. Every movement brought a sharp pain to her battered body. It screamed in protest. The gentle roll started her ribs throbbing. Merciless aches and pains invaded her from her head to her toes. Her bruised cheeks ached, along with her cut lip and swollen nose. She closed her eyes. Another moan slipped through her lips.

"Hey, you okay?" Sarah asked.

Billie was surprised to hear her voice. She glanced at her and then closed her eyes. Lifting her hand, she gave her the thumbs-up signal.

"I'll call Eve," Sarah said. "Maybe she can give you something for the—"

"No, I'm fine," Billie assured her.

"The hell you are." Concern laced her tone.

Billie rolled her head and looked over at her. "Honest, us cops are made of steel, remember?"

Sarah stared hard. She offered a half smile. "Oh, yeah, how could I forget."

Billie smiled. "So, how are you doing?"

Sarah shrugged and glanced at her bandaged shoulder. "A lot better than you, by the looks."

"Don't you believe it." She looked away and closed her eyes.

"I hate to be the one to tell you, but Bland made a good punching bag out of you."

The comment brought another smile to Billie's lips. The cop rolled her head towards her and met her eye, knowing there was no disrespect in the comment. "Would you like to tell me something I don't know?"

Sarah gave a short laugh and turned away. She gazed up at the ceiling. "Well, now that you mention it, I would." She looked the detective in the eye. "I know I said it before, but I owe you an apology as big as a mountain." Billie went to say something, but Sarah lifted a hand and silenced her. "Hear me out, okay? I want you to know how sorry I am for coming down on you in the truck. Not only the punching part but the whole crazy madness side of me you never want to see again, right? I really didn't mean it. I guess you're the closest thing I have for letting off steam, if that makes any sense."

Billie studied her remorseful expression. "Yeah, it does. Look, forget it, okay? Like I said, it was a tight situation, enough to send anyone over the edge."

"I can't forget it. I *won't* forget it. I know I have trouble showing it, but I really do appreciate all you've done for me. Right from the beginning you've been a strong leader, a great role model, only we were too blind to see it, at first. You've been a tower of strength to us, to me. I know I took a long time to accept it, and probably longer to tell you, but, without your perseverance and endurance, or your patience towards me, I know for a fact I wouldn't be here now." Locked on Billie's fixed gaze, she fell silent, allowing the words time to settle. "I'd like to apologise for being such a bitch, and I want to thank you for everything you've done." Another pause. "I just wanted to let you know, that's all." She turned away.

Billie, surprised and a little lost for words, felt privileged. She respected Sarah's sincerity and honesty. Watching her a moment longer, she regained control of her emotions and found an answer.

"You know, with all that built-up steam in your system, you could have taken Bland out and saved me the trouble."

Sarah snorted. "Huh, I doubt that very much. Besides, you did such a fine job I'd hate to see you lose your credibility."

"You're so kind."

"Aren't I."

A small hush engulfed them.

"Sarah?" Billie said on a more serious note. She held no grudges and gladly accepted Sarah's apology. "Thanks for opening up to me. You've just made it all worthwhile."

Sarah looked at her. She nodded and smiled. "Yeah, it feels good, I have to admit." Breaking from the cop's gaze, she looked over the room. "So, how did we get back here? The last thing I remember is lying in the dirt with my shoulder throbbing. Did the guys drive us back in the truck?"

Billie smiled. "Not quite. Would you believe Dave, John and Mark, my partner, arrived just after you passed out."

"They did?"

"Dave and Mark turned up here about an hour after Bates grabbed us. John guided them in a general direction where he thought we might have gone, going off what we'd told him about our trip."

Sarah's eyes widened. "Shit. They were lucky to find us."

"Tell me about it."

Eve poked her head around the door. Her face lit up in surprise. "Will you look at you two? And here I was thinking you were resting." She walked in beaming. Her gaze shifted from one to the other.

"We *are* resting," Billie said with a weak smile.

"Yes, I can see that." Stepping to the cop, she looked at her with a perturbed expression while studying her bruised face.

Billie remained silent, confused about what was on Eve's mind. When Eve finally elaborated, it wasn't what she expected.

"So, I hear you've been out fighting with Bland."

"Where on earth did you hear that?"

"Oh, I have my contacts." Her voice broke. Tears flooded her eyes. "Oh, Billie..."

Billie reached out and squeezed her hand. "I'm fine, Eve, stop worrying."

"Stop worrying? You forget I had to watch everything in the shed that night – *everything*. With that picture etched in my mind, I'll never stop worrying."

The detective nodded. "I know. It wasn't fair. You shouldn't have been put through it."

"Excuse me, but I'm well aware of that. The point is, neither should you have been. And now that I know it happened again..." She shook her head, squeezing Billie's hand tighter. "Thank you."

"For what?"

"For bringing my girl back to me. Thank you very much."

Billie gazed at her with compassion and nodded. "You're welcome."

Eve wiped a tear away and exhaled a shaky breath. She cast a watery look over at Sarah. Sarah returned her gaze with an encouraging smile.

"Anyway," Eve said to Billie, "now that you're awake, I may as well check you over."

"May as well." Billie smiled, happy to take her mind off the lingering nightmare. "I don't suppose you'd have anything to eat?"

A laugh slipped through Eve's lips. "Eat? Well, I guess I could whip something up for you." She winked and turned to Sarah. "How about you, young lady? Are you hungry?"

"Maybe. I'm not a guts like some of us," she said, shooting a mischievous look at Billie.

The detective smiled.

Eve looked affectionately at her. "If you can hold on for a few minutes, I'll check your stitches first."

"Sure, I guess I can hang out a little longer."

"Good."

After assessing and dressing their wounds over a casual conversation, Eve fetched them a light breakfast. Dave and Mark called in to see how they were. Sarah looked them over with interest, more so Mark. Billie realised it was the first time she'd had a chance to be introduced. The officers stepped forward and shook her hand on Billie's introductions.

"Thanks for coming to get me out, and the girls," Sarah quickly added. "The fact you're here assures me this nightmare is definitely over."

Dave nodded. "That it is. You can rest easy and concentrate on getting better."

"That won't be a problem, believe me."

"Good."

Mark smiled. "It's nice to actually meet you, in person I mean. All we've had is your photograph and folio. It's been like chasing ghosts."

"So, you've been stalking me then," she teased.

He chuckled. "Yeah, I guess I have. Can't say I've ever stalked so many women before, and all at once."

"Hmm, you have nothing on Bates, that's for sure, so this time I'll let you off."

"Glad to hear it. Unfortunately, it didn't really get me anywhere, other than running around in circles."

"Let it be a lesson to you," Billie put in, catching his attention. "Too many women bring too many problems."

He smiled and walked over. "Only if they're all like you."

"Good."

Dave joined them and pulled a rolled paper from under his arm and unfurled it. Sitting down either side of Billie on the bed, he and Mark held it up in front of her. She easily recognised it, or at least some of it. It was a detailed map of northern Queensland. Dotted lines indicated tracks weaving in and out of the almost uncharted area. She could see how they'd gotten lost in their run for freedom. Only an experienced navigator could follow it. Many places had warnings written in small red print – "Track overgrown" or "Impassable in wet conditions", "Extreme care needed". Bates certainly had known where he was going, but then again, he'd used it enough times.

Billie studied the map closely, tracing back over the area they'd travelled. Even on paper, it looked confusing. Using the few landmarks and towns they'd visited, she guessed at which way they'd come. She pointed out the tracks on the western side's coastline. A couple of times she paused at crossroads, needing to consider which way they'd taken. Finally, she stopped at the end of a dotted track halfway up the large peninsula.

"I'm pretty sure Bates' camp would have to be around here somewhere."

Dave nodded. "That's great, babe, you've been a big help."

"What are you up to?" she asked, watching him roll up the map. Gut instinct guided her in a rough guess.

"I intend to bust this operation once and for all. I've got help on the way. They should be here by mid-afternoon. We plan to hit this place before they know anything about it."

Even without his strained tone, the determination was apparent on his face.

"Dave, I can help if—"

"No, Billie, you've helped enough. You need rest, and John has already agreed to you staying here as long as you need to. Besides, we have to move fast on this before they disappear. Maybe we're already too late, but I'd like to make sure. After we finish up there, we'll come back for you guys, okay?"

She glanced at Mark.

He reached out and stroked her hair. "Dave's right. You've done your bit. You need rest. Don't knock it."

"I knew I could count on you."

"Always."

She nodded a hesitant nod. As much as she hated to admit it, she was in no condition to go with them. "Fine. Just make sure you get them," she said to Dave.

"Oh, we will, believe me. Don't panic if we're away for a few days. I want this set up properly. If anyone's still there, they won't know what's hit them." Leaning down, he kissed her on the forehead. "Just take it easy and enjoy the break. We'll see you soon."

Mark squeezed her hand. He looked over at Sarah. "Keep a close eye on her, Sarah. She's likely to try anything."

"Huh, don't I know it." She smiled.

Mark glanced at Billie. "Take it easy."

The two officers left.

Sarah sighed. "I hope they catch every last one of them."

"Don't worry. If they're there, Dave won't let anyone go. You can count on it."

Chapter Twenty-Eight

A few days passed. Sarah and Billie recovered quite quickly. They'd spent the first couple of days in bed being spoiled and waited on. After that, Eve just about had to strap Billie to the bed to keep her there. Now both were back on their feet, growing stronger with each passing hour. Their stints out of the bedroom gradually grew longer.

Sarah relaxed on the verandah in a chair with Jane and Casey, her arm hanging comfortably in a sling. Happy to be up, she still tired easily after a couple of hours. The chair she'd laid claim to had become her second bed.

Jane glanced at the two girls. "So, what happens when you guys get back home?"

"I guess we'll have to chase up our old jobs," Sarah said, exhaling a disheartened sigh. "I'm sure Rose will have us back." For some reason she didn't feel all that enthusiastic about returning to her job. Having been away from that lifestyle for the past few weeks, particularly under such threatening circumstances, had changed her outlook on life, and her occupation. She'd been on the game for so long without a break, other than when she was in jail, she'd simply accepted it for what it was. Now, something had changed. Something was missing. The enjoyment of giving herself to men was gone. The incentive was gone. Terrific. Without that job, she had no other. So where did that leave her? Hopefully, she'd get over this, once she was in Sydney and busy again.

"So, you'll go back to her?"

Sarah shrugged and turned from Jane. She stared pensively out at the horses in the stockyard to hide her feelings. "That's all we know. What else can we do?" The dispirited answer lacked confidence. As happy as she was about the whole situation coming to an end, there was a sad element accompanying it – their friendship with the cop could also be coming to an end and that thought left a void in her heart.

"My only other option is to go back to stealing cars," Casey said with a faint smile.

"What? You wouldn't, would you?"

Casey chuckled. "Naw, probably not. Looks like Rose it is."

"Shit, don't tell Billie that," Jane said.

"Come on, she'll either accept us the way we are or not at all," Sarah said. "There's no point in hiding anything from one another now."

Jane looked sharply at her and then nodded. "Yes, I know that. I'm sorry." She looked out to the horses. "Hell, it's all so different now, now that we're getting back into the real world again. Huh, I have no job to go to, or a place to call home, other than that dive of a room Bates found me in. I'm not even sure if it's still mine. The sleazy owner has probably rented it out to someone else, even though I paid two weeks in advance, which would be up by now. Can't say I'm looking forward to going back to that."

Sarah glanced at her. Her heart went out to her. "Yeah, I hear you. It won't be easy, that's for sure." Deep down, she knew they'd always be the way they were, the way they'd always been. How could they change now, after so long? None of them knew anything else, and no one would give them a job with so many convictions against them anyway. Their futures were on a one-way road, obviously the wrong one, and, unfortunately, one they couldn't get off.

Billie and Kate stepped out from the house and strolled towards the girls along the verandah. Billie moved a little stiffly. Her black eye was slowly fading. Most of the swelling on her face had subsided and her cuts were healing well. She seemed little affected by it. She looked over the three lounging girls under a casual gaze.

"Great life some people have," she teased, sinking down in a chair beside Jane.

"Careful, McCoy, you are in no position to give us cheek," Casey said with a mock scowl.

Sarah smiled. "That's right. I think we could handle you quite easily at the moment."

Billie's head shot up. She looked from one to the other, caught out by their quick returns. She raised her hands in surrender. "Hey. Okay. I'm sorry I spoke." She flashed a smile. Casey nodded.

"Good, keep it that way."

"That's what I like." Sarah smiled at Casey and Jane. "Control over cops."

Billie looked at her, meeting her eye with a challenging but merry look. Shaking her head, the cop gave a laugh. Now was a good time to back off. To come into it with these three banded together would only attract more retorts. She rested her head against the chair. Blowing out a contented sigh, she watched Kate take a seat on the top step. The farm girl leant against the post facing her guests.

"Oh, and while we're on the subject," Sarah went on, "Don't forget you owe us a drink."

Billie looked at her with a surprised look. "What subject? What drink?"

"You know very well what drink I'm talking about."

"Come on, Sarah," Casey said. "Bland did give her a hiding. Maybe she knocked some sense *out* of her."

Billie turned to her ready to argue her defence – only Sarah beat her to it.

"True, but maybe another bashing now might jog her memory" She eyed the cop with a mischievous look.

Jane gave a short laugh. Kate giggled from her front row seat.

Billie glanced at the girls. They had her outnumbered and they knew it. Fine. They could have their fun – this time.

"What's it going to be, McCoy? You want another beating?" Sarah asked with a twisted grin.

Billie met her gaze. "Huh. You guys are so funny, aren't you." She smiled.

"Yes," Casey exclaimed, shooting a fist in the air. "That's twice in two minutes we've made her back down."

All eyes turned her way. Delight lit up Casey's face as she bathed in the rare victory.

"Yeah, you're right." Sarah turned to the detective with a wide grin. "Not so tough after all, McCoy?"

"Hey, come on, give me a break," Billie yelped, turning from one to the other, meeting their impish looks. Her gaze rested on the smiling Kate, imploring help from her. "Kate, back me up here."

"Why?"

"'Why?' she asks?" Billie said in astonishment. "Huh, trust me to think I could count on you. Thanks a lot."

The girls broke into warm laughter.

"Ha! Looks like you're on your own," Sarah said.

"So what else is new?"

Her reply drew more laughs.

Finally, Kate took the heat off her. "Okay, Billie, I'll give you a break." She looked at the other three. "Who wants to come horse riding?"

Immediately, all laughter died. The girls stared with set gazes, a little horrified by the question.

"Horse riding?" Jane said with uncertainty. "I don't know how to ride. I mean, I've never had a go before."

"Me neither," Casey added.

Kate looked from one to the other, her eyes wide in surprise. "Well, there's a first time for everything. Come on, I'll teach you." She jumped to her feet.

Jane looked at Casey and shrugged. "Why not?"

Casey hesitantly nodded and stood with Jane. She took a step towards Kate and stopped. Turning, she looked at Billie and Sarah. They sat watching, making no effort to follow.

"You guys don't mind, do you?"

Billie glanced at Sarah. Her dumbstruck expression said it all. Even if they'd been up to it, she doubted very much this city girl would have taken up Kate's offer anyway.

The detective smiled at Casey. "Go for it. We'll watch."

"Yeah, I've never been that keen on horses," Sarah said.

"Too bad. You'll be missing out on all the fun," Jane said, her eyes sparkling with excitement.

"Gladly." Sarah smiled and sank deeper into the chair, blowing out a relieved sigh.

Jane turned to Casey. "What party poopers. Just because they have a few little hurts, they use it as an excuse to sit on their arses all day."

"Oh, tell me about it," Casey said, starting down the stairs with her. "We have to nursemaid them all the time, at least *they* think we do. Get me this, get me that."

Her voice faded out of earshot as they walked away. They climbed through the rails into the yards. Kate had already caught one horse. Billie and Sarah watched Kate bridle two more and start to saddle them up. Jane and Casey stayed close, listening to her advice while patting the horses.

Giving a light scoff, accompanied by a shake of her head, Sarah slowly shuffled forward to the edge of her chair. "Damn. Now that all the hired help has gone, I'll have to get up and get my own drink. You think they would've had the decency to ask us if we were comfortable first before they left us high and dry here."

Billie turned to her with a smile playing on her lips. "It sure is inconsiderate of them."

"My sentiments exactly." Blowing out a heavy sigh, she struggled to her feet. "So, now that I'm up, would you like a drink?"

"Love one."

Sarah returned her smile accompanied with a curt nod. Billie looked out to the yard. The horses were saddled. Kate led one each to Jane and Casey. Looking nervous, they listened to what Kate was telling them.

"I'll keep an eye on our cowgirls. They're likely to break their necks."

The smile dropped from Sarah's face. She stared out at the yards, a look of concern tensing her features.

"Hell, I hadn't thought of that. What if they can't handle the horses? They might be too wild. You can never anticipate what a horse is going to do. They could bolt or..."

Billie couldn't hold in the short laugh.

Sarah looked at her in surprise and then relaxed. The smile sheepishly returned to her lips. "Cute, McCoy. You're full of jokes. I should make you get your own drink."

She turned and walked off before the cop could come up with any more smart remarks. Billie chuckled and sat back, relaxing. Now that the dangers had passed, the girls were much more at ease. She liked them a lot and knew the feeling was mutual.

The three cowgirls mounted their horses. After taking up the reins and listening to a final piece of advice from Kate, they were ready to leave. Jane and Casey steered their horses somewhat uncertainly out the gate. They sat rigid in the saddle, gripping the pommel and reins with both hands as if their life depended on it.

Kate, whom they'd invested their faith in, led them out sitting relaxed and confident. She turned in her saddle with a huge grin on her face at the sight of her two tense trainees. Turning back, she guided her new recruits out into the paddock away from the house.

Jane bravely lifted a hand from the saddle and gave Billie a quick wave. The detective smiled and returned it. Casey only offered her a grin. She was too busy hanging on to lift a hand. Again, Billie chuckled. She shook her head, watching them ride off. It sure was a sight to see.

The cop rested her head back and closed her eyes. In a sense of total relaxation, time meant nothing. If she fell asleep before Sarah returned with the drinks, it didn't matter. Nothing mattered at the moment. This was a time of rest and recovery, a well-deserved break.

A crash in the kitchen brought her out of the doze with a start. Her head shot up. Glass breaking? It sounded as if Sarah had dropped the drinks. Guessing she might need a hand to carry them, or probably to clean them up, the detective climbed to her feet. Strolling through the living room, she pushed the kitchen door open and stepped into the room.

"You know, you only have to call if..." She stopped dead. Her senses jumped to full alert as she fought to take control of the shock stifling her. Chet Riley, the third brother she'd tangled with in the street saving Kate, had Sarah pushed up hard against the cupboard holding a short wide-bladed knife to her throat. He sneered at the detective. A cold vindictive look of hate filled his eyes, daring her to provoke him.

Sarah's apologetic gaze was also on her, peering over the hand clamped across her mouth. Billie heard the door click shut behind her. She looked over her shoulder. Two brothers stood in front of it – Paul and Geoff. They'd been with Bates the night of their kidnapping. These two had eluded the police and gone into hiding, until now. Great. Both leered at her hungrily, like a pack of wolves with a cornered deer.

"You try anything smart and you can say goodbye to your friend here." Chet pushed the knife harder against Sarah's neck. She gasped and lifted her head to avoid the point.

Billie forced herself to stay calm. Beneath her nonchalance, she tensed ready to spring into action. "Take it easy, I'm not trying anything, okay? What's your problem? What do you want?"

He snorted a wry laugh and nodded. "What's my problem?" His voice sounded almost hysterical. "I'll tell you what my problem is. *You're* my problem, that's what. You'll pay for what you did to Tony and Jack, believe me. You've ruined everything."

Billie studied him. These boys were obviously a close-knit family, but was their visit fanned by an act of brotherly love or merely an excuse for revenge, to pay her back for the other day in the street? Either way, they were stirred up about it.

"They shouldn't have sided with Bates. They knew the risks and they broke the law, just like your brothers here."

"Shut up," he snapped.

Sarah gasped.

Billie lifted her hands. "Okay. Just take it easy with her, all right?"

"Shut *up*, I said." His tone rose through clenched teeth. "And I mean without argument."

Worried for Sarah, Billie did exactly what he wanted and kept quiet. Chet's gaze momentarily left hers, his scrutiny drifting over her marked face.

Billie met Sarah's eye. She looked scared and worried, and had every right – they were in big trouble.

"Looks like you've already had a taste of what you deserve, but I'm going to give you more, you bitch."

Billie focused on Chet. He nodded.

"Get your hands behind your back."

She stared at him, knowing all too well what his intentions were.

"Do it or I'll cut her," he barked.

Casting another glance at Sarah, slowly Billie moved her hands behind her. Paul and Geoff stepped to her. Rough hands quickly tied them.

Chet smiled. "Good." He turned and released Sarah. The knife dropped from her neck. Almost instantaneously, he rammed her hard on her wounded shoulder with the heel of his hand. She squealed a shrill cry. Crippled by the pain, she sank to the floor against the cupboard.

Billie leapt forward. Anger and worry for Sarah drove her on. She'd smash his face in if she could get to him. The brothers grabbed her from behind, denying her the opportunity. They yanked her back and held her.

"You bastard." She struggled to break free.

Chet smiled and strolled closer – and stepped straight into her kick when she struck out with both feet after dropping her weight into the two brothers' arms. Chet crashed to the floor with blood gushing from his busted lips and rearranged nose. The knife flew from his slackened grasp, sliding across the wooden floor out of reach.

"You little bitch," Paul spat. He heaved her onto her feet and, together with Geoff, threw her backwards into the wall by the door. Billie hit it hard with her shoulder. A groan slipped from her lips. Lurching forward from the rebound, she almost tumbled over. Catching her balance, the detective looked up. A fist swung at her. With perfect timing, she turned her head. It missed her jaw and flew past, smashing into the wall behind. Paul screamed and staggered backwards, nursing his shattered hand.

Geoff raised a fist. A deep frown furrowed his brow. His eyes flared, the fury clearly visible. Billie kicked him between the legs. He stopped instantly, his wide eyes almost bulging out of their sockets. Clasping his family jewels, he fell back a step. Billie kicked high, clubbing him behind the ear and knocking him to the floor.

Her body screamed in protest. Gritting her teeth against the searing pain across her ribs, she turned to Chet as he rushed at her. She spun on one foot, bringing up the other, stretching it out fast and powerful to deliver a kick to his solar plexus. The impact halted him in his tracks. The air was forced from his lungs. He doubled over, fighting to catch a breath. Before he could recover, she kicked him in the nose. He was flung backwards onto the table. Landing on his back, he made no effort to get up.

About to follow him, Billie was yanked to a halt by a hand on her shoulder. Spinning her around, Paul swung a punch with his good hand; his other hung uselessly by his side. In a desperate bid, Billie ducked. Instead of catching her fully on the jaw, the fist nicked her on the cheek. The blow dropped her onto the large table. Without the support of her hands, she had no chance to regain her balance. Landing on the corner, the momentum carried her across the tabletop and dumped her on the floor.

"You're gonna pay, you bitch," Paul Riley growled. "My brothers shouldn't be in jail, especially because of you."

Billie looked up. The words seeped into her dazed mind. He was coming at her, and fast. More alarming was Chet's discarded knife in his hand. He raised it above his head. Still half winded from the fall, she knew she had to act now.

Paul plunged the knife towards her chest. Billie forced herself to roll. The knife buried into the floorboards where she'd been only seconds before. Instantly, she brought in her knees and kicked out hard, hitting him in the shoulder. The force slammed him into the cupboard before dropping him to the floor. Unfortunately, he ripped the knife from the floorboards as he fell back. Still within reach, Billie knew he posed a serious threat while he held the knife. She kicked him in the ribs but still he refused to drop the blade. Again, she kicked him. He gasped, riding the blow. Before she could pull her leg back to launch another kick, he suddenly grabbed her foot and locked it firm. With a crazed look in his eye, he stabbed the knife into her trapped thigh.

"Agh!" Billie cried.

Paul's face twisted into a snarl. Yanking the knife out, he raised it, preparing to stab her again. On instinct, Billie smashed her free leg into his face, twice, busting his nose. He fell to the side. Her bloodied leg slipped free from his unconscious body.

"McCoy, look out!" Sarah called.

Billie automatically rolled on Sarah's distressed warning. Chet lunged at the cop armed with another knife. The blade narrowly missed her, burying into the floorboards. With a frustrated growl, he yanked it free and stabbed at her again. Again, Billie rolled, staying just ahead of him as he lunged after her on his knees, trying to pin her to the floor.

A chair suddenly smashed across his back before bouncing to the side. Chet jumped and squealed in pain. He jerked to a halt and looked over his shoulder. Sarah, swaying on unsteady legs, picked up another chair one handed. Grunting, Chet climbed to his feet.

"That hurt, you bitch." He started for her.

Sarah threw the second chair at him before retreating a step. Chet deflected the flying chair and continued towards her. Backing off, Sarah tossed whatever she could lay her hands on: bowls, plates, pots, glasses. He easily dodged her missiles, all the while laughing.

Appreciating Sarah had come to her aid, Billie knew her friend was in big trouble and badly needed her help. The cop went to get up but gasped when a pain tore through her wounded thigh. Denied any help from her hands, she couldn't push herself up. She dropped to the floor, weak and breathing hard. She gave a frustrated cry. On top of the pain in her thigh, the wound on her ribs ached from the strain she'd put on it. This time, she'd pushed herself too hard.

Chapter Twenty-Nine

The sudden jar into the wall halted Sarah's backward retreat.

Chet grinned and moved in. Refusing to give in to him, Sarah threw a punch. He caught the fist and held it tight in his large hand. She fought like a wild cat to break away, to hurt him, but it was no good. Still weak, and with one arm incapable of doing anything, she was no match for him.

Chet cackled at her futile efforts. "Come on, girly, give me all you've got."

The taunting words and mocking smirk across his animated face motivated Sarah to do just that. She drove out a foot, kicking him wherever she could. Chet jumped with a yelp but maintained his firm grip. He slammed her against the cupboard, pinning her with his body. She couldn't fight at all. An evil chuckle slipped through his lips. It turned Sarah's blood cold. His hot breath pulsed on her cheek.

"Now, you listen good 'cause I'm gonna tell you how it's going to be. First, I'm going to mess up that pretty face of yours." He lifted the knife, and using the tip, slightly nicked her cheek. The razor sharp blade instantly drew blood.

Sarah sucked in a gasp. As frightened as she was, and, doing her best not to show her pain, she stared into his cold eyes, refusing to give in to his torment.

Chet's other hand suddenly dropped, groping in between her legs. It was so unexpected it threw her into a wild struggle. No matter how hard she tried, she couldn't break free or stop him. The more she fought, the more excited he became. As quickly as he'd started it, he stopped, removing the hand. All the while he leered at her.

"I can take you so easily and there is no way you can stop me." A high-pitched cackle followed the soft-spoken menacing words. His tongue spilled from his open mouth and slid up her cheek in a wet, drooling lick. Sarah tried to pull away, unable to stop the disgusted gasp slipping through her lips.

Chet laughed. "Then," he said in the same unsympathetic quiet tone, "I'm going to show you how big a man I am. I'll make you feel like I'm cutting you in half and you'll be begging for me to stop."

A cold shiver slithered down her spine. Her stomach was so tightly coiled she thought it would cut off her air supply. Even though she worked with men and did for a living exactly what this creep threatened to do to her, his intention of rape shook her. Again, she struggled to push him away, cringing from his touch. Her efforts only seemed to stimulate him more. Another laugh hissed from his lips.

"Then, if you're lucky, I might kill you quickly – maybe a stab in the heart." He flashed a smile. "No, why make it too easy? Maybe I could give you another mouth under your neck here," he taunted in a sinister whisper, the knife tracing an invisible line across her throat. "You'd be trying to breathe but you'd be drowning and choking on your own blood." His eyes were wide and excited. "Or I could slit your stomach so you could watch your insides fall out. That'd be interestin', wouldn't it?"

Sarah was scared. His threats hit hard. There was no doubt in her mind she was staring death in the face, death that promised to come with a lot of pain. This guy was crazy. She didn't put it past him one little bit to carry out his threats, and the worst part was she was powerless to stop him. But, no matter what, she wasn't about to show him that. Vainly she kept up her struggles.

"You sick bastard."

It didn't come out as harshly as she would have liked. He laughed and then slapped her. Sarah flew into a frenzied attack. Chet struggled to hold her. An evil grin lit up his face, and then it was gone. Brutally, he whacked her on the wounded shoulder.

"Ahh!" Sarah fell into him. Her body shut down under the stress, failing to support her. Now, nothing mattered but the pain. It wrapped itself around her like a thick heavy blanket, smothering her.

Chet dragged her up and held her. She stood gasping hard with her eyes closed tight.

"Well, that talked to you, didn't it," he sneered. The familiar cold laugh slipped through his lips. "Now, where should we start? How about your face?"

The cold blade rested against Sarah's cheek. She was completely at his mercy, too weak and in too much pain to defend herself. In the back of her agonised mind, she accepted it was over. This creep had won.

Just as Chet Riley geared his morbid plan into action, his right leg unexpectedly gave way under him.

"Aghh!"

He lost his hold on Sarah and collapsed to one knee. Deprived of his support, she slid to the floor beside him. Chet, gasping in pain, looked around behind him.

Billie stood over him. Watching him manhandle Sarah had given her the strength she'd so desperately needed, enough to get her up on her feet.

Chet snorted a growl and swung the knife in a backwards strike. The detective dodged it and kicked out. Her foot slammed him under the jaw, throwing him to the side to his hands and knees.

Billie winced. She'd had to put weight on her wounded leg to deliver the kick. Using the rage to drive her on, she kicked out again, giving him no time to recover. Chet took it solidly on the nose. He crashed to the floor onto his back. Billie hobbled after him, kicking the knife from his hand. He lay still, out cold. She turned to see if the other two posed any further threat. Both lay unconscious where she'd left them.

She returned her attention to Sarah, who sat crouched low with her head down, groaning and clasping her sore shoulder, none the wiser they were out of immediate danger. Billie's stomach tightened. Her heart went out to her, but she couldn't help her, not yet. The cop turned her attention to Chet. He and his brothers would be a threat should they wake. She needed to have control over them. Picking up Chet's discarded knife, she jammed it in a drawer with the blade sticking upwards. Leaning against the drawer to hold it secure, she positioned her hands and used the blade to carefully slice through the rope. Once free, she tossed the knife and rope on the bench and searched through the remaining drawers below. She found what she was looking for in the third – a roll of Duct Tape. Using the knife to cut it, she secured each of the Riley's hands and feet. Though a temporary measure, it'd suffice until help arrived.

By the time she'd finished, her defences were weakening, draining the strength from her aching body. Doing her best to ignore it, Billie limped to Sarah. Her hurts seemed to flood through her system all at once. It hit so quickly it almost caught her out. She fell into the wall on her shoulder beside Sarah. Without it, she would have crashed to the floor. Turning so she leant on her back, she rested her head on the timber and closed her eyes, fighting to overcome the wave of weakness swamping her. Reluctantly giving in, she slid down the wall, managing to sit upright against it. A gasp left her lips. Immersed in total concentration, she strived to regain some energy and bring her breathing into line. Too weak to help Sarah, instead, she sat with closed eyes, forcing her body to relax.

The moments quietly slipped by.

"Billie?" Sarah gently said.

The cop opened her eyes at the touch of her hand on her arm. She rolled her head towards her. It wasn't hard to read the concern in Sarah's expression. Sarah attempted to say something but stopped. Billie offered a weak smile. She didn't need to hear what Sarah wanted to say. In fact, she didn't have to say anything. Her thoughts and gratitude shone all too clear in her troubled expression.

"How do I...? Where do I...?" Sarah hesitated. She turned away, lowering her head.

Billie could understand where she was coming from. "It's okay. It's over."

Sarah's gaze shot up. "The hell it is. I won't ever forget this."

Billie read her solemn face. Sarah was taking it hard, in fact, having trouble dealing with it. She'd been so frightened at the time she'd truly believed she was going to die.

"Does this mean I miss out on another of your lectures?" she teased in an effort to lift her spirits. "My, you are slipping."

Sarah blurted a sob. "For the moment, you're off the hook, but only until I get my strength back."

Billie managed a slight nod. "I can hardly wait. So how about you? Your shoulder took a good whack."

"Two in fact. Yeah, it's easing." Sarah seemed distracted and stared at her behind an unwavering gaze. "Damn it, McCoy, don't you ever stop?"

Billie rested her head back and gave a laugh. "Certainly not around you guys."

"Shit." Sarah lowered her head and shook it. "I honestly don't know how you keep going."

Billie rested a hand on her knee. "I had a lot to fight for. We've been through too much to let it end here."

Sarah looked at her. A smile crept to her lips. She nodded. Her eyes watered. "What the hell are you trying to do to me? I have a reputation to live up to..." The words faded. On the verge of tears, she caught her bottom lip with her teeth.

Billie was touched by her show of emotions. She squeezed her leg. "Hey, I promise I won't tell anyone."

Sarah sobbed, wiping her eyes. Nodding, she looked at the floor.

Warmth rushed through Billie's veins. At last, she'd broken through and reached her, and was happy with what she'd found. Her instincts were right about her. Beneath the hard surface, there was a caring human being.

"And while we're on the subject, I want to thank you for pulling Riley off my back with the chair. You took a big risk doing that. I appreciate it."

Sarah looked at her with a weak smile. "Sure, as long as you don't go doing it again. You scared the shit out of me."

"Hmm. I guess that makes us even."

"Even? How the hell do you work that out?"

"Come on. I nearly died when I walked in here and found you with a knife at your throat, and then at the end there when Riley had you pinned against the wall. I didn't think I was going to make it in time."

Sarah stared in awe. She nodded. "Okay, so we're even. Let's keep it that way."

Billie smiled. "Deal."

The smell of smoke was strong. Smoke? It took Billie a moment to register smoke hung in the room. Turning, she looked up behind them. Thin spirals of black smoke escaped through a crack somewhere on top of the wood stove. She looked at Sarah. "This is your doing?"

"Yeah. I thought it might help."

"Help? By smoking us out?" A touch of mischief laced her tone.

Sarah held her gaze, failing to fall to the cop's teasing. "I threw a pot of lard in the fire to get John's, or someone's attention to come and help. I figured if they saw the smoke, they'd be straight here to investigate..."

Billie's broadening smile stopped her. "You really think they'd come?"

"Anything was worth trying, and with the way you were taking so long playing with these creeps, I figured I'd better take a hand."

Billie gave a laugh but before she could comment, voices distracted them.

"Billie? Sarah?" John called from beyond the walls.

The girls turned toward the door. The sound of rapid, heavy footsteps hurried across the lounge room. Sarah looked at Billie with a wide smile planted on her lips.

"See, my idea worked. It wasn't as crazy as it seemed."

Billie smiled with her. "Okay, so you got lucky."

"Ha! Not luck, sheer cleverness."

John and the girls burst through the door and jerked to a halt, taking in the scene with stunned looks.

"What the..." Casey gasped.

"Who are these guys?" Jane said, looking over the sprawled, unconscious intruders.

John grunted a low growl. "The rest of the Riley clan. Damn the bastards. How dare they come into my house."

"Hell." Jane dashed forward. Casey, John, and Kate followed. The four crouched in front of the wounded couple examining them with worried stares.

"We saw the smoke. What happened?" John asked.

"Are you two all right?" Jane's anxious gaze darted from one to the other.

"We are now," Billie said. "You really came running because you saw the smoke?" she asked John, still having trouble dealing with how it had alerted him.

He looked a little surprised. "Well, yeah. It was dark black and pouring out the chimney. I figured something must be wrong."

Sarah smiled at Billie. "Told you it'd work. Good plan, huh?"

Billie turned to her with a half smile. "More like arsy," she corrected.

"Man, I don't believe this," Casey said, looking around at the men. "It must have been one hell of a fight."

"Yeah, you could say that."

"Shit, it's a good thing you didn't come riding with us," Casey said, turning back to her.

Billie frowned, confused. "A good thing?"

"For Sarah, I mean." A flicker of a smile touched her lips. "I mean it might have turned out a lot differently if you hadn't been here to help her against these creeps."

Billie nodded. "I guess so." She hesitated, still baffled. "Maybe we could discuss this tomorrow, you know, when my *new* bruises and cuts don't hurt as much and my head's clearer so I can understand your reasoning regarding 'a good thing.'"

Casey chuckled. "Yeah, sure." She looked at Sarah with a mischievous smile. "Cops. You have to explain every little detail to them."

Sarah smiled. "Tell me something I don't know."

"Come on, let's get you two out of here," John said.

Limited with his arm in the sling, he slipped a hand around Billie's waist. Jane leant forward and took hold of her from the other side. Together they hauled her to her feet. The detective winced. She stood favouring her leg and had to lean into them. She held her ribs in an effort to ease the sharp aches.

Casey and Kate helped Sarah up.

"Hell, we leave you two alone and this is what you get up to," John mumbled. Distress oozed from his voice.

"Have you–ever thought about–putting locks on the doors?" Billie asked, striving to get on top of hurts standing had heightened.

"Locks? With you around? I think I need bars."

"That's g-good." She attempted a smile.

"Yeah, now concentrate on getting out of here, okay?"

The two convalescents were helped out of the kitchen. Eve met them halfway to the bedroom, hurrying in from the front of the house. Her breathing was heavy, as if she'd been running.

"Sorry, I couldn't keep up with John to get here sooner. What's happened?" With wide eyes, her fretful gaze jumped from Billie to Sarah as John gave a brief account of the Rileys' visit. A horrified expression paled her face. "My goodness. I'll get the first aid."

John and the girls sat Billie and Sarah on their beds. Casey sank down with Sarah. Jane and Kate sat either side of the detective, ready to help Eve with whatever she needed.

"This looks like a knife wound," Eve said after examining Billie's bloodied leg.

"Good guess," the detective confirmed, leaning forward with her hand still holding her ribs. Eve gently pulled the hand away and lifted the shirt to look at the bandage.

"There's no blood, but that doesn't mean you haven't torn the stitches."

"I'll leave them in your hands, Eve," John said. "I want to get back to the Rileys."

"Yes, go. I'm fine with this."

John turned and strode out the door.

"What did they want?" Jane asked. "Why did they attack you guys?"

Billie looked at her. "To pay us back for locking up their brothers."

"You're kidding?"

"What do you mean 'us'?" Sarah said. "They only wanted you, not me." All eyes turned her way. "You're the one who laid the charges on their brothers, and you were the one who dropped them in the street and made a mockery out of them. Not me. I had nothing to do with it. Hell, I didn't even see them the other night. No, believe me, they definitely wanted you. I just happened to be in your . . . unlucky company at the time."

"Oh, really? You sure riled them enough to turn on you, if I remember correctly, without any help from me," Billie carelessly said with a faint smile.

"Only because I was trying to save your arse."

"Ah huh."

"I can't believe they had the nerve to come here in broad daylight," Casey cut in. "You two are lucky to be alive."

Sarah looked at her. Slowly, the smile faded from her lips. "Yeah, ain't that the truth. They sure put the wind up me, I'll tell you."

"So what happened?" Kate asked.

Sarah looked at her and then around the expectant faces. "They were waiting for us. I don't know how long they'd been there or how they got in, but they definitely meant business." She shuddered. "You guys had only just left," she said, looking from Jane and Kate to Casey. "They jumped me when I went to get us a drink and then lured McCoy in."

"Mm, I walked straight into their trap, that's for sure." Billie winced when Eve touched her wounded leg.

"Looking at your wrists, I'm guessing those bastards tied you, right?" Jane said, lifting her gaze from Billie's rope burned wrists. "And you still beat them?"

"I couldn't have done it without Sarah."

"Oh, yeah, I was a great help. I felt like a goat amongst a pack of lions," Sarah said.

"You did great."

Eve looked up, catching Billie's eye. "I'm afraid this'll need stitches. I'll be back in a minute." She stood and walked out.

Billie looked at Jane. "What does she mean by that?"

Jane smiled and rested a hand on her arm. "I've no idea, but it can't be that bad."

Kate nodded. "Mum is great at fixing wounds up. Don't worry about it."

Billie couldn't for some reason share her confidence. Eve returned carrying a small syringe. Stopping in front of the girls, she prepped it.

Billie watched her squirt some of the clear fluid out the end. "Are you licensed to use that?"

Eve smiled down at her. "Now, Billie, I was a nurse remember, and I've used this on my family a number of times."

"Honestly, It's not that bad—"

Eve leant over and squeezed her cut leg. As gentle as she was, the slight pressure caused the detective to wince and lean forward with a gasp.

"Does it look bad to you, Jane?" Eve asked behind an innocent tone.

"Yeah, it does." Unease thinned the hesitant answer.

Billie sat back and glanced at her. Jane watched her with an unsettled look. She flashed a smile. The cop returned it.

"Thanks for your support."

Eve pushed up her sleeve and wiped a spot on her upper arm with a soaked alcohol pad. The detective turned and watched.

"So how come if you're fixing my leg, you're stabbing my arm?"

Eve slid the needle in. Billie flinched.

"It's to help you relax so I can work on your leg without hurting you." In a matter of seconds, it was done. Eve straightened and smiled.

"Ah huh." Billie, unconvinced, rubbed and studied her arm where the needle had entered.

"Now lie back and let the drug work," Eve said. "It'll be over before you know it."

Billie looked at her sharply. "Lie back? What exactly did you give me?"

"Just a mild sedative. I didn't have a local so this is the next best thing."

"You think so?"

"You're starting to turn into a sook, McCoy," Casey teased from the other bed.

Billie looked at her. "Sook?"

"Sure. It was only a little jab. Hell, it isn't even a big needle. What's wrong with you?"

"I have a thing about needles, big or small."

"My, how the mighty warrior has fallen. The last of the tough cops."

Billie's body already began to grow heavy. Kate looked at Casey with a smile playing on her lips.

"Come on, Casey, give her a break. Everyone has their weaknesses."

"So true, Kate, so true, and I think we've just found McCoy's."

Billie had all intentions of contending the jesting remark, but suddenly found no desire or energy to do so. Her mind grew fuzzy, her drive dwindling. Lowering her head, she closed her eyes, rubbing them with her fingers. The girls' voices seemed such a long way off. Without lifting her head, she struggled to answer.

"Maybe Eve . . . could give you two . . . a shot." Every word was an effort. Before she knew it, her eyes refused to open. Her hand dropped down and her head sank lower onto her chest. Jane and Kate had to quickly grab hold of her to stop her falling forward. Billie slumped against Jane as sleep invaded her mind and body.

Chapter Thirty

Jane's stomach twisted. She looked at Eve for confirmation, for reassurance that this was how Billie was supposed to react.

"Don't worry, she's okay," Eve said with a warm smile. "She won't be out for long. Lay her back so I can get to work."

Trusting the calm words, Jane nodded and glanced at Kate. Gently, they pulled Billie back and lowered her onto the pillow. They lifted her legs onto the bed, making her comfortable. Jane watched her, unable to quell her concerns. She hated seeing her like this.

Eve leant forward and lifted an eyelid. "She's out."

"Boy, that works fast," Casey said, her stare fixed on the detective's sleeping form.

Eve glanced at her. "There's no need to worry. She'll be fine. Jane, why don't you sit with Sarah and Casey while Kate and I fix this leg?"

Jane looked at her and then to Kate who smiled.

"It's okay, Mum knows what she's doing," she assured her.

Jane nodded. With a final glance at Billie, she hesitantly stood and moved across to the girls, sitting down beside Sarah. They welcomed her with brief smiles. After watching Eve start cleaning Billie's leg, Casey turned to Sarah.

"So, how are you holding up?" she asked Sarah. "How's the shoulder?"

"It's not so bad now. That bastard hit it twice pretty hard."

"Don't worry, I'll check as soon as I'm finished here," Eve said, shooting her a glance followed by a smile.

"Thanks." She sighed. "Now I can understand what McCoy went through when her wound kept opening up. Even today it slowed her up. I don't know how she kept going, or how she got to me in time to pull that creep off me before he started into me." Sarah's voice was quiet, subdued. She gave an insecure laugh and then a sudden sob. "She was tied and wounded but somehow she still took him out."

Lowering her head, she started to tremble. She clasped her hands together tightly.

"Sarah?" Casey slipped an arm around her.

Jane, just as concerned, rested a hand on her leg.

Sarah looked up and stared at Billie. Her eyes were watery, her voice strained. "I guess it's starting to sink in what he intended to do. He was..." Her words faded. Her widened eyes seemed glazed.

Jane tensed. Sarah sat rigid, staring ahead. No doubt the shock had caught up with her. Doing her best to contain her anxieties, Jane glanced at Casey. Looking just as distressed, Casey hugged Sarah tighter.

"Hey, it's okay. It's all over. Come on, we're here for you now."

Casey's words had no effect. Sarah sat frozen, her gaze fixed on the other bed with a tormented look on her taut features.

Eve and Kate turned and looked over after hearing Casey's concerned words. Surprise washed across their features at the sight of Sarah in a stunned state of shock.

Jane shot a confused look at Casey. She turned to Sarah. Her face was expressionless, as if chiselled in marble. It was as if her mind had emptied, been invaded by some alien forces. Fighting to hold in her worry, Jane took her hand. Gently, she squeezed, rubbing her thumb back and forth in a comforting gesture. In a calm and collected voice, she attempted to reach Sarah using her own tactics.

"Sarah? Remember after my night of horrors, when you and Billie came to get me out of that room with Smith? I was so scared. You two were like a godsend, a dream come true. You got me out, you saved me, and you have no idea how you helped me with that talk we had while we were driving. Remember, when it was just the two of us in those early hours of the morning? You helped me get over it a lot faster than I'd ever been able to do on my own, if ever I'd been *able* to do it on my own. Talking it out seemed to ease the burden. I felt so much better, and I had you to thank for it. Now, I'm ready to listen to you, so, come on, talk to me. Let me help you, the same as you helped me. Please, Sarah, I know you want to, and I know you can do it. Try, for me, and Casey."

Sarah showed no reaction to Jane's words, at least not at first. Slowly, she turned and looked at her. After a long moment, she nodded.

Jane cast Casey a relieved glance. She returned it with a grateful nod before focusing on Sarah.

Sarah picked up her story where she'd left it, carrying on as if she'd never stopped. "He was going to carve up my face..."

Casey and Jane glanced at each other. Now Jane knew where the scratch on her face had come from.

"Then . . . he said he'd rape me . . . and if I was lucky . . . he'd kill me quick . . . but then he changed his mind . . . said it'd be more interesting making me suffer a slow and painful death." Her voice was barely a whisper. "He joked about cutting my throat or opening my stomach..."

Casey took her other hand and held it tight.

Sarah kept on. "I was so scared. I really believed it was all over. McCoy was down and wounded..." She shook her head. "Another minute and I would've been..." Her voice faded. "And then it was over. Billie had taken him out."

Casey hugged her tight, holding back her tears.

Sarah sucked in a shaky breath. "The odds were against us. Those bastards were going to kill us – simple as that. They tried, they really did, but Billie was too good for them. She had to do it all on her own. I couldn't help her. Shit, I can't believe we came through it."

"We've come through too much not to have made it," Jane said with a quiet, sincere tone.

Sarah looked at her and blurted a short laugh, only it came out more like a sob. She turned and stared across at the detective.

"Funny, that's what McCoy said."

Jane smiled. "Well, it's true."

Sarah glanced at her with a flicker of a smile before returning her attention to Billie. "She went through a lot to help me. I don't know how she does it."

Jane followed her gaze, watching Eve stitch up the cop's thigh. Sarah's words stirred her own feelings towards the detective. Regardless of the odds, Billie was always ready to fight for them.

"Yeah, it's a bad habit she seems to have," she murmured.

The girls fell silent. Jane's thoughts drifted over the last couple of weeks, contemplating how lucky they were to be alive. Many times over, they could have met with their "great maker", that inevitable fate which, on numerous occasions, had come so close to achieving its purpose. They'd slipped past "death" itself. Life now looked so different, and she knew she had Billie to thank for it.

Eve finished stitching the detective's leg. She checked the wound on her ribs and nodded. Leaving her to sleep, she threw a light rug over her. She turned and crossed to Sarah sitting between her friends.

"Okay, let's take a look at you, shall we?"

No argument came. First, she checked her shoulder. Taking it out of the sling, she carefully unwrapped it. Fresh blood darkened the flesh around the wound. Jane had a clear view of it. It had opened a little but didn't look too bad. Eve strapped it up after cleaning it. She then cleaned the cut on Sarah's cheek and placed a small plaster over it.

"There. Now, what you need is rest," she said. "Come on, lie back."

Sarah submitted to Eve's gentle pushing. "I won't argue."

"How long will Billie be out?" Jane asked after Sarah lay settled, finally breaking free of her sombre mood.

"Oh, at least another half hour yet." She turned to her daughter. "Kate, why don't you finish that ride you started. These guys look like they need a distraction for a while."

"No, I'd rather wait—" Jane started.

Eve cut her off adamantly. "There's nothing else you can do here other than keep Sarah awake. Some fresh air will do you the world of good."

Jane stared at her. She turned to Casey, who nodded. Eve was right. All they could do was wait, but not in here.

"Come on," Kate urged, encouraging them to their feet. "You were just starting to get the hang of it."

"We'll be okay," Sarah said.

Jane shot her a look.

Casey nodded. "Okay, just for a while." She glanced at Jane. "Come on." She took her by the arm and escorted her out with Kate. Jane cast Billie a final look before disappearing through the door.

* * *

Billie stirred. Slowly, she rolled her head and sucked in a breath. Her eyes flickered and sluggishly opened. When they focused, she found Sarah sitting beside her.

"Well, I'm glad to see you're not going to sleep your life away after all," Sarah said with a relieved smile.

Billie wet her lips. Her voice was weak. "With you around, I doubt it."

Sarah nodded. "You know me too well, and that's scary."

A faint smile flashed across Billie's lips, and then it was gone. She looked at her more seriously. "Should you be up?"

"I'm fine. You don't have to worry about me."

Sarah's answer came with too much confidence, a sure sign she was disguising her true feelings, but Billie didn't push it. Sarah seemed to be in reasonably good spirits after such a close call.

"Well, that's good to hear." She closed her eyes. "Hell, I thought Eve was only going to relax me, not bowl me over."

"You *were* relaxed, totally," Sarah said. "Besides, she sewed you back up as good as new."

"Ah huh. And I thought you were on my side."

Sarah nodded. "Of course I am. Most times."

Again a forced assurance laced her tone. Billie stared at her, the words sending her mind to the kitchen incident. Maybe it *was* time to talk about it. "Yeah. So how are you? We did have a close call."

Sarah's smile faded. Her lips tightened. Fear flashed in her eyes. Then it was gone. She shrugged. "My shoulder's not hurting that much now. I'm doing all right."

Billie's gaze didn't falter. "That's good, but what about up here?" she said, touching a finger to her temple.

Sarah blew out a breath and lowered her head. "Okay, I guess. I had a few shakes and tears earlier, and I guess I freaked out for a moment, but, after talking it through with Casey and Jane, I feel a lot better for it." She looked up at the detective and flashed a smile.

"Are you sure?"

Sarah nodded. She stared at Billie with a strange expression. "Damn it, McCoy, how the hell do I thank you? That creep meant to carve me up without a blink of an eye. If it wasn't for you..." Gratitude and strain shone in her eyes.

"Forget it, okay? You don't have to keep thanking me."

"But I want to. Thank you," she said sincerely.

Billie nodded and smiled. "Anytime. Now, why don't you try and get some rest."

Sarah stood. "Good idea. You've kept me awake long enough now."

A laugh slipped through Billie's lips. Sarah's smile was more gracious, her demeanour more relaxed. She ambled across to her bed and settled herself against the two pillows.

Billie closed her eyes, giving into the exhaustion haunting her. Her leg throbbed, and her body ached, but nothing mattered except for the desire to rest. Almost immediately, sleep engulfed her, drawing her away from her hurts into a welcome world of nothingness.

* * *

The following day, a helicopter's drone drew everyone out from wherever they were. The boys raced over from the horses in the yards, watching excitedly as the chopper set down to rest. As soon as the blades and motor stopped, they rushed over.

Dave climbed out and greeted them with a smile. "You're welcome to check it out, boys, but I'm trusting you not to touch anything, or fly away in it. Deal?"

"Deal," they chorused with broad grins. They raced over to it.

Grinning, he strolled across to his welcoming party. "Hi, guys."

The girls eagerly greeted him.

"Hi, Dave."

"Hi!"

"Lieutenant," John said with a nod, shaking his hand. "Good to see you back."

"It's nice to be back."

"So how'd it go?" Billie asked, trying not to sound too anxious. "Where's Mark?"

"It went well. Mark stayed in Cairns to tidy up. We'll meet him there." His words slowed as his focus drifted over her freshly bruised face, and then to how she favoured one leg. He glanced around, looking with more interest at the subdued watching faces. His gaze returned to the detective. "Everything okay?"

"Sure."

"Well, it is now," Casey said.

Dave looked at her. "What do you mean, now? What's happened?" Raising his eyebrows expectantly, he turned to Billie.

"Oh, it was nothing really. We managed to clean up some . . . untidy ends while you were gone."

"Untidy ends? Such as?"

"Oh, you know, things like, well, like those Riley brothers you were looking for. But you don't have to worry, they're locked up snug as a bug in town." She smiled.

"The Riley brothers? What are you talking about?"

"They kind of visited us looking for our hero here," Casey said with a nod at Billie.

Dave's face paled. "You're kidding?"

John picked it up and filled him in and, backed by Billie, Sarah and the girls at different times, the story spilled out.

"Hell. Why didn't we see that coming?" Dave asked in astonishment. "Are you sure you're all right?"

"Dave, I'm fine, honest," Billie said.

Exhaling a long sigh, he nodded. "Seems we can't leave you for a minute, can we?"

"Guess not." She smiled and tucked her arm through his. "So, now you know my story, tell me yours." She led him to the house, limping along beside him. Except for Tom and Janda playing around the chopper, everyone squeezed into the lounge room. Mary and Julie sat on the floor in front of their parents. Settling down with coffees all round, Dave filled them in on his adventure.

"Thanks to your directions and detailed description of Bates' village, we, with the help of the Cairns police, slipped in and surrounded it. Everything went to plan. We arrested everyone involved without any bloodshed and netted local and overseas buyers illegally in the country for their dirty dealings, including the sheik. Apparently, he delayed his departure on Bates' word he would return with Billie," he said somewhat strained, glancing at the detective.

"Bloody hell. No wonder Bates started shooting us," Sarah said. "We were expendable. He was only interested in keeping the sheik happy."

"Yeah. Anyway, for more good news. We uncovered the files on every missing girl, going back over the last three years. It could possibly lead to their present whereabouts, and, more importantly, their freedom, which in turn will also lead to more arrests of the men who bought them. No one will be getting away with anything."

"That's the best news I've heard in a long time," Jane said.

"Amen." Casey sighed. "May they all rot in hell."

"So, when are you leaving, Dave?" John asked, taking a sip from his coffee.

"As soon as the girls are ready. We have a long way to go."

"So soon? Wouldn't you like another night to rest before you take off?" Eve asked.

Dave smiled and glanced at the girls. "Thanks for the offer, but I think the guys would like to get home."

"Can you believe it?" Casey grinned and looked at Sarah. "We are finally going home."

"It sure is hard to comprehend," she replied, shaking her head.

"You certainly deserve it," John said.

"Yes, you do. We'll miss you though. I feel like I'm losing part of my own family." Eve's eyes watered. She gazed at the girls with an affectionate smile.

A brief silence filled the room.

"That's probably because you opened your heart and home to us," Billie answered, her gaze fixed to Eve sitting holding hands with John. "Thank you very much, for everything. You've both done so much for us. If you hadn't taken us in, we'd probably still be on the run."

"Oh, Billie, it was the least we could do." She smiled and wiped a tear from her eye.

"Billie's right," Jane said. "You didn't have to do what you did. We were a sorry looking bunch when we turned up here, enough to put anybody off. We're all very grateful for your generosity, believe me."

"It was a pleasure." Eve smiled and turned to Kate sitting beside her. She slipped an arm around her. Kate looked depressed, no doubt hating the thought of them leaving.

Janda and Tom marched into the room like two soldiers. Everyone turned to watch them. Just inside the door, they split up. Tom strode to his mother's side and sank down between her and John. Janda crossed to Billie. He made no effort to sit. Instead he stood in front of her with a sober stare. From the way he nervously changed from foot to foot, she knew he had something to tell her, something she might not like.

"What is it, Janda?"

"I wanted to—it's just that—I mean..."

Sensing his uncomfortable hesitation, she sat forward and took his hand. "Hey, it's okay. What are you trying to tell me?"

Janda sheepishly glanced at Jane, Sarah and Casey sitting watching. They offered him smiles behind their intrigued stares. He looked at Billie. "Well, I just thought, maybe, well, I–er–I do want to go, but, well, I have nowhere to go once we get there and, well, Tom and I were talking and..."

"Mum, can Janda stay here and live with us?" Tom finished for him.

Everyone stared at him, caught out. One by one, they turned to the apprehensive boy in question.

Janda looked over at Eve and John. Gently pulling free from Billie's hand, he faced them, standing rigid and anxious. "I know it's a lot to ask, but I'd really like to stay. I'll do jobs and help with anything, no questions asked. I can do lots of things."

Eve smiled and caught John's eye. Striving to conceal his smile, he turned to the nervous boy and cleared his throat with a couple of short deep grunts.

"Tell you what, Janda," he said in a matter-of-fact tone, "if you can talk the cop and the girls into giving you up, I'd love to have another man around the house."

After taking a moment to comprehend the full meaning behind John's long-winded answer, Janda slowly smiled. He spun and faced Billie, the silent question lighting up his face.

For a minute, the detective stared at him, studying his energised features. She'd never seen him so excited. It wasn't hard to see this was what he really wanted. Her smile disappeared. She blew out a heavy sigh.

"I don't know, Janda. I was kind of counting on you to help me out with this case once we got home." She turned to the girls. "What do you think, guys?"

Cued on Billie's lead, Sarah took up a solemn tone. "He'd be leaving us with a big load, having to fill in all the details without him. I can't help feel like I've been . . . dumped."

"*And* betrayed," Casey added.

"Not to mention jilted," Jane said, casting a grave stare at the stunned boy.

The smile faded from Janda's face. "No. I didn't mean to upset you." He looked from one to the other. "If you want me to come, I'll come."

His troubled face finally broke the girls up. They burst out laughing, unable to maintain their pretence any longer. It started everyone off, everyone except the two boys. It was only their innocence and trust that failed to warn them they'd been tricked.

"Of course you can stay, Janda, if that's what you really want," Billie said, putting him out of his misery.

He looked hard at her, confused by her supportive words. "So you really don't mind?"

"We only want you to be happy, and I think you'd be very happy here."

His face burst into a huge grin. "Thank you. Thank you." He hugged her tight. Quickly, he moved to the girls and wrapped them in hugs.

"Just don't forget us, okay?" Casey said warmly.

"No way." He looked from one to the other. "Wow, this is great." He turned to the grinning Tom before his gaze fell on John and Eve. They watched him with affectionate smiles. He dashed across the room and hugged them. "I won't let you down."

Eve smiled. "We know. It'll be lovely to have you in the family."

"Come on, Janda, let's go play," Tom called, jumping to his feet. The two boys raced out.

"Well, guys, we should start thinking about heading off too," Dave announced after the kids disappeared out the door.

"I guess we're ready when you are. It's not as if we have a lot of packing to do," Sarah said, turning to her friends with a smile.

Casey grinned. "I knew there had to be some advantage to travelling light."

Ten minutes later, the gang sauntered out to the chopper. Billie used a walking stick, only because Eve had insisted. The cop gave up arguing and thanked her for it and, after giving it a go, was surprised how much strain it took off her leg.

Slowing to a halt beside the chopper, Eve faced the girls.

"Well, good luck and take care of yourselves." She paused, looking at each of them. In that brief, lingering delay, tears filled her eyes. "Oh, I am so going to miss you girls." Stepping forward, she hugged them all. Without another word, she stood back. John moved in and hugged them.

"Thanks again," Billie said after he let her go.

"It was a pleasure." He nodded with a smile. "And thank *you* for bringing us our daughter home, and cleaning up our town."

"Anytime. And if either of them gets out of hand again, just call me."

John laughed. "I'll hold you to that."

"Good."

The girls said their goodbyes to Mary and Julie before they surrounded Kate standing to the side. From the look on the farm girl's face, Billie sensed she was already missing them. Sarah hugged her. Kate held her tight, being careful not to squeeze her shoulder.

"Hey, anytime you're in the big smoke, don't forget to look us up, okay?" Sarah said.

"I sure will. I am so going to miss you guys." She released Sarah with a sob.

Jane smiled. With teary eyes, she hugged her. "Same here. You've spoiled us no end."

Casey hugged her next. "We'll keep in touch."

"You'd better." Kate let her go. She quickly wiped her watery eyes. A shaky laugh slipped through her lips. "It's been so good having you here."

Casey's voice thinned. "It's been great. Thank you so much."

Putting up a brave front with a smile, Kate turned to where Billie leant on her stick patiently waiting. For a brief moment, Kate simply looked at her, silently thanking her.

"And as for you, please look after yourself," she said in a strained voice.

Billie nodded. "Don't I always?"

Stepping forward, Kate embraced her. "Thank you for everything." She held her for a long minute, expressing her gratitude.

When they stood back from each other, Billie smiled. "Look after those boys."

"I will, and make sure you keep these three out of trouble," she said, indicating with a nod towards the girls. Billie looked at them. They smiled as if butter wouldn't melt in their mouths.

"Ha! Now you're asking for the impossible," the detective said, turning to the farm girl.

"Kate, don't you mean the other way around?" Jane asked. "I mean, we're not the ones always in trouble."

Kate giggled. "Maybe you have a point there."

Billie chuckled. Dave put his arm around her and looked over his passengers.

"Okay, guys, let's get moving."

The girls gave their hosts a final rush of goodbyes and climbed into the chopper. Sarah, Jane and Casey slid into the rear seats. Billie took the front beside Dave who awkwardly settled his lanky frame into the pilot's seat.

"Bye," Kate called yet again.

Everyone responded and waved back. Eve, John and the two girls walked to Kate. John wrapped his large arm around her shoulders. Eve stood on her other side, slipping an arm around her waist. Julie and Mary stood beside their mother with wide smiles.

The chopper whined to life. Its rotor blades began to spin, gaining in speed until they became a blur. The loud drone of the engine grew with it. The wind from the spinning blades stirred the dust, swirling it in a thick cloud and forcing the family to move back. They had to shield their eyes from the sudden dust storm. After a few moments, the chopper lifted. The Cauldrons stole looks through the thinning dust. Ten metres off the ground, the chopper banked and glided smoothly towards the east to begin its trek home. Janda and Tom sprinted out from the yards, jumping and waving madly, chasing it in a race.

Billie and the girls waved, and then the boys were lost from their vision as the chopper picked up speed and height.

Chapter Thirty-One

Some hours later, Dave set the chopper down at Cairns airport. The girls stared out the windows while he deftly shut down the motor. The noise died. The blades revolved in a free, unengaged spin above them, slowly losing their momentum without the powerful motor's thrust driving them.

Workers went about their jobs, assisting and servicing the different aircraft parked on the ground. They ranged from the small Cessnas up to the passenger jets. Further in the distance, the larger Boeings and Airbuses stood out on the tarmacs of the international airport.

The sun shone brightly, bathing the sky in a clear magical blue. It painted a refreshing background to the crisp clear day, highlighted by the neatly cut green grass and thriving gardens surrounding the buildings. The scenic mountain range behind portrayed a picture of splendorous beauty, a picturesque glory for the mind to absorb – had anyone been in the mood for such indulgence.

Dave turned in his seat, glancing at his tired passengers. Jane, Sarah and Casey hadn't said a word in the last twenty minutes or so. It seemed emphasised without the roaring of the chopper's motor and blades overhead. He looked at Billie.

"We'll have a few hours here. I've arranged for a car to take you to a motel where you can freshen up and change. We're on the seven o'clock flight to Sydney." He looked at his watch. "It's now two fifteen so we'll have to be back here in about four hours."

She nodded. "Sounds good." She cast a friendly smile over into the back. The girls nodded their acknowledgement with forced, distracted smiles. Billie checked her surprise. She'd expected a more enthusiastic response. Failing to offer any comment, they turned their attention out the window, away from the cop's scrutinising stare.

Billie strived to understand their mood. Here they were almost home, free to live their lives in their own space, however and wherever they liked, yet they seemed preoccupied. The elation of being back in civilisation just wasn't there.

"You guys okay?" she asked, offering them an opportunity to explain their odd behaviour. All eyes shot to her, filled with surprise.

Sarah nodded. "Sure. Why shouldn't we be?"

Billie watched her, pensive. Her gaze jumped to the other two. Their troubled expressions badly betrayed them. The cop knew them well enough to know there was definitely something bothering them. Before she could push it, Dave interrupted.

"Come on, let's go." Opening his door, he jumped down. The three girls filed out after him.

Billie blew out a breath. She used her door to exit and joined the gang on the tarmac. The girls stood watching the jets land and take off in the distance. A dark blue Toyota van sped towards them, following a side road on the other side of a high wire fence. It pulled up beside a personal gate thirty metres away. The horn sounded a short sharp beep.

"There's your lift," Dave said, glancing at it. "We want to get out of here as discreetly as possible. As far as we know, the press hasn't got wind of your story, but it's only a matter of time. Come on." He strode towards the waiting van. The three girls cast it a brief glance but didn't follow.

"So, this is really it," Casey muttered.

Billie had stepped off to follow Dave but Casey's words pulled her up. She looked over her shoulder, a little confused and a little concerned. Casey almost sounded anxious. Why? Wasn't this what they wanted? To be going home? The detective glanced at Jane and Sarah. They looked to be in the same frame of mind. There they stood, where she'd left them by the chopper, returning her gaze in silence with strange expressions.

"Okay, something's wrong. What is it?" Billie asked, turning fully around to face them.

The three stared at her, offering no explanations. The detective leant on her walking stick and considered their behaviour, trying to see through to their hidden anxieties. Their silence only heightened her concern. Holding off pushing too hard for an answer, it was better to let them come to her, to freely explain this unusual behaviour.

Casey sighed and ambled over. Stopping in front of her, she held Billie's gaze only for a moment before casting a glance out to the busy tarmac. She looked back at the detective's battered face and blew out a breath. Still seeming unsettled, she glanced over her shoulder to Jane and Sarah.

Curious, Billie followed her gaze. The two girls stood side by side, watching on. What was going on here? She'd never seen these three looking so lost and . . . speechless. What could possibly be on their minds more serious than what they'd just survived? They had their lives back so why weren't they rejoicing?

Casey cleared her throat, at last making the effort to explain. "The problem we have is, it all seems like a bad dream," she started, turning to the detective. "Like it happened to someone else."

Sarah and Jane moved forward with some uncertainty, coming in on Casey's left.

Casey continued with more confidence now that she had backup. "Now that it's behind us, all the frustration and the fear, the danger and the not knowing what's going to happen, all the horrors we had to face and the strain of everything, and, well, you know, the whole complete package wrapped up in that nightmare, now that we're finally safe, it seems hard to . . . come to terms with. We know how lucky we are to be here, alive, and . . . I don't know, for some crazy reason, it all seems to be hitting harder now." Casey's quiet voice became strained by the time she'd finished. She glanced at

Sarah and Jane. They nodded in encouragement. Casey turned back to Billie. "Look, what I'm trying to say is, we are truly grateful to you. We owe at least ninety-nine per cent of our freedom, and our lives, to you."

"Ninety-nine point nine," Jane corrected.

Billie glanced at her and then back at Casey. At last she understood what was bothering them. With this understanding came a sense of relief. She'd expected a much bigger problem from the way they were behaving. They were suffering delayed shock, which was only natural. More than that, they felt indebted to her. That was the big hurdle these three struggled with. She couldn't believe it. To her, it seemed such a trivial reason. She'd done it because she'd wanted to, for them, and didn't expect anything in return. It merely proved they really did care about her and thought a lot of her.

"We wouldn't have made it without you," Sarah said.

Billie looked from one to the other and shook her head. "We made it together, remember? We *all* put in."

"Maybe, at times, but, without your strength to carry us through, we wouldn't be here now."

Billie cast sympathetic looks at the three sombre faces. Guilt obviously haunted them, no doubt for the way they'd first treated her and for their lack of support at some crucial times. Her help had been unconditional which, at the moment, seemed to rub salt into the wound.

She smiled. "Come on, cheer up. It's behind us. We won, and you should be proud of that. We beat the odds together."

"We hear what you're saying, but you're missing the point. It's just that, well, we have an attack of the guilts," Sarah said. "Well, at least, I do. I was the one on your case the whole time, and don't deny it. Why the hell you just didn't flatten me or give up on me, I'll never know."

Casey gave her a nudge in the ribs with her elbow, shooting her a reprimanding look. "Don't be a hero. We all were, sometime or other."

"Come on, guys, we've been through all this before," Billie said. "I'm just as grateful to you. We worked as a team, and a good one . . . eventually," she added, bringing a smile to the girls.

"That doesn't make it any easier," Jane argued. She glanced at Sarah and Casey before continuing. "I think what we're trying to say is thanks, in a big way." Her quiet tone held sincerity. "Thank you so much – for everything."

Billie looked at her friends in silence. She nodded. "Listen, I'll make a deal with you. You guys cheer up here and now, and I'll buy you that drink I promised, now that we *have* finally made it, as long as you can handle being in public with me," she added. "I mean, I'd hate to give you a bad reputation for hanging out with a cop."

The girls smiled.

"What, you had doubts?" Casey teased. It brought light chortles from her friends.

"I wouldn't be surprised if she called Bates in herself back in Willowbank, just to get out of having to spend money on us," Sarah said before Billie could answer.

"Damn, and it didn't work," Billie threw back. "But there's still time, we're a long way from home yet."

"Hmm," Sarah contemplated. She turned to Casey. "Like I said, never trust a cop."

"You are so right."

Jane giggled. "Don't let them get to you, Billie. You have my backing one hundred percent."

Everyone looked at her with wide smiles.

"Well, now, I'm scared," Sarah said.

"And so you should be." Jane grinned.

"Thanks, Jane, but these two are far from 'getting to me,'" the detective assured her.

"Billie?" Dave called.

She turned. He stood by the waiting van. A second car pulled up beside it. Two men climbed out with cameras as soon as it stopped.

"Uh-oh, press. Looks like we've been busted. It's time we were out of here."

"Good idea."

The two men intercepted them as they walked through the wire gate.

"Detective McCoy? Could you tell us what happened? Is it true Captain Bates was tied up in a slave trading racket?"

Dave stepped in between them. "There will be a press conference in a day or so, okay? Not now." While he talked to the reporters, forcing them away from the van with his arms outstretched, the girls climbed in.

"Come on, Lieutenant, give us a break."

The other guy took a couple of photos before the girls disappeared behind the security of the car doors. The tinted windows gave them complete privacy from the outside world.

"Sorry, guys. See you at the conference." Dave turned and slid in beside the driver. The instant he was in, the Toyota pulled out, leaving behind the stunned reporters watching with unwavering stares.

* * *

The girls arrived in Sydney late that night. Word had already leaked out, drawing the reporters in like flies. Mark faced the waiting press alone, distracting them while the girls made their exit. Thanks to the help of security, they slipped out of the airport unnoticed.

Dave led them to the waiting car he'd arranged. A pall settled over the girls as he weaved through the familiar city streets. Billie glanced at the girls in the back. They sat locked in thoughtful trances, watching the hookers and dealers hanging off the footpaths as they drove through King's Cross. The cop knew this was their area, their life, their source of income. It was back to the real world, to the world of looking after themselves in the sleazy side of town.

"You guys okay?"

The quiet question drew all eyes to her. The three girls offered faint smiles.

"Yeah, sure, we're good." Sarah answered after glancing at Jane and Casey.

Billie held her gaze for a moment. The despondency in Sarah's tone spread across her features. That despondency permeated the car. Billie couldn't deny it touched her too. The fact they were splitting up, going their own ways hit hard. She would miss their company, dearly, and she knew the feeling was mutual.

"Good." Though her reply lacked certitude, Billie didn't push it. She returned their smiles and faced the front.

Sarah and Casey were first to be dropped off. Following Sarah's directions, Dave pulled up in front of her unit.

Sarah sighed. "This is it. Home sweet home." It was a unit in a block of six – nothing much to look at but big enough for what she needed. Casey had opted to stay with her for the night. There they sat, staring out at the street, hesitant to leave the car.

"It seems ages since we've been here, doesn't it?" Sarah said.

"Centuries," Casey mumbled. Opening her door, she looked at Dave. "Thanks, Lieutenant, for everything."

Sarah smiled. "Yeah, thanks again, Dave."

"You're welcome. Take care."

Billie and Jane climbed out with them. The four stood on the footpath gazing at the unit block. Noises and voices from the neighbouring units filled the air. In the distance, sirens sounded. A few cars drove down the street behind them. The city seemed extra loud after weeks in the bush.

Sarah and Casey faced their two friends.

"Well..." The next words caught in Sarah's throat.

Jane nodded. "Yeah." Stepping forward, she grabbed Sarah in a hug. "This is horrible."

Billie and Casey embraced. Words didn't seem appropriate, and releasing their emotions in actions seemed to help. After everyone hugged each other, they stood back, looking at one another somewhat apprehensive.

"Are you sure you guys are going to be all right?" Billie asked.

"Yes, now stop worrying," Sarah said.

"Can you get in? I mean, do you have a—"

"Yes, I have a spare key hidden."

"Do you want us to come in for a while? Just to make sure everything is okay?"

"No, it's late. We'll be fine. Go home and get some sleep."

"Okay, we're going." Billie smiled with a nod. It lacked buoyancy.

"Take care," Jane said. Despair roughened her voice. Her stare locked on the two girls. Casey and Sarah looked at her, just as depressed.

"You too. Hey, we'll see you soon, though. The cop owes us a drink, remember?" Sarah said.

Jane's face brightened. "Exactly, and we won't let her forget it either." She smiled at Billie.

"Oh, yeah, that drink. First, I'll have to check my schedule to see when, or even if, I can fit you in..."

Casey laughed. "Get out of here."

Billie smiled. "Come on, Jane. Let's go before we wear out our welcome."

"Huh, I think you're already too late." She turned to Sarah and Casey. "See ya, guys."

"Bye."

Twenty minutes later, Dave pulled up outside Jane's terrace unit. Sitting in the back with Jane, Billie glanced out at the building. The dull streetlight and lengthy shadows only added to the terrace's uninviting semblance. She turned to Jane who stared glumly at the old building. Billie sensed her misgivings, guessing what she was thinking from the reluctance she showed in leaving the car. Her abduction, the insecurity, the lack of welcoming this dive of a place offered would all be on her mind.

"Are you okay?"

Jane glanced at her and gave a faint smile. "Yeah, fine." She opened the door, and paused, looking at Dave. "Thanks for the lift, Dave, *and* everything else."

He nodded a curt nod. "I was happy to help."

She smiled. Casting a glance at Billie, she went to climb out. The detective grabbed her arm, preventing her from leaving.

"Why don't you stay with me for the night if this place gives you the creeps."

Jane stared at her. Breaking Billie's gaze, she glanced at Dave. He sat patiently waiting behind the wheel watching them.

"It's very tempting, but, no, I'll be fine. I have to face this on my own sooner or later. This is the first step to restoring my confidence, my life. If I don't do it now, I'll never do it. This is my home, and, as bad and dreary as it is, I have to accept it. Thanks anyway, I really appreciate it," she said.

Billie studied her. She was proud of Jane. Despite being disheartened, Jane was determined to move on with her life. Nodding, Billie let go of her arm. "Fine, if that's what you want. You have my number. Don't hesitate to call me – *any* time."

Jane nodded with a smile. "I will, thanks." Leaning forward, she hugged the cop. "Stop worrying, I'm okay."

"Sure." Billie climbed out with her. "Do you want me to come in with you?"

Jane shook her head. "No, it's okay. Thanks anyway." Turning, she walked up the steps. At the top, she looked back and flicked Billie a quick wave before disappearing through the scarred front door. Billie leant on the car and blew out a breath, watching her go. She couldn't stop worrying about her, about all of them. If only she could do something to help. At least Sarah and Casey had a job waiting for them, and more comfortable apartments, but Jane had nothing. She'd only been here a day before Bates had grabbed her.

Taking hold of her growing anxiety, the detective opened the passenger door and slipped in beside Dave, pulling the door closed behind her.

He rested a hand on her shoulder. "Come on, let's get you home. You're worn out. I'm sure you'll feel better in the morning, and so will the girls. You can ring and check on them if you're still worried."

She looked at him. Nodding, she laid her head on the headrest. "I know. I just wish I could do more for them, give them something to look forward to, to live for." Anguish knotted her gut.

Dave squeezed her shoulder. "You've done more than enough. They now have their lives back. Isn't that what's important?"

She lifted her head and looked at him, ready to argue the point, and then stopped. A tired breath escaped her. She nodded. Letting her head fall back, she slipped into a silence while Dave drove her home.

Chapter Thirty-Two

Three days later, Sarah and Casey hesitantly entered the foyer of the police department. Both female and male officers walked in and out of the spacious area. Some cast them curious looks, others ignored them. Being among so many cops made Sarah feel uncomfortable, lifting her guard even though no one knew who they were. The grudge she carried was hard to bury. Neither she nor Casey had ever had a pleasurable moment with a cop – other than Billie, Mark and Dave of course. Now, here they were at the front desk right in the middle of head office.

Both girls were dressed casual in tailored jeans wearing a touch of make-up. They looked nothing like the two girls who had been plucked from the far north. Sarah's arm was out of the sling but she still nursed it protectively. Her bruises had almost faded, the make-up helping to disguise them.

Some of the younger male officers turned, staring at them in passing, admiring their slim figures and attractive presentation. An elderly sergeant walked to the front counter and met them.

"Can I help you?" His gruff voice did little to settle Sarah's already panicky nerves.

"Would Detective McCoy be in?" Casey asked.

The officer studied them for a moment, doing his best to hide his surprise at the request. He picked up a phone and punched in some numbers. He waited a few moments before speaking. "Sergeant Whitley here. Is Detective McCoy up there? Okay, thanks." He hung up and looked at the girls. "No, not as yet I'm afraid."

Casey cast Sarah a glance and then asked, "How about Lieutenant Edwards?"

The desk sergeant failed to contain his surprise at this request. "Lieutenant Edwards?"

"Yes," Casey answered politely. Sarah inwardly smiled. It wasn't hard to see this guy was having trouble comprehending how two young attractive strangers like themselves and Dave could have anything in common.

"I'll check," he said with some reluctance. Again he picked up the phone and punched in the required numbers. He briefly spoke to someone. His gaze drifted to the girls as they listened. "Sorry, you're out of luck there too I'm afraid. He's in a meeting," he explained, hanging the phone up. "You could wait over there if you like," he suggested, pointing to a vinyl bench seat by the wall in a corner. "He shouldn't be too long."

They looked in the direction he indicated. Casey nodded.

"Thanks."

Taking up the sergeant's offer, the girls sat down on the bench. Since arriving home, they hadn't seen Billie due to the fact she'd been kept busy with press and paperwork. She'd been in contact with them a couple of times on the phone to check on them. In their last conversation, they'd arranged to meet today in her office. They'd arrived early so guessed she shouldn't be too far away.

Sarah, sitting tense and stiff, and very much on edge, watched the foyer like a trapped animal.

Casey flashed a smile after glancing at her. "Relax, it shouldn't be for long."

"I'm relaxed, okay?" Sarah affirmed, the answer sharp and unconvincing.

Casey nodded, taking no offence. "Yeah, I can see that."

Sarah looked at her then exhaled a sigh. Distractedly she picked up a magazine from the low table beside her and started flicking through the pages, too tense to actually read it but it gave her something to do. Suppressing a smile, Casey took another and sat back with it in her lap.

The foyer was busy. Officers and civilians were coming and going. A young cop in uniform strode in. His solid and stocky build filled out his uniform in a snug fit. Everything that could be polished was polished, right down to his shoes. The spic and span, spotless look supported his creaseless blue attire. The number one haircut distinguished his features to appear butch and authoritative.

Glancing at the girls in passing, he abruptly stopped and stared. Casting a casual look over one shoulder and then the other, he crossed to the waiting visitors. He stood watching them without a word.

The girls looked up from their magazines when they became aware of his presence. Sarah checked her uneasiness. It wasn't hard to read his over-exaggerated commanding expression. The self-centred look conveyed only one interpretation – to strip them down. Immediately Sarah sensed trouble. This guy was the fitting prototype of the police officers she'd come to loathe.

"Let me guess. You two are the reffos rescued from the jungles up north, aren't you?"

Sarah stared blankly, hardly surprised by the question and his belittling tone. He was exactly what she'd assumed. As soon as she'd laid eyes on him, she knew he was going to be a smartarse. He proved it the moment he opened his mouth. Give these thickheads a uniform and their heads grow to match their exaggerated egos.

Quietly and with distaste, Sarah answered. "And what's that supposed to mean?"

"You heard me." He cast a quick look around behind him before stepping in closer and leaning forward with a sneer twisting his face. "Don't think you'll get any special privileges just because you spent a few days with McCoy."

The unmistakable tone in his voice expressed his dislike and jealousy of Billie. Sarah now knew this was closer to his motives for jumping on them rather than their involvement in bringing Bates to justice. He'd obviously clashed with Billie in the past and was using them as an avenue to get back at her. Either way, whatever his reasons, he'd succeeded in stirring up his targets.

Sarah jumped to her feet and stared him in the eye. "And what would you know about it?" she spat. "Taking a wild guess, I think you might be a little put off by us and Detective McCoy catching a wanted criminal out, particularly a corrupt police officer."

Casey was instantly by her side, protective and ready to stand up to this bigoted law enforcer.

Lifting an accusing finger, the officer shoved it in Sarah's face. "Be careful how you speak to me. You could find yourself in a lot of trouble, something I'm sure you're already familiar with." He glanced at Casey before going on. "I know you and I know what you are – once a pro, always a pro. You lot can't stay out of prison and I'm sure it won't be long before you're back behind bars. Your game of playing hero is over, not that I expect you did much anyway to catch Bates out. You'll be back where you belong in no time."

"What's the matter, Constable..." She hesitated while she read his name badge. Her gaze returned to his. "Bodey. A bit sour we did your work for you?"

His face reddened in discomfiture. "Maybe I could do a little digging to find a reason to get you back in a cell faster."

"You bastard," Casey cut in ahead of Sarah. "We don't have to take this shit, not from you or any other stinking pig here. We are clean now and you have no right to slander us."

"I told you to watch your mouth," he threatened, his stare burning into hers. No comeback met him. Satisfied he'd put her in her place, he reinforced his status. "You need to show some respect or I might have to teach you how. I have friends in places you wouldn't believe."

"I'd doubt you'd have friends anywhere, not ones you didn't have to pay."

"It must really hurt your macho ego to know that us *pros* defeated the whole police force by catching Bates out after three years," Sarah spat, drawing his attention from Casey. "Especially when he'd been doing it right under your noses the entire time. Oh, and let me correct you, we had a lot to do with Bates' demise."

The officer's eyes narrowed. "You know, I've got a good mind to slap a charge on you for insubordination. A night in the slammer would soon cool you two down and teach you some respect for the law."

"Try it, you weasel," Casey challenged, her resentment blinding her perception of where she was and who she was talking to.

Sarah was quick to back her. "We have every respect for the law – just none for you." After what they'd been through and the people they'd had to face, this guy was nothing more than a pigheaded nobody. The fact he was in uniform or who he represented did nothing to deter her. "Why don't you get back to what you were doing and stop bothering us or *we* might teach you a lesson in respect when we put in a complaint against you regarding police harassment." He glared hard but didn't comment. Sarah acted on it. "Now, we are patiently waiting here for Detective McCoy and Lieutenant Edwards, so if you want us to take this further, Constable Bodey, by all means, we will."

"Don't try to threaten me using McCoy and Edwards. They won't be able to help you should I lay a charge on you."

"Fine, go for it," Sarah said, taking up his challenge. "Then we'll see who will come out on top."

He stared, weighing up her threat. Casey watched on, firing a hard glare in support of Sarah's challenge. Sarah maintained her resolute expression, hardly believing she was doing what she was doing. This shithead could indeed arrest them but it was obvious he was afraid of Billie and Dave. Bodey's features twitched in his silent debate in which avenue to take. At last he backed off.

"Sit down and stay out of my way," he snarled.

"Pleasure."

He turned and strode off. Sarah exhaled a tense breath and sat down, doing her best to settle her shot nerves. "What an arsehole," she spat.

Casey sank onto the chair beside her. "And they call themselves cops."

"Shit, I need some fresh air." She jumped up. Her rage soared way beyond control after the way Bodey had treated them. Her nervous gaze darted around the foyer. "Man, we don't belong here." She ran a hand back through her hair and then stepped towards the door, struggling to come to terms with what had happened. Casey caught up to her. They walked out and marched across the car park in silence. Reaching the car, Casey pulled her up by the arm.

"Wait up a minute, will you?"

"Can you believe that? Typical bloody cops. *Typical*," Sarah exploded, ripping her arm free. Shaking her head, she looked away, away from Casey's supportive gaze.

"Hey, I agree, okay, but you're forgetting one thing."

"What?" she snapped, directing her unsympathetic look at her friend. Casey ignored the harshness, both in her tone and her eyes.

"Our statements, that's what."

"They can shove them up their arses for all I care."

"Sarah, you know as well as I do we have to write them out."

Sarah glared in a steady stare, considering the words for a long, silent moment while battling to decide what to do. Coming up with a blank, she sat down on the bonnet and folded her arms, exhaling a heavy, frustrated breath.

Casey sighed and stood looking at her. The short silence forced itself upon Sarah, rudely intruding on her flustered thoughts. Feeling her friend's eyes on her, she glanced up when Casey failed to make any further comment. Casey watched her with a strange yet expectant look.

"Now what?" Sarah demanded in a gruff tone, knowing from the disturbed expression on her face something else bothered her.

Casey sighed and looked around the car park. Finally, her gaze returned to Sarah. Another sigh slipped through her lips. "Don't get me wrong here, okay? You have every right to be mad at that bastard, just as I am," she said. "He shouldn't have spoken to us like that. It was unprovoked and—"

Sarah wasn't in the mood to go over it again. Shaking her head in annoyance, she leant forward to stand up, "Don't start on about—"

Casey pushed her back. Her hasty actions cut Sarah off. "Listen to me for a minute. The thing is, we promised Billie we would be in today. We have to write up our statements."

"We can call her and change it. I do not feel like facing any more cops today."

Casey raised her eyebrows. "Are you talking about Billie?"

"What?" Sarah had to check her surprise. "No, of course not. Yes, she's a cop, but that's not what I meant."

"Good. You had me worried there for a minute." She flashed a smile. "The thing is, Billie will be relying on us to turn up. You have to do it today whether you want to or not."

Sarah suddenly couldn't answer. After a brief silence, she tore her gaze from Casey's with a frustrated grunt and inattentively watched the traffic passing by out on the busy street while struggling to control her confused emotions. She knew Casey was right but with her hatred for cops like Bodey driving her on, she found she was too upset to commit herself. She shook her head. Once again, her pride stood in the way.

"How come you're not supporting me here?" she pressed, looking at Casey with a frown. "You always have when it comes to cops."

"Well, that was before we had a cop for a friend, wasn't it," she joked. Sarah made no reaction to it. Casey pushed on. "Sarah, you know we don't have a choice. They are waiting on our statements to finalise this case."

Sarah could only stare. As hard as she tried, she failed to come up with a feasible answer to dispute it. "Damn it, this is all so crazy," she breathed, dropping her gaze and staring at her feet. She knew she was kidding herself. She couldn't deny Billie was indeed their friend and was relying on them to fill out their statements.

"Yeah, that it is." Casey's tone had mellowed.

A voice suddenly interrupted them. "Sarah! Casey!"

The girls looked out over the rear of the car. Jane walked towards them through the rows of parked cars with a wide friendly grin on her face.

"Hi, guys!" The enthusiasm was strong in her greeting. She quickened her pace to reach them.

"Hi!"

"Hey, hello," they responded, returning her smile somewhat subdued. Jane's arrival brought with it a warm welcome. Sarah had to admit it was good to see her. Until now, she hadn't realised how much she'd missed her. The bright happy look across her merry features was enough to drag anyone out of the dumps. Jane's bruising had almost disappeared. Her eye was still a little dark and a yellow, fading bruise stood out on her cheek. She, too, had used light make-up in an effort to conceal it. Sarah stood to meet her. She and Casey gave her a hug.

"Hey, it's good to see you're out of the sling," Jane chirped to Sarah. The excitement was clearly expressed in her voice.

"Yeah, it's a lot better now."

"I have missed you guys so much."

"Same here," Casey said. "You're looking great."

"And so are you." She turned to Sarah, her smile broadening. "It'll be so good to catch up with Billie. I've missed her too."

"Yeah, same here." Sarah's smile faded. The thought of returning to the cop station injected a sombre tone in her voice. Jane stared at her confused. She looked at Casey. She didn't appear very happy either.

"Uh-oh, something's wrong. What is it?" she asked, looking from one to the other.

"Nothing," Sarah answered, almost too abrupt. It caught Jane's attention, the blunt reply betraying her badly.

"Don't give me that. Something is worrying you. Hell, what's happened? And why are you sitting out here in the car park?"

"It's nothing, just drop it."

The harshness in Sarah's tone drew a concern into Jane's gaze. She studied her two friends under a pensive stare.

"Please, we've been through too much for you to simply shut me out. I care about you guys and I can see you are both upset. Come on, tell me what's wrong."

The girls held her stare. Jane's speech might have been short but it packed a powerful punch. Casey glanced at Sarah, nodding a curt nod. Sarah sighed. Jane was right. They *were* friends and she had every right to know.

"Okay," Sarah started, turning to Jane. "If you want to know, we just got our arses kicked in there, that's what."

"What are you talking about?"

Casey took over when Sarah hesitated. "Some young cop recognised us, both from our trip up north and from our past. Well, he certainly knew about our past, that's for sure. Anyway, he started into us for no reason other than to throw his weight around. He couldn't put us down quick enough and started threatening us. The thing is, he stirred us up so much, we gave some back. It was starting to get pretty nasty," she explained. "He was going to arrest us."

Shock highlighted Jane's face. "You're joking."

"I wish I was. He was such an arsehole. He doesn't deserve to be wearing a uniform, let alone representing the law."

"And that's why I hate cops. There are way too many like him," Sarah spat. When the girls failed to continue with the story, Jane looked at them confused.

"And . . . then what happened?" she prompted.

Casey shrugged. "Surprisingly, our hothead friend here turned his threat around by throwing Billie and Dave's names at him, explaining how if anything happened to us, he'd have to face them. She sure put the wind up him because he backed off after that. We were so pissed after dealing with him, we stormed out of there." A light smile touched her lips, emphasising her dimples. "This is as far as we got."

Jane stared wide-eyed. "You didn't speak to someone about him?"

"No. I told you, we were too shit off."

"But why didn't you wait in there? Billie will be wondering where we are."

"Hey, you weren't there," Sarah cut in, her sharp tone defensive and abrupt. "That creep was way out of line to speak to us the way he did. He was such an arsehole." She shook her head at the thought of it. "I could've smashed his face in, then and there. The whole place is full of them. We had to get out before I did something I'd regret."

Jane, remaining calm, backed off. "Okay, take it easy, I'm on your side, remember?"

Sarah glared intently and then blew out a breath, checking her temper. Jane was right. Taking it out on her was not going to help the situation. "Shit, I'm sorry."

Jane nodded, happy with that. She turned to Casey. "So, you know you have to write up your statements, right?"

Casey glanced at Sarah before facing Jane. "Yeah."

A playful smile sprang to Jane's lips, inspiring an attempt to shed some humour on the subject and ease the tension. "Well then, what are we waiting for? Come on." Turning, she walked towards the police building – only to stop after a couple of steps. She looked over her shoulder. Sarah and Casey hadn't made any effort to follow. Jane turned and faced them. Folding her arms and tilting her head, she silently challenged them to accompany her.

Casey and Sarah returned her gaze. Undeterred by her stern look, Sarah struggled with her hurt emotions. Going back in there was too big an ask.

"Don't you think you at least owe Billie a statement?" Jane put to them.

The girls' lingering stares didn't flinch. Finally, Casey turned to Sarah, her resigned look filled with defeat.

Sarah sighed. The mention of Billie brought her thoughts back into perspective. "Yeah, I guess you're right." She glanced at the building in question and exhaled a nervous breath. "Fine. Let's do this."

"That's what I like to hear." With a smile and supportive nod, Jane turned and led them into the foyer. The girls bravely lined up at the front counter. Jane politely asked the desk sergeant for directions to Billie's office. He glanced at Sarah and Casey.

"She came in a few minutes ago."

Sarah couldn't answer, not when she was so apprehensive about being here. Casey did it for her.

"Thanks, that's good to hear."

Nodding, he turned to Jane and explained where they had to go. Thanking him, they rode the lift up to the top floor. It was a silent and smooth ride. When it bumped to a gentle halt, the girls stepped out and looked around.

A large open room met them, spanning a good quarter of an acre of floor space. Divider walls about six feet high separated it into a maze of offices. Directly in front, a wide hallway faced them. The full length wall on the left had several doors along it, offering the rooms behind it more privacy. The place was a mumble of noise. An older officer ambled towards them, or rather to the lift they were exiting.

"Can I help you?" he asked in passing, noticing the lost expressions on their faces as they looked around. Then he stopped, his gaze locking on the three faces. A smile lit up his. "Hey! Aren't you the girls who helped Billie nail Bates? I ought to shake your hands." So he did. Quickly he took each of the dumbfounded girls by the hand and shook them. "Great job – doing Bates in I mean. I never did like that man."

"Thank you," Jane answered with a smile, glancing at the other two. "Could you please tell us where we could find Billie?"

"Sure. Boy, it's so good to have her back. We all missed her." Turning, he pointed down the hall. "Go straight down here and her office is the fourth on the left."

"Great," Jane said.

"Pleasure." With that he left, disappearing into the lift.

Jane turned to Sarah with a playful smile lighting up her face. "'Arseholes' you said."

Casey and Sarah both looked at her with faint smiles tugging at their lips. Feeling she'd just been made out to be a liar, Sarah wasn't about to give it up so easily.

"Huh. It wouldn't surprise me one bit if McCoy hadn't paid him to do that," she mused.

Jane couldn't hold in the laugh. The two girls smiled. At last they were beginning to relax.

"I couldn't have said it better," Casey agreed, her smile widening. She slipped an arm around Sarah's shoulders. "Never trust a cop. Isn't that our motto?"

Sarah looked at her with a chuckle, appreciating her words of wisdom. "Definitely."

Feeling quite united, they turned to Jane with triumphant looks. Jane shook her head. "Come on."

Chapter Thirty-Three

Billie sat on the edge of her desk beside her chair facing the large window overlooking the city with a spectacular view of the harbour, a postcard scene that could hold anyone's eye for long moments. But she showed no interest in it. Her focus was on the papers in her hands. A quiet knocking behind caught her attention. Her head shot around. Jane, Casey, and Sarah stood in the doorway. They seemed a little on edge, no doubt brought on by being in the company of so many cops. She could imagine their discomfort riding the lift up and walking through the maze of offices, and officers, to find her.

Since arriving home, Billie hadn't seen the girls. It warmed her heart to see them now. She'd missed their company.

"Hey. Hi, come in," the detective said with a smile, placing the papers on the desk. The three girls entered on her invitation. She noticed Sarah's arm was out of the sling and their bruises had almost faded, hidden by light makeup. Billie walked around to meet them, favouring a slight limp. Out of the four of them, she carried the most tell-tale signs of their horrific adventure; her blackened eye, cut lip and bruised chin and cheek were slowly healing. She moved a little stiffly from the wound on her ribs and leg but overall, felt refreshed and revived, and happy to see the girls.

Jane smiled. "Hi. It's so good to see you." She hugged her.

Casey hugged her next. "It is, but man, it's an adventure just trying to find you."

"Why couldn't you have an office on the ground floor? Do you know how many cops we had to mingle with? And you know how much I love cops," Sarah said with a teasing tone, giving her a hug after Casey.

Billie chuckled. "Do you good. I should show you around, introduce you to some of my associates."

"Ah no thanks. Let's not rush this." She exhaled a heavy sigh. "I've already met one of your fellow officers, who believe me, almost turned me away from here for good."

Billie held her gaze, picking up on the seriousness of her comment. "What are you talking about? Who?"

"Oh, it's nothing, forget it."

"Yeah, we'd rather not discuss it," Casey put in.

"Nothing?" Jane queried. "I think it was a little more than nothing." She turned to Billie. "I found them fuming in the car park and believe me, they were upset."

Billie looked from one to the other, "Okay, what's happened?"

Sarah shrugged. "It's okay, now. Besides, if we tell you, I know you'll charge downstairs and jump on the arsehole, who I must say deserves it, and who might I add, has a big grudge against you, which is half the reason he jumped on us, to get at you, besides the fact he wanted to throw his weight around to scare us . . . and possibly arrest us," she finally finished. Billie stared, striving to piece the cryptic explanation together.

"Are you saying someone hassled you downstairs?"

"Hassled? Yeah, you could call it that, and believe me, I was so pissed, I was out of here. You have Casey and Jane to thank for changing my mind."

Billie's voice hardened. "Who was it?"

"Like I said, you'll go after him and then he'll think I sent you, not that I care."

"Why would he think that?"

"Maybe because I mentioned you would. He backed off quick smart after that, so really, you've already done your piece. He was afraid of what you could do to him."

Billie was gobsmacked. The first time Sarah steps foot in the station and some smartarse has to hassle her? Talk about lousy timing. She turned to Casey and Jane. Casey responded to her stunned reaction.

"Sarah's right, he was an arsehole, but she put him in his place very professionally. You would have been proud of her."

Billie turned to Sarah, who had a faint smile on her lips. Glad she wasn't affected by the uncalled attack, she injected a playful tone into her reply. "Is that so?"

"Yeah. I can't believe even you have enemies here."

Billie chuckled. She nodded. "There's arseholes everywhere, and at times, they need bringing into line, which I can't do if I don't know who it is."

"You have that many who don't like you?" Casey asked, surprised. Billie smiled.

"They're only the ones I know about. There are a few individuals here who don't think I should be in the squad."

"You're kidding," Jane cut in, unable to hide her surprise. "You would have to be the biggest asset in it."

Sarah nodded. "I'll say. You're right though. This guy sure sounded jealous of you so he'd fall into that category, so next time you cross paths with Constable Bodey, give him one for us."

"Bodey? Shit, he *is* an arsehole. We've clashed a few times, and yes, he definitely believes a girl has no place in a squad like ours."

"We guessed that," Casey said.

"Ha." Billie focused on Sarah. "Well, I'm glad you sorted him out, and I'm glad you're still here. I'm sorry it happened."

"Yeah, me too."

"Don't let him get to you. He is as corrupt as they come and if a chance ever comes up, I intend to nail him."

"Good. Do it hard."

"Definitely."

Sarah nodded and then sighed. "All I have to do now is adjust to being in a building full of cops."

Billie smiled. "You're doing great."

She gave Billie a smile and then looked around. "So, you have your own office. That's impressive."

"I don't know if you'd call it impressive."

"Oh yeah, I'd call it impressive." Jane moved to the window and admired the view.

Casey walked around the desk and joined her. "Okay, I can see why you have the top floor. Hell, how do you get any work done when you have this to distract you?"

The spectacular view of the harbour presented a striking scene. The clear blue water was sprinkled with small white dots – boats. Busy ferries shot up and down between them. Even from this distance, the mighty harbour bridge boasted its image, an image that labelled Sydney all around the world. Its arched length spread majestically over the marine playground like a protector, an ambassador.

"That's probably why I'm always behind," Billie joked. "Hey, you guys look great."

"It's amazing what a long soak in a tub and rest can do for a girl," Sarah said distractedly, gazing at the view.

"Ain't that the truth. Like a coffee or tea?"

"Coffee's fine," Jane answered, backed by nods from Sarah and Casey. The girls wrote out their statements over the hot brew and friendly talk. The time passed quickly. After reading and approving their statements, Billie put them to the side and sat back in the chair. She gazed across the desk at her friends.

"You know, I've been doing some thinking since we arrived home. Now, tell me if I'm out of line here but I'm just trying to help, okay?"

"What are you talking about?" Casey asked. Curiosity laced the question.

For a moment, Billie was hesitant. What she had to say might upset them but it was a risk she was willing to take. "I'd like to help you find steady jobs."

A brief silence hung over them. Wrapped in surprise, the girls stared hard. Sarah broke it.

"We already have steady jobs," she quietly reminded her, a slight touch of resentment invading her voice.

Billie's gaze shot to hers. Like always, Sarah would be the hardest to tackle. "Just answer me this. Are you happy doing what you're doing? Can you tell me it's truly what you want to do?" Billie had sensed she and Casey were apprehensive about coming home to their jobs, and Jane had nothing to look forward to and really no direction to head in. Worried if they weren't given a chance, they'd slip back into the life they'd only ever known, and they deserved more than that.

Sarah sat forward on the edge of her chair. Her eyes narrowed. "You're right. You're *way* out of line."

Without shifting her elbows from the armrests, the detective lowered her head and cupped her hands over her nose and mouth. Gently she blew into them, patiently waiting for the onslaught. She knew these girls too well and prepared herself for what they had to throw at her. It was a touchy subject and needed to be handled carefully.

As usual, Sarah didn't let her down. "Just because you're a cop doesn't give you the right to run our lives."

Billie looked up over her hands, meeting her irritated stare. Considering her words, she dropped her hands and raised her head without altering her gaze. "Hear me out, okay?"

"Forget it, I've heard enough. I get good money for what I do and I do it well."

"I don't doubt that, but do you plan to keep desperate men happy for the rest of your life, no matter what the price, facing the risk of abuse and violence or catching some disease? Do you *want* to spend the rest of your life in and out of prison?"

Sarah jumped to her feet and leant forward clasping the edge of the desk. She glared at the detective. "Is this what it's all about? Are you afraid we'll embarrass you if we're caught, afraid we'll mar your big reputation? Don't worry, I promise I won't let on I know you if it comes to that."

Billie stood, raising her hands in defence. "Will you calm down for a minute?" She hobbled around the desk.

Sarah pushed off the desktop and shook her head, running a hand through her hair. "Bloody hell, I don't believe you. Already you're pulling rank and trying to change our lives. Well, we are not interested. You hear me?"

Billie stopped in front of her. "I'm not trying to pull rank on you. I just want to help give you another opportunity to better your future, that's all, honest. I care a lot about you guys and I don't give a shit what people think about our friendship. All I'm asking is for you to hear me out. If you don't like it, there's nothing to lose, is there."

Sarah's glare held no leniency. "Forget it." She went to move off, but Billie caught her arm and looked her in the eye.

"Please."

The simple word stopped Sarah in her tracks. She held the cop's gaze, speechless. Turning away, she lowered her head, blowing out a heavy breath. Billie knew a couple of weeks ago Sarah would have instantly told her to shove it, but that was before she'd come to mean anything to her.

Sarah looked up and, for a long moment, stared at the cop. She turned to Jane and Casey. The two girls sat rigid, watching.

Jane nodded at Billie, feeding off Sarah's hesitancy. "Okay, we're listening."

Billie returned her attention to Sarah. She released her arm. "If you were given the chance to do something else, what would it be?"

"I told you, I don't *want* to do anything else."

"You've never had a desire to be someone, to do something you'd really enjoy? A childhood dream maybe?"

"No . . . I don't know." Frustration, confusion, and hope were all rolled into her tone.

"Come on, there must be something."

Sarah glanced at the other two. They sat watching intently with a touch of curiosity in their stares.

"A jeweller," she said with uncertainty, facing the cop. "I've always had a thing about shaping and designing stones and rings and, you know, jewellery."

Billie nodded. At last, she was making progress. A faint smile played on her lips. Deep down she knew she'd safely got over the first major hurdle. Sarah was playing the game.

"All right. That's good." She turned to the others. "How about you, Case?"

The girl cast a hesitant look at her two friends before looking at Billie.

"Well, after growing up as a car thief and safe opener, I'd love to do something involving locks and electronics. I've always wanted to design a lock that'd fool the best of thieves. Anything with electronics, I'd be happy."

Billie gave a short laugh, nodding her approval. "Jane?"

There was no hesitation with her, not now after the other two had given their answers.

"I've always dreamt of being a hairdresser."

"Okay." Billie flashed a quick smile and turned, strolling back around the desk. She sank onto the chair pondering over the answers. Placing her elbows on the armrests and interlocking her fingers, she lowered her head in thought.

"So where did that little exercise take us?" Casey asked after a lingering silence.

The detective looked up. Her gaze drifted to each of her friends, meeting their questioning looks. She leant back in the chair. "I'm not making any promises, but I may be able to start you on your dreams."

"What?" Sarah blurted. She sat down with a frown, grappling with what the cop was saying.

"Ha, that's crazy," Casey said. "No one hires crims these days, *no* one."

"Maybe you've never pushed hard enough or the right buttons."

"No, forget it," Sarah said. "We don't want you getting us a job on your good name."

"I understand that, and I'm not saying I will. What I *am* saying is I may be able to help you get a foot in the door, a chance to prove yourself, prove that you're dedicated and reliable workers. I may be able to offer you an interview, that's all. You might not get past that stage, but, at least, it's worth a try. You've certainly got nothing to lose by it."

The girls held her steadfast gaze while considering the offer.

"We'd like to be able to believe you, Billie, but Casey's right. No one is going to hire us with our records," Jane said.

Billie shrugged. "Like I said, you've got nothing to lose, have you." No one challenged her. "Give me a week, okay? If nothing comes of it, I won't bring it up again."

The three girls looked at one another.

"I guess it can't hurt to give it a try," Jane said. Casey nodded.

Sarah sighed. "Whatever." She turned to the detective. "I'm sure it's going to be a waste of time, but it's your time." Shooting Jane and Casey a quick glance, she returned her gaze to Billie. "A week you have."

Billie smiled. "Thanks, I'll do my best."

A knock at the door distracted them. Dave walked in.

"Hi, guys, how are we all?" Dressed in a suit and tie, the formal attire made him appear sophisticated and important, the role of lieutenant shining through. He looked totally different to when they'd first met him.

"Hi, Dave."

"Hi."

"Good, how are you?"

"I'm fine," he answered, waving them down in their seats when they started to get up. "Have you settled back in all right?"

"Yeah, more or less," Casey said.

Sarah nodded. "We're doing okay."

"I'm glad to hear it." He cast Billie a quick sideways glance. She acknowledged it with a slight nod, knowing exactly the reason behind his visit. He had good news, very good news in fact. She almost found it hard to remain composed.

Dave turned to the visiting girls and dug into his coat pocket. "I just stopped by quickly hoping to catch you. I have something here you might be interested in." He smiled and passed Jane an envelope, only because she happened to be the one sitting closest to him. Hesitantly Jane took the offered envelope and stared at it.

Casey and Sarah looked on with baffled expressions.

"What is it?" Sarah asked, shooting her gaze between Dave and the held envelope.

"Well, as soon as Jane opens it, you'll know, won't you."

They turned to each other and then looked at Billie. She smiled and shrugged her shoulders.

Jane ripped open the envelope and pulled out a folded letter. With a brief glance at Sarah and Casey, she unfolded it and read its contents. Her eyes widened. Her mouth dropped open. She stiffened, staring at the paper in her hands.

"Jane, what is it?" Casey asked. When Jane failed to answer or even acknowledge she'd been spoken to, Casey gently pulled the letter from her hands and positioned it between her and Sarah. The girls read it for themselves.

Casey sucked in a breath. Sarah's face paled.

Dave chuckled. "I've just come from a meeting confirming the entitlement of the reward on solving this case still stands. As you can see, it does, and as you three played an extensive part in bringing it to a head and ending it, I've persuaded the authorities that the money is rightly yours."

The girls looked at him wide-eyed.

"Ours?" Jane whispered.

"But . . . but this says the reward is three million dollars," Casey stammered.

"There must be some mistake," Sarah said in an unrecognisable voice.

Dave smiled. "It's no mistake, believe me. You've earned it."

"But that means the split is one million each," Sarah said in astonishment.

"Yes, it does. Your maths is good. It started off as a million but as the case blew out over time with no leads, an extra mil was added each year. That amount of money still failed to entice anyone to step forward with information."

Casey shook her head. "Dave, we can't accept this."

"Sure you can. It's for a job well done. You should have the money in about a week. You can sort out the details with Billie sometime in the near future." He struggled to keep a straight face at the three girls' mystified looks. "Like I said, this case had been going on for too long. The reward was offered to help quicken it up, but, even with that incentive, no one could help us. Bates had every detail covered and, as you know, didn't leave a trace of evidence behind. Without your help, he would've kept getting away with it."

"But..." Jane stopped. She seemed unable to find the right words to say.

"Come on, you guys should be proud of yourselves." Dave smiled, looking from one to the next. "You did us cops a favour, and a big one."

Stunned, Jane looked at Billie. The cop smiled, making no effort to intervene. Jane turned to the lieutenant. "But, Dave, you're missing the point here. Billie did most of it. Hell, you may as well say all of it. She was the one who brought down Bates, *and* Bland. This money should be hers, not ours."

"I can't take it," Billie said. "It's illegal for cops to claim rewards. Besides, I don't need it. I'd rather see you three have it. You deserve it. Consider it compensation if you like, for the misery and hurt Bates put you through."

Casey shook her head, struggling to get the words out. "You don't – need three million bucks?"

"Ha," Billie said with a grin, enjoying the stunned state her friends had slipped into. "It is a lot of money, I agree but, no, not really. My parents left me enough funds to live very comfortably on."

"Okay, then we split it four ways," Jane said, throwing another avenue in the mix.

"Honestly, I legally can't take it. The money's yours. It's all arranged, so enjoy it. As far as I'm concerned, you've earned every cent of it."

A brief silence met her along with three pairs of wide, staring eyes.

"Damn it, McCoy, don't do this to us," Sarah finally said, shaking her head.

"Do what? It's rightfully yours. End of story." She flashed a smile.

Again the girls fell silent. They turned to the lieutenant.

Dave, looking uncomfortable under the scrutiny of their piercing gazes, glanced at his watch. "Well, I've got another meeting to get to. Thanks, guys, for a job well done."

"Dave–hell–thank you," Jane feebly answered.

"Yes, thank you so much. I can't believe you've gone to all this trouble just for us," Casey replied in a daze.

"It's a pleasure, and, believe me, it was no trouble. In fact, I hardly did any of it. Billie's the one who was behind it. She remembered about the reward and chased it up."

All attention swung her way. The girls expressed only looks of overwhelming respect and gratitude.

The detective shrugged and flashed a warm smile. "Well, I'd rather see it go to you than some do-gooder."

The light insult brought instant smiles to their faces. Jane gave a sob of joy. Tears welled in her eyes. Sarah shook her head. Casey stared intently at Billie.

"Okay, guys, I'll catch up with you later," Dave said, breaking the silence. "And, Billie, get home as soon as you're finished here."

"I will."

He nodded. Casting the three girls a brief smile, he turned towards the exit.

"Bye, Dave," Jane said.

"Thanks again," Casey added.

Sarah cleared her throat. "Yes, thank you."

"Take care, guys." He disappeared out the door.

The girls looked at the detective, the astonishment still haunting their faces.

"Shit, Billie, why?" Sarah asked.

"Why what? The money? I thought I made that clear. You deserve it, simple as that."

"The hell we do. How can you say we deserve it? We were more of a burden than a help."

Billie stared at her, the smile fading from her lips. She glanced at the other two. They sat watching, absorbed, obviously supporting Sarah from the looks on their strained faces. The detective sat forward, focusing on Sarah. "Okay, let's get this straight once and for all. You were *never* a burden, do you hear me? Sure, there were times when things seemed hopeless and went wrong but not through any fault of yours. They were difficult times because of the circumstances, not because of any of you. We got through them, together. You guys were there for me when I needed you and helped me more than you'll ever know. We had our moments, true, but I never once considered you a burden – and still don't."

The brief hush that followed weighed heavy. The girls stared with solemn faces. Billie inwardly smiled. She'd bowled them over, and, hopefully, buried this subject for good.

"Now, I don't want to hear any more about the reward, okay? It's all been finalised and it's all yours, to do with as you please." Still no reply met her. She'd never seen them looking so . . . stunned. Maybe she'd hit them a little too hard. Resting her elbows on the desk, she smiled. "You know, now that you've come into money, I think it gets me off the hook for buying you that drink, and, seeing as you're so eager to give it away, you're welcome to waste your share on me. How about *you* do the shouting instead?"

At last she had a reaction, the very one she was fishing for. Snapping out of their dazes, the challenge in her words inspired a response.

"What? No way are you getting out of that promise, reward or no reward," Sarah shot back at her. "You are going to buy us that drink whether you like it or not, and we intend to drink you under the table, so make sure you come loaded."

"Too right. You've been sitting on this promise for far too long so you're not sliming out of it now, understand?" Casey said.

Billie's smile widened. Yes, it was a response she was well used to. Glad to see these two on top of it again, she turned to Jane, waiting for her opinion on the matter. The girl flashed a warm smile.

"Sorry, but I'm with them this time. I've waited too long for this drink, so you're not backing out of it."

"Aren't you supposed to be on my side?"

"Don't throw that at me. This was your idea, may I remind you."

Billie shook her head, grinning at her friends. "Huh, just the answer I'd expect from you guys."

"Good, then you know that's the end of the argument, isn't it," Sarah said.

"Fine, I know when I'm beat. Let's make a date then. How about this Friday night?"

Casey nodded. "You're on."

"Okay, sounds good."

"Can't wait. Let us know where and when."

"Will do."

"Good." Jane stood. "And on that note, we should leave so you can get home and put your feet up."

The girls walked to the lift under a casual conversation.

"I'll be in touch," Billie said as they stopped in front of the closed doors.

"Sure." Jane stared at her. Solemnity washed the warmth from her features. Biting on her bottom lip, she stepped forward and hugged the cop. "Billie, thank you so much, for everything."

Billie smiled. "Like I said, it was a pleasure."

As soon as Jane let her go, Casey readily took up her spot.

"Same goes for me. Thank you."

Billie returned her hug. Standing back, the cop smiled and looked at Sarah. The girl shook her head, grinning. She stepped forward and hugged her.

"You damn cop. Thank you."

They held each other for a few moments. Billie appreciated the unconditional friendship that now bound them.

"You're welcome." She let her go.

Sarah, Jane and Casey looked at one another with contented smiles.

"Okay. Well, we'll see you soon." Sarah pressed the down arrow beside the lift. The doors opened with a quiet hum.

"Will do."

"See you." Jane smiled and stepped into the lift. Sarah and Casey followed. They waved her goodbye and then the doors slid closed.

Billie sighed, revelling in the wash of emotions surging through her. This was the closest she'd ever been to these girls, and it felt good. They *were* good friends. Turning, she strolled to her office with her mind fixed on the girls. Reaching the room, she remembered her earlier promise about finding them jobs. Walking to her desk, she pulled a diary out of the top drawer.

"Shit, this had better work." She flipped through the pages of contacts she'd collected over the years, searching for someone who might be of help to her.

Chapter Thirty-Four

The days passed quickly. Bates' case was finalised and so was the girls' money. Billie chose a respectable pub for dinner and celebrations on the harbour for the long awaited 'girls' night out'. Newly restored, it boasted a clean and modern looking bar and restaurant, complemented by a serene and well-kept beer garden. Boats cruised the harbour's peaceful waters.

Billie stepped out into the beer garden and looked around. Jane, Sarah and Casey sat at a table amidst a cluster of palm trees. She sighed. Trust them to be early. She descended the wide steps and joined them. "Hi, guys," she said with a smile.

They stood and gave her hugs with warm greetings in return. Sitting back down, a waiter appeared beside Billie carrying a tray with a bottle of iced wine and four glasses. He set it down on the table.

"I hope you don't mind. I took the liberty of ordering us a kick starter," she said with a grin. "The best bottle of champagne in the house."

Jane's eyes lit up. "Champagne?"

"Aren't you going a little overboard here?" Casey asked, watching the waiter fill their glasses.

"No, I don't think so. We have a lot to celebrate, don't you think?" The detective held up her glass in a toast when the waiter left, smiling at her newfound friends. "Well, here we are at last. I'd like to propose a toast to our freedom and team effort, and to a long friendship in the future."

"I couldn't have said it better," Jane said, cracking a smile.

"Cheers," Sarah and Casey chorused, tapping each glass in turn before taking a sip.

"Ooh, that is a nice drop," Sarah praised.

"And definitely the best," Jane added, smiling at Billie.

"It so is," Casey agreed. "And I have to say it's a nice place you picked." She sat back with a contented sigh while gazing affectionately at the detective. "I'm glad we left it up to you."

"Yeah, it's quite relaxing." Billie looked around. The crowd was growing, filing out from the pub in groups and filling the seats. Turning to the girls, she put down her glass. "Oh, I almost forgot." She picked up her handbag and dug into it. The girls set their champagnes down, watching with mixed curiosity and surprise. The detective pulled out three envelopes and passed one to each of the girls, smiling at their sceptical looks.

"What's this?" Casey asked, turning the envelope over in her hands and studying it. Other than her name written neatly on the front, it was unmarked. Studying theirs, Sarah and Jane were just as hesitant to open them.

"They call them envelopes," Billie said. The girls looked up.

Casey smiled. "Go on."

"Ooh, you are starting early, aren't you?" Sarah chuckled. The detective sat back with a smile and took a sip of her champagne. Sarah looked at Jane and Casey. "I don't trust any envelope coming from a cop anymore. Remember the last one?"

"It's a bit hard not to," Jane said, casting Billie a wary look. "What are you up to now?"

Billie's smile widened. "You guys are so untrusting."

"Only around you. After your last effort, we know you can't be trusted."

"Let's say I like to keep you on your toes. Now, you won't know what's in there if you don't open them, will you?" she teased, getting back to the subject on hand.

The three looked at her and then turned to one another. Together they opened their unsealed envelopes and began reading. Billie took another sip, calmly waiting for their reactions. One by one, the girls' mouths dropped open in shock.

"Now, remember, you only gave me a week, which I didn't end up using anyway, so I hope they're okay," Billie said, watching the girls. No one showed the slightest interest in her comment.

"Holy shit, I have an interview with Hair City Salon for a traineeship," Jane whispered in awe, her gaze fixed to the letter.

"Mine's at King's Electronics. I don't believe it."

"Mine's at Roués Diamonds," Sarah said in a thinned voice. She looked up at the smiling detective. "But how? How did you do it?"

"Haven't I taught you never to underestimate a cop?" Billie said with a light-hearted tone.

The girls failed to bite. They stared blankly, looks of disbelief etched across their faces.

Billie gave a laugh, thoroughly enjoying herself. None of them had expected anything to come out of their agreement the other day, especially after the distraction of the reward. They'd given her their permission to persist in this only because they knew she wanted to, not because they expected her to find anything. Now they were having difficulty believing it.

"Okay, so it was a little tricky," Billie went on after her question failed to achieve a response. "And I swear I didn't step out of line. This is only an interview. It's totally up to you to get the job on your own merit. You may have to start at the bottom and work your way up, but at least you'll have a foot in the door, and your future in your hands."

"But how...?" Jane asked.

"Yes, tell us," Casey said.

Billie gave another laugh. "So some people owed me a few favours." She shrugged. "After I gave them a rundown on your profiles and personalities, not to mention how you helped bring Bates' racket to an end, they agreed to meet you. Simple as that."

The girls sat silent with unwavering stares. One by one, they slowly smiled.

"I'm not entirely convinced it was 'as simple as that', but I do have to say I'm impressed." Sarah grinned.

"This is wonderful." Jane looked at Sarah and Casey. The two smiled broadly. Jane turned to Billie and shook her head. "I swear, if you do anything like this to us again... I mean, first the whole episode with Bates, and then the big surprise of the reward, and now this. Damn it, McCoy, I don't think I can take any more surprises."

"I promise I'll back off. I'm all out of them for the moment."

"Good, keep it that way. You've done far too much for us already."

Casey held up her glass. "I'll drink to that." She swallowed a large mouthful.

Sarah smiled. She looked at Billie with a sober expression. "I owe you an apology," she said sincerely.

"You do?"

"Yeah, for doubting you. I should've known. Thank you for this. We won't let you down."

Billie nodded and smiled. "I know."

Sarah returned it and then frowned. "Oh crap."

The girls turned to her, confused.

"What's wrong?" Casey asked.

"How will we explain this to Rose? She was so happy to have us back and now we could be leaving again, for good."

Casey nodded and then shrugged. "I'm sure she'll understand."

"Either that, or you could simply stay with her," Billie teased. Sarah looked at her. A smile played on her lips.

"No way. I intend to prove to you I can do this."

The cop smiled. "Good."

The night rolled on and so did the bottles of wine. Somewhere in between, the girls managed to fit in a meal. Last drinks were called over a speaker system, drawing the night to a close.

"I say we continue this back at my place," Casey said in high spirits. "Seeing it's the closest," she added when the girls turned her way.

"Good idea. I love trashing your joint," Sarah said with a merry giggle.

"Yeah, the night's still young after all." Jane bubbled with merriment.

Billie nodded with a broad smile. "I'm in."

After stocking up with a couple of bottles of wine, the girls caught a taxi to Casey's. She led them through the front alcove and across to the living room. A three seater and two single chairs surrounded a coffee table. The kitchen was behind the lounge room, divided by a narrow breakfast bar. A hallway led off to the right. A door sat opposite the lounge, half opened, exposing a bedroom inside. Billie guessed it was Casey's room after she pushed open the door and offloaded her handbag in it.

The girls sank into the lounge chairs. The wine was opened and the party continued. The four were completely relaxed in one another's company with no discrimination about jobs or social status.

Finally, the night's events start to take effect. Weariness and overindulgence set in. Casey climbed out of the chair clasping her near empty glass and looked over her guests. Billie and Sarah sat slouched on the three seater nursing their drinks in their laps. Jane was on the single opposite sitting with her feet tucked underneath her and her head resting against the lounge. Looking worse for wear, she'd drifted into a meditative trance.

"Okay, this is a once only offer," Casey said. "Seeing as it's too late to be out on the road, *and* the fact you are in no condition to *be* out on the road, I guess you guys will have to stay the night."

Sarah grinned. "If that's an invitation, it sure is a lousy one."

Casey smiled at her. "You're lucky you're even getting one."

Sarah laughed. "Hey, if you hadn't brought it up, *I* would have."

"Yeah, I'm sure you would. Now, I have two beds and one lounge. Who goes where, I'll leave up to you to decide," she said, looking from one girl to the next.

"Well, I'm never one for sleeping on lounges, and one of those beds in there already has my name on it," Sarah said, shooting Billie a look. "I mean I've slept in it heaps of times before now."

The detective smiled. "It's never too late to change. I sleep on my lounge all the time."

"There you go, it's yours then, seeing how you're so used to doing it. What do you think, Jane? Don't you think it suits McCoy?"

Jane met Sarah's question with a warm grin. She rolled her head towards Billie. "Sarah's right. You've bought yourself a lounge."

Billie gazed at her in thought. A faint smile played on her lips. She shook her head. "You know, I liked you better when you used to stick up for me. How is it you always side with these two layabouts now?"

"Who are you calling layabouts?" Casey squealed.

"That's it, McCoy, you've just earned your bed. Don't bother getting up," Sarah said in a stern tone behind her smile. Pulling a cushion out from behind her, she tossed it at her.

Billie caught it one handed and smiled back. "Huh, did I have a choice?"

"*Now* what is she on about?" Sarah asked, glancing at Casey and Jane.

Casey grinned down at the detective. "Who knows? Cops are so hard to figure out."

Jane giggled from her seat. Billie gave a light chortle and nodded. She knew she wasn't going to win this, as usual. Propping the pillow Sarah had tossed her against the one she leant on, she brought up her legs and stretched out on the lounge, resting her glass on her stomach and her feet in Sarah's lap.

"Well, then, if that's the case, why don't you get off my bed so I can get some sleep, unless of course you'd like to massage my feet."

A laugh slipped through Sarah's lips. "Now you're pushing your luck." Lifting Billie's feet, she clambered out from underneath them and stood. Immediately she swayed. "Whoa." She clasped her head. "I think I've been sitting too long."

Casey stepped to her and rested an arm around her shoulders. "What sort of excuse is that? Has it occurred to you that you may have been drinking too long?"

"What? No way."

"Ha. I think you're just getting old. You can't handle your grog anymore."

Sarah looked at her. "Old, huh? At least I'm on my feet, more than I can say about the cop."

Again, the girls giggled, their gazes drawn to Billie where she lay relaxed.

"What, now you want me to carry you to bed?" she asked.

Sarah smiled at Casey. "Hey, there's a thought."

"Er, you can give me a hand if you want," Jane said from behind them.

They turned to her meek and hopeful voice. She sat expectantly watching them, her head resting on the seat looking as helpless as a baby. The girls chuckled.

"Now you look like you *do* need a hand," Casey said, dropping her arm off Sarah.

Jane's eyes widened. "It shows that much?"

"And more."

Casey and Sarah took her by the arms and hauled her out of the chair. Jane staggered between them before regaining her balance.

"Thanks. I don't think I could've done that on my own."

Billie smiled. "Told you you should've grabbed the lounge." She closed her eyes. "Then you wouldn't have had to walk so far to find a bed."

"Just say the word, Jane, and we can have her out of there, pronto," Sarah said in a sinister tone.

The girls chuckled.

"If she gives any more cheek, I'll definitely think about it."

Billie looked up to find the three watching her. She let the challenge pass.

Jane flashed her an affectionate smile and turned to Sarah. "Anyway, now that I'm up, I think I can probably make it."

"Good. I hope I can." Sarah smiled.

Casey nodded. "Okay, let's do it."

Jane smiled down at the cop and then plucked the almost empty glass out of her hand. "Night, sleep well."

Billie recognised the challenge in her eye. About to contest her actions, she let it go. "You too."

They shuffled off. Billie listened to the moans and groans as they disappeared into the hallway. She smiled. Contentment washed through her. It had been a great and memorable night, one she guessed was only the start of a lot more to come. She felt fully accepted by these girls, so much so, it was as if they'd been friends for years. Everything she'd given to bring this friendship together now seemed worth it. She'd never had friends like them, not where she could be so open and have such a good time. Always too busy with work, this was all new to her. With these thoughts on her mind, she closed her eyes. The comfy lounge already lulled her.

After some minutes, a soft velvety bundle landed on the detective's chest. She jumped, snapping out of her doze. She looked up. Casey grinned down at her with a mischievous glint in her eye.

"You weren't asleep, were you?"

Billie eyed her suspiciously. "Asleep? Naw, not now."

Casey chuckled. "Thought you might like a blanket."

"You're too kind."

"I am." Smiling, Casey shook out the blanket and laid it over the cop. "There. Anything else I can get you?"

"No, you've done pretty well, thanks."

"Good." She flashed another of her infectious smiles. "Okay. Goodnight then."

"Sure, see you in the morning, or should I say in a few hours. I wouldn't be surprised if the sun's not already on its way up."

"Shit, I hope not. I'd like *some* uninterrupted sleep. Night."

"Night."

Casey turned out the lights, plunging the room into darkness. Under a peaceful silence, Billie drifted off into a welcoming sleep.

Chapter Thirty-Five

Sarah stirred from her sleep. Aware of the building heat in the room, her eyes opened. She glanced over at Jane, only to find her bed was empty. Sarah sat up and groaned. She clasped her head, striving to ease her pounding headache and hold back the queasiness threatening to overcome her. Warily she stood. A bout of dizziness instantly gripped her. She shot out a hand and leant into the wall to steady herself.

"Shit." She closed her eyes. Gaining some control, she shuffled out the door. Jane stepped out of the bathroom opposite. She looked pale. "You okay?"

Jane sighed. "I am now. At least, I think I am."

"Come on, I'll make you a coffee."

"Sounds good."

The girls shuffled into the kitchen. Sarah did a quick sweep of the lounge room. Billie slept under her blanket undisturbed. There was no sign of Casey. She filled the jug and turned it on. Jane sank onto a stool at the breakfast bar. She propped her elbows on the tabletop and rested her chin in the palms of her hands. Her eyes closed.

Sarah smiled. "You do this often, don't you?"

Jane glanced at her. "All the time." As if the words drained her only energy, her eyes closed again.

Sarah watched her with an affectionate smile. She looked around, searching for something that might pep Jane up. Her gaze fell on Billie. A cheeky grin twisted her lips as an idea sprang to mind.

"You know, seeing as we're up, I think it's time, and only fair, that the cop should be as well. Don't you agree? I mean, why should she get to sleep any longer than us?"

Jane looked at her blankly. A frown crossed her brow and then, as if finally deciphering Sarah's meaning, her head lifted out of her hands. Slowly, she turned to the lounge where Billie lay relaxed. She looked at Sarah with an impish smile. "Hmm, that's quite a selfish thought, but you do have a good point."

Sarah grinned. "Exactly." Turning, she spied a small alarm clock on the shelf. She picked it up and adjusted the settings.

Jane sat up straighter. "You're not . . . going to do what I think you're going to do – are you?"

Sarah met her questioning brown eyes. "You know me far too well." She flashed a roguish grin. Jane smiled, a sign she wanted to be in on it, and then it was gone.

"Wait." Spinning around on her stool, she stood and crossed to the cupboard. Pulling out a cup, she half filled it with water. She turned to Sarah and tapped her top pocket. A shallow rattle sounded. "Panadol I found in the bathroom. I think a certain cop may require these." The smile sprang to her face.

Sarah nodded with a smile. "She'd better or I'll make sure she does."

Jane gave a laugh. "Let's do it."

The piercing high-pitched buzzing broke the tranquil silence. Billie jumped, waking instantly to the loud ringing in her ear. She sat upright. Half stunned, she looked around in bewilderment. What was going on?

The two pranksters burst into laughter. Sarah, crouched beside her, collapsed back on her heels, totally out of control. Jane sank onto the single lounge chair, doubled over in merriment.

"Man, her reflexes are good," Sarah stammered in between laughs.

"Especially after a night like last night." Jane giggled, watching Billie with watery eyes.

Understanding hit Billie like a slap in the face. Too stunned to retaliate, she slumped against the lounge, the listlessness catching up with her. Rubbing her tired eyes with the palms of her hands, she let the girls have their fun. At the moment, they had the advantage. They'd had time to gain some control over their hangovers.

"Man," she breathed. Striving to come to grips with the shock of her wakeup call, the escalating throbbing in her head didn't help. She fell onto her stomach and closed her eyes. "I must be in hell."

Unfortunately, any hopes she might have had of her two tormentors taking the hint and leaving her alone fell flat.

"Good morning," Jane said, overcoming her giggling spasm. She rested a hand on Billie's back and gave her a slight shake. "Here's your morning kick-starter. Panadol all round. The cure to all headaches after a heavy but great night," she said in a sales pitch banter.

Billie half opened her eyes. Jane knelt beside her holding an open palm in front of her face with two white tablets. In the other hand, she held a glass of water. Uninterested, Billie closed her eyes.

"I can't do it," she whispered.

"Sure you can," Sarah said. She took hold of Billie's arm and started lifting her. "Come on, first you have to sit up."

Jane gave her a hand. Together they sat Billie up. The detective clasped her ribs, absorbing the minor ache. She rested her head against the seat. Through half opened eyes, she looked at the two smiling faces in front of her.

"Why are you doing this? Can't you find someone else to pick on?"

Their cheeky grins broadened.

"Don't worry, Casey is next," Jane said. "Now, take these." Again, she offered the glass and pills to her. Billie couldn't deny she needed something to help ease her aching head. After swallowing down the pills, she rested her head back and closed her eyes, nursing the glass in her lap. Except for her pounding head, she was beginning to take control of her lethargic body.

"What's going on? Did I hear an alarm clock?" a sleepy voice said from across the room. Billie looked over. Casey leant on the doorjamb of her bedroom, rubbing the sleep from her eyes.

"Damn it, we're too late," Sarah said quietly to Jane as her friend staggered towards them.

"Too late for what?" Casey asked, nursing her head. She sank into the lounge chair opposite Billie.

"Don't ask," the cop said. Sarah and Jane took a seat on the floor. Their guilty expressions and twisted smiles gave away their innocence.

Casey looked at them. "What are you two up to?"

"Up to? Us?" Sarah asked. "Nothing. Why?"

Billie looked at her. "Huh. I certainly don't need enemies when I have you two as friends."

"Well, I did try and warn you." Sarah smiled and stretched out on her back with closed eyes. "Shit, I've forgotten what the morning after was like."

"Tell me about it." Casey sighed. "What time is it?"

Sarah lifted the clock in her hand and read it. "10:42."

"Day or night?" Casey asked. The girls chuckled.

"Day," Jane said. "How's your head? Would you like some Panadol?"

"I'm fine. It's nothing I can't handle. I think a coffee would be good though, I mean if you're offering." She backed her request with a grin. Jane smiled.

"I wasn't but seeing you asked so nicely, sure." Taking the glass from Billie's lap, she climbed to her feet and headed for the kitchen.

Casey grinned. "Hey, great night though, until now that is."

"Sure was." Sarah tapped Billie's leg. "Hey, McCoy, I had you wrong. Socialising with a cop isn't so bad after all."

Billie smiled at her. "Yeah, and I had you wrong as well. Once a crim, always a crim." Picking up one of her pillows, she sat forward and belted it into the unsuspecting Sarah's face.

"Hey," the girl yelped.

"Stick an alarm clock in my ear, huh?" Billie pounded her with a sudden energy inspired by this small act of revenge and pleasurable fun. Sarah squealed her protests. Curling into a ball, she did her best to protect herself from the onslaught. Her voice rose with the increasing torment.

"Cut it out, McCoy."

"Geez, Sarah, you'd better work on those reflexes," Billie teased. "They're–a bit–slow," she said in between hits.

"Case, do something," Sarah yelped in a desperate plea.

"I am. I'm watching." She laughed.

"Casey!" Sarah yelled more sternly, only to be whacked again. "Damn it, McCoy!"

"Okay, okay," Casey said with a suppressed giggle. She climbed out of the chair and picked a pillow up from the lounge. Billie kept a wary eye on her. With Casey backing Sarah, the odds against her would definitely rise. She'd have to change her plan of attack.

Casey raised the pillow. With her arm in mid-air, she glanced at Billie and gave a wink. Billie was caught out. Unless she was mistaken, it was a sure sign of an allied force. Did Casey plan to side with her rather than Sarah? So it seemed.

With an excited squeal, Casey laid into Sarah with her pillow. Sarah yelped, more in surprise than discomfort.

"What are you doing? Casey? Damn it, I'll kill you Reynolds, you hear me? Both of you, I'll kill you! Jane?" she called as a last option, her tone frantic.

Billie couldn't stop laughing. Sarah rolled around the floor, trying to slip past their assault. She cursed them every time they blocked her with blows. Finally, Billie had to let up. Her ribs ached. She sank onto the lounge with a hand supporting them.

Casey slumped beside her, laughing and panting from her efforts. Sarah slowly sat up, somewhat dishevelled. Her gaze shot from Billie to Casey, wide-eyed and distrustful.

"You side with a cop? A cop? Before me?" Disbelief raised her tone.

Casey shook her head, striving to control her laughter. "I couldn't help myself."

"Couldn't help...!" Sarah blew out a snort. She looked at Billie sitting forward supporting her ribs.

"A bit sore, are we?" she said without any harshness.

"It was worth it," Billie gasped.

"Sure was," Casey merrily said. Her laughter ignited. Within seconds, it took control, doubling her over in a giggling fit, which in turn, started Billie off.

"Shit, don't, Case." The more she laughed, the more it hurt but she couldn't stop. As it involuntarily engulfed her, she doubled over out of control.

"Oh, go ahead. Feel free to laugh on my account," Sarah said. "I hope it hurts, McCoy."

Billie simply shook her head, unable to stop. She rested her head on her knees in an effort to ease the pain and slow her laughter. Finally, after a few long moments, she gained some control and sat up, casting a warm smile at Casey. Casey grinned with a victorious glint in her eye. Billie turned to the watching Sarah. Her gaze darted from her to Casey, looking in no mood for forgiveness.

"I hope you've had your fun," she said. "You've just rekindled my headache. Those pillows are hard, especially after such a big night."

Again, laughter threatened to start Billie off but somehow she suppressed it to a few giggles.

"Headache?" Casey teased. "Mine seems to have gone. Fancy that."

Billie had to fight to keep her amusement in check. Casey definitely wasn't helping.

"Well maybe I could fetch it back for you," Sarah said. "At twice the strength."

The chortles didn't let up. Even Sarah was having trouble containing them. Jane walked in carrying a tray of mugs. She placed it on the coffee table centred between the lounge chairs.

"Okay, guys, time out. My shout."

Graciously the girls took the mugs of coffee Jane handed out. Sarah looked at Billie.

"Truce, okay? I think we're even. Hell, I should've known you'd come back at me."

Billie smiled. "Good. Maybe you'll remember that in the future."

"Yeah, maybe. Or maybe I'll remember to have *reliable* backup," she said, shooting a look at the person in question.

Casey smiled and grinned at Billie and Jane.

Sinking back in the chair, Billie relaxed. Giving a contented sigh, she sipped her coffee with a smile, happy to be in the company of these girls.

Chapter Thirty-Six

The girls passed their interviews. They were so excited they took Billie out for dinner to celebrate. For the first time in their lives, they held a true job in their grasp. Billie was equally happy for them, and glad to see them settle on the right side of the law. Her gamble had paid off.

With support from her friends, Jane found a nice unit to move in. As the weeks slipped by, the friendships grew stronger, bonding the girls like sisters, a family. Once or twice a week they met for a meal, a drink, a movie, whatever, providing Billie wasn't tied up on some undercover assignment that saw her disappear for days on end. Sarah, Casey and Jane worried about her during these times. Despite having had firsthand experience with her in such dangerous situations during the Bates episode, they were always relieved to see her return home in one piece.

On a clear and coolish evening, Sarah pulled into The Swan Hotel's car park. She and the guys had arranged to meet here for drinks. Locking the car, she'd only just started towards the Swan's entrance when a cold and distinctive voice behind halted her in her tracks.

"Hello, Sarah, it's been a long time."

Sarah's heart leapt. The hairs on the back of her neck stood up. There was no mistaking the voice, or the menace associated with it. Slowly, she turned. He stood level with the boot of her car, dressed how he always dressed – in a dark suit. His short black hair was smothered in oil and combed back, emphasising the thin angular face. One thing she knew for sure; if he was here, then so was trouble.

"Finch," she said quietly. Finch had been her pimp for a few years when she'd first started on the game – a long time ago. He was a sleaze but unfortunately an extremely powerful man in the underworld, the type of guy you couldn't turn your back on. "What are you doing here?"

"Looking for you, baby. My, you look as beautiful as ever." His gaze briefly ran over her.

Sarah, stunned, struggled to cope with the shock of seeing him after all these years. "What do you want?"

For a minute, he simply stared. His voice softened. "You know, clients still ask for you even after all this time. You were my pride and joy. You've built yourself a good reputation over the years, and I believe I had a lot to do with that."

Sarah lowered her head, hating hearing what came out of his mouth. She wanted to run, to get away from him, but experience had taught her you never ran from Finch.

The pimp took a step towards her. The movement shot Sarah's head up. She stared into his dark heartless eyes.

He flashed a shallow smile. "As I remember, we made a pact. I allowed you to go, to 'spread your wings' I think were the words you used, and you agreed if ever I asked you back, you'd honour my request. Well, now I'm asking you back, and very nicely in fact." A twisted grin lit up his face.

Every nerve tensed tight at the thought. Sarah turned away, closing her eyes. Everything he said was true. How stupid she'd been to agree to his terms, but, at the time, she'd been so desperate to get away, it seemed the only avenue of escape. Damn it. Why, after all this time, did he want her back? Now, when she'd finally left that life behind?

"So," he went on, "It's time to repay me. Seeing how you've severed yourself from Rose's employ, I'd like you to work for me again."

The invitation cut deep. Turning back, she glared at him. Not surprised he'd found out she'd quit her job with Rose, what he was proposing hit hard. She shook her head. "No. Just leave me alone, okay? I'm clean and I want to stay that way."

Finch made no reaction to her words. He moved closer. "Tell you what, I'll even give you a pay rise. I'm sure your salary has dropped since you took on your . . . apprenticeship."

Sarah tensed. He knew about her new job? Of course he'd know. Finch knows everything. She called his bluff. "That pact was years ago. A lot has changed since then. I really appreciate all you did for me, but money's not the issue here. You can't expect me to drop my career for something we verbally agreed upon so long ago. I'm sorry, Finch, I'm not coming back. I can't, not now."

Finch looked around. A soft chuckle slipped through his lips. He stepped forward, closing the gap. It took all Sarah's willpower to stand her ground and not turn and run. That could prove to be a fatal mistake.

He flashed a smile and then sighed. "Rumour has it you're hanging with a cop."

Sarah's heart skipped a beat. What did Billie have to do with this? Hell, was she now in danger? "Rumours are rumours. You can't believe everything you hear," she said thinly.

Finch smiled. With no warning, he grabbed her and slammed her hard against the car door, holding her firmly. Caught unawares, Sarah fought to break free.

"Don't forget for a minute who you're talking to," he growled savagely. When she refused to stop struggling, he slapped her. Anger overrode her fear.

"You bastard. You don't own me."

Finch rammed her into the door a second time. Sarah gasped and stood still, glaring hard. Finch inhaled deeply, as if soothing his rage. He continued in a calmer tone.

"Now, I'm prepared to give you time to think about it. You have..." He glanced at his watch. "Five hours. I want to see you and Casey at the Red Lady tonight at midnight."

"What? Casey? Are you crazy? Casey won't work for you and neither will I."

He grabbed her by the chin. His eyes narrowed. "Do you forget what I can do to you? To Casey? Or maybe to your new cop friend?" His hot breath fanned her lips as he spoke.

"You don't need us. There are plenty of other girls you can pick from."

His fingers tightened on her chin. "I don't *want* other girls. I want you and Casey. Or do I have to force the issue with some unnecessary accidents involving your friends?"

Sarah knocked the hand from her chin. A stifling wave of anxiety and helplessness descended upon her. She suddenly knew she couldn't win, not when he held her friends' lives in the balance. Crushed, she turned away.

Finch' voice cut in on her thoughts. "I'll ask you again. Will you come and work for me?"

Sarah closed her eyes tight. What choice did she have? Her head bobbed in a slight nod.

Finch released her. "Good. Good girl." He straightened her clothes. Numb, Sarah couldn't speak. Hate had already started to eat away inside her. She'd been kidding herself she could put her past behind her and hold down a decent job.

"I'll see you tonight at the Red Lady. Don't be late." He flashed a smile and patted her cheek. Instantly she yanked away from his touch. With a chuckle, he walked off.

Sarah fell against the car and closed her eyes, letting the shock wash through her. Hell. What had she done? How could she tell Casey they were now working for Finch? How in hell could she ask her to give up her job, a job she loved doing, to work for a creep like Finch? How could she explain it to Billie after all the effort she'd put into finding them their jobs? She'd promised her she wouldn't let her down. Ha. What a joke. She'd just let her down big time. Her stomach knotted. Not only was hers and Casey's life ruined, Billie's welfare hung under a cloud of looming danger, and there wasn't a thing she could do to change it.

To be continued...

Don't miss out!

Visit the website below and you can sign up to receive emails whenever Carol Marvell publishes a new book. There's no charge and no obligation.

https://books2read.com/r/B-A-IHEIB-ZMEBF

BOOKS 2 READ

Connecting independent readers to independent writers.

Did you love *Providence Road*? Then you should read *Cold Bars*[1] by Carol Marvell!

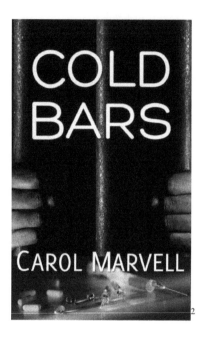

[2]

There are some things in life that will bond you as friends. For Detective Billie McCoy, surviving a kidnapping and sex-slavery ring with two ex-prostitutes and a drug trafficker is one of them. Naturally, once the girls were home safe, Billie used her connections to help Sarah, Casey and Jane find their dream jobs on the right side of the law. But she soon learns she can't protect them from the past, and it's not long before an old flame of Sarah's comes knocking, wanting his best girls back in the game. Sarah declines his offer, but in doing so sets off a chain reaction that lands Billie in hot water. Framed for drug use and possession, Billie learns the drugs are related to a much larger drug syndicate, one that is entrenched in the prison

---

1. https://books2read.com/u/49J61J

2. https://books2read.com/u/49J61J

system. Billie and the girls form an agreement with the police; they go in undercover to bring their attacker to justice. It's a risky operation. The last undercover cop to enter the system was found dead just three days later. The girls begin to gather their evidence, working together as inmates. But when Billie is exposed, their mission suddenly turns to one of survival. Billie becomes a new target and her enemy is desperate to eliminate her. Can she survive the inmates' onslaught? Can she get the evidence she needs before it's too late? Even with her friends' support, they will need each other more than ever to walk out with their lives.

About the Author

Carol lives on a property outside the small country town of Childers in Queensland, Australia. Married with three grownup children, she is now retired from working in a primary school as a Teacher Aide, where she also looked after the library and drove the school bus. Most of her life Carol has played in a four-piece band with her husband and they have now formed a duo after the band folded. She loves to travel, both abroad and in Australia, which she is now discovering more of in her caravan. Fishing, camping and gardening are some of her favourite hobbies.

Read more at https://billiemccoy.blogspot.com.

Milton Keynes UK
Ingram Content Group UK Ltd.
UKHW040835141024
449705UK00006B/265